SWORD OF DIPLOMACY

SOVEREIGN STARS
BOOK 7

BLAIR C. HOWARD

FROM BLAIR HOWARD

The Harry Starke Genesis Series
8 Books in Series as of 2024

The Harry Starke Series
24 Books in Series as of 2024

The Lt. Kate Gazzara Murder Files
20 Books in Series as of 2024

Randall And Carver Mysteries
2 Books in Series as of 2024

The Peacemaker Series
3 Books in Series as of 2024

The O'Sullivan Chronicles: Civil War Series
5 Books in Series as of 2024

FROM BLAIR C. HOWARD

The Sovereign Star Series
7 Books in Series as of 2024

Copyright © 2024 Blair C. Howard
Sword of Diplomacy : Sovereign Stars Book 7
Printed Cleveland, TN, USA
Library of Congress Control Number: 2024926482
Paperback Print ISBN: 979-8-9908529-6-9

For Jo

PROLOGUE

ABOARD USF WARSHIP Thorn
    Defender-Class Cruiser
    Fighter Bay 3

Meera Seleure was seated against the hanger wall with Commander Danis Morian, twin sister of Commodore Richard Morian, Commander of the USF Avenger.

"He's just... always there, you know?" Danis said, not for the first time. "And then the war started, and... and then we were thinking each other's thoughts..." she trailed off, staring across the hangar at the guards.

Meera had raised three rambunctious children, so she understood what Danis was going through, at least to a degree. *Well, maybe not that twin connection*, Meera thought. *But she knows nothing. So she has lost her lover. But she knows nothing. How could she know what it is like to lose a son, as I did?*

Meera's son, Sorge, had died in battle against the Swarm, and she'd fallen apart. She'd been emotionally devastated, and had to rely on her daughter to help her get through it, but then her TK powers manifested, and she'd fought back.

Meera couldn't fault Danis for losing herself. She knew that eventually, she would get past the pain. And, though Danis complained about her brother—he cast a long shadow —they clearly looked out for one another. She hoped Danis would be able to reclaim her life soon.

One of the guards saw Danis staring at him and he snapped his rifle into the port position and stepped forward. "What are you staring at?" He yelled.

"Put that down!" Meera snapped at him. "It's bad enough we're arrested—!"

"Get away from us, you son of a whore," Danis screamed at the guard. "I am a commander in the USF and I demand to be treated as such. "

The guard stood transfixed. Meera saw several other guards had started over before freezing in place.

"Danis, what are you—?" But Meera began, then realized Danis could influence these guards because she, Danis, was a Psy, and a strong one.

Then Meera felt a powerful electric shock, and she hit the floor. Her vision swam and her ears rang.

When she was able to look up, she saw Danis being yanked away by a guard in a weird helmet and when Danis struggled; he shocked her with a tase baton until she fell to the floor beside Meera.

"Danis?" Meera mumbled. "It's going to be all right." Danis didn't answer her. The guard hauled her upright, now assisted by several other guards.

"Didn't anyone check her ID?" the guard with the helmet barked as he locked his helmet over Danis's head.

"We confirmed she was a commander and a senior pilot off Avenger," one of them replied. "Didn't want to rough up an officer and get ripped for it."

"She's a Psy, you idiots!" the helmet-less guard snapped. "She could have marched you all out the airlock! You were told to confirm each ID!" He tapped his wrist pad. "Control, we have a confirmed Psy on board. She's down and restrained. I need escorts to remove her. And you can send some replacement guards," he added, glaring at the hapless soldiers.

By the time Meera could sit upright again, the guards had changed and Danis was gone.

Meera tried to stand. "But why did you have to—" she asked, but before she could complete the question, something struck her head and she stumbled forward.

"Keep quiet, traitor," the guard said.

"Hey, leave her alone!" a voice roared. And a storm of particles streaked past her, pummeling the guard's armor.

It must be Jude! Meera thought and turned to see the one-armed hunter inside a whirling dervish of discarded metal.

How is he doing that with his restraints? she wondered.

The guards took aim, but Jude was strongest with small objects. The debris pelted their armor.

"Jude, watch out—!" she yelled, but she was too late.

The guard came from behind and stabbed his tase-baton inside Jude's empty prosthetic-arm socket. She couldn't imagine his pain as he screamed, his debris cloud falling to the deck. Then the guard applied the baton forcefully to Jude's skull. He fell forward, and one of the guards stabbed his arm with a medical infuser.

"We should have tranked all the prisoners," one of the guards muttered. "Then we wouldn't have these problems."

"That stuff can cause seizures, Gerrick," another guard remarked.

"What do you care, Aron?" Gerrick snapped. "These people are the traitors? What do we care?"

"Just because they were on the ship doesn't mean they're rebels," Aron replied.

"You mean like how they spaced Captain Paris?" Gerrick laughed. "Yeah! Right. They're real stand-up types."

Meera knew the truth about Captain Paris—she'd been removed to another ship. But she didn't dare speak, lest Gerrick tase her or use tranquilizers. She waited until Jude had been slumped against a wall. Once the guards left, she slid closer and tried to support his head. He may have murdered people at Ikalven, but he had just tried to protect her, and she was grateful. She closed her eyes, trying to chase the brutal images on Ikalven away. When he awoke, things would be different. She was certain she could... could... and she drifted into unconsciousness.

When Meera awoke next, she was in a prison cell, alone.

———

ONE MONTH LATER

Councilor's Offices
Orso Royal Palace, City of Som Orsi
Planet Caerus, Orso System

DUKE GYRICH RUTTA once dreamed of rising to the highest pinnacle of government, to rule millions and spend billions, and take whatever he pleased.

That seemed beneath him now. His new dreams of ruling over people like a god were ever closer, yet still just out of reach.

His shoulder began to ache, and he touched the ⚡⚡ marks under his shirt. They throbbed a summons to his new master's will. He didn't know where she was, but the dull pain pulled him forward along the grand hallways past the Palace servants' quarters, into the smaller, deserted passages where the servants rarely went until, finally, he found himself in the old guest quarters. A door opened, seemingly of its own accord, and he stepped inside.

The room was dimly lit, and the opulent furnishings had been removed. His master's servant was eccentric, but he understood he required absolute obedience and that was all that mattered.

Obedience now would give him power over people's lives, power to crush his enemies, literally. So he followed orders and knelt, barely able to stomach the indignity.

"What honorific may I call you today?" he asked the figure reclining on the chaise lounge.

A slip of a boy was feeding her arrantberries. The master's servant was clothed in her usual fashion in a sheer black dress trimmed in iridescent blues. The dress was revealing, and at least a century out of fashion. Her elaborate hat, black with a dark bird perched upon it, only accentuated her bizarre appearance. But she always wore skinthins under the filmy dress to conceal her figure.

She stood and waved the servant away, and Rutta once again beheld the emaciated figure, the sunken eyes a reminder of months, possibly years, of starvation. But those eyes burned with a purpose, or was it fanatic devotion?

"What did you call me yesterday?" she asked, her voice thin and rasping.

"Mistress Helot," he replied.

"I am no one's mistress!" she snapped. Rutta didn't flinch; she often behaved as though her titles were insults. "I am my own woman now that I serve the One King."

"Then what may I call you?" he asked, resisting the urge to grovel. A Duke did not grovel, though he did bend knee when it suited his purposes.

Rutta waited as she mulled over his question. It was pertinent—the wrong title would send her into a fury. Her displeasure burned.

"You may call me... Lady Helot today," she replied.

"Oh, Lady Helot," Rutta intoned in false submission,

11

"you have summoned me to your side. What request may I fulfill that your hands are unsoiled?"

"Oh, get up, Gyrich," she said with disdain. "No need to crawl around on the floor. We have business to discuss."

Rutta stood, relieved that today wouldn't be a haughty Helot day. "Lady Helot," he began again. "You summoned me?"

"Quite right," she said briskly. "I have received new instructions, and while I could easily accomplish them myself, he offers you the opportunity to serve and prove your loyalty."

"Anything the One King commands," Rutta said sincerely. He didn't try to shield his thoughts. His thirst for power, even over Lady Helot, was obvious to her Psy talents. She had never cared about his desires, except when he'd wondered what she really looked like naked. Then she'd clutched his ϟϟ scars with her bony fingers and the feeling he was being burned alive had made it perfectly clear she wasn't interested in lust.

"You will take me to your prisoners," she said bluntly.

Rutta blinked. "Um, which ones, Lady Helot? There are so many—"

"You should know which ones I mean!" she snapped, and he cringed. But before he could offer apologies, she replied, "The ones who have just arrived on your ships, of course. The One King has use for them, and I am to make certain that all of the pawns are moved to their respective places. Ha!"

Rutta cringed at her laugh.

"I will accompany you for the rest of the day," she said. "You will wave me through all the security checkpoints. I will visit whomever I wish, and then we will return. Do you understand?"

"Assuredly, Lady Helot," Rutta agreed.

She walked past him toward the door, and he caught a whiff of her scent. She smelled of darkwood cologne, and musty clothing stored too long. But he trotted along behind her, trying to catch up with her.

Whatever mental tricks she used, he wouldn't follow her like a hound.

He'd been assured the chance to rule, and he wouldn't allow anyone to consider him a servant, even if his new strength came from this... One King.

———

RISING TIDES GROUP Psychiatric Facility
    Resdon Military Facilities Annex
    Som Orsi, Planet Caerus

LANCE-SERGEANT DASCHER BIKK hated his new guard job.

"Why do I always get the boring stuff?" Second-Corporal Nejaz called from his station chair.

"If that were the case," Second-Corporal Donda called from the break table, "you'd never get out of the chair!"

"Look," First-Corporal Sen grumbled as he dealt the next hand. "Someone thinks it takes a four person shift to do this. If you don't like it, transfer and dig a ditch."

Nejaz muttered something to himself no one could hear.

"I wish Arthon was here," Donda mumbled. "At least he enjoyed himself."

"Because he takes all your money," Sen pointed out. "Nejaz complains when he loses, and when we let him win, and when he gets monitor duty."

Bikk sighed as he looked at his cards. He'd been shoved into this job after one of the guards turned traitor, and his supervisor was demoted. Now he spent his days watching a vast cell block filled with mental patients sitting around doing nothing, and then write a bare-bones report about it.

The traitor guard, Arthon Daire, had come in off-shift with two civilians and broke out two patients. That was the official story, anyway. Now, Arthon Daire was at large, along with the civilians and the "patients."

So, they played cards while someone paid very close attention to the monitors.

"Hey, something funny's happening," Nejaz said.

Bikk set his mostly full-house down and walked into the monitor room. He saw the patients on-screen, exiting their comfortable little rooms to stand on the former prison walkways and stare intently at the ceiling.

"Oh, yeah, you're new. They do that sometimes," he explained to Nejaz. "They haven't done it for almost a week. It's usually once every few days."

"What are they looking at?" Nejaz asked.

"Nobody knows," Bikk admitted. "They stare at the same spot, then shuffle back into their rooms. It's not a big deal."

"Pardon me, sir," Nejaz said, "but do you realize how crazy that is?"

"Corporal," Bikk replied, "I don't rank high enough to realize anything. I just write the reports."

"Well, shouldn't you mention that they're doing this?" Nejaz asked.

Bikk looked again. He could have sworn the patients were looking east. Now they were looking south-east...

He could see their heads moving slowly, as if they were tracking something.

He looked at the ceiling, trying to spot what they were staring at, but he saw nothing. The patients continued to slowly turn their heads until they were facing west-south-west.

"Well, that was weird—" he began, but was cut off when the patients began to sing.

The sounds were unlike anything he'd ever heard before. Discordant, high-pitched, wavering. It sounded like a hundred flutes playing underwater.

"Um..." Nejaz said as the noise continued, "what are they doing?"

"I have no—"

The noise stopped. The patients had stopped singing.

"—idea," Bikk finished nervously.

Then they all turned and filed quietly back into their rooms.

"So... what are we going to do?" Nejaz asked.

"You go play cards awhile," Bikk said as he sat down at the terminal. "I think I need to fill out the report right now."

———

Shuttle T-4159
Entering Caerus Atmosphere

FOREIGN COULD FEEL its minions now.

They called out as Foreign came closer, atmospheric friction vibrating the shuttle's hull in a glorious counterpoint to the thrumming chords of devotion it could sense below.

Foreign guided the shuttle through Caerus's atmosphere toward Awega City, a mere four-hundred-twenty-two kilometers away. It would have preferred to land closer, in Som Orsi. But the security at the Resdon's military launch facility was too strong. No matter how it manipulated the data, the humans would be watching, and Foreign couldn't affect the humans; only its minions.

Foreign was fortunate to have taken this body. Not only was Foreign born an Imperator, a biological computational construct that served its master the Will, but this human could think like a computer itself—herself, it amended. Its body was a female named Kasa Su Mei, and sometimes other names as well.

These humans are so focused on their identities that they ignore their higher purpose, Foreign pondered, *to serve something greater than themselves. And since they won't do that, they must be removed.*

Foreign reached out through the shuttle's navigation computers, made contact with the Farda Launch Facility, and corrected the shuttle's displayed trajectory to appear as a flyby. All facility computers were instructed to ignore Foreign's approach, and to guide Foreign around any flight paths, and a landing pad was cleared of personnel with just a few lines of code. It wondered at how humans could leave themselves so open to such an attack.

Foreign landed without incident and walked onto the landing pad, and from there to the parking area where it scanned the vehicle registry to find the gravcar that had been parked there the longest, enabled it, and then drove to the exit. For a moment, Foreign was surprised at how easily driving a gravcar was. The body's memories must have aided the process.

Foreign cleared the gate without incident and drove directly toward Som Orsi. The human roadways were left behind and, though the verdant landscape held little fascination for it, its human host surged with some kind of unfathomable emotion.

It will be a simple matter, Foreign mused, ignoring the pitiful human's feelings. *Why do the humans make their roads go anything other than in a straight line? This is more efficient.*

After an hour, the vehicle slowed and sank to the ground. Foreign glanced at the onboard computer—an insultingly simple technology—and saw that the vehicle was drained of power.

Foreign reached out to tap the world's communications grid, but there was no signal. Without a transmission device like the humans carried, communication was impossible.

Perturbed, if such an emotion could apply to an alien biological computational construct, Foreign exited the vehicle, and began to walk toward Som Orsi.

It will be a simple matter, Foreign corrected itself, *once a suitable location for communication and transport is reached.*

CHAPTER
ONE

ELIO LORNE, once prince of the Orso kingdom, now sat in a simple chair in the ship's almost spartan guest quarters, the usual diplomatic suite denied him, as so many things were. He wore a metal circlet designed to suppress his formidable Psy talents, the thin neural mesh hidden by his tousled hair. He wore metal bracelets and a collar disguised as a man's choker designed to null his TK abilities, abilities powerful enough to smash a grav truck and throw the debris more than a kilometer.

"Do you think we'll have time to sightsee?" he asked his faceless guards.

No one answered. They never did. They simply stood quietly, an imposing sight in their smooth and stylish royal armor. But Elio had grown up seeing such things, and knew there were ordinary men and women behind those half-visored helmets.

Elio looked over his travel itinerary one more time. He had three meetings that day, then a public appearance with the governor tomorrow before leaving. That was quite a lot considering he was to arrive at 1100 hours local time.

His room's annunciator chimed. But instead of walking over to answer, he eyed the door as one of his honor guard stepped forward instead.

"The ambassador is preparing for his meeting," the guard said.

The voice on the other side was pleasant and female. "I just wanted to relay Captain Carrica's—"

"The ambassador has no time for formalities," the guard snapped.

"Very well," the voice on the other side replied. "The captain informs the ambassador that we are twenty minutes from final approach. Please make any preparations now, as the shuttle must be ready on time. They will not let us stay on approach for the Stationary Moon very long."

"Understood," the honor guard said, and stabbed the button to cut communication off.

"You didn't have to be rude to that officer," Elio commented. "She's just doing her job."

The guard turned quickly, and Elio saw his mistake. This was the honor guard's team leader, with a Blade Sergeant's dagger-pierced chevron insignia on his arm. He'd not offered his name, nor did he wear an ID tag.

"Get Squad D up," the blade sergeant ordered. "Shuttle in ten, everyone. Only take gear in bag three." Then he fixed Elio with a glare. "And I'm just doing my job," he growled. "My job is to keep a pampered noble on schedule. He can't do that if he chats up every female ship's officer."

Elio frowned at him. "I don't spend a lot of time chatting—"

The blade sergeant cut him off. "You'll spend no time. You have a job to do, and you'll do it. You will not run off and flirt with someone and disappear like you did before."

"Listen here," Elio snapped. "Whatever you think you've heard about—"

Elio saw everything around him yank forward. He looked around and found the chair was now almost a meter away. *Did he just shove my chair with TK?*

When he looked up, the blade sergeant's visor loomed in his face. "Listen here," Blade Sergeant repeated. "Whatever you think you can order, you can't. Pack up and get to your shuttle. You've a busy afternoon."

Six years ago, Elio might have been cowed. Two years ago, he might have retaliated. Today, he remained passive. He simply stood, never letting his eyes leave the blade sergeant's face-plate. "If I do the job, it's because I want to. I asked for this job because it needed to be done. If your job is to keep me in line, don't harass other people for doing theirs."

Then he turned away and gathered his things, knowing the blade sergeant was only a handful of centimeters away. He didn't need Psy to feel the man's rage boiling, but Elio would not be cowed, nor would he retaliate. His power wasn't to be used to fight his own people, and he would follow this man as best as he could.

"Squads A and B, on me," the blade sergeant ordered. "Squads C and D take the rear. You'll have to catch rack time when we get to quarters."

Placing tired guards in the rear made no sense to Elio, but he gathered his bags and followed the blade sergeant out of the room. Suddenly, he remembered the papers upon which he'd been jotting his notes. He reached out with a wisp of TK and pulled the papers through the door just before it closed. He let them flutter to the ground just in front of C Squad.

"Sorry," he said. "Let me just grab those."

He could see the confusion on their faces.

He snatched up the errant papers and caught up with the front squads quickly.

"What's the holdup?" the blade sergeant barked.

"Just dropped some notes," Elio said truthfully.

"I swear, you nobles are useless," the blade sergeant mumbled. "Can't even pack your own bags..."

The guards began marching along again, but Elio had to hide a smile.

They thought he was helpless, imprisoned by his restraints. But where the circlet kept his thoughts close, the bracelets were another story.

———

Ataraxis's Hanger Bay

THE BLADE SERGEANT insisted on arriving early for departure. Elio stood outside the shuttle while Squads A and B searched for contraband in the cabin. He could hear the blade sergeant questioning the pilots about their course.

I don't know what his orders are, Elio thought, *but he's too obnoxious by far. I'll bet they're from Duke Rutta.* Gyrich Rutta had watched Elio grow up from a headstrong boy into an independent man. While there was no love lost between then, Elio wished he could at least respect the petty tyrant's drive. *But he's all selfishness*, Elio thought.

A barked order from the blade sergeant and Elio and his guards boarded the shuttle and they took their seats. With two minutes to spare, the shuttle launched, and the Ataraxis angled away to join the other ships in parking orbits around the twin planets.

And he watched Hebe and Gany spin slowly around their common epicenter, at which sat his destination—the Stationary Moon, Remanor.

Where Hebe was a lifeless rock plagued with dust storms, and Gany an opaque orange ball of swirling clouds, the tiny moon was bursting with signs of life. Elio had visited Remanor once before and was looking forward to the bounce of lower gravity again.

I bet Danis hasn't been here, he thought in a moment of cheer. *Wouldn't it be fun to go where she could fly without a fighter? The glider rentals would—*

But he hadn't seen Danis for forty-three days, and his guards would deny him any of the bounce. *And even if they don't, the blade sergeant certainly will,* he concluded.

So he simply gazed out the view-ports at one of the unquestioned jewels of Orso. The lush forests were dotted with tiny cityscapes, like an uncut emerald wound with criss-crossing silver wires. The poles of the planet glimmered with power where the twin gravitic amplifiers maintained the moon's habitability.

There was a moment of static over the speakers as they passed through the intense magnetic field where the planetary fields overlapped, and the odd loose ferromagnetic item slid across the cabin or lifted into the air before settling down again.

"This is the pilot," came a calm, reassuring female voice. "We are on approach to land in the Remanor Dignitas District landing port. If you haven't done so already, please fasten your harness and wait for the shuttle to complete its landing cycle before preparing to exit. Thank you."

Elio double-checked his harness. None of the guards did. They just watched him intently.

This undivided attention is creepy, he wanted to say. But anything might be construed as a distraction, though to little effect. So he returned to watching the beautiful Remanor come closer. He could feel the heat of the sun beating down even before they slipped into the penumbra underneath Hebe —one of the downsides of building a habitable world so close to a star.

As soon as they docked, the blade sergeant stood up, along with Squads A and B.

Elio blinked. He hadn't noticed them unfastening their harnesses.

C and D were a little slower to rise, but Elio didn't keep them waiting. He gathered his bags—an easy chore in the light gravity—and joined his honor guard at the base of the ramp, where they'd already moved into a respectful formation. And amid her own honor guard, the governor of Remanor stood waiting.

"Greetings, Prince... I mean Ambassador Lorne," the governor said. "I am Maybella Friah. Welcome back to Remanor." From her expression, the use of his former title wasn't a mistake.

"It's wonderful to be here," he said. "How did you know it wasn't my first time?"

"I checked our records, Ambassador," she replied. "But I remember when you came before. It was quite a spectacle for the week that we entertained the... most eligible bachelor of Orso. All the young ladies were quite smitten."

She'd glanced at his honor guard before she finished. Elio wondered if she had been about to mention his father. "So, were you one of the young ladies?" he asked in jest.

"I'm afraid not," she replied. "I was old enough not to

entertain the fancies of a man ten years my junior." She smirked.

"By my honor, I wouldn't have guessed," he replied, and meant it.

"Well, there's no sense waiting for the sun to come up," she said. "Why don't we retire to the wardrobe and prepare for your meeting?"

———

122nd Floor, Comsidus Room
Aestim Building, Dignitas District
Moon Remanor, Hebe-Gany System

ELIO KNEW the wardrobe rooms were all culturally different. Here on Remanor, they were divided, multi-person rooms, like changing rooms in the boutiques of Orso.

I can't blame them, he thought as he changed from ship-boards to something more befitting a visiting dignitary. He had to balance himself carefully in the low gravity; sudden movements could be dangerous. They're on a moon and considered prime real estate at that. No one wants to take up extra space. And my schedule is so tight that I have no time to freshen up properly. Once again, I sense the presence of Duke Rutta's petty hand.

He pondered how Duke Rutta had managed to time his arrival and concluded that Captain Carrica had specific instructions. The sharp-eyed captain wasn't Elio's enemy, but if he took such orders, then he was no ally.

Yet, Elio reminded himself as he finished tying his cravat. *He isn't an ally yet. But he is still a citizen of Orso, and I must treat him as such.* He couldn't afford to view some of his people as allies and some as enemies. The only enemies he had were the Council of Regents. And the alien invasion, of course.

Attired as an ambassador, Elio Lorne stepped out to be greeted by a guide and, of course, eight armed guards.

"A-a-ambassador Lorne?" the guide squeaked. "These soldiers insist on accompanying you. I tried to explain that it's against protocol, but—"

"I understand," Elio explained. "But they are with me, I'm afraid. Blade Sergeant, perhaps we could enter the room with two guards? The rest could wait just outside."

"My orders are to ensure—"

"Yes, yes," Elio interrupted before he could spell them out. The guide was skittish enough. "But I have a job to do here. And it's more difficult if you're hovering." He hoped that implying "overprotective babysitter" might sway the blade sergeant's ego.

It seemed to be working. He saw the pride cross the blade sergeant's face.

"How many entrances here?" the blade sergeant asked the guide.

"Entrances? Oh, um... I think there are only the three," the guide managed.

"Windows?" Sergeant added.

"No, none at all," the guide replied.

"Squads, break into pairs, take those entrances," the sergeant barked. "Pairs on both sides, constant contact. No entrance or exit without reasonable assurance."

I wish they could lose the helmets, Elio thought. At least they could look human. But he wasn't meant to see them as human.

"Well, there you go?" Elio said and allowed his patient guide to take him to his first meeting. They reached the door, and his guards slipped away. The guide opened the door, and Elio swept in behind him.

He saw Governor Friah talking among delegation members. And he recognized all the obvious players.

Standing next to the Governor was a well-dressed man, slight of build, with impeccably tailored clothing. His hands moved while he spoke, fingers curled, index straight. His index fingers twitched every time he made a point. As if pulling a trigger, Elio thought. This was Wex Andreys, the weapons manufacturer from Maress.

Across the room were two more figures, one swathed in voluminous and overlapping purple. While it had been some time since he'd last seen her, he recognized the woman in purple as Iola Cesat of Eos's textile concern. Her colleague was none other than Creg Granos of Tyche, solid and stolid, as befitted the mining colony's Extrock office. Granos's face revealed nothing as Iola chuckled, likely at her own joke.

He saw others, but the governor called the meeting to order. Elio checked his chron. It was 1200 hours. He sat in his designated place and wondered what the first order of business would be. As host, Governor Friah had first choice.

"Welcome, everyone," she said. "We have a number of items on the agenda, but I'd like to ease into things. Let's discuss our upcoming quincentenary. It isn't every year a planet celebrates five hundred years of settlement!"

Everyone around the table chuckled.

"We have a lot of things to plan for, and I'd like to know what to expect from each of you," the governor continued. "That will segue into the trade disruptions, and how we can resolve them."

Elio glanced at his notes. The quincentenary was scheduled post-luncheon. He'd hoped to excuse himself early to attend the next meeting between the banker's guild representatives and off-planet Seyshore Industries, who were restructuring themselves. With all that was happening, it was unlikely they'd reach any substance until 1500 hours, and then he'd be rushing to the banker's meeting at 1800.

Elio managed not to groan. It was going to be a long day.

———

Comsidus Room's Foyer
Aestim Building

"THIS BLOWS VACUUM," First Corporal Drella Simond grumbled to herself.

She and her Squad D partner—some brick-head marine second corporal she hadn't known before being assigned to this detail—were guarding at some sort of party of the elites.

Her helmet's heads-up display tracked sudden movement. *Merely service personnel*. She thought. *Why treat Prince Elio like this? He never did anything wrong. Not like his screw-up father.*

Drella spoke her mind—ten years of reprimands had cost her three promotions. Her supervisors hadn't appreciated her attitude toward Orson Lorne—*May he rot in peace,* she added to herself. His poor decisions had cost Caerus dearly multiple times. He'd coughed himself to death, years too late, but Prince Elio should have ascended the throne and fixed everything.

It's probably good if I didn't gush over him, she thought. *I've heard there's a purge of the old loyalists. My reprimands are probably the only thing that got me here.*

She'd fought near Prince Elio during the Battle for Som Orsi. He'd been cut, bleeding, filthy, and raging at the enemy on the front lines. He might have died trying to turn the tide of battle, but for a team of TKs working alongside him.

I wish I could have manifested some TK, she thought. But instead, she was a normal marine, just turned forty, with a list of offenses that had left her working alongside bullies and thugs.

Well, she thought as she heard Elio try to discuss trade something-or-others with an obviously disinterested elite. *If he needs a friend, he has one in her, for all the good I can do.*

———

Comsidus Room
 Aestim Building

"If we have no further questions concerning the quincentenary," Governor Friah concluded, "then we should move to discuss the trade disruption."

Finally, they get to serious business. Elio might have complained a few years ago. Now, this meeting seemed to be little more than an affront to those suffering and dying.

"First, allow me to thank our esteemed host," Creg Granos began. "But terming this a trade disruption sounds more like an accusation—"

"Remanor depends on shipments we receive from other planets to vitalize our economy and living spaces," Friah countered politely, interrupting him. "When we fail to receive shipments, it isn't just harming our economy, it's endangering our populace."

"I fail to see how a failure to receive mine tailings constitutes a threat to your people, Governor," Wex Andreys commented wryly.

"Our people are involved heavily in attempting to

terraform a planet," Governor Friah retorted. "Our economy has been tied to that goal for seventy years. Our population is growing too large for the moon to support comfortably. Hebe needs to reach at least five percent sustainable surface before we can move people to the planet. Without the polar gravitics, the situation is hopeless."

"But you already have the polar emitters completed, don't you?" someone asked.

"They are ninety-three percent functional," Friah corrected. "But those stations would provide a minimum necessary amount of atmospheric containment. Without bringing them to minimum functionality, creating a polarized reflection field is useless."

Elio had tried to research this quarrel, but it seemed he still had a ways to go. So he discreetly pulled up a window on his wrist pad and tried to research "polarized reflection fields" as the discussion spilled into argument.

This isn't going very well, is it? he wondered as voices began to raise.

CHAPTER
TWO

OFFICERS
Bautan Beta-Max Penitentiary
Iseria Badlands, Planet Caerus

MICHAEL JADERN SWUNG his sledgehammer straight and true. His blow cracked a sizable chunk of stone.

Another prisoner ambled over and lifted the stone away. He'd soon have his turn on lifting duty. The hammer was a coveted position, since it allowed one to beat out their pent-up frustrations.

Though I suspect some want to use it on a guard, too, he thought as another armored soldier walked past. The rock quarry had sunlight—the climate-controlled exercise yard let few rays through, though Jadern took it better than most. He was a starship commander—

I was a starship commander, he reminded himself, fingering his ID patch. *Now, I'm just Prisoner 1045.*

Jadern had served under Richard Morian on the Defender-class cruiser Avenger for most of his career. Richard was a good commanding officer and a good friend. Now, the Avenger had disappeared, along with all hands. Jadern might have been one of them, except he'd replaced Captain Paris on the cruiser Thorn, after her vengeful orders caused her officers to mutiny. Almost everyone aboard Thorn had been arrested by the United Sovereign Fleet, and any native Orso citizens forced to swear allegiance to the new king of Orso in exchange for their freedom. The non-natives, no small number, had been reprimanded and sent to their home systems.

However, bridge officers had been an exception. For leading the mutiny, they had been singled out for punishment. And Jadern, replacing the captain who had "suspiciously" disappeared along with the Avenger, had received the harshest punishment of all—stripped of his hard-earned rank, cashiered, and sentenced to twenty years in a non-military, high-security prison. Here, the guards had no qualms against beating unruly prisoners with tase-batons. Their armor was designed to stop electric shocks if prisoners gained a baton—unless their armor was damaged. By a hammer... Now that was something different.

From the way prisoners eyed the guards, Jadern wondered how many lives he saved every day by keeping the hammer from their hands.

But he found the quarry in his dreams. The other prison "jobs" weren't physical and offered little chance of escape. But he was USF Navy—their training regimen required hours of menial work. He did his jobs without complaint.

Maybe that's why I dream of it, he wondered. *If I've taken responsibility for my work, then I belong here. That's... not comforting.*

A large, heavily muscled prisoner approached. His name was Zam. Jadern had seen Zam "reprimanded" by the guards. "Your turn's over, shrimp," Zam snapped.

"Happy to oblige," Jadern replied, holding the hammer out.

But Zam didn't take it.

"You kidding me, little piss?" Zam sneered.

Jadern was confused. "Pardon?" he asked, eyeing Zam's muscles.

"Oh, I'm so sorry," Zam mocked. "Pardon my obliging. I just talk like I'm better than everyone else."

Jadern held his tongue. "Thank you for my chance to beat rocks," he said carefully. "Your turn, like you said."

"Hear him?" Zam said to a few others nearby. "He's happy. He's thanking me. He's giving me the hammer."

"Is there a problem?" Jadern said evenly.

"Not anymore," Zam said, and hauled his meaty fist back for a blow.

Jadern lifted the hammer from the ground ten centimeters, then crashed the heavy head down on Zam's boot.

The prison garb was tough, but lacked the safety features of those protecting the guards. So the cheap leather crumpled under the blow, and so did Zam's momentum.

"OOW!" Zam screamed as he bent forward by reflex. "You bastard, I—"

But he never did say what he planned, because Jadern lifted the hammer handle straight into Zam's jaw.

Jadern heard the crack! as Zam's teeth smashed together.

Jadern dropped the hammer. He knew two things would happen in quick succession now.

Zam shook off his stupor and roared incoherently as he lunged toward Jadern. That meaty fist now connected solidly, but Jadern turned slightly and took the blow on his shoulder blade instead of his face. The sound of cracking fingers was followed by sharp pain.

Suddenly, Jadern felt the shock of a taser. The guards had intervened and were punishing the entire crowd.

Jadern fell to the ground, not wanting to provoke anyone. But Zam bellowed in rage and attacked the guards. The flash of tase-batons grew brighter as they adjusted their attack. It took five guards to subdue Zam before he slumped to the ground.

"Take the big one back to his cell," one of the guards ordered. Jadern noticed the red chevrons on his shoulder—a guard sergeant, maybe? "And take 1045 to the warden's office. She'll speak to him."

"What's special about—" Jadern tried to ask, but only received an electric shock for the trouble. He clutched his shoulder, wincing as that pulled his bruises.

"You just assaulted another prisoner," the red guard laughed. "Why do you think we're taking you out?"

"For the record," Jadern tried to reason, "he hit me first, so —" But he received another shock. "I didn't lay a finger on him —AAAH!" This time, the shock was agonizing and prolonged.

"For someone so quick, you don't seem too smart," the guard said, amused. "Go ahead, 1045, say something funny. I'll keep clapping."

Jadern took the hint and shut his mouth and began the quiet, painful walk to the warden's office.

———

Bautan Beta-Max Penitentiary
Administrative Offices

Jadern didn't have to wait long before he was called into the warden's office. But once inside, things took a turn for the strange.

Jadern had visited the warden before—no prisoner came into Bautan without an interview. The warden sat behind her desk, her straight hair clipped short to her jaw line; her face lined from years of draconian rule. Yet she sat quiet and still.

Behind the hard-edged woman stood two figures. One was a smirking man in expensive clothes. He looked familiar. The other was a tall, slender woman seemingly dressed in somebody's historical wardrobe. The black gown might have been enticingly revealing, but Jadern was too experienced to let an attractive woman distract him. And the room had a strange, musty odor to it he didn't remember from his previous interview.

"Warden Jesna, you have assisted us well," the smirking man said. "You may leave us alone now."

With a smooth compliance that Jadern also didn't recall, the warden simply stood and left, not even acknowledging the order to leave her own office.

"What's this meeting about—" Jadern started to say, but then fell inexplicably silent. He opened his mouth in an effort to try again, but the question slid from his mind even as he tried to grasp it again.

"Oh, no, handsome man," the slender woman said. "We can't have you asking questions. We need you to answer them. The first question is, what happened to the Avenger?"

"Nobody knows what happened to the Avenger," he replied easily. He'd answered that question plenty of times.

"He's telling the truth," the woman said to the smirking man.

"All right then," the man replied. "Tell me, Michael Jadern, did that bastard Morian have any plans to escape that would allow anyone plausible deniability?"

"None," Jadern answered so quickly that he might have frowned if the woman hadn't given him such a disarming smile.

"Duke, this is my realm of expertise," she chided. "I already understood that. Now, handsome man, what about any orders Commodore Morian gave you? Surely he had some words for you at the end?"

Jadern felt his head ache as his mind flashed back to those fateful minutes, as four capital vessels prepared to flee the Ras Algethi system under enemy fire. But Richard hadn't said a thing to him.

"What about before that?" the woman asked. The headache grew deeper as Jadern found himself tracking back over hours, even days. Richard had barely spoken to him after he'd taken command of the Thorn.

"I'm sure he wasn't ignoring you," he heard the woman say. "He must have been very busy, after all."

"Yes," Jadern replied, rubbing at his temples. But now it was out in the open. Why had Richard cut him off like that? Did he give me command of Thorn because he trusted me, or because he wanted me off the bridge?

"Then again, you wouldn't have been there, but for him," the woman suggested. "And you wouldn't be here, either."

She's right! Jadern realized as his headache peaked. *I'm in prison because Richard disobeyed orders. It was easy to believe we were right at the time, but I'm in prison and he's avoiding punishment.*

Suddenly, he couldn't believe that Richard was dead. Richard had escaped the consequences and left a patsy in his stead.

The headache disappeared entirely, and a rush of well-being enveloped him. He'd seen through Richard's deceptions!

The man suddenly spoke up. "Michael Jadern, I am Duke Gyrich Rutta," he said in very officious tones. "It's true that Richard Morian and I didn't agree, and he was very convincing to others. But you have seen through his charade so I'm offering you the chance to leave this pit."

Disgust for Richard, his onetime friend, welled up inside Jadern. "I'll take it. Whatever you want, I'll do it. Just don't leave me here getting beaten for his mistakes."

"No, we don't want that," Duke Rutta said. "In fact, I'll do one better. Swear loyalty to the new king, and I'll help restore your rank. We'll give you a ship—a destroyer, maybe? It will be a significant step for your career."

Captaining a ship again? he thought. From a twenty-year prison sentence to landing on a bridge? I'd be a fool not to!

"Yes," Jadern said. "I'll take any oath you ask."

"You see, Duke Rutta?" the woman said. "I told you he'd be reasonable. Let's see if the sister is amenable this time."

Jadern glanced at her, but she drifted from his mind. He had a hundred things to think of now. He had no time for a woman in hundred-year-old fashions, or her cryptic statements.

If not for Richard Morian, I wouldn't be here now, he assured himself. *So there's no reason to pretend any loyalty now. He got what he wanted. Now it's my turn.*

———

Bautan Beta-Max Penitentiary
[CLASSIFIED]
Solitary Block, Cell A

Danis Morian awoke to find herself in the same blank, featureless cell as she did for countless days on end. She sat up on the strange block of a bed, soft but with rounded edges that she just sank into. She wasn't quite certain how long she'd been held captive. They only delivered meals while she slept, so she might get two meals a day or four without knowing. There wasn't much to do besides eat and sleep, though she never felt like doing either. The quietude was becoming a distraction all its own.

How would I know it's the same cell? she wondered. *Maybe every time I sleep, they move me to a similar cell, just to see if I respond.*

It was a thought she'd woken to a dozen times. It was days since she'd spoken to anyone. She'd been sitting in the hanger with another woman, worrying about Richard—she'd never even gotten the woman's name. Then the guards had hauled her off to some stuffy colonel, but that was... Now, the idea that she was helpless also affected her internal reasoning. She was very much alone.

More than alone. For the first time in six years, her Psy was gone. She couldn't sense any minds. It was like losing a lullaby.

How didn't I notice that connection? she wondered. *I always felt Richard—it was like we heard each other from the womb. And I always felt Elio nearby, but I never wanted to stop sensing him. Why did I not notice the presence of... everyone else?*

But now, it was all gone.

How are they doing it? She wondered. *Is it a machine?*

She thought about the prisoners they'd taken in the raid against Ikalven Mining Station. *There were a lot of PsyOps in that station,* she mused. *How were they being kept prisoner? Did Richard—*

The repeated thoughts of Richard brought back the last contact she'd had with him. She'd overheard a thought that sounded like he'd sacrificed pilots to gain a military advantage.

But any denial she might have mustered was cored out of her by the fact that he'd disappeared.

He's not dead, she told herself. *He can't be. Richard just... showed up later, or somehow escaped. I'm sure of it.* She fought back the tears, but it was no use. No matter how hard she tried to convince herself that he'd survived, she always found more tears.

What's wrong with me? she wanted to scream. *Why can't I push past this... helplessness? Why can't I get myself out?*

But looking around the room, at the featureless walls with no opening, she wanted to despair all the more. She buried her face in her hands, unwilling to look at the walls anymore.

"I trust you're willing to talk?" came a completely unexpected voice.

She looked up in shock. There was a man in her cell.

"How did you get in here?" she demanded.

"The same way you did," he remarked. He sat down on a chair that wasn't there before. "Would you like to talk?"

Danis had no idea how long she'd heard nothing but silence. Simply hearing a human was gratifying. But no one on this ship was a friend. "I... suppose it depends on what you want to talk about," she replied carefully.

"Well, that's better than the last time," he said with a smile.

That smile seemed familiar. "Have we met before?" she asked.

"Oh, I'm glad you remember," he said. "They tased you hard after our last meeting. I was afraid they'd damaged you."

She was recollecting something... "You asked me if I wanted to talk," she said, the pieces coming back.

"And do you remember what you said?" he prompted.

Danis remembered the bulky helmet, the snide remarks from the guards. She'd spit on this man, and when the guards flinched, she'd lunged forward to headbutt his stupid face—

She kept her face carefully composed. "No, I don't," she lied, looking to see if there were any telltale bruises she could spot.

His expression said he didn't believe her. "My name is Commander Bali Escalle," he said. "I was sent to find your brother and bring his ship back."

And now I remember why I spit on him. This time, Danis asked, "What do you expect of me?"

Escalle smiled. "To speak out against that mission you were part of. Richard was everyone's commodore. You couldn't help that he dragged you along after he was ordered to stand down. You couldn't ignore orders to fly after he attacked another government—they were firing on your only refuge."

Danis was flabbergasted. "So you want me to denounce my own brother, and the former prince of Orso for ordering the mission, and... what? You'll reinstate me as squadron commander? Maybe promote me, give me a wing of fighters?"

"You certainly deserve it," Escalle said. "You've achieved spectacular results these last six years. You've led an impressive number of attacks against the Swarm, and you've earned the respect of your military leaders."

"Except you," Danis stated.

"Ah, there you're mistaken," he said. "I hold you in high esteem. I'd be honored to have you on my flight deck, though it's the marshals in Central—"

"You have no respect for me, or my intelligence, or my loyalties," Danis countered. "If you had a shred of respect for me, you'd know that I am loyal to my brother—" she shoved the thought of him sacrificing pilots aside—"and loyal to the true crown of Orso. Elio Lorne is the only royalty I ever bent a knee to, and he's done more to prosecute this war than any dozen politicians you could name. Two dozen, even. So I'll save you the trouble. You'll never get any cooperation from me, and it will be the same for anyone who served under Richard."

Escalle shrugged. "Perhaps. But plenty of people aboard the Thorn didn't serve under him. They are willing to listen. I came to you as... a courtesy. And we've already received a great deal of help from you, Danis Morian. You led us all the way."

"What are you talking about?" she snapped. "I never—"

Audio began playing, as if from the very air.

"Dear Elio," Danis heard in her own voice. "I've been worried sick ever since we left Caerus. I've been desperate to talk—"

"How did you get that message?" she demanded as she fought tears.

"We knew about Elio's special accounts," Escalle replied as the message droned on. "Yours, and the TK Knights. We waited until someone used one of them and then followed the signal back through the Slipgate network."

"If you... ever get this... I'm sorry," her traitorous voice continued. "I should have tried harder—"

"I'll leave this on," Escalle said with a smile. "It's too quiet in here."

"No—wait—!" Danis cried out.

But he, along with his chair, disappeared.

Danis scrambled off the bed and looked everywhere she could touch, but there was no trace.

I'm not in a cell, she thought. *I'm in a halo simulation.*

"Because I... I hope I hear something soon," the message ended, and Danis felt like a coward for not saying I love you instead.

There was a moment of silence. She braced herself.

"Dear Elio, I've been worried sick—" she heard again.

And then again.

And again.

CHAPTER
THREE

Enlisted
Bautan Beta-Max Penitentiary
[CLASSIFIED]
Solitary Block, Cell F

Jude Cabeus was gratified to awaken. He had another chance to see Maila. He had another chance to hold Tag and Posie. Even with one arm, it was the best feeling in the world.

He missed his family more than anything else, and he hated being a soldier.

As before, he was in a featureless white room. It had a soft, smooth block of a bed with no corners, no loose pieces.

No hard, blunt edges to strike against.

Always look for the weapon, his father's voice had once whispered in his ear. Everything has the potential to be a weapon, if you can figure out how to use it.

"Bet he never got stuck inside this room," Jude muttered. Not that this was really a room. It had been convincing for the first few minutes, but he'd been here ten days and thirteen hours. And the smells... Ten minutes had been long enough to detect his own scent. But it was the same antiseptic clean as the first day.

I wonder how the real one smells, he mused as he pushed himself from the bed with his one arm. He lowered himself to the floor, using only his legs, and began a series of simple stretches. Maila was always teasing him for fidgeting, needing to move. *I'd feel bad for whoever sponges my body, but... I didn't choose this.*

The stretches relaxed his mind—they were structure, familiarity, purpose, and whatever that hellhole of a camp had taught him, Jude couldn't sit still. While he stretched, he reviewed likely locations aboard a Defender-Class cruiser he might be being kept. *Ten days is more than enough time to make the trip to Caerus*, he thought, but then passed over the thought. Once he'd judged the likeliest prison cells, he reviewed memories of Orso's prisons. Most Caerus prisons were built around the same square layout—entrance hallway to Admittance, then a long hallway to the rear, which branched off left and right into detention wings. Each wing was accessible by a single hallway, making a choke point during escape attempts. Jude was trying to determine which threat-level he might be in when a man appeared, as if by sorcery, in a wooden chair.

"Good morning, Jude Cabeus," the man began an obviously prepared speech. "my name is Bali Escalle, and—"

"It's 1600 hours," Jude interrupted without looking up from his quad stretch. "Maybe 1630."

The man started and glanced at his wrist as though expecting to find his wrist pad in the simulation. "Um, how do you know that?" he asked, too politely.

"The guard told me," Jude replied, and the man's eyes bulged before his expression settled into a tiny sneer.

Jude was gathering information. He'd noted the man's

insignia, but his flared emotions showed he wasn't prepared to hold a real commander's rank.

"I'm here to offer you a deal," Escalle began, but Jude interrupted him again.

"You only have one thing I want," Jude snapped. "Something I don't have here in your simulation. So let me out. Once I'm out, showered, given clothes that I select, and cook my own food, I will listen to deals. Otherwise, I will punish you until you accept."

Jude was done stretching. He tucked his legs under him, resting on the balls of his feet not two meters away.

Escalle held up his hands in mock helplessness. "I'm afraid things aren't as simple as that—"

Jude sprang the distance in a single leap, crashing his one hand into Escalle's neck. His knees collided with Escalle's chest, knocking the chair backwards from the impact. Jude landed on top, the commander's eyes bulging before he disappeared, chair and all.

"I wonder what he thinks of that?" Jude muttered. He'd been in halo-sim combat training before, and he'd felt the rigidity of the sim body. No easily broken skeleton, but a hard body mass with a soft layer of skin texture. He assumed that the sim's pain functions had been decreased, since the commander had said nothing—

The sim screeched with static before he was dumped back into his body.

BAUTAN BETA-MAX PENITENTIARY
   [CLASSIFIED]
   Solitary Block, Cell K

. . .

MEERA SAT IN HER CELL. Aside from the helmet and bracers she wore, she wasn't uncomfortable, though she thought she'd like a good scrub in the hydro soon. The cell was dingy and worn; the mattress was flat and squeaked when she lay down, and the door had a shuttered window.

She was beginning to miss the company of the other TK Knights.

They weren't always the most expressive bunch, she thought. *Well, except for Proose, with his crazy dancing. And Elaer's juggling act with all her wire tentacles. And... and...*

Vecht had been reassigned after the Battle of Odin. Jude had become withdrawn and violent. Rauf and Beko both died in the Battle for Som Orsi. Andra? She had no idea what had happened to her. And Klaus—

I don't want to think about him! she wanted to scream, but he was there now, and she would have to deal with him.

Klaus, her almost-lover. She'd hesitated, and she'd been right to. He'd kept secrets from her. Klaus had been deployed with her son Sorge before the Battle for the Slipgates. They had been friends until Sorge's death. Klaus had learned all about Meera from him. Then Klaus had used that information to romance her, but she'd never overcome her reluctance to date someone so young.

But she had begun to love—

You can't love a lie! Meera tried to be adamant. If Klaus had lied to her, how could she trust him? How could he misunderstand so much if he loved her?

I didn't want to bring up bad memories, he'd pleaded. As though she blamed her son for dying!

Klaus had survived that crash, Meera thought. He received a medical discharge. How did he survive? What medical problem? He never seemed injured to me. The things she'd accepted were thrown into question, but it didn't matter because she'd turned her back on him.

But... did I do the right thing?

The shutter on her cell door opened.

"Meera Seleure?" a gruff voice asked.

"That's m-me," she replied.

The shutter slammed shut, and the door opened. A man walked in, massaging his neck. He was wearing a crisp military uniform with an assortment of pins and ribbons. She didn't recognize most of them. But she did recognize the pair of starburst insignias on the shoulders. He was a starship captain.

"Hello," the man said. "My name is Commander Bali Escalle. I'm here to discuss the terms of your release."

"My release?" Meera could hardly believe it. "Finally. I knew there had to be a mistake. I was just—"

"Silence," Commander Escalle snapped. She quieted immediately. "I am authorized to offer you the following terms. We will release you contingent on the following: first, that any statements you give concerning your previous mission be strictly worded in accordance with the briefing you will receive. Second, you will be on paid medical leave for one year, or on permanent medical discharge with one year's pay."

"That would be—" Meera started to say, but she caught the hard look in the commander's eye, and quieted.

"Third, you will wear an inhibitor to control your TK abilities. You will still have TK, but vastly limited compared to what you were wielding in war. The government has decided that recent combatants need to be kept under control."

Meera wanted to argue, but she couldn't argue against their fear of her using her full strength. She was dangerous.

Wait, she thought. *If they're taking me off duty, and they're putting these things on me permanently...*

"Fourth," Escalle stated, "you will not contact any of your former crew members. Any intentional contact will be seen as an act of sedition."

"Sedition?" Meera said, trying to remember what that meant. "How can talking to people I worked with—"

Escalle glared at her. "We've had enough. The government spent fifty-two billion to send my flotilla out to arrest Morian. You were a contractor, and we're terminating your contract. So the only reason for you to talk to them is to stir up resentment and trouble. Read the scripts for your interviews and go home to a nice quiet life. The government will take care of this."

Meera hated every word, but they held the ultimate trump. If her infant grandson Stevian got sick, it would only take minutes of hospital delay to force her hand—a simple "accident" or "mix-up."

"I—I accept," she replied.

Escalle's glare softened into a smirk. "Glad you see it our way," he said. "Someone will be by to formally release you. Clothes will be provided for you. Your duffels will be returned in two weeks once we've searched them."

Meera wanted to ask what contraband she might have, but decided against it. He was riding high on his authority.

"Be glad you had a cell," he added, waving at the cell. "Some people were dealt with far more harshly."

He knocked on the door, and the guards opened it. He didn't look back before it clanged shut.

Meera looked around her cell once more. She had nothing to do but wait.

If this was nice, she wondered a hundred times in that hour, *what did they do to the others?*

———

BAUTAN BETA-MAX PENITENTIARY
[CLASSIFIED]
Solitary Block, Cell F

Jude screamed again.

Pain engulfed him. He was being tased repeatedly. He tried to lash out, or roll away, but he was strapped down, immobilized. Finally, the shocks subsided, and he stifled a moan. He would deny his torturers any satisfaction. Before he could blink, he found himself back in the simulation, clean but aching.

He didn't wait long before another man and chair materialized. But it wasn't Commander Escalle.

"Marshal Marrion," Jude muttered.

"Since when is 'Dad' not appropriate?" his father asked.

"I left because of you," Jude answered. "I left the military, I left Som Orsi, I left the entire continent, just so I wouldn't have to talk to you."

"You could have stayed away," his father observed.

"Don't bother," Jude said. "I can predict this conversation. If I stayed away, I'm a bastard who would burn the world. If I enlisted again, I'm a foolish idealist."

"Actually, you were already a fool," his father said. "You let that idiot woman sway your thinking."

"You leave my mother out of this," Jude snapped. "Your mission was an abomination. You set me up to be a patsy, and my life was worth no more than that of a pawn."

"Patsy?" His father laughed. "You left just when things were getting interesting. You would have been whisked from scrutiny, and made a key player. Instead, I wasted years setting up Ugo Tan to replace you."

"The mission was to murder the royal family," Jude replied. "What a patriot you are."

"A patriot has loyalty to the government, not individuals," his father snapped. "And what's happened in six years? Orson refused to face the threat. Elio flittered away, and the fleet pulled away from Central Command. Now this regency takes advantage of my work and has set up a puppet we can control."

"I'm surprised you didn't just have them killed," Jude muttered.

"I spent months putting you in place for an assassination," his father said. "I can't move against them now without suspicion."

Jude knew that was true. They'd carefully crafted "Jude Cabeus" to pass every level of scrutiny, and he'd worn the mask for over a year before abandoning his mission.

"Let me be blunt, Wayn," the marshal said. Jude flinched at his old name. "You want to go back to your harlot and her brats, go ahead. Yes, I know about them. But if you want to live in peace and quiet and far, far away from me, then you have a job to do."

"I have no interest in anything you—"

"You'd better be interested, boy!"

Jude's head rocked sideways from a blow he never saw coming. His ears ringing, his head aching, he looked up at the man standing over him.

"How... did..." Jude managed to say.

"This is a sim, remember?" his father said. "Your body's defenses are reduced to nothing, while mine are superhuman. No sense having a repeat of your tantrum with Bali, is there? Or letting you use TK on me."

His father grabbed his jumpsuit collar and hoisted Jude into the air like a sack. "Now, I'm working with this Regency. And they want two men dead. You find these men and kill them. One of them has a son, an admiral. When I explain how the Regency killed his father, he will immediately join our side, instead of sitting on his fence."

"And I'm protected from all that fallout?" Jude demanded.

"Absolutely," his father replied. "Just kill them, then go

back to your mud and bugs." He dropped Jude on his prison bed.

"So I just use what you taught me?" Jude said, hoping to get a little rise out of his father.

No such luck. "I taught you to blend in on a dozen planets, to be a spy without peer," his father replied. "Now you live in a stick hut."

Jude didn't know if he wanted to trust his father, but... then he realized he didn't have a choice. Not if he wanted out of his prison. "Fine," he agreed. "Who are the marks?"

The wall of the sim changed to a viewscreen. Two pictures appeared, one of them with a very familiar eye patch.

"Colonel Avrum Rosst," his father said, pointing to Jude's former commanding officer in the TK Knights. The pictures showed front, profile, and three-quarter views. A second set showed him without his eye patch "He was slated to receive a replacement eye before the Regency seized power. He may have found a way to receive one. And the second is retired Air Marshal Teyn Grig."

Teyn Grig... The plan became clear. "Teyn Grig?" he asked. "His son is Huis Grig?"

Jude knew Admiral Grig's reputation—a fierce warrior with a quick temper.

"If you tell him his father is dead, won't he fire on the palace from orbit?" Jude asked.

"I'm reasonably certain that he won't," his father replied. His smile was cold, though, and Jude felt a shiver run down his spine and through his missing arm.

My arm. "What about my arm?" he asked. "The mission would be easier with two arms."

"Didn't I teach you to fight with one arm tied behind your back?" his father asked with a chuckle. When Jude didn't respond, he scowled instead. "You'll have a basic model, no onboard weapons. You can kill them with a regular gun—in fact, if you steal one and discard it, it can't be traced back to us."

Jude looked at the images. He hated everything his father stood for. But... the Regency had already killed citizens and ignored the war in order to maintain power. As much as Jude hated it, his father would make the war a priority. And with Elio probably dead, there was no one left to fight for Orso's survival.

If there was one thing Marshal Jonn Marrion knew, it was how to survive.

"I'll take the job," he heard himself say. Bile crept into his throat.

"Excellent!" his father said. "Oh, and the arm will have a TK inhibitor."

"Why shouldn't I have TK?" Jude demanded.

"My personal safety," Morrison sneered. "And it will be locked on. Only a specialist will be able to detach it. When you get out of this simulation, apologize to Bali. He isn't mine, and I don't want him holding a grudge. Understand?"

How did I agree to this brush-fire plan? "Yes, sir," Jude replied.

He was back in the Orso military after all.

———

Bautan Beta-Max Penitentiary
Administrative Offices

HELOT SAT SILENTLY, occasionally twitching or smiling. When she opened her eyes, Duke Rutta ventured a comment. "So, did it go well?"

"Those two soldiers have no defense," Helot said. "The woman is too broken inside to resist. The man with one arm fought me, but his father is a dark symbol of authority for him. He will do what we need."

"And Jadern is working for us now," Rutta said. "But what about Danis Morian?"

"She bears closer examination," Helot said, a strange look in her eye. "She resisted me, even though she isn't trained. I will break her eventually."

"And what about my idea?" Rutta pressed. "Did you implant my suggestions?"

Helot stared into his eyes, and Rutta held that gaze.

Finally, Helot responded. "Since you believe it will serve the One King as well as yourself, yes I added your suggestion to the plan. If Elio Lorne comes home his days are numbered."

CHAPTER
FOUR

ONSLAUGHT
Orbital Station Auspex
Hebe-Gany L2 Point

MILENDA SHAE STARED at her screen.

She didn't expect anything to happen, but she'd heard too many stories about the Swarm appearing while people were distracted.

Perversely, she was now obsessed with watching every monitor nearby. If she watched everywhere, then, by logic, the Swarm couldn't surprise them. There should be constant vigil on every sensor, every vector to the outer planets. She understood she was wrong, and yet she still checked every screen the moment its operator stretched, or went to the facilities, or turned to chat.

I can't fault them, Milenda tried to convince herself. *They don't believe that they can prevent an invasion by staring at screens. I don't really believe it either. This is a healthy para-*

noia, I'm sure. So I'll politely ask Galez to shove it the next time he asks me to see the station psychologist.

Suddenly, she heard alarms. She glared at the screens, daring any of them to be the culprit. But none of the screens within sight were the cause.

"We have unknown vessels approaching from in-system!" she heard Galez yelling across the room. "Signatures match possible Swarm contacts. I repeat, we have vessels coming from beyond the inner planets!"

The bastards are invading! Milenda thought right before she had another thought. Nobody was watching the inner system sensors! *I was right!*

———

135TH FLOOR, Caissier Room
Aestim Building

ELIO'S last meeting had been less than stellar. He'd been unable to help with the trade dispute. Governor Friah had argued, rightly, that if the various systems had honored their agreements, Remanor wouldn't be in financial straits or scrambling to find protection. Wex Andreys had critiqued Governor Friah's predecessor for disregarding citizens' safety to continue terraforming, and Friah hadn't campaigned to enlighten citizens about the expanding conflict.

Given the choice between terraforming or building additional defenses, Elio wouldn't have chosen the United Sovereign Fleet as their only defense force. The leaders in the USF—the ones he trusted completely—could be counted on one hand. Most of them had led forces during the Invasion of Odin. Finally, the meeting had devolved into a shouting match before Elio hacked the lighting controls and flickered them, calling for a recess until tomorrow. Grateful to be away, he'd fled to his next meeting with the banking guild, and that one hadn't gone any better.

The dry accounting of assets and infrastructure for Seyshore Industries left him with little to do until the actual negotiations began. As ambassador, his job was to arbitrate a fair balance between bank interests and company production, and he hoped it would be a simple task. But after the arguments over trade... well, he wasn't expecting much.

At least I don't have Squad A looking over my shoulder this time, he thought. Blade Sergeant had rotated Squad A, and himself, into their makeshift barracks in the room near Elio's own. I don't envy them. Hot-bunking four shifts in a two-bed suite sounds miserable. So now he was left without Blade Sergeant's infectious charm, replaced by Squads B and C who were watching the doors, while Squad D was standing nearby as unobtrusively as possible. Which meant that they just looked out of place, instead of threatening.

"Now," the banking representative droned on, "if you'll look at page one-hundred seven, paragraph forty-three, subsection F, you can see that—"

Alarms began to blare, cutting him off. Amber emergency lights glowed as the overhead lights dimmed.

"What's happening?" Elio demanded.

"We have a planetary alert!" the banking host declared. "A fleet of Swarm ships is attacking Remanor!"

Elio's first instinct was to fight, but he checked that reaction. He wasn't aboard a ship; he didn't have a fighter, and he didn't have a commando group; just a few guards.

"Everyone listen!" he announced. "We're on the hundred-and-nineteenth floor. We need to evacuate to the lower floors immediately."

"What if the building collapses?" someone yelled back. "We'd be trapped in the rubble, or crushed to death!"

"And what do you think are your chances," Elio asked, "if you're near the top floor when the building topples?"

Elio heard no complaints, so he took the lead. "Form a line and make your way out! We're going to the stairs. Yes, stairs. If the building shifts, the lifts will stop working. Everyone, open every door and yell for evacuation. We have to find as many people as possible."

His guards immediately crowded around him. He expected them to resist, but they followed him. He breathed a sigh of relief.

One factor in their favor was Remanor's low gravity. Everyone loped along the hallways. The offworlders had some difficulty adjusting, but the natives glided like ballerinas in slow motion, alerting their fellows and moving on. Once they reached the stairs, people took steps four and five at a time, gently wafting to the lower floors. Several offworlders stumbled and fell, but even those weren't hurt. And the building tremored and Elio was instantly alarmed.

"We need to move faster!" he shouted to those having trouble keeping up. "Those plasma blasts will take out the support structures. If we're too high—"

There was a brilliant flash as a plasma beam cut through their stairwell. Elio shielded his face from the burst of heat that scorched his skin. When he opened his eyes, the blast was several floors above.

Bodies toppled down the shaft, dozens of them. The bankers stared at them in horror.

"Get moving!" Elio ordered as another plasma beam cut through the building, burning through the structural supports. Debris rained down the stairwell. A severed girder fell, clanging against everything in its path, heading right toward Elio's group.

———

Drella heard the ominous creak and looked up.

A massive section of girder pinwheeled in the light gravity as it fell toward her.

Drella's HUD calculated the trajectory. The landing above would deflect the girder, but it would take half the platform and all of D Squad with it.

She had to protect the prince! She threw herself in front of him and tried to push him to safety, but Elio's body didn't move. His eyes were closed, his hands extended, trembling. The choker and bracelets glowed fiercely, a sign that they were working at full capacity to restrict his powers. She turned to find the girder hanging in the air as if by steel cables.

He... caught the girder with TK. Drella couldn't believe it. All his restraints, and he can still... do that?

Strain etched across his face, Prince—Ambassador Elio set it on the landing just below.

He turned to D Squad. "Can you take my restraints off?" he asked, his face a sheen of sweat.

Drella stared at him for a moment, dazed, before she shook her head.

"This is life and death here!" he snapped. "I give my word on House Lorne that I will submit myself again."

"Sorry," Drella muttered, shame burning her face. "Only the Blade Sergeant has the hash code."

"Fine," Elio groaned. "Get moving. No sense waiting for the sky to fall." And he took to the stairs again.

Drella looked to her lance sergeant.

"D Squad, follow," he ordered, launching down the stairs. "And... keep quiet, if you can."

Drella nodded. She would protect the ambassador. She owed him a debt, and there was no way she'd rat his secret out.

———

HASH CODE? Elio turned that information over in his mind several times as he took the stairs carefully. *There isn't a normal lock. A hash-encrypted electronic key can't be hacked, but it might be duplicated. Why would they choose that?*

The answer was obvious.

Because I could release a simple lock with TK, given enough time.

He filed the information away, hoping he might free himself at need, but only at need. *If I don't prove myself trustworthy, I'll never have an opportunity.*

The building shuddered under another plasma blast. Elio heard creaks and groans and chunks of building began to rain down the stairwell. Too many to deflect!

He reached a landing and turned automatically, but there was only a door. He faltered for a moment—

One of the guards slammed into him from behind, crashing him into the wall just as a shower of metal and glass landed where he'd been standing.

He pushed away from the wall. "Thank you," he gasped, "but we need to assist anyone else on the stairs—"

The groaning turned into a piercing shriek as he looked up. The stairwell above the fortieth floor disappeared as the upper building canted sideways even in the moon's low gravity.

Three-quarters of the building tore away from its base with a mind-rending screech.

Debris crashed down what remained of the stairwell. And then, all was quiet, and Elio could see the night sky. High above, blocking half the stars, the yellow swirls of Gany drifted into view. It might have been beautiful, but for the death and destruction around him.

Elio allowed his guards to bustle him underground, where the survivors cried, whimpered, or begged family to answer their comms. For many of these people, the terrors had only just begun.

Elio scanned through the crowds until he found a man wearing a security uniform. He strode over, his faceless guards having to shove their way through the grieving crowds. He wondered how that looked to the common people. Probably bad, he decided.

"I'd like a report, officer," Elio stated. "What's going on up there?"

"It—it's already over," the young officer stammered.

"What do you mean?" Elio asked.

"The Swarm attack," the security officer replied. "I just got the message. They appeared from sun side and flew past the picket ships in orbit. They went right for the city, and the pickets couldn't fire without hitting it. By the time our fighters launched, the Swarm had already left. They just... flew back toward the sun and disappeared."

Elio resisted the urge to demand more. This officer wasn't a military resource, just a scared young man. But if what he said was true...

The Swarm had never struck a target and fled. Their tactics were changing, and that was alarming. An enemy with overwhelming forces appearing unexpectedly and changing tactics, avoiding previous mistakes, was something entirely new. It was something to fear.

———

Emergency Shelter, Floor U-3
   Aestim Building

. . .

D Squad entered the shelter and found chaos.

Drella's HUD tried to track everyone to classify their threat level. She could barely see through her visor, or think over the hundreds of voices. It was so distracting!

The thought of the thousands of people plummeting to their deaths chilled her. *But then, I'm alive. We're alive, she thought.*

She spotted C Squad entering after them. Their Lance Sergeant Sidray spotted her. They exchanged nods. Drella gave the signal for we have a target. Sidray signaled we have exit. And then the ambassador found a security officer, who relayed some information she couldn't catch.

Drella's chest pumped against her armor as the word safety took new meaning. She'd never been so frightened. In battle, she could kill the enemy. But a collapsing building? That had no enemy except time and gravity.

Drella turned to her partner. "I don't know what C Squad saw," she whispered, "but we keep our mouths shut, right?"

Her partner shrugged. "Far as I'm concerned, the Fish ranks over Sarge. Ain't gonna talk."

"Make sure nobody else—"

Suddenly, D Squad's comms crackled to life. "I want a report now!" Blade Sergeant's voice bellowed loud enough to make Ambassador Elio flinch.

"D Squad here," she reported. "Underground shelter, floor U-3. Target Fish safe and accounted for. D Squad is whole, C Squad visually confirmed."

"C Squad here," she heard, both on her comm and from somewhere nearby. "Shelter, U-3, guarding the door."

"Did you run comm checks?" Blade Sergeant demanded.

"Sorry sir." She hated giving him any reason to berate her, or anyone else. "We're just grateful to be alive."

"What about B Squad?" Strike Sergeant asked. "Have you confirmed them?"

"Um, no sir," she replied. "But... they were in the conference room—"

"I know where they were!" he bellowed. "You were on floor one-nineteen! Everything above three-seven is gone!"

Drella's stomach sank. B Squad, dead? Just... gone, just like that?

"Location, sir?" she inquired. "We'll bring Target Fish to you and—"

"No," he ordered. "Building security will escort you. No need to risk any incompetence. Out." The comm clicked off.

"I'm sorry about that," Ambassador Elio murmured next to her. She hadn't realized he was listening.

"He's... he's just... "Drella didn't know what to say.

"He's that way with everyone?" Elio finished for her.

Everything was out of control. The building collapse, B Squad's loss, the dressing down... Drella had known these four squads only for a month. Someone had contacted her, offering her a place in the Redemption Unit. She'd jumped at the chance to get reassigned. And guarding an ambassador seemed like the easiest post.

"By the way... "Elio added. "I'm 'Target Fish'?"

Drella hoped her sudden blush wasn't visible. "The, um, Blade Sergeant named you that. He said you, um, always had your mouth open, like a copper-finned trask, and nothing important came out."

The ambassador actually smiled! "He sticks to his opinions, doesn't he?" Elio said. Drella couldn't answer.

Of course he can't see me blush! she thought. *I'm wearing my helmet!*

A pair of security officers appeared. "Ambassador," one of them said, "we have orders to lead you topside. The rest of your guard is waiting for you."

"I'm sure they are," Elio replied. His shoulders slumped as they left the throng of weeping, mourning people.

Whatever could be done to help them, it wasn't in Drella's power, or his. She'd joined Redemption to take charge again. Now she felt even more helpless than she had before.

Ataraxis's Bridge
193,000 km above Hebe

Captain Bhor Carrica watched the last Swarm fighters flee out of range. He thumbed the comm control at his station.

"Ataraxis, stand down to Level Three," he ordered, his voice broadcast to the entire ship. "I want repairs underway immediately and battle assessments in thirty minutes." He looked at his bridge crew. Most of them looked shocked. Carrica himself was perturbed by the abrupt end to the conflict. "I am announcing an immediate shift change," he continued. "Anyone on station during the attack gets four hours rest, then report to your supervisors. I want everyone else sharp and on duty for twelve hours. That is all."

He turned to his first officer. "I'll be in my ready room. Take the conn, please."

"Aye, sir," he said, taking Carrica's place.

Captain Carrica stepped into the quiet solitude of his ready room. Unlike most captains, he'd had his rooms decorated on his own budget. Fine furniture, antique bronze sculptures, wall hangings his wife had picked out while on vacation in Auspicia. The ready room was decorated to relax him, and it did. It also served as an appropriate setting for diplomatic events, and it reminded him of happier times, if he could keep his recent memories at bay.

Peaceful Mind is a powerful name for a diplomatic ship, Carrica thought. *As important for us as for our guests.*

But his intention wasn't to find peace. Far from it. He placed his halo over his thinning hair and contacted his superior. Then he waited. And waited.

It was almost five minutes later when Duke Gyrich Rutta finally appeared. "Bhor Carrica. It's good to see you," the duke greeted him. "Why are you contacting me? Did His Ambassadorship fall down a hole?"

Carrica winced at the duke's quip. "My duke," he began, "the twin planets were the victims of a Swarm attack. It didn't last but an hour, but the damage is... substantial. We must delay departure. Remanor called for assistance under USF Code Fifty-Five, paragraph—"

"Nonsense," Duke Rutta interrupted. "That only applies to military vessels. You are a diplomatic ship."

Carrica hesitated. "With due respect, that's a narrow point. The Ataraxis was a military vessel, and its towing capabilities would help recovery operations or the transportation of refugees—"

"But that isn't your job," Duke Rutta stated. "Your job is to ferry the prince. And if leaving makes him look tactless, even better. The last thing I need is for Elio to rally ten thousand people."

Carrica considered that. "Then, why is he even—"

"You have your orders," Duke Rutta snapped. "Move on and don't be late." The duke disappeared.

Carrica sighed and removed his halo.

"I think I've dug myself in too deep, Pieda," he whispered to the stars. "When that Redemption officer came around and said I could have a second chance, and that I could end my career on a peak, instead of..."

A tear trickled down his cheek.

"What do I have left? You're gone. Deena and Meret are

gone. It's enough to break any man. Must I sacrifice my honor, too?"

He closed his eyes, but the last images of his wife and children flashed by, over and over, hours before the Battle of Som Orsi.

"I've lost enough, haven't I, Pieda?"

But the stars didn't answer.

They never did.

CHAPTER
FIVE

Wilderness, ENE from Awega City
Location Unknown, Planet Caerus

Though cardinal direction was simple, geography provoked Foreign's outrage constantly. Hills, valleys, rivers, forests—all of it blasphemous to the Will's notion of perfection, and all difficult to circumvent.

The first day, Foreign found the human body was subject to debilitation by sun, movement, and thirst. It needed frequent rests, culminating in a lack of sense organs permitting night travel. It was beyond inefficient.

The second day, Foreign learned that human bodies were also debilitated by rumbling torsos. In consulting the information gleaned from its prisoners on Odin, it decided this was hunger and could be solved by seizing handfuls of plant and masticating it into pulp. But, the plant "grass" was difficult to swallow, and caused unpleasant oral sensations.

On the third day, it realized certain plants aided the body

more than others. Now Foreign favored tree bulbs and the occasional ground-gourd. Its energy replenished; it surged forward vigorously; at least for part of a day. Then the hunger and resting needs began again.

On the fourth day, Foreign located a human settlement from a glimmer of network connectivity. It reset its path toward the signal. Soon Foreign located a smooth paved pathway, clearly intended for vehicle travel, with signs announcing locations and amenities. In the distance were buildings. Computers and travel were finally at hand!

It stepped onto the roadway. There was a slight push away from the surface, as though Foreign were being lifted slightly.

Gravity is partially negated here? Foreign accessed the distant network signal and made a query, something it hadn't thought to do days ago. The roadway masked a gravity-deduction device that allowed vehicles to travel long distances more efficiently. So that was why the gravcar had died so quickly—it was pushing against an uneven surface with soft, compressible vegetation. Also, Foreign was surprised to note, the roadway concealed a magnetic-induction line, its purpose to supply power to a vehicle's power supply. The original roads might have circumnavigated natural obstacles, but the new ones protected the material-intensive mechanisms the humans depended on to ease their lives.

Lives that will be burned from existence, and their works crumbled to dust in a fraction of their pitiful lifetimes. Foreign didn't muse rhapsodic over the human's pitiful accomplishments when compared to the magnificence of the Will.

Still, Foreign had accomplished a great deal of travel, and was now rewarded with arrival at a suitable location for communication and transport—

Riverbol, 2 km, the sign read.

Foreign paused and accessed a map. Riverbol wasn't even a

minor metropolis. Riverbol was descended from ancient water travel and trading. Its location near several mining centers had kept it from disappearing completely. But most importantly, it was only forty-two kilometers from the Farda Launch Facility.

Foreign had traveled four solar cycles and thirty-nine point six-five kilometers? Less, technically, since that was the distance for roads. Foreign checked its records again, this time for human endurance and capabilities. This human Kasa Su-Mei's body was not inured to the rigors of travel.

A large grav truck was approaching Foreign's position. Foreign stepped onto the roadway, accessing the grav truck's systems and commanding the simple engine to stop.

The grav truck barreled toward Foreign.

Foreign attempted to command the vehicle again, but it was already shut down.

How is it still moving—?

The grav truck slowly veered to one side before rushing past Foreign with the force of a storm gale. It drifted some ninety meters further down the roadway before stopping in the grass nearby.

Foreign tried to walk, but its human body was shaking. A complex cocktail of chemicals had released into the brain before the truck narrowly missed Foreign's body.

Is this... fear?

Foreign tried to delete the chemical emotions, but to no avail. *Even if I could order this body to stop manufacturing chemicals, Foreign decided, it will be hours before they are purged. Humans are inferior. It is good that they will be destroyed.*

After a moment of computation, Foreign realized the mistake. The truck had stopped driving forward, but the momentum hadn't been halted. Foreign's shutdown order had also interfered with the truck's safety-braking system.

It was Foreign's fault. It had made a mistake that almost cost the Will its valuable tools.

Another chemical surge forced emotional response. This time it was... guilt?

A woman got out of the grav truck and made her way back to Foreign. "Hey, what's the matter wit ya?" the woman yelled. "Don't ya have any common sense—?"

Foreign turned to face the woman, and the trucker blanched. "My goodness—Dearie, what happened to ya? Was ya attacked or something?"

Foreign accessed the body's ability to speak. "I—I walked through the woods, and the river, and the fields."

"You look like you ain't had nothing to eat in a week!" the woman declared. "How did ya get lost so bad?"

"I have eaten," Foreign replied. "Grass and fruits, and gourds. My vehicle stopped working."

"Where'd you lose it, hon?" the trucker asked. "Can I give you a ride back?"

"I lost it four days ago," Foreign declared. "It is not on a road. It will be difficult to find."

"Stars and moon," the trucker said. "Well, I can at least give you a ride. Where are you heading?"

Foreign nearly ended this polite talking. It should be easy to abandon this woman and command the grav truck to go to Som Orsi. But...

The human had knowledge of this world. Foreign had been tasked with learning about human minds, but knew little about their technology. If this human woman could provide travel, and screen others from identifying Foreign's host, it would make things easier.

"I am going to Som Orsi," Foreign answered finally.

"Oh." The woman seemed disappointed for a moment, then gave a big smile. "Well, I can take you as far as Bariell. I turn north after that, but if I get ya three hundred klicks closer, it won't be half so bad. Maybe we can even get you a bus into the city, right?"

Foreign tried to imitate the woman's facial expression. "Right."

"Well, let's get a leg up," she declared. "I'm Selkie. What's your name?"

"I am Foreign," Foreign replied.

"Forann," Selkie repeated. The sound was distinctly different to Foreign's ears. "I ain't heard that name before. It sounds kinda foreign to me—oh, I'm sorry! I bet you get that a lot around here."

"No," Foreign answered.

"No? Ah, well." Selkie ushered Foreign into the grav truck. "Now buckle up. I ain't getting cited for safety noncompliance. That little camera there will rat me out to home office if I don't lay down the law."

Foreign saw the tiny lens embedded in the dashboard. It must be destroyed, or my presence will be detected! Foreign deduced. It tried to shut the device down remotely, but the camera was somehow unconnected to the truck's other systems.

"How will it rat you out?" Foreign asked.

"It records everything," Selkie explained. "Once I drop the truck at the depot, some AI system scans through the entire trip in about five seconds, and cites me for anything wrong. I'll get one over you, but I can argue with the shift super about it, get off easy. I ain't never left a half-starved woman on the road, and I ain't starting now."

The grav truck rumbled to full power, and Selkie edged back onto the roadway.

Foreign felt the body give a slight smile. Three hundred kilometers in a few hours, and transportation after. Som Orsi would be a short ride away.

Then Foreign felt a strange sensation, a buildup of pressure in the throat that expelled violently, over and over.

Foreign clasped its throat. It felt... pain? It wished to shut off pain, but inefficient human bodies didn't allow that.

"Oh, my," Selkie clucked from the next seat. "That's quite a cough. Did you catch something out there in the woods? Best I drop you near a med center first. You need to get that checked out."

"I must not delay long," Foreign stated. "I must go to Som Orsi immediately."

"If you say so, dearie," Selkie answered.

———

Rising Tides Group Psychiatric Facility
Resdon Military Facilities Annex

Lance Sergeant Dascher Bikk walked into work just behind Corporals Dondo and Nejaz and were about to enter the locker room when his wristpad dinged a message alert.

"What's it, Bikk?" Dondo asked.

"I'll check it once we get on duty," Bikk replied. "It's probably nothing."

"I think it's an official message, boss," Dondo insisted as he clicked his riot armor in place. "See the light? It's flashing blue."

Bikk looked at the indicator. Official, huh? He wondered if this was finally the response to his report. But he didn't want to remind Dondo or anyone else of that particular day.

Bikk strapped his wrist guards in place. "If it's official, I might as well get paid for reading it, right?" he asked.

"Ha!" Dondo clapped him on the back. "Whatever, Bikk." And he pushed Nejaz out of the room.

Bikk was tempted to pull it up right then but forced himself to put on his riot armor. *It's nothing important,* he insisted. *If it was important, I'd have received it a week ago.* All he'd received in response to his report was a confirmation; nothing mentioned the strange occurrence. He'd sent two other reports since then, with queries attached, hoping they might share some details. *Have they finally acknowledged the problem here?* he wondered.

Bikk and the others arrived at their station to find Sen already there, as usual. His unit waited by the guard station until 1557, then led everyone inside and one official changing-of-the-guard dance. Later. he was seated at the console for first watch, while the others set up the game in the break area. Nejaz had brought something called Colonists of Canton, and it beat playing cards for amusement.

As they started announcing their antes, because this group would gamble on anything, Bikk finally pulled up the message.

From the Desk of Commander Denk Tonhous, the message began.

I got a commander? Bikk thought. *Maybe they did take me seriously.*

Lance Sergeant Dascher Bikk.

You are hereby ordered to cease investigation into the Rising Tides Group Psychiatric Facility.

Security's role is to file reports about any unusual incidents, not to investigate them.

Speculation about any such incidents is an actionable offense, and may cost you your clearance.

Your predecessor was reprimanded for a similar breach of building security.

Any further remarks on the subject of the Rising Tides Group Psychiatric *Facility will result in full-unit disciplinary action, and possibly discharge.*

Let me make this abundantly clear, Bikk. File reports. Don't ask questions.

Bikk could hardly believe it. *First the zombie horde choir. And now this?*

He sat back in the chair, listening as the other two argued over starship routes and commodities exchanges.

It's like they have a bubble, Bikk thought. *They just stay in a little bubble, until the aliens show up. When the aliens are gone, they just... go back to normal. But this is far beyond the time when ordinary citizens should know what's going on, let alone the people who are watching over these prisoners-of-war.*

These humans were captured on an alien-held planet. The aliens fought with overwhelming force in every encounter, but did the humans manage to pull one over on them this time?

Bikk didn't think so.

———

OFFICE OF MILITARY Affairs
Orso Royal Palace

"COMMANDER MICHAEL JADERN?" an aide called.

Jadern stood and followed the aide through the double doors deep in the heart of Military Central Command into the Office of Military Affairs. His dress shoes padded against the carpet as he walked. It was the short nap he would have expected but for its colors: crimson, gold and cobalt, the colors of the Orso kingdom's flag. After walking down a featureless corridor, the aide tapped a panel, and the wall slid open, and the aide stepped aside for him to enter.

"Thank you," Jadern murmured and stepped through. As

soon as he'd done so, the aide shut the door behind him. *Huh? I guess I'm facing this on my own,* he thought.

He stepped toward a small conference table where two distinguished men in sharply pressed uniforms were seated. Both had the severe expression of high military rank, though their ages were very different. Each had numerous medals, though the older officer had fewer than his younger associate; both wore marshals' insignias.

Two Marshals? Jadern wondered. *How did I rate a pair of marshals?*

He stood silent, perfectly still, at attention, waiting for one of them to speak. He'd served two decades, been shot at by human and Swarm vessels, charged into the fray with naught but a sidearm, and had been imprisoned simply for following his commodore's orders.

Richard Morian...! He checked his anger. This was no time to muse about betrayals. This was the first step to correct the injustice.

Finally, one of the men spoke. "Well, I suppose I should get this out of the way," the younger man said. "Hail King Targer Lorne, the true King of Orso."

"Hail King Targer Lorne!" Jadern repeated obediently. "The true King of Orso!"

Despite that, the men simply waited once more. Jadern held himself still, waiting, uncertain.

Finally, the younger marshal spoke.

"Commander... Michael... Jadern," he recited slowly. "This must be an interesting change of scenery for you, isn't it?"

Jadern hesitated. "Sir?" he asked cautiously.

"No need to dissemble, Commander," he explained. "I'm Marshal Shon Erviette. I signed your prison order."

Jadern felt the other officer's gaze upon him and quashed any reaction.

"He holds himself well, doesn't he, Jonn?" Erviette said to the other man. Whoever "Jonn" was, Jadern caught a flicker of... annoyance? Maybe he resents being here? Despite their equal rank, Jadern wondered if they got along.

"Well," Erviette said, "no use sitting all day. Commander Jadern, you were convicted of aiding and abetting Richard Morian's flight from duty and justice. For the record, how do you plead?"

"Sir," Jadern breathed out in a rush, "I have been, had been, Commodore Morian's first officer for almost five years, and served under him for sixteen. Yes, I obeyed him in the moment. And then I followed him because that was my job. Looking back, I see I might have made mistakes—"

"Yes, yes. Following orders, like you said." Erviette folded his hands together. "And how do you feel now?"

"I... feel betrayed," Jadern admitted. "I never noticed before, but he wasn't the—" Jadern stumbled over the word friend. "—officer I thought I knew. I'm glad to be back."

"Mm-hmm," the older man said. "You've been recommended by Duke Gyrich Rutta. His position in the government is such as to warrant this interview, but not enough to land you a berth. I... ahem, we are at our own discretion in the matter."

"What Marshal Marrion means," Erviette said, "is that we don't answer to the Councilor of Aristocratic Affairs, though we like to maintain a good relationship. We've brought you here to determine if you are fit to serve."

Jadern wanted to say something, anything, even beg forgiveness for his error in trusting Morian. But he stood his ground, silent. No breach of discipline would cost him this chance.

"I will serve the Crown in whatever capacity you decide, Marshals," he declared. "Even if that is to break rocks in the prison yard again."

Erviette grinned. "Look at him, Jonn! Exactly as Rutta said. Masterful discipline, Commander. You may stand at ease."

Jadern widened his stance slightly, folded his hands behind his back, still ramrod straight.

"Do you think he's a good fit for your Redemption Unit, Marshal Marrion?" Erviette asked.

Marshal Marrion gave Jadern the most critical once-over he had ever endured. "I can do a lot with him," he said. "Have you ever captained a vessel of the line, Commander?" When Jadern hesitated, Marrion added, "I mean before this incident."

"No, sir," Jadern said, suppressing a sigh of regret.

"Well," Marrion continued, "I'd like to give you the opportunity, Brevet Captain Jadern. I have a small capital squadron. I'll give you the Torrent. She's an older Guardian-class cruiser we recommissioned. Let's see how you handle her."

Jadern's heart leapt in his chest. *I have a chance! Finally, after all this time, my own ship!*

"You'll serve under Commodore Vandu and the battleship Tsunami," Marshall Marrion continued. "The other cruisers in your squadron will be Captain Lavare's Deluge and Captain Seder's Alluvion. Is this offer satisfactory?"

Jadern couldn't help but loose a sigh of relief. "Absolutely, Marshal. It is... a dream come true."

Marshall Marrion looked to Erviette. "Excellent! The Tsunami task force will tour the Orso system for another two months, and then she'll be ready for patrols. I trust you'll have Torrent well in hand by then?"

Jadern flushed with relief. "Yes, sir. You can count on me."

Marshall Marrion gave him a look. "Yes, Captain, I trust we can. I want your bags packed and ready by 0800 tomorrow.

Your dock assignment will be sent to your wristpad. Do Orso proud, Captain. Dismissed."

Jadern saluted, turned and left the office. A different aide than before guided him through the featureless halls once again before they reached the lobby. "Good luck, sir," he said, though it lacked any real emotion.

It doesn't matter, Jadern thought as he exited the building. *Hitching myself to Richard's star almost cost me everything. From now on, I make my own way.*

CHAPTER
SIX

Avrum Rosst sat alone, before a viewscreen, in a decrepit warehouse. He had awakened before everyone else, as usual. After thirty years of military life, he woke at reveille with or without the instrument.

Som Orsi was like any metropolis, with official and unofficial districts. Lockwith, the owner of this warehouse in the back alleys of Geartown, called this the Rat Cellar. It was reasonably clean, with empty three-by-four meter shipping containers for private rooms.

Better than some combat postings I've experienced, Rosst thought with a smile, remembering his deployment to the mining planet Tyche twenty years ago.

The viewscreen showed information for an ocular implant. It showed a polished ceramic orb, cradled in a gold-alloy socket that allowed it to mimic normal motion. The implant used a series of enhanced vision gates with a working iris that closely matched his own eye color. It also had a neck-band sensor that would connect wirelessly, displaying information from other directions simultaneously. Lockwith assured him it would arrive soon, through one of his most trusted associates.

Rosst had lost his eye during the Battle for the Slipgates around Caerus, when a viewscreen shattered in his face. He'd opted first for a simple replacement, with enhanced magnification for reading. Now he was a fugitive, so more options were available. Lockwith had also recommended a black-market surgeon working on the border of Geartown, but Rosst had only agreed after grilling the hacker woman, Verso, about the choice.

"Rrreally, she has a fine reputation down here," Verso had purred. "But there was an indiscreet scandal involving her husband? She was upset about it, and then he turned up dead. I wouldn't ask her for details."

Rosst kept strange company nowadays, but these people had rescued him and his fellow prisoner at no small cost. Whatever their real aims, they wanted the Regency Council disbanded, and Elio Lorne on his rightful throne.

"A watched pot never boils," a familiar voice purred behind him. He swiveled the chair to find Verso elegantly dressed, a silver throw over a deep violet dress that only hinted at her form, with a ruffled hem that clung to her ankles. He suspected tensathread, a simple trick to allow the fabric to gather closed.

"Well, there's nothing to watch here," he said. "You are a sight for a sore eye, but you look upset. What's wrong?"

"I am frustrated," Verso replied. "But if I prey on Deno's emotions, he will still reject me. So I have reluctantly decided to be a friend."

"That dress looks... friendly," Rosst commented.

"I was unwilling to leave my favorites for the Regency's

thugs," she pouted. "I packed other clothes, but sometimes a woman likes to feel... womanly. Besides, the young lady is without a role model. However unsuited I am to raise children, little Pinari shouldn't grow up to be ignorant."

"Does Deno appreciate that?" Rosst asked. "We can't afford a fight."

Verso gave him one of her knowing smiles, and Rosst felt a brief stirring. It had been a long time since he'd enjoyed the benefits of a woman. "The children are almost twelve now. He'll appreciate it soon. Since we have an elderly mother and a blushing bride—"

"Careful," Rosst warned. "I believe the Presdon woman is my age. And if the lass needs a woman to guide her through biology, the bride should be enough."

Verso gave him a look and shook her head. "Neither of those women has what that young girl needs."

"I'm surprised you're so vehement about this," Rosst said. "This has nothing to do with why we're here."

"Those women aren't involved," Verso insisted. "They're superfluous to our agenda."

"Those women are involved because of someone else's agenda," Rosst corrected. "And since your original agenda was to impress a man who moved on and got married, I find it difficult to listen to you moralizing on the subject. Now, do we have any actionable intelligence we can work with?"

Verso's face seemed set in stone, but she replied, "I left some watch-keeping programs running through the night. If there's any information, I'll know as soon as you get out of my seat."

Rosst stood smoothly and turned the chair toward Verso. "As the lady wishes."

Verso pushed past him and dropped into the chair in a manner not quite befitting her formal attire and called up several screens of her own.

Rosst smiled, then turned and walked to the door. But as he was about to leave the prefabricated room, he saw the other child, Faxil, leave his family's cargo container. Rosst had never dealt with children, so he respected Deno Avestan for taking care of them. That said, handling children was like picking scabs—it felt good... until everything came apart.

There was a sudden storm of old-fashioned key-clacking. Rosst turned back and saw the screens shifting rapidly as Verso changed from one program to another.

"If only I had a decent setup here!" she snapped as she did things on the screen that Rosst could barely track.

"We might... have... a—!" Verso tapped a final key, and the screen dissolved into static before going blank. "Problem," she finished with a sigh. "At least it's minimal now. The system is resetting."

"What happened?" Rosst asked.

"The palace has an impressive computer team now," Verso explained as the screen lit up again, this time with a colored logo. "Every backdoor I established in their systems was attacked simultaneously. They almost found our location. They probably know we're in the city. That isn't immediately fatal."

"What about the information we've collected so far?" Rosst asked. "How much of that was false or compromised?"

"Hard to say," Verso said. "Without knowing how long they watched, it's impossible to say. We should probably consider it all useless."

Rosst swore and kicked a box off the step.

Verso sighed. "So, what's the plan, then?" she asked, just as Faxil bounded into the room.

"Goood morning... Hey what's wrong?" Faxil asked. "Why are you guys so unhappy?"

Rosst sighed. "Hey kid, go wake everyone up gently," he replied. "We need to have a meeting. Tell them..." He glanced at his wristpad. "Um, 0930 is fine. We should let everyone get some coffee, if nothing else."

As Faxil trotted off, Verso said, "I think it's going to take a lot more than coffee."

———

Faxil skipped from one temporary home to the next. He knocked politely beside the entrance curtain. The air inside smelled a little like synth. "Mister and Missus Presdon?" he said. "They're having a meeting in twenty minutes. They'd like—"

"Look, kid," Mr. Presdon muttered. "Quit with the Mister and Missus bit, okay? It's me and my mom in here."

"Well, what should I call you?" Faxil asked.

"Ferg and Emila are fine—"

"He can call me Mrs. Presdon," came a voice behind Ferg. "He's a boy. He needs to be respectful."

He sighed. "Fine, Mom. So that's Ferg and Mrs. Presdon, please, Faxil."

"Okay, Mr. Ferg," Faxil replied. As he left, he heard them continue the quiet argument.

"Why shouldn't he call you Mr. Presdon?"

"Because Mr. Presdon was my Dad, Mother."

"Your father has been dead for eight years now—"

"But he's still Mr. Presdon, okay?"

Faxil hoped they would quiet down soon. Even spread out as they were, everyone could hear them. Mr. Ferg seemed to be always bothered about something.

He crept quietly toward the Daire's area, Mr. Arthon and Ms. Bree. It was furthest away from everyone else. "They just got married," his dad had said. "They want their privacy."

When Faxil asked why they needed privacy, Dad stopped talking.

Pinari said she knew why, but she wouldn't tell Faxil. Nobody would, but Mr. Ferg and his mom argued more than Mr. Arthon and Ms. Bree did. He thought they should have some "privacy," too.

He rapped on the side of the container before reaching the double doors. One of them was left ajar for air, he supposed.

"Mr. and Mrs. Daire?" he whispered. When they didn't answer, he said louder. "Hello? Are you awake?" He nudged the door, and it gave a slight creak.

"No, wait!" Ms. Bree's voice was surprisingly loud.

"It's just me, Faxil. I need to—"

"Don't come in!" Ms. Bree squealed.

"Stay out, please!" Mr. Arthon called. "Look, what is it, Faxil?"

"Mr. Rosst says we have a meeting," Faxil reported.

"Umm, tell him I'll be there in ten minutes?" Mr. Arthon said.

"It isn't for twenty minutes," Faxil replied.

"Whatever," Mr. Arthon said. Before Faxil could leave, though, he heard Ms. Bree's voice again.

"Arth, can I go to the meeting?" she asked.

"It's just a boring—"

"But I want to," Ms. Bree interrupted. Faxil could almost see her little quivery lip and he smiled.

"Fine. Let's get dressed," Mr. Arthon said, like he didn't want to. "I was hoping you'd stay like that a little longer."

"Aren't you tired of seeing me naked yet?" Ms. Bree whispered, and Faxil's face grew hot. He fled toward Mr. Grig's room. Thoughts of Ms. Bree naked made him shiver. She was only a little taller... he could kiss her if he was on his tiptoes—

What? Faxil didn't really want to kiss Ms. Bree. *It must be those net shows Pinari's always watching,* Faxil thought. *They're always kissing on those shows. Maybe... they have a quiet trailer... so they can kiss? Naked?*

After Ms. Bree had arrived, Mrs. Presdon had insisted that they "make things official." Faxil thought that was silly. They always looked googly-eyed at each other. it was obvious they were together. But Ms. Verso used the computer to submit an official Marriage Certification, as official as a hacker could, anyway. Then Mrs. Presdon insisted on a wedding.

Ms. Verso had provided a dress, though Faxil thought if Ms. Verso had worn it, her long legs would hang right out. On Ms. Bree, it was almost too long. Mrs. Presdon had talked for a minute, saying romantic love was easy to find, but married love needed a foundation of respect and cooperation. Ms. Bree loved all the attention, and they'd made a cake out of stuff Mr. Lockwith got. But they hadn't made a cake since.

He knocked on Mr. Grig's container, and a sharp voice said, "Enter." Faxil did, quickly.

Mr. Grig shared a container with Mr. Rosst. There was a cot on each side. Each one had a small table, and a small trunk at the foot. The room was otherwise bare.

"I suppose there's a meeting?" Mr. Grig said.

"Yes, sir," Faxil replied. "At 0930 hours."

"Avrum found something," Mr. Grig said.

"I don't know," Faxil said. "They weren't happy."

"Hmm, well." Mr. Grig never said much. "You're dismissed, son." Faxil jogged away.

Mr. Lockwith was the last person besides his dad. Faxil found the office where he usually stayed. Mr. Lockwith didn't talk to the others much. Faxil heard him say mean things, but he owned this warehouse. If he didn't like them, why did he let them stay?

He opened the door. "Mr. Lockwith?" he called.

The office smelled bad, like sweaty guy and synth. It reminded Faxil of Mr. Ferg's apartment. Mr. Lockwith was lying on an old couch. He was wearing one of those shirts he liked, open all the way down. He had a pillowcase draped over his face.

"Mr. Lockwith?" Faxil asked loudly, and the man fell off the couch and said bad words.

Mr. Lockwith yanked the cloth off of his face. "Kid? What the star-blazes are you doing here?"

"Mr. Rosst said there's a meeting at 0930," Faxil reported.

"And... I'm supposed to be there?" he asked.

"Mr. Rosst told me to tell everyone," Faxil replied.

Mr. Lockwith took a drink of synth from a bottle on the floor. Faxil didn't think it would help, but Mr. Lockwith stumbled to his feet. "Fine. Let me just..." He tugged at his clothes. "I'll fresh up a little first."

Faxil returned to his own container-home to find Ms. Verso talking to his dad. "So, can you make your famous pot of coffee?" Ms. Verso was saying.

"I don't know," Dad said with a quick smile. "Do you want people to sleep tomorrow?" But Faxil could see the way Dad didn't really smile. It was just an old joke he always told.

Except Faxil had never heard it, and Ms. Verso was being really friendly. She was laughing and teasing him, just like Inoiae always did before.

Then he realized that Ms. Verso was talking like the ladies on Pinari's shows, who were trying to get kissed.

Faxil decided he needed to keep a closer eye on Ms. Verso.

———

Avrum Rosst stole Deno's first mug of coffee and sipped it.

"Gah!" he muttered. "This is like my second wife, bitter and angry. How do you make this garbage, Avestan?"

But the man only laughed. "Trade secret, Rosst. If I told you, you'd have no reason to keep me."

Rosst saw the other warehouse denizens gathering and put his comments away for later.

"Attention, please," he said before anyone could start chatting. "Those who need coffee, help yourselves. It's bitter, but I'm told it can jump-start a fuel cell." Two people started fixing cups, and the others started talking.

"Hold comments. We're starting now," he warned them. "As you know, we've been trying to hack the Regency's computer systems. Well, that blew up a half hour ago. Verso had to crash the system before they could find us, but we're pretty certain we got away clean, but we have to consider all information received until now as suspect, if not poisoned. I wish I had better news."

"Then why'd you wake us?" Lockwith complained, drinking his coffee from some bowl with a handle. Rosst wanted to slap him sometimes, but Lockwith was providing everyone here a hiding place and resources out of his own pockets; however illegally they happened to be lined.

"He's got a point," Fergal Presdon said. "If there's nothing we can do about it, then why bring it up?

Rosst could barely stand the man's complaining. Presdon had been a guard on his cell, not that either of them had known. But again, Presdon had risked his safety to free Rosst and Grig.

Rosst took a pull from his own coffee. It was still nasty. "You never leave a soldier to wake up to enemy action. Or civilians, either," he replied, glancing at the varied faces. Only he and three others were soldiers. "If anyone has an idea how we might be able to get viable information from inside the

Palace, or recruit people to our cause, we'd like to hear it. So, drink some coffee, and put some thought to it. Because..."

He didn't want to say it, but it needed to be said.

"... if we don't figure something soon, we'll never root the Regency out."

He watched as they milled around before trudging back to their makeshift rooms. Some grouped together to chat—the Avestans and the Daires. No one had gone back for more coffee. He shrugged.

"Oh, well, more for me," he said, and helped himself to another cup.

Yep, he thought. Just as bitter as the first one.

CHAPTER
SEVEN

Restless
   Universal Public Annex
   Cerchier Collegium
   Outskirts of Som Orsi

JUDE CABEUS SAT at a public research terminal with his face in his hands. He'd been working since 0600, trying to gain some insight into the people he sought.

He missed the forest. It talked to him, whispered secrets he understood. He tracked his prey with the natural instinct of a man pitted against the natural cunning of the beast.

The months away from his family, first in Som Orsi and then on Planet Odin, had not been a hunt. The Swarm had no instinct, no cunning. They were mindless killers, and Jude had become the mindless killer his father had trained him to be. That was too apparent on Ikalven Station where he'd killed without remorse for the humans that had died. Only after Avenger had been captured did he realize that.

Jude's new prey, on the other hand, had their own

instincts. They could hide in the urban jungle, could disappear into the concrete warrens. A natural hunter had little chance to find them.

However, Jude was also trained to infiltrate. So he'd cloaked himself in the garb of a thief, Som Orsi's underclass. He crawled through alleys and grime as they did, and tried to understand the mind of his prey. Paranoid, protective, hidden movements, traits that spoke of vermin, rodents scurrying around in the dark, stealing whatever they could. Even if the military men didn't adopt those traits, they had fallen in with someone who had. That person would make decisions, guide them to safety.

A brief conversation with the palace security showed either surprising apathy or witless incompetence. They hadn't followed up on the vehicle in the security footage. Identity scans for the perpetrators were less than sixty percent certainty. Just in case, he also ran the identified phenotypes of the criminals. In a city of over seventeen million people, that left point four percent of the population, or almost seventy thousand people. I need something more to go on! he fumed.

He opened another search, but then noticed the time. It was 1325, and he was mentally exhausted. He sighed, gathered his things, and left for... home.

Ha, he thought in disgust. It will never be my home. He fought the urge to run to his wife and children and take them as far away as possible.

But Marshal Marrion wouldn't have any trouble at all finding them.

———

Esse, Monere District
    Som Orsi

. . .

MEERA SELEURE HEARD the knock at her door and shuffled away from a late breakfast. She opened the door to find a young delivery woman.

"Two Class 4 private packages for..." the woman looked at the label. "Seleure, Meera. That you?"

"Yes," Meera sighed.

"I need to see identification," the woman said. "Sorry."

Meera tapped her wristpad and called up her identification. The woman scanned it, her device blipped, and she slid a pair of large boxes inside. "Thank you for using Imperial Express," she recited. "Need it this day or the next? ImperiEx." Then she was gone.

Meera thought about using TK to drag them, but her fingers stroked the choker necklace she wore. Her inhibitor collar. She longed to dig underneath it, tear it away—

Two weeks and a day, Meera thought as she dragged the boxes. *They said two weeks.* She opened the seal and pulled out several small bags. They contained her clothes from the barracks. She'd liked the base. It created a new sense of self after the wreckage of her life. Divorce, depression, the loss of her son; all those memories. She'd been happy to forge a new path.

And now I've returned. She thought as she opened another bag and found personal items, neatly folded and arranged. She wondered who might have handled her intimates. *It must have been a female soldier. That would explain the folding.*

She spent the morning putting everything away, content to be occupied. And Lifia's life had continued uninterrupted; her classes had kept her busy, especially while her mother was away.

I need to clean up the table, she thought. *Lifia shouldn't come home and find me moping. She's shouldered my burden long enough.*

Meera pulled out her rolled-up exercise shirts. Memories of those early days in the Perceptual Expansion Unit rushed back. Twenty trainees, physical drills, sprinting, weightlifting, martial arts. Their time had been short, their faces were a blur. She couldn't remember all their names. But the TK training had marked her out, the first accidental surges that had pushed her up the chain until she became a TK Guardian... along with Klaus.

She pushed the memories of Klaus away. She didn't want them. She had a family, a son, a daughter, a daughter-in-law and a grandchild.

Stevian! she thought with delight. *All my messages to Gesc and Dusti, and I've barely visited. Visiting them would be wonderful.* She sent a message to Dusti before she cleaned the table. She had a goal now.

It was twenty minutes to Gesc's house in Signa. His house was virtually identical to the dozens nearby, but Dusti had made it their own. The garden was liberally flowered, cardimums if she recalled, in every color. They made a double rainbow, starting with blues at the edges and culminating in twin bursts of sunny yellow flanking the front door. Meera thought it was all too artificial, but it was striking and recognizable. She reached the door and pressed the annunciator.

"Dusti? It's Meera," she said, but the door opened before she finished.

"Look, Stev!" Dusti said with a smile. "It's Grand-mommy"

Stevian gurgled with delight as Meera held him. He touched Meera's face with damp fingers.

"Oh, don't wipe your fingers on Grandma," Dusti tried to scold.

"It's fine!" Meera laughed. "If I didn't like it, I wouldn't have had three."

She waited for Sorge's death to wash over her, but it was only muted sadness. *It's been two years now,* Meera thought. Maybe fighting in Sorge's war made his loss easier. She didn't know, but she had a grandson to play with. Stevian's fingers found her collar and tried to pull.

"Stev, don't pull on Grand-mommy's necklace," Dusti said playfully.

"No need," Meera reassured her. "It... won't come off."

She enjoyed playing with Stevian, wiggling his feet and making faces while Dusti bustled around. After three children, Meera understood all about chasing one mess after another. She could give Dusti some peace to settle her house.

———

Dregs Border Zone
Greasetown

JUDE CABEUS FOUND himself in the situation he'd dreaded. Backed into a dead-end alley with punks flashing weapons, two pipes and a chain. The leader carried a wicked knife.

"Look, you gotsa metal arm," the leader said. "We reconn you got plenty credit. Hand it, and we gone."

Jude doubted that promise as much as his faith in the punk's schooling. "I got this after an accident," he said, trying not to provoke any violence. "You know, like from medical insurance?"

"Hear dat?" the leader called back.

They laughed and closed the distance.

And no TK, Jude thought as he prepared. His training guaranteed survival but bodies attracted questions and he couldn't risk exposure.

He charged forward, startling the punks who expected fear. Jude seized the blade in his metal grip, rolling the edges of the blade to nearly useless, and ripped it away.

Jude caught the first pipe in his mechanical hand, yanked hard, and kicked the punk. He heard the chain rattle and pulled the punk into its path before shoving him into the chain-wielder. Both ran, one of them crying over a fractured humerus. He glared at the leader.

"Are you staying?" he growled, trying not to breathe hard.

The leader ran.

Jude slumped against the wall. He hadn't fought hand-to-hand like that in years. Even in the Knights, his TK was a powerful tool for keeping his distance.

Once he had his breath back, he walked back to his new lodgings, his current lodgings.

Jude walked up the stairs to his pest-ridden apartment. The elevator had been broken since before the Swarm invaded.

He took a flash-dried meal from the cabinet. It didn't matter what—it was all terrible. He opened the pull tab and added some "city water," and sat while it was absorbed into his food. *How do city people live on this mess?* he wondered.

He sat at the scuffed table in a battered plastic chair, eating a lunch that turned his stomach. Barely food, nothing natural. He longed for the days in the forest, eating ants with a stick. He used a steam device to sterilize his bedsheets, as he did every time; he was no food for insects. He lay down and ignored every itch the stifling apartment presented.

Maybe I can do better tonight, he thought, and drifted into a nap.

Signa, Monere District

"MEERA, IS EVERYTHING OKAY?" Dusti asked.

Meera felt ashamed that Stev was crying. "Dusti—I'm sorry. I mean, I didn't mean..."

Dusti wrapped her in a hug before she could leave.

"Hey there, Grand-mommy, it's all right," Dusti murmured in a soothing tone. "We all have our tough days. I know, I know."

Meera felt useless, doubly so because Dusti's voice made her feel calm. "This isn't how it's supposed to be," she murmured in Dusti's ear.

"Many people feel that way these days," Dusti whispered, "and they're right. We've all suffered in this war. But it's not our fault. We do what we can." Dusti finally let go and picked the now quieted Stev up.

Meera's past battles came slinking back. Som Orsi, then Odin, Ikalven Mine, the attack on Planet Hydra. It was an incredible time, but it lasted only six months.

And now I'm... removed, Meera thought, *I have more to give.* But something inside her was empty.

Dusti sat down to nurse Stevian, and Dusti said, "Gesc didn't want me to say, but after Sorge died, he broke down, too."

"Why didn't he want you to say?" Meera asked.

"Meera, you were kind of a wreck," Dusti said. "He didn't want to burden you. He went to a group called TraumAnonymous instead, and they helped him."

"TraumAnonymous?" Meera repeated, frowning.

"Yeah, that's some name," Dusti agreed as she switched Stevian to her other side. "But they helped him. He talked about his feelings without being, you know, him. The manly man, the strong support he needed to be a brother, you know?"

Meera remembered Gesc practically living at her house, even though he had a pregnant wife at home. Then, after two weeks, he suddenly disappeared, and Lifia came back and started doing her schoolwork from home.

"He thought everything fell on his shoulders," Dusti continued. "They made him realize that it wasn't on him. He needed to stop being the support. He had to realize that. Meera, you need to work through some things, too. You need to be you; not what others need you to be."

Dusti layed the sleepy Stevian down in his crib, then rummaged through some papers. She handed Meera a card. It read—

TraumAnonymous
Dealing with the feelings
Be the you that you want to be.

"Please go visit them," Dusti said. "I know something bad happened, and Lifia said you won't even talk about it."

"I'm under... I mean, I've been told... not to discuss it," Meera said. It was the closest she'd come to admitting she'd been threatened into silence.

"But there are other things to discuss, I think," Dusti reminded her. "Gesc worked through those things until he became the man I married again. You should give yourself the same opportunity."

Meera flipped the card over. It had a list of times and places. One was that afternoon, at the social hall near her home. "Very well, Dusti," Meera found herself saying. "I'll do it."

She stayed a while longer, chatting with Dusti. It was good not to be alone, but...

Dusti can't fill the pit inside me, Meera realized. So she concluded the chat, said her goodbyes, and headed home.

At an intersection, she glanced at the card. The meeting has already started, Meera told herself. I... shouldn't interrupt. It wouldn't be polite to barge into the meeting late.

Comforted by her evasion, she drove home. She hadn't lied. She would just... go another day.

———

Universal Public Annex
Cerchier Collegium

Jude's unfulfilling breakfast settled painfully into his stomach and gurgled, but he'd decided to find the escape vehicle and he wouldn't allow himself to be distracted.

The prisoners had escaped in a military transport. So he tracked down the vehicle model they'd used. It was an RVX troop transport, and it had been in civilian hands, which was unusual. There were no official sales for such vehicles to civilians, so he broadened his search. He located ten scrapyards in Som Orsi's vicinity that accepted military vehicles. Three of them had RVX transports, but they were listed as "gutted on arrival." Given the dates, they were scrapped after the Battle of Som Orsi, meaning destroyed by the Blue's plasma weapons. No likely candidates there, just a list of common salvage.

Two others had accepted RVX transports before and since those dates. Most were listed as "stripped after arrival." All the usable parts were removed for sale before the body was recycled.

The hunt became interesting. There were no recorded sales of RTX transports, but there were three sales of "retired surplus" and "stripped vehicle" from two salvage yards that took RVX trucks. The sales were two different companies, but his search turned up connections between the companies. Shared ownership, no matter what their letterheads claimed.

The surplus prices didn't matter. Whatever was listed was likely to be false. But it provided Jude with a list of twenty-seven factories, warehouses and businesses to visit, out of roughly forty thousand such buildings in Som Orsi. Far better than seventy thousand people.

Jude reported this information to his handlers and began to study the different building's blueprints. Perhaps I can narrow it down, he thought. If I guess what they need, I can rank their probability. It was more work, but there was no quick way to investigate twenty-seven buildings.

CHAPTER
EIGHT

FRIVOLOUS
   Unknown Location "Rat Cellar"
   Som Orsi, Planet Caerus

Hours later, Rosst sat nursing his sixth cup of coffee. Verso was still at her computer, occasionally swearing quietly. She was still wearing the dress, though her hair was coming loose, and the dress limp. He hadn't noticed the daytime heat, but he wondered if Verso preferred a cooler environment.

He decided to try tact. "Excuse me, Miss Verso," he began, then shook his head. Maybe it wasn't his place.

"What is it?" she snapped.

I suppose I'm stuck now, he thought. "I thought you might like to take a break to—"

"I don't have time," she complained. "I've been monitoring the networks since we lost the Palace. There's activity, and I'm betting we're targets."

"Is it safe to have an active connection to the network?" Rosst asked. "Not my field, but better safe than sorry."

"Is a sniper likely to get shot in bed?" she countered. "Of

course there's risk. But if we don't monitor, then we won't know if they find..."

She trailed off. Rosst rushed to her side.

"They found... my server..." she mumbled. But before Rosst could ask what could be done, she typed a string of what looked like gibberish into her computer. All her screens blurred, changed into multicolored squares, then went black except for one showing the basic start menu.

"What did you do?" he whispered.

"I severed it," she said. "Every connection is gone."

"But why?" he asked. "Couldn't you fight off whatever they sent?"

She shook her head. "No, Rosst. They were there, physically. They found my safe place and entered my main server room. I... I destroyed it all."

A tear trickled down her face. Rosst couldn't imagine years of work, thousands of work hours, removed in a moment because of the danger. Danger because she risked everything to save two prisoners. Rosst being one of them.

After several minutes, Verso tapped a few commands. Another window lit up, this one different. It showed only a few icons, but nothing more. She clicked, typed commands, and a video opened.

Opposite the camera, he saw a large server array. Lights twinkled like a miniature city, and several physical monitors flashed readouts every few seconds.

Then a group of soldiers broke down the door. Several others entered, unfolded chairs and sat down at the monitors. They weren't soldiers. Others looked around the room—until they found the camera.

A soldier stood center frame, held up a slip of paper with a message scrawled on it.

WE WILL FIND YOU!

Then the screen went dark.

———

FAXIL SPENT the rest of the morning with Pinari. It wasn't time for her vids yet; ever since they'd gotten there, she had refused to miss any. *Why does she get so attached to those vids?* he wondered as they explored one corner of the warehouse. Sometimes, Faxil remembered being chased by aliens through a place like this. But Pinari was here, and he couldn't look like a scaredy or she'd hit him. Just a little, not like the old days before Inoiae and Dad adopted her.

Almost everyone seemed to have forgotten that there was a world outside. Mr. Arthon and Miss Bree were in the kitchen area, making lunch for everyone. Mrs. Presdon often cooked, and her food was pretty good. She'd been teaching Miss Bree cooking, though Ms. Verso made a face if Mrs. Presdon talked about being a good wife.

"So, what do you think they talk about?" Faxil asked as they peered out from behind some boxes. This corner was the filthiest place in the warehouse, but they'd run out of places to explore.

"Who?" Pinari asked.

"Mr. Arthon and Ms. Bree," he replied.

"She's a missus now, right?" Pinari poked him with a little wooden stick. "They talk about grownup stuff, probably. Boring stuff, like groceries and politics."

"Well, yeah, but…" Faxil worked up the courage to say it. "Do they kiss and stuff?"

"Of course they kiss and stuff," Pinari scoffed. But after a moment, she added, "What do you mean by 'stuff'?"

"Just… stuff," Faxil shrugged, trying not to look clueless.

He shouldn't have bothered. "You don't know anything, do you?" Pinari laughed.

Of course, she noticed. He felt his face turn red. "I know

lots of stuff! Just not... that stuff. How did you learn about it, anyway?"

"At my aunt's," Pinari said. "Believe me, you don't want to know that stuff, anyway."

"Um... I mean... of course I don't," Faxil managed to say, before adding, "I mean, except I... I haven't... ever... kissed a girl?"

"Really?" Pinari took a step closer, then another. Faxil got nervous, but Pinari grabbed his wrist and pulled him closer, until their noses touched. He could feel his whole body trembling.

"Yeah," she whispered. "You never got this close to a girl."

Faxil gulped.

"Tell you what," Pinari said, "we'll play a little game. I tell you something I want and if you bring it to me I will give you a kiss."

A shiver of dread or thrill ran through Faxil's body. "What... what happens if I don't bring it back?"

"Oh." Pinari thought a moment. "Then I punch you in the gut."

"But," Faxil quickly added, "it has to be something in the warehouse. That I can actually bring." He couldn't let Pinari make the rules as she saw fit.

She sighed. "Fine. I want a Murple juice pack."

Faxil scampered off. He easily found a Murple juice in the kitchen area. Mr. Lockwith always complained about the food costs, yet there was always plenty of food.

"Whatcha doing, Faxil?" Mr. Arthon asked, and Faxil jumped a little.

"Um, nothing?" Faxil stammered. "Just, um, getting some juice."

"Well, enjoy it," Ms. Bree said.

Just as he tried to leave, his dad saw him. "Hey," Dad said. "We're having another meeting. I want you there, okay?"

"All right, Dad," he said. "I... just need to... give this to Pinari?"

"Tell her to come too," his dad said.

Faxil brought the juice back except... Pinari was gone.

"Pinari?" he called.

"Over here," she hissed from his left. "Keep your voice down!"

Faxil went behind some rusty security fencing to find her. "Gimme," she said, reaching out.

Faxil pulled away. "The deal was I get a... a kiss, remember?" Faxil reminded her. "And then we have—"

Pinari tried to grab at the drink, but Faxil jerked his hand away.

"Give it!" she demanded, lunging forward.

Faxil dodged to the side, used to her attack now. But she slapped his arm; Faxil stumbled to the side and Pinari shoved him against the wall. She quickly pressed herself against him so he couldn't escape. She tried to pin his arms to the wall, so he stretched them to both sides.

Now they stood there, faces almost touching. Faxil felt her chest heave as she caught her breath.

"We have a meeting," he said breathlessly.

"Give it to me," she panted as she tried to creep her fingers past his wrist, but her arms were just shorter than Faxil's.

"You promised me a kiss," he reminded her.

"Hey, kids? Come on," Dad called, and he glanced over.

Pinari snatched the juice from his hand. "Got it!" she said, but Faxil's hands were free.

He yanked her closer and kissed her.

He held her there for a long moment, waiting for some sort of understanding to arrive, some secret of the universe to unravel.

Pinari stared into his eyes and wondered if she was thinking the same.

She blinked. And then she punched him in the gut.

"Jerk," was all she said as she turned and walked away.

Faxil rubbed his stomach. "It barely hurt," he whispered to himself, smiling, as he followed her to the meeting.

———

Rosst waited until everyone had arrived.

"I have an update," he began. "Things are... not good. Verso's secure server was just taken down. Everything we've done was through her systems, and they're gone. We can try to co-opt someone else's system, but their security won't be as good. At least, that's what she tells me."

"There are five people on this planet that are as good as me," Verso said. "None of them owe me any favors, so anything I do without asking will be noticed."

"We've found ourselves a tight spot to wriggle into, and we can't back out," Rosst said. "How do we move forward?"

No one spoke.

"I understand that—" he began.

"What's the point?" Fergal Presdon blurted, interrupting him. "We locked ourselves underground, and for what?"

"As I recall, Presdon," Lockwith drawled from the rear, "you were garbage, fleeing your many mistakes."

"Says the professional criminal!" Presdon replied. "And why are you here?"

"I have several legitimate businesses—" Lockwith began.

But Rosst lost patience. "Enough!" he snapped. Everyone jumped, except Teyn Grig. The former Air Marshal.

"We are the only coordinated insurgency on the planet," Rosst said. "Anyone else is inexperienced or was deemed threat enough that the Regency crushed them early on. Verso kept us safe, but that shield is broken now. No offense, Verso."

"None taken," she answered.

"We need a window of opportunity," Rosst continued. "The public was primed to reject Elio Lorne for years, and I believed some of it myself. The Regency sowed seeds of dissension long before their takeover."

"So how do we fight that?" Arthon asked.

"We need to sow our own seeds," Rosst replied. "How do we convince the populace that the Regency isn't the answer? How do we convince them Elio Lorne is their only hope of surviving this war? Unless some other kingdom pulls their heads out from between their knees, Prince Elio and Prince Tarak are the only royals doing something besides reacting. The Regency captured Elio and told Tarak to make exhaust. We're the only people still trying. So we need to come up with something, and quickly."

He gazed out over the small crowd. "So, if you have any ideas, right now's the time to air them."

———

ALL THE ADULTS murmured to each other. Faxil hadn't thought this was so serious.

"I wasn't thinking at all," he muttered to himself.

The grown-ups always seemed serious to him. Sure, they were living in an old warehouse, but he'd lived through an alien invasion. Two, in fact. Their old apartment building almost fell down, and his new mom was a soldier who disappeared, and the bully who pushed him around was now his adopted sister. What did he know about normal anymore?

Pinari... he'd kissed Pinari. He still didn't know what it meant. They were like brother and sister, family. And sometimes family kissed each other. No big deal. It was just a game, right?

But it didn't feel like a game to him—

Just a game.

The thought kept rolling back and forth in his mind.

Just a game.

Just a game.

Pinari had claimed it was... a... game.

"Wait!" he said, almost shouted. "What if we can convince people with a game?"

He saw everyone was staring at him.

"What?" he asked nervously.

"What do you mean, a game?" his dad asked.

"I just... I mean..." Faxil wasn't going to mention the kiss. Never ever. "I just meant, we could hide it in some kind of puzzle... or something."

"What good is that supposed to do us, kid?" Mr. Fergal snapped.

"People like to play games." Faxil didn't know what he was saying. He just wanted everyone to stop staring at him. "People think games are important. Like, my dad is always trying to guess what Thunderball players are good, and put them on his team."

He looked at his dad. He looked embarrassed. *Maybe because he doesn't always pick the best players,* Faxil thought. He was uncomfortable with all the attention, but he continued, "Halos have all sorts of games. So I thought, what if people played a game and we told them about the bad stuff that was happening? Then they'd believe it more, because it... was... in a game?" The more he thought about it, the less sense it made.

"Hey kid," Mr. Fergal said. "Just... stay out of the grown-up conversations, okay?"

"Leave Faxil alone," Mr. Arthon said.

"Yeah!" Mrs. Bree added. "The little man's just trying to help."

Mrs. Bree called me a little man? Faxil felt a bit of pride seep back in—

"He's just a kid, and it's a stupid idea," Mr. Fergal insisted.

"If you dress up the truth as a fairy-tale, then nobody will believe it."

Before Faxil could try to pull away, he felt a hand on his shoulder. He looked up and saw his dad give him a smile.

"Ow!" Mr. Fergal suddenly yelled, and Pinari appeared at his side a moment later with a big dumb grin on her face. Mr. Fergal leaned over, scowling and rubbing at his leg.

"Enough!" Mr. Rosst shouted. "Presdon, be civil or be quiet. Avestan, keep your children leashed. We don't need distractions."

"Actually," Ms. Verso said from behind Mr. Rosst, "the boy has a point."

Mr. Rosst turned and looked back at her. "What do you mean?"

"Psychologically speaking," Ms. Verso said, "he's right. When we enjoy something, we associate it with ourselves. Then we find like-minded others and form a community. If we created something that people could claim as their own, it could sway the masses. Once people get excited, suppression guarantees it spreads like wildfire. People will find out why it's suppressed. And once we reach critical mass, we send the message to revolt."

"Now wait a minute," Dad said. "Revolt? We're only trying to expose the cover-ups."

"A revolt is going to be messy," Mr. Arthon said. "And cost lives. Real people who don't have training."

Mr. Fergal spoke up next. "Look, this is crazy and if you pull it off, people will get shot over it. I was there, remember?"

"Yeah, sure." Mr. Lockwith gave Mr. Fergal a shove. "You were doing the shooting—"

Mr. Fergal punched Mr. Lockwith, and they started fighting. Dad and Mr. Arthon pulled them apart, still trying to kick each other.

"Settle down!" Mr. Rosst roared. "Or I'll lock you both in the closets, you hear me?" But they didn't stop.

Mr. Grig walked between them and kicked Mr. Lockwith in the stomach. The skinny man doubled over, and Mr. Grig turned in the other direction. "When we got here," he said to Mr. Fergal, "I told you I owed you exactly one favor for throwing your career away. Is this the favor?"

"Um, no, sir," Mr. Fergal whispered.

Mr. Grig kicked him in the stomach, too. "Next time, don't," he said as he backed away and let Mr. Lockwith and Mr. Fergal stand up.

"If it works," Mr. Fergal wheezed, "you won't have an army. If a million people play this game, only a thousand will do anything. And a thousand people will die."

Mr. Rosst turned toward Ms. Verso. "Well?" he asked. "What do you have to say?"

Ms. Verso gave him a wintery smile. "We just need to be imaginative," she replied. "We're not providing a story. It's a piece of identity to grab. They'll want to be involved. So we should involve, oh, Deno, Arthon and Bree, and the children. They're the ages we need to target."

"What about me?" Lockwith said with a cough.

"Lock, dear, you're older than we need," Ms. Verso replied.

"I'm not that much older—"

"But you don't believe in the plan," Ms. Verso said. "You're also drunk."

"I'm not that drunk," he argued.

"Enough," Mr. Rosst barked. "Grig and I will sit in on planning. If you can explain it to us, and there's a good chance it'll work... Well, we'll see. We'll meet back here in an hour, Avestans and Daires."

And with that, the meeting was over.

CHAPTER
NINE

Ataraxis's Guest Quarters

After a week of staring at the walls, Elio was fit to burst. He'd seen no one but his guards since they boarded. Blade Sergeant rarely graced his room but had provided him with a different guard.

Why won't he spend time here? Elio wondered.

Why did it take a week to make a four-day journey?

What did Blade Sergeant know about the stairwell?

He couldn't ask anyone.

"Why is this taking so long?" he finally complained. "Why haven't we reached Tyche yet?"

One of the D Squad guards glanced around nervously. Then she whispered, "Station-keeping orbit, two days."

"Two days?" Elio murmured. "But why? Shouldn't I be talking with the representatives? I am, after all, the ambassador?"

The woman looked up at her squad-mate, who shook his head. She sighed. "I don't know exactly why."

Elio understood. She had an idea, and if she shared it, it meant trouble. He'd noticed D-squad being nicer to him: privacy in the refresher, an occasional smile or "You're welcome," if he thanked them.

But life continued as before; interminably boring. He was growing used to fuming silently and finding ways to pass the time.

He once again pulled up an org chart for the mining operations. He still couldn't believe an Orso kingdom holding was so entangled in corporate nonsense. The planet had representatives present from Orso. The three companies with grants to mine, Extrock, Metaglione, and Zeetsteel, each had corporate interests there. These interests had a network of supervisors that reported issues with labor. And in a situation that bordered on irony, the corporate interests were opposed by a union of workers from all three competitors.

"I should be down there," Elio muttered to himself. "That's what I should be doing. I could have spent days with these people, learning about what they needed."

There was a knock, and the guard opened the door without hesitation and Blade Sergeant strode in with a grimace on his face.

Elio was shocked at the man's appearance, though he carefully hid his reaction. Sergeant's uniform showed a slight rumple. There were bags under his bloodshot eyes.

"I wasn't aware you were coming," Elio drawled.

Blade Sergeant's anger was visible. "I have four soldiers dead and another recovering from the building collapse," he barked. "I see you avoided injury."

Elio glanced at D Squad. They studiously stared ahead. *So they didn't report that I used my TK*, Elio thought.

"Well, you have two hours," Blade Sergeant grunted. "Your meeting starts at 1500 hours."

"Two hours?" Elio asked, feigning ignorance. "How long have we been here?"

Blade Sergeant shrugged, though Elio could have bet that the man knew to the minute how long it had been since they'd arrived.

"Why wasn't I told?" Elio asked. "The ambassador should be building connections with local interests, in personal meetings or over halo."

"Your halo use is restricted," Blade Sergeant said. "And it's obvious why. Your freedom has a price and can be curtailed for any reason. Just remember that."

Elio thought of the dead soldiers at Resdon Airfield. Dozens of loyal men and women, killed by their own comrades at the orders of the Regency Council he was obliged to serve.

"I understand the price," Elio snapped. "But I have real responsibilities. Humanity must take this war to the next level."

"Spare me the act," Blade Sergeant growled. "Practice your speeches for the easily duped... But, then, if you step out of line, you won't be giving any. You'll simply disappear, and I won't... I won't... hesitate."

He turned smartly and walked to the door. "Two hours!" he barked as he left, and the door slid shut.

What was that about? Drella wondered for the tenth time as D Squad led the ambassador to his shuttle, the Goodwill. C Squad secured the perimeter, and once Drella had Elio seated, C Squad entered and took position. The Goodwill floated through the containment field and out of the docking bay. But Drella felt nervous.

D Squad had decided not to report the event in the stairwell. The ambassador had saved their lives, and obviously he meant to stay peaceful. But Blade Sergeant had been antagonistic from the first. It was a small spark of rebellion, but Drella refused to let that spark die.

Drella glanced out the shuttle's window and fought the urge to give a low whistle. The surface of Tyche was unlike anything she had ever seen before. The rocky surface was pitted from asteroid strikes, and the atmosphere lent a murky haze. A high carbon dioxide atmosphere absorbed most of the visible light. It looked like twilight without stars.

The Goodwill landed on a platform machined almost to glass. "This is your pilot," the intercom said. "You are advised to wear your breathers. The air is chewy today."

Everyone donned the atmospheric filter masks. Drella expected Ambassador Elio to pull out some fancy rig, but he accepted the same style mask as everyone else. C Squad exited first, and then D Squad and Elio.

Drella felt a heft to her step. The planet had about five percent heavier gravity. The slight poof to her uniform showed an atmosphere of .93 standard, which should have been breathable, had the atmosphere been nitrogen-oxygen instead of mostly carbon dioxide caused by the smelting processes on-planet. Tycho's air wasn't breathable, and without terraforming it never would be.

Five minutes later, they walked through the airlock doors into the first administrative building.

C Squad marched quickly forward, and Drella assumed they'd been given a more detailed briefing. *And it isn't the first time, either.* She thought back through the last few days. The other squads always seem to know before we do. D Squad was the last to know the trip details. *We were the last to know about leaving Remanor,* she thought, *and I thought they might leave us behind. That would wreak more havoc on the four-shifts a day guard duty, but I wouldn't put it past the blade sergeant to order it.* They were hard pressed to cover the shifts and sleep without B Squad. A Squad was in the rack now, and from the looks of him, even the blade sergeant needed to sleep.

Something is going wrong, Drella thought. *And if the blade sergeant won't tell us what it is, then someone needs to figure it out. I guess I just elected myself, didn't I?*

———

ZEETSTEEL ADMINISTRATION OFFICES
Planet Tyche

ELIO and his guards passed through into the airlock. The doors cycled shut and the green light flashed, so they were able to remove their masks.

If there wasn't so much carbon dioxide, Elio thought, *it wouldn't be habitable at all. Nothing kills industry like blizzards at a hundred below zero.*

Inside the colony, concrete beige and rust predominated. The anteroom had a three-meter-high ceiling with no windows. Ancient steel girders wrapped in a concrete base supported the ceiling.

"Hello, hello," a man with black hair said as he swept into view. "Welcome to Zeetsteel Mining! I'm Spel Darian, Sorting Supervisor First Grade, and I will be your guide. Please, follow me." And the man turned on his heel and took off at a brisk walk, and they all followed him.

Elio frowned. This man was thin, not very muscled, wearing office casual and a gold circlet. He was obviously not a miner.

"I'm sure you have questions," Darian continued as they walked, "but we'll cover everything you need. Right this way, yes-sirs, certainly..." They passed through a large arch, odd for an industrial building, Elio thought.

Darian shook his head. "Oh, my manners. I'm so sorry. You need your halos!"

Elio reached down to pull his halo out.

"Oh, not those," Darian explained. "We have our own. Many miners have them, too. Except the ones who don't," he quipped.

He took several circlets of striped bronze instead of plain gold from the shoulder bag he was carrying and offered one to everyone. None of the guards seemed interested. "Pri— I mean, Mr. Ambassador," Darian corrected in dismay, "certainly you will take one?"

"What is it?" C Squad's leader finally demanded.

"Your environmental upgrade!" Darian didn't wait for Elio to respond, but placed it on his head before any guards could react.

The moment the circlet touched Elio's head, it activated. The grimy walls and depressing atmosphere disappeared. The room was now an office lobby. The walls were marbled stone, the floors intricate mosaics, the girders elegant pillars that stretched upward to a gabled ceiling. Rich sunlight streamed through massive windows...

The view disappeared as he felt hands touch his head again. A D Squad guard yanked him backwards while C Squad's leader grabbed Darian. "What did you do?" C Squad's leader demanded, pulling his sidearm.

"No!" Elio shouted, seizing the soldier's elbow. "It's all right, Sergeant. It's just scenery. May I have it back, please?"

The lance sergeant frowned. "I don't like this," he muttered. "We had no advance instructions about such things."

"It was an oversight," Darian said. Elio noticed a shake in

the man's voice. "We wear them constantly. Some people sleep with them."

"Lance Sergeant?" Elio said. "I'll take that back now." Reluctantly, C Squad's leader handed it to him.

Elio placed it back on his head. The room's architectural style was Late Alastor Revival, angular spirals that curled into each other. It hurt his eyes, but it was better than the reality. "I'll keep it. Will there be other sense manipulations?"

"Just overlays to existing structures," Darian explained. "And your sense of smell is... adjusted to improve the experience. Nothing more."

"But sir—" the lance sergeant tried to protest.

"If I'm to do my job," Elio said, "I need to see their world. Each squad take two halos and pass them around so everyone knows what differences there are. It will keep you on your toes."

The lance sergeant still wanted to protest, but he was outmaneuvered. If he argued, Elio's authority was negated; if he didn't... "Yes, sir," he answered. "And, as ordered, the squads complied."

Four guards put on halos and gave startled reactions. "I'm certain you will be pleased with your stay," Darian said as they continued.

Elio passed several pieces of artwork and magnificent sculptures. Any business lobby in Som Orsi would be pleased with such surroundings. "Where do these images come from?" he asked Darian.

"They are recreations of a sector office," Darian said. "It would be nicer if..." He shook his head. "It's easier to program a simulation. I understand Orso has teleconferencing? This is similar."

Elio thought of Prince Tarak's system on the Reaper. But this was... light-years ahead of Orso's applications. "We have some similar projects, actually," he admitted. "I look forward to seeing what else you'll show me."

"I must show you to your room now," Darian demurred. "Your meeting will be in..." he checked his wristpad, "forty-five minutes? Please take the opportunity to refresh yourself."

"Thank you," Elio said, still gazing at the decorations. "Tell her I'm looking forward to it."

———

Drella wasn't impressed with her room. Unfinished walls of gypsum panels. Cheap plastic furniture ridged like wood. The ash gray rug was thick and real enough. *Probably works wonders for hiding stains*, she thought.

The room probably looked quite different with the halo, but it wasn't her turn.

It doesn't matter, she thought. She wasn't a decorator, and she was puzzling over D Squad's lack of involvement. But Elio didn't stay long. After a clothing change, they left for his meeting.

The skinny little supervisor walked quickly, chattering about this wall hanging or that piece of modern art that she couldn't see. There were strange plants everywhere, with dark, almost black leaves. She brushed one deliberately with her elbow. It moved, the supple twigs constricting like a grasping hand. And she wondered where such plants were found, and why they were there.

The soldiers wearing halos were distracted, which made her glad she wasn't wearing one. The building was strange enough that she thought she needed to be aware of their surroundings in real time. But those with halos continued to gawk.

Then she noticed that C Squad led the way, ignoring

Darian, even keeping ahead of him. *There's something going on here,* she thought.

They arrived at an office suite. The walls and floors were nicer than the ambassador's room, but not by much.

"I will announce you to Executive Sti," she heard Darian say. "She's pleased that you're here, Ambassador."

———

THE OFFICE WAS SUMPTUOUSLY DECORATED, and Elio appreciated the fine taste before remembering the halo. *But how much of it is real?* he wondered.

"You can take that off, if you like," the smartly dressed woman behind the desk said. "I paid dearly for my office."

Elio took the halo off and felt guilty at his flash of doubt. The room was just as he'd seen. "I'm sorry if my expression—" he began.

"I'm Ajena Sti," she interrupted. "And I have little time for the niceties. Do you know why you are here?"

Elio felt embarrassed. This woman was direct and sharp. "I do not," he admitted. "I took this position under—"

"Unlike you," she stated. "I have sources of information in several kingdoms. I have a problem close to home, and I've spent a year trying to get your government's attention."

"What's the issue?" Elio asked.

"Metaglione is the issue," she said. "Right before the Battle of Som Orsi, there was an accident at your shipyards."

Elio frowned. "The shipyards were attacked by—"

"Days before that. There was a secret project, something I haven't unearthed. Whatever it was failed, and Metaglione was a supplier. It was probably a subset of their dealings for the Vindication Fleet. Between the accident and... your other troubles, Ambassador, Metaglione lost their contracts."

She paused, but Elio held his questions.

"I see you are a man who doesn't need to hear himself talk," she said. "How refreshing. Arbo Crenhauser is a Metaglione executive. He oversaw the Orso military contracts. Now, he's stuck out here."

"An odd choice of words," Elio suggested.

She smiled. "I was promoted from district director, and I put space between myself and an annoying suitor. Arbo was living in a penthouse in Som Orsi before he lost one and a half billion a year. And for that, he received a mere slap on the wrist. But now Metaglione is shipping again, like they did for the Vindication Fleet. And Arbo Crenhauser is preparing to leave."

"Who are they shipping to?" Elio asked.

"I don't know," she admitted. "But it isn't Orso."

Elio's head spun. Was this another move from Prince Tarak's elusive One King? Having failed to steal the Vindication fleet, were they building their own?

Before he could ask questions, his halo began vibrating. Several of his guards reacted in alarm.

"What's going on?" Elio demanded.

"The Swarm just popped out of nowhere," one of them declared. "They'll be over the mining complex in ten minutes!"

Outside the office, Elio could hear klaxons.

"Sir!" the guard ordered. "We need to get you to safety!"

CHAPTER
TEN

BREAKOUT
Zeetsteel Administration Offices
Planet Tyche

The entire complex shuddered, and Drella froze in panic. Suddenly, chunks of concrete ceiling fell into the office. Drella jumped forward and pushed Elio out of danger. Debris smashed into her, and she fell.

"My legs!" she screamed. Pain lanced through her, and something spread under her. *I'm bleeding. But I can still feel my legs!* she thought. *I only need some regen therapy, instead of spinal reconstruction. If I make it to the ship*, she reminded herself as someone pried the weight from her legs. She cried out as something gouged another wound.

"What happened?" she asked, but her ears rang too loud to hear. She tried to stand, but the pain was too much, and she collapsed.

She could hear intercoms blasting instructions. "Can someone help me?" she asked. "I'm hurt."

"Stars, but you're a whiner!" a C Squad soldier complained. "You think you're the only injury?"

"Show some respect, soldier. Two people are dead," Elio said. "And comms aren't working."

Drella glanced over at the largest debris pile. A large shard of ceiling that had crushed her lance sergeant's ribs. Of the other, all she could see was an arm and a surprising amount of blood.

"Executive Sti," Elio said, "what's the construction of these buildings? Reinforced concrete? Secure-grid through the walls?"

"I'm not an architect!" Ajena Sti snapped. "But if you look at that damaged section, you can see rebar and metal mesh. So maybe you're right."

They're dead, and I'm half crippled, Drella thought. *How are we supposed to get out of here?*

"These walls are a Faraday cage," Ambassador Elio stated. "It's not the best—"

"We can't use our comms!" the complaining C Squad leader yelled. "How are we supposed to call for help?"

I need to focus! Drella told herself. *What should I do...?* She could feel shock creeping in.

"We... we usually—" Sti was flustered. "We have a building intercom network. It has security—"

"Then tell us the passcode," Ambassador Elio said.

"Um, can someone tape my leg?" Drella begged. I need to get mobile. If I don't move, shock will drag me under. "Wrap something around it so I can walk, please!"

Hanson of C Squad, the only soldier with medical training, started on her injuries. She saw the tear in his sleeve, the blood beneath. She heard the hiss of field anesthetic.

"Your arm looks... bad," she mumbled, not knowing what else to say. "Can I... help?"

"It's fine, but thanks," he replied, as he probed inside her wound.

He's looking for fragments, she thought, woozily.

It should have hurt more, but the anesthetic was taking effect and the worst of the pain was dissipating rapidly.

She barely felt Hanson tightening the compression bandage, but when he pulled her to her feet, she found she could manage her balance well enough.

"Just... don't try to move too fast," Hanson warned her. "That leg needs serious attention; it will buckle if you push through the Nullicon."

"Whatever you say, doc," she replied.

He turned his eyes away. *Too quickly*. She thought. *Did I offend him? Hah! But this is the Redemption unit, so he must have a story, she decided. Maybe I can ask him later.*

"I don't know what you plan to do, Ambassador," Ajena Sti said. "But my datapad says we're to follow directions to the shelter. I gave you the passcode, so now you can call—"

"Hey, I got something on comms!" C Squad's Lance Sergeant Sidray called.

"...is Captain..." Elio wrinkled his brow in concentration. He could barely hear. "All personnel... report to... aboard ship. I repea... sonnel to..." and the transmission died away into static.

"Personnel," the lance sergeant said. "That's us."

"We're not the ones they mean," D Squad's ranking corporal argued. "He means the supply crews reporting to duty stations."

"You heard what Blade Sergeant ordered last time," Sidray said. "Extract the Ambassador instead of hiding him. So get the shuttle over here, and we'll extract him."

"Wait a minute!" Elio snapped. "He can't mean in the middle of an invasion!"

Drella saw a cold look in the lance sergeant's eyes. "He said especially if there's an invasion. We got reamed for taking you to the basement last time. You're not calling the shots, sir! Director lady. Where's the nearest landing pad?"

"There's...a private executive pad," she stammered. "I can show you."

"Great. Mig, call the shuttle, code 11592, tell them north-west corner and follow my beacon."

What does he mean? Drella wondered as they all filed into the hallway. *Will he fly the shuttle out during a fight?*

"Get moving, people," Sidray ordered. "Target Fish goes in the net. First try."

With plasma everywhere, bullets and missiles? Drella couldn't believe what she was hearing. *How the stars will we survive that?*

———

Ataraxis's Bridge

When the Ataraxis had arrived in Tyche orbit two days earlier, Captain Carrica had expected a pair of modern cruisers and a dozen older destroyers. His briefing had been specific. Instead, He'd found only two destroyers, Steadfast and Reliant. The rest were diverted to nearby systems to help recover from other Swarm attacks.

The destroyers were to accompany the cargo vessels as a defense against piracy, or more likely, a Swarm attack. They were also converted to carry four F-30s on the hull, the cost of extra pilot pay being less expensive than replacing the aged warships. The fighters launched quickly and freed their guns to fire. A pair of destroyers was enough to drive off a cruiser. Fourteen warships and seventy-two fighters would have been a force to reckon with. But, in all, they had just three destroyers and eight fighters.

"Sir, we have incoming!" the comms officer yelled. "Vessels from solar north, bearing one-five-three toward Tyche!"

Carrica followed the heading on the holo map. One-five-three was directly in line with the inner planet Agathos. As he watched the penumbra around Agathos, he could see ships twinkling like crystals as they caught the sun. A dozen, then two, appeared on the map. Then the system updates synced with the holo map, and the enemy force became clear.

This was an invasion fleet, and all he had were the three destroyers and eight fighters to hold back the Swarm. The first wave of the enemy closed the distance to Tyche quickly.

"All guns, fire on targets of opportunity!" Carrica bellowed. "Comms, contact the other destroyers. We need to coordinate our defense. We can't hesitate. Helm, bring us closer to the destroyers. We can't let them hit the colony! Where did these bastards come from?"

"Tracking, sir," the sensors officer called. "It's in system. Calculating likely gravitational—"

"Calculate and broadcast it!" Carrica snapped. "Someone needs to know how the enemy dropped in."

"And if we're lucky," he muttered to himself, "we won't float into the dark star itself."

Carrica didn't profess any profound religious bent, but even he knew better than to disrespect the keeper of the dark star. Like a spider, the keeper of the dark star sat at the center of his web and drew unwary souls along the threads. It was said that for every mistake you made in life, you would see a thousand different possibilities of that decision after death.

How many mistakes can I make now? he wondered as he continued to spit out orders, making split-second decisions. His crew served admirably, and they coordinated with the other destroyers to send a hail of projectiles toward the hard-hitting ballistas. But one of them smashed into the Reliant, taking out the port weapons array.

"Tell the Reliant to roll a hundred and eighty degrees!" Carrica ordered Comms. "Weapons, cover Reliant's field of fire. Do we have any more scattershot missiles?"

"We have five M-99's, sir," Weapons answered. "Should we hold them in reserve, or...?"

"What reserve?" Carrica asked. "If those ships get through, we won't have time. Fire all into that breach, two-second intervals, point two degrees between!"

He felt the tremor as each missile launched as upward of a dozen enemy fighters shot through the breach. I hope the timing is right! he thought, anxiously.

Successive detonations shattered the enemy flight, but didn't catch the ballista that followed them.

"Sir, the ballista is on our heading!" Navigation called. "It's going to ram us!"

Carrica felt his voice hitch as he called, "Weapons, fire on —!" He paused. It had closed too quickly. But then it exploded in a ball of brilliant blue fire and a hail of shrapnel that slammed into the Ataraxis's shields.

"Thanks for covering our plate, Axis!" he heard, and recognized the voice of Reliant's captain on the comms. He'd avoided the dark star by only a few moments.

I'm not ready to face that again, he thought, his hands trembling as he checked his readyboard. The holo map showed progress, but it wasn't looking positive. The attack had comprised two waves, fighters first, then ballistas.

Three destroyers and eight fighters aren't enough to hold back this... trickle? It's not even a true invasion, he thought, frowning. *A few dozen fighters and eight ballistas. Even so, we don't have the strength!*

Was this the enemy's plan? he wondered, *to thin us out and then attack us when we're weak?*

"Sir! Anomalous energy burst!" Sensors reported. "Heading is—!"

A brilliant flash of light illuminated the bridge, almost overwhelming the viewport's polarizing filters. It looked, for a moment, like the end of the world.

"ATTENTION!" the ship comms announced. "This is Commodore Fermi Lier, captain of the USF Resolve!"

Zeetsteel Administrative Offices

There was no arguing with the C Squad leader. But the D Squad leader's reaction showed there was something else in play, but Elio just didn't have time to figure that out.

"Very well," he said to the lance sergeant. "How should we handle this?"

"You agree with this?" D Squad's new leader exclaimed. "I don't have orders to—"

"It doesn't matter," Elio interrupted. "We're not fighting over the escape plan. If he's in charge, then we follow. Each squad is down by one, so I suggest we combine squads for now. The walking wounded can stay on either side of me, you two as front and rear guard—diamond formation. The leaders can scout ahead."

"Why shouldn't I take Hanson instead?" the C squad sergeant argued. "The Dork Squad corporal can stay behind."

Elio fixed the sergeant with a steely glare. "If Hanson is the medic, he should tend the injured, and you need a lesson in survival. Cooperate, or I'll report to Blade Sergeant that you refused."

"He wouldn't believe you," the sergeant said. "He thinks you're an idiot. And so do I."

"That's irrelevant," Elio replied. "Once everyone here explains things, your version collapses."

"Can we get to the shelter?" Ajena Sti wailed. "The air smells wrong. It's Tyche's atmosphere!" Her cool composure was gone, stripped away by the collapsed ceiling, the dead bodies, and the sudden reality of war. "There's a repair function, but the hole is too big..." She trailed off into weeping.

Elio sniffed the air. "She's right. Sergeant, let's get moving."

"You're not in charge here!" the sergeant insisted.

Hanson reached over and yanked the sergeant's shoulder. "Sidray, we don't have time for your shit! Do as he says."

Sergeant Sidray glared at Hanson, but stepped back. "Fine. Corporal Dink, follow me. We're trailblazing."

As they both walked off, Elio said to Hanson, "Is the corporal likely to argue with him?"

"Not sure," Hanson shrugged.

"Director Sti," Elio said, "if you'll accompany us?"

Ajena Sti wobbled over and clung to Elio's arm. "We'll get you somewhere safe," Elio said, but she was shivering and didn't seem at all comforted to him. *I wish I could promise her something,* he thought, *but I don't know what these soldiers will do in a crisis. All I know is they don't work well together, and that's... not what we need right now.*

The area outside Sti's office was badly damaged. They hobbled into the hallway, where the air seemed clearer. The executive landing pad was mercifully close, with two soldiers injured and a hysterical civilian standing by. Elio and the two squads caught up with their leaders at an intersection. The landing pad was seventy meters away.

"Let's ditch the lady here," a C-Squad soldier said.

"Nooo..." Sti shouted.

"No," Lance Sergeant Sidray said, "we might need to have someone ground-side to stand them down. She goes with us."

"You mean as a hostage?" Elio asked in shock.

"No, of course not," Sidray replied. "She's a director, right? Executive privileges, including letting the shuttle through. Don't worry, Director, you'll be back here in twenty hours, hopefully. Get her to the shuttle."

"Lance Sergeant, you can't take this woman," Elio tried to explain. "It's against three regulations I can cite—"

"You don't order me, Ambassador." Sidray gestured with his rifle. "D Squad, lead these august superiors to their ride."

D Squad hesitated. "Now!" Sidray ordered.

"ATTENTION!" the intercoms blared. Everyone jolted in surprise. "This is Commodore Fermi Lier of the USF Resolve! All craft will remain docked, all fighters will return to their hangars! Disobedience will result in death!"

"Ignore that! Everyone on the shuttle!" Sidray demanded.

Elio was dumbfounded. "You can't ignore that! A ship's captain in a war zone outranks almost anyone. It's suicide!"

"You're not listening!" Sidray ranted. "This is supposed to put my career back on track, and I won't let you—!"

There was a sharp thud, and Sidray collapsed. Elio blinked as he saw the female soldier, with her leg bandaged to the knee, with her rifle stock still in the air where Sidray's head had been.

"Thank you... I mean, I'm sorry," he said to the rest of the two squads," Elio said. "But I subdued this man without thinking. You'll need to write in your reports that I refused to disobey a USF captain."

They all nodded. Elio noticed a stray tear on the woman's face. "I'm sorry," he said. "I haven't thanked you for saving me yet. What's your name?"

"It's um, Drella, sir," the soldier replied. "First corporal Drella Simond."

"I owe you dinner sometime," Elio said. "Stars, I'll buy everyone here dinner if we live through this."

———

Ataraxis's Bridge

Fermi Lier? The Resolve? Carrica looked at the holo map. Between Tyche and its large outer neighbor, Tethys, a single blip had appeared. Then another, and another, all accompanied by immense bursts of light and energy.

"All craft will remain docked, all fighters will return to their hangars!" the pronouncement continued. "Disobedience will result in death!"

"Pull back!" Carrica ordered. "Give the fighters cover to reach safety!"

"All USF ships and citizens, remove yourselves from our field of fire!" Commodore Lier ordered.

But before the Ataraxis could even clear the zone, the holo map showed the Resolve firing projectiles that streaked into the battlefield, missiles that eerily followed the enemy fighters. Ships that jinked sideways found themselves still targeted, and were quickly destroyed in an eye-searing flash of iridescent blue fire. Carrica marveled at the effectiveness of the missiles. Then the comm board lit up with a priority vid.

"This is Commodore Fermi Lier of the Alastor system. The hostiles have been neutralized. Alastor places this system under emergency protection, until we can be relieved by USF or Orso forces, per USF Regulation 18.5, Emergency Martial Aid, Paragraph Four, Declaration for Rendering Assistance. I require a meeting in three days with all plenipotentiaries to discuss terms. Please use comm frequency 108.1 to coordinate the meeting."

The image disappeared.

"It's over," Carrica whispered. "We're... alive?"

"Orders, Captain?"

Carrica turned to find his first officer looking at him expectantly.

He took a deep breath and tapped the comm switch. "Carrica to all hands. Well done," he announced to every corner of the ship. "We... made it."

He released the switch. "You... you have the conn, Commander," he ordered.

"Aye, sir." His first officer's tone left no doubt of his opinion on that.

Carrica didn't care. He went to his ready room, but this time he ignored all the rich tapestries and fine furniture. Instead, he collapsed on his divan and wept. Terror, relief, joy, trepidation; he did not know which was driving his emotions.

I was dead. The thought echoed through his mind. *I was dead; I was going to die. Everyone was going to die.*

"Oh, Pieda," he murmured into the cushion. "I'm so sorry."

CHAPTER
ELEVEN

INTERVENTION
Royal Meeting Rooms A-3
Orso Royal Palace
Som Orsi

"I call this meeting to order," the king stated. And his councilors took their seats.

Eroa Lorne, Queen of the Orso kingdom, watched from the sidelines as her husband managed the kingdom he had inherited only months ago.

"Thank you for your time today," he began. "I'm eager to hear your reports."

Eroa winced. Targer was a decent person—she might even say simple—but he didn't know how to command. She'd been raised to command in any given situation. She could steer one person, or a dozen, or a thousand if she so desired. Targer could not.

She had expected to marry some insignificant elder noble, settled and stubborn. She'd trained to entice such a man, please him, manipulate him to her will. Her mother had overseen her training. She'd practiced seduction under Mother's watchful eye. But her marriage lacked any artifice. Targer was who and what he was, and she despaired.

"Those are promising numbers," Targer said, and Eroa stifled a groan. She'd gone over those reports with him last night. She'd hoped her point had been taken, but evidently Hal Merca had spun the bookkeeping to make his ledgers look... beneficial. Orso was reducing its trade with neighboring kingdoms, not increasing it.

Being himself isn't enough, she mused as Sandir Comex discussed materials production. As queen, Eroa had access to most secure files, and there were military programs being shuttered or locked down. Promising new designs from every corner of the kingdom weren't even being considered. The council constantly contracted rather than expanded their interests. She wanted to storm in and demand, Why aren't you more concerned about the alien threat?

Targer had asked her not to attend these meetings and his councilors manipulated him at every turn. Targer paraded and gave kingly blessings and bestowed awards while she was behind the scenes reading every industry report, finding every hint of corruption, and leveraging them to her advantage. At any moment, she could seize power and turn these councilors out. They would bow before a real queen, and she'd remake the kingdom.

She needed a Lorne child in her belly, and her husband dead. She would declare herself regent and dispose of these bastards. That was expedient. She could practically hear her mother agreeing.

But every time she thought of killing Targer for his throne —though she'd be doing the kingdom a favor—she felt sick. He never wanted to be king! Her emotions wailed. He doesn't deserve that. The Regency pushed him into it. He took the crown out of a misplaced sense of duty!

But he was willing to try, even while drowning in his own machinations, and that, for some strange reason she couldn't fathom, made her care about him. He was, she knew, little more than a clumsy puppy, but he cared, and he was so sincere. She'd never met such a person.

She needed to help Targer, not kill him, she suddenly realized, and that was a much tougher project than it sounded, but she was determined to make it work, somehow.

———

KAILITHA MEMORIAL HOSPITAL
 City of Bariell
 Planet Caerus

TWO WEEKS. For two weeks, Foreign had been trapped. It had a mission! It needed to reach Som Orsi! But the miserable female machine had abandoned it to this... hospital.

Foreign tried to command the machines to do its bidding, as it had aboard the space station. But its control was as erratic as human coughing, which was abundant. Its body felt weak and useless. Is human medicine hindering me? Foreign wondered before another fit of coughing took hold of her, stripping its throat raw with pain.

Foreign didn't understand why humans didn't welcome the Will's oblivion. Why didn't humans destroy themselves? Nonexistence must be better than diseases.

"Oh, hello there, Forann," said the human called Nurse. There were many such humans simply called Nurse, but this one had been checking Foreign constantly, ever since the human Selkie brought it to the hospital. "Comin' to catchup your folder. Betcha feeling better yet, huh?" Nurse tapped the datapad on Foreign's bed.

"I am not functional!" Foreign complained. "How long until I can travel to Som Orsi?"

"Oh, that infection got pretty bad, dontcha know," Nurse replied. "Them little forest buggies carry all sorts of nasty little things. I think we need another few days and flush those little germs outcha system."

"I should not have germs at all!" Foreign insisted. "This body should maintain peak efficiency. Humans are miserable!"

"Aintcha speakin' the truth, lassie," Nurse replied wistfully. "Sometimes we do fall down a little. But the point is to get back up again, you betcha."

Nurse made a note on Foreign's datapad. "Well, we be seein' you this afternoon. Best get some sleep, dontcha know. A good rest is best for what ails ya." And with that, Nurse was gone again.

Foreign wanted to scream. Foreign wanted to demand they pump inferior chemicals into this body to make it functional again.

But, someone decidedly not Nurse had explained that another outburst would land Foreign in another hospital where patients didn't leave peacefully. So Foreign marinated in negativity, waiting until Nurse's next visit. It was, after all, the only thing it could do.

It glared at the vid projector. The channel changed several times. Foreign could manage that much. But there were only insignificant news stories and puerile fictions.

This planet's vid programs were execrable. By themselves, they were reason enough to exterminate the material universe.

————

ROYAL ARCHIVES, Auxiliary Access
    Orso Royal Palace

. . .

QUEEN EROA LORNE strode into the royal archives section. This small room was conveniently close to the Royal Quarters. It was quiet and staffed day and night by two Royal Librarians. They were there to aid anyone in the royal family, but Eroa was certain they were an additional layer of security. They had watched her diligently throughout her studies.

She was looking into an inspiration, or was it perhaps premonition? She knew King Targer Lorne had been born a bastard, the illegitimate son of King Orso Lorne and his physician, Kiaro Chiru. But he was Orson's second bastard child. His first concubine, Fugie Crowe, had fled to the Independent Militia of Free Planets. Among the IMFP, Sasha Crowe, her bastard daughter, had risen to the rank of ship's captain, a testament to her bloodline. But she had been disinherited along with Elio Lorne; Sasha had once threatened to exercise her right of succession, so the Regency had revoked it.

But how many children did Orson Lorne father? she wondered.

Those records were locked behind encrypted access codes. Only military secrets were more protected. Such information could be dangerous to the king, were it to be exposed and thus make the king subject to blackmail, or extortion. Assassination threats were always a danger, of course, but, finally, Eroa was able to access the files for Orson's known children: Sasha Crowe, Elio, and Targer. Sasha's file was woefully outdated; lacking information beyond her tenth year. Elio's records were exactly as she expected, since the palace physician had constant access. But five years ago, his records became spotty. *A consequence of his jaunts into space with his girlfriend*, she supposed.

Eroa thought of her mother, Cythia Disiac. Once Eroa had begun training to seduce a future husband, the impenetrable wall between them had fallen, and now her mother confided in her as a friend. Her mother had attempted to wed Elio Lorne years earlier, and Eroa sometimes wondered what being the daughter of a queen would be like. Mother's decisions made more sense now, but still, Eroa wondered...

Wondering is for fools, she told herself. I will find and fight any dangers to the kingdom. *We can't have half-blood heirs fighting over the throne!*

For several hours, she worked to access the encrypted files, and when she finally did, she encountered her worst fear: there were no less than twelve more bastard Lorne offspring. Each no more than a year or so apart. All had Orson Lorne's genes. All were borne to various women in Som Orsi before the war. Once the attacks on Caerus began, the records were only rarely updated. Some missing altogether. And all these records bore the same signature...

Targer's mother. Royal Physician Kiaro Chiru.

I need to have a very frank discussion with my mother-in-law, Eroa decided.

———

KAILITHA MEMORIAL HOSPITAL
   City of Bariell
   Planet Caerus

"FINALLY, YOU WILL LET ME LEAVE?" Foreign demanded as a different Nurse pulled the various tubes and needles from its arms.

"Against our better judgment, yes," Nurse replied. "You've said many times you wanted to leave. But we weren't allowed to discharge you while you were sick. We have rules, you know."

"Don't your rules state I am allowed to self-discharge?"

Foreign demanded.

"Only if you are not a danger to yourself or others," Nurse replied. "And you needed to run the full course of treatment to avoid leaving while still infectious. Really... I mean, how did you manage to contract ubilaeteis? Swimming in a swamp, were you?"

Foreign chose not to answer that question.

"Whatever, darling," Nurse said. "You don't have to tell me nothing. But I'd dearly love to put you down in the kitchens for a month to cover some of the expenses. You haven't made your stay here easy, and I don't like giving fools a free bed when there are... more deserving people."

No human deserves that, Foreign thought. *This Nurse is a pestilence upon the humans. Perhaps if more were like the other Nurse...*

Foreign was... perplexed, or something akin to it, if such a thing was even possible. Did it truly believe that some humans were worth saving?

Surely not, Foreign decided. *Some humans may have more worth. The way some minions follow the Will's instructions better than others.*

"I am happy to be leaving," Foreign announced.

"May you live many years of healthy life," Nurse replied, and left. Foreign pondered these words. Was she truly wishing for good health? No, this Nurse might rather harm Foreign.

Ah! Foreign finally decided. *Nurse wishes me to never return!* Then Foreign, for the first time in its existence, actually felt something. Was it shame? Shame that the human didn't like it?

There is no time for philosophical ramblings! Foreign decided. The Will was absolute, and Foreign would see the Will's commands were carried out.

Foreign left the room and approached the place where nurses sat. Before, it found that the door only opened by a switch, operated behind the counter. But with a thought, the switch clicked and Foreign pushed the door open. At last! It wanted to scream, but emotions were human weakness.

It marched out into the bright sunshine. All around Bariell, humans bustled to their businesses or employments. Others were shopping, buying food or other items.

None of it was organized. None of it felt purposeful. It was like watching insects scurry around, looking for leaves. Foreign had observed insect behavior many times on the hike to Riverbol. Ants, like humans, scurried mindlessly and to no purpose.

Foreign's human stomach rumbled. I should have made Nurse bring me something to eat, it grumbled. It spotted a human food vendor and walked over. It scanned the offerings listed, but didn't recognize anything from the hospital. The serving man handed a wrapped bundle of food to a customer.

"What is the thing you serve here?" Foreign demanded.

"Back of the line, scrub!" someone shouted.

"Please wait your turn, ma'am," the serving man said. "It's the 1500 rush, but I have plenty."

The other humans stared at Foreign, so it made a show of meekness and went to the back of the line. It watched each human approach, wave their wrist device over a little box, and receive their food. Once it was able to approach, it asked again, "What is the thing you serve here?"

"This is a takdo stand," the man said. "Costs eight. Pay at the reader." He turned to fetch Foreign's order.

Foreign waved its naked wrist over the reader, but nothing happened. So Foreign reached out and manipulated the box to give a beep, like the other humans had received.

"Thanks, here you go," the man said, and handed over a... takdo?... in a small paper sleeve. Foreign walked away quickly, before the human noticed its deception.

Foreign meant to walk straight to the place where

conveyances might travel to and from, but its legs quickly tired. I have had all the resting! it complained. Why does this body have no stamina? It found a place to sit down, next to a water mister. Feeling human hunger pangs, it decided to eat.

Flavor exploded across Foreign's stolen tongue... and pain! It was hot! Foreign spat the burning food out on the ground, and looked at the steam twisting and boiling out of the tiny hole left by Foreign's mouth.

A flying scavenger swooped down and snatched the fallen food. It looked at Foreign before flying away again.

That was beautiful, Foreign thought as the creature escaped with its prize. Foreign didn't know where the thought came from. Just another material-universe animal. It didn't matter how the creature was constructed. The Will had ordered the destruction of this universe, and it would carry out its wishes.

It looked at the takdo, which showed less steam. It tried another bite. The flavors once again filled Foreign's mouth. This wasn't grass, or fruit, or gourds. This was full of fat, and meat, and fried vegetables, and savory herbs that lent a twist upon its tongue. A small moan of pleasure escaped its lips as it bit into the food again, and again.

CHAPTER
TWELVE

Control
Councilor's Offices
Orso Royal Palace, City of Som Orsi

Duke Gyrich Rutta reclined in opulence, his Palace offices decorated with the finest carpets and hangings to be found in the Orso kingdom. Some were over five hundred years old. His family was rich and storied, entrenched in the highest levels of the kingdom for generations.

And Elio, that idiot child, would have shed me and the other councilors like dead skin. Rutta had seen it in a vision. His Sight was growing stronger, but no matter what futures he saw, they branched into two paths.

In one, he was stripped of power and influence to spend his final days on only two or three estates, with barely enough money to employ a hundred or so servants in each. Practically destitute!

In the other, he saw himself battering Elio's TK aside. He fought Elio in the streets, each of them flinging grav cars and building debris at each other. But Rutta always prevailed. Always.

But how can I receive TK? he wanted to demand of his new liege.

Suddenly, Rutta felt another vision coming. He closed his eyes and beheld... himself, kneeling in the throne room before Helot garbed in a black gown.

At first he felt disgusted with himself; how could he kneel? Then Helot touched his head, and a brilliant light shone around him.

This is where I receive TK, isn't it? he wondered. He felt urgency, as though it would happen soon.

He pushed himself up from his divan and made for the door. He wasn't yet used to the Sight, but he was compelled to see what was coming. He couldn't shake the feeling of urgency.

He walked blindly, but soon he grew confident. If he was called to the throne room, he would go. He'd been there a thousand times. Ten thousand. It was as familiar to him as his penthouse in the Monere District, or his offices in the palace.

At the end, he practically ran. Only the barest propriety kept him from dashing headlong. He found the massive throne room empty, its columns bare, tapestries absent. It felt strange. Why was the room so stark?

Then he saw Helot, just as he'd seen her in his vision. Her dress was more inappropriate than ever, a deep V-neck to her navel, the entire bodice sagging from her emaciated figure. Her skin was clearly visible. She wore no skinthins today. A long train was slashed up to her narrow thighs, again showing her meager flesh. She wore a long, draped funereal veil.

"Lady Helot?" Gyrich said during the quiet moment.

"Gyrich," she whispered, the sibilant sound echoing in the empty chamber. "You came to me."

"I saw you in a vision," Rutta blurted out.

"I was told you'd find me here, or not." Helot shrugged her bony shoulders. "But since you've arrived, it is time to prove your allegiance to the One King."

"Of course," Rutta said without hesitation. But how could he give his word in such a way as to—

"Stop," Helot commanded. "Or he will not grant you the gift."

"What do you—"

"Do you think he is ignorant?" Helot gave a dry chuckle, almost a wheeze. "The One King can make use of you. But he has decided to grant you the power of TK. In return, you will do whatever he commands."

"Will I hear him?" Rutta asked.

"He will relay his messages as he desires," Helot said. "But you will kneel, now. Praise the One King of Power, who reaches across space and time. And serve him, in exchange for your power."

Rutta was confused. "But didn't I already—"

"You will swear on your life!" Helot's voice cracked against the stone. "His marks remind his servants of their place. But you... you need something more."

She pulled the right side of her bodice open. Atop the shriveled breast lay three marks, ⅄⅄⅄, one aside the next. "Place your hand upon my marks and give your vow."

Remembering her anger when he had, briefly, wondered about her body, he reached up and cupped her limp, leathery breast. He winced without thinking, remembering the pain her touch had inflicted through his scars. But nothing happened.

Until she clawed her nails through his shirt, grasping his scars and causing him pain like he'd never experienced before. It felt like being flayed alive by glass shards while being drowned in molten lava.

"Tell him you swear!" she commanded.

"I swear to the One King!" he screamed.

"You will obey him!" she ordered.

"I obey the One King in all things!" he insisted.

"You are his to use!" she screeched.

"I am his puppet!" Rutta bellowed.

"You will kill for him!" she laughed.

"I will murder the entire city if he tells me to! Please make it stop!" Rutta begged.

Helot tore her hand from his chest. Rutta looked to find pinpricks of blood staining his shirt. He ripped the shirt open to find a third ⚡ branded into his skin. After the torturous sensations of her touch, that pain was only a little less excruciating.

"In this symbol of loyalty to your old king, you have given loyalty to a new one," Helot said. "Now, he gives you his first command."

"What is that?" Rutta asked.

"You will kill someone for him," she stated. "Anyone. A servant. A noble. The boy king himself, if you wish. Or find a beggar in the streets. Use your TK if you wish. But to prove yourself, you must murder someone, or you are useless to him."

She waved to the door. "Go. You have until sunset." She reclined onto the throne. "Now, I must return to my duty. The little bird must see the light of a different sun before she will fly to us."

Rutta crept away, wondering who Helot's "little bird" was.

———

BAUTAN BETA-MAX PENITENTIARY
   [CLASSIFIED]
   Solitary Block, Cell A

. . .

"DEAR ELIO," Danis's own voice mocked her again for the... She didn't know how many times.

The message to Elio still played in her cell. She knew it wasn't a real cell. But it was still a cage. She'd never liked seeing a bird in a cage.

Her voice droned on. Danis could barely stand it anymore.

"I've been worried sick ever since we left Caerus," it repeated. "I've been desperate to talk, but we never stay in one place for very long. I had that strange dream just for a moment before we jumped."

Her last memory of him was a fleeting vision as Richard pulled an untested Slip out of Caerus space. After that had been days of boredom traveling, and bouts of vicious dog-fighting.

"There's been a lot of fighting. I know you worry about me flying missions without you. I really wish you were here."

At the beginning, she'd just wanted to talk to him. She'd wanted him nearby more than she wanted out of the cell. But after uncounted days in here, that had begun to change.

"Sometimes I get scared, and you're not here to hug it away," she muttered.

That would have sickened her five years ago. Danis had had time in her birdcage to wonder about the past few years. She'd clung to feelings and emotions she would have shunned before. Many of those memories were now linked to her voice talking about herself.

She hated weakness.

"I wish I knew what you were doing. But what could be going wrong? I mean, you went back to be the king, right?"

It was hard to remember exactly what she'd put in her message before. She didn't quite recall this part. But the last thing that had happened on Caerus was the announcement that the old king had died. *So Elio is king now, right?*

"What does your coronation mean for us now? Every time I thought about that, I shoved it away."

If Elio was king, then he'd abandoned her. After all, there was nobody else who could be king. Except Elio's sister Sasha Crowe, but she'd never seemed interested in tying herself to Orso politics.

Nobody else could be king. Nobody else at all.

I still want to be a pilot. I wish you were still a prince. But we're all born to be something, right? I just never thought I'd have to choose. Do we really have to choose?

She'd had plenty of experience before Elio came along. She'd didn't want to be tied to anyone. "Free as a bird in flight" had been her motto back then. She didn't want to clip her wings.

Then a sweet, slightly bumbling, really hot prince had fallen into her life. How could a girl say no?

Except she was locked up, and her lover had left her to die. His choice seemed clear. He'd chosen the throne.

"If you... ever get this... I'm sorry. I should have tried harder. I don't want to stop flying, but... royals do crazy things, too. Like you, always running into battle? Maybe... we can talk about that. Sometime. Someday."

She should have had that talk. She should have stopped the relationship before they'd reached this point. She was angry with him, sure, but she was disappointed in herself.

She was weak. She'd never suspected that kind of weakness was within herself.

"Because I... I hope I hear something soon. End."

And that was the clincher right there. She'd balked at saying how she really felt in a supposedly private message on a supposedly secure server.

Maybe if I'd said the real words, he'd have changed his

mind... No. A man who would leave any woman to languish in prison... after days of battle, and nights of passion... he was scum. And if I ever get out, I'll cut off his...

———

Primary Throne Room
Orso Royal Palace

Helot laughed in the still air of the throne room.

"Good little bird," she cackled. "Fly to your new home. I have a different king for you to serve."

She heard the bustle of servants preparing to enter the room and dress it for the day. She watched as they entered the throne room, carrying tapestries and banners to hang in the alcoves and from the rafters. They never noticed the crone lounging in the highest seat of their kingdom. Helot had simply whisked away the image of her presence.

"Now she must be turned against her brother," she whispered to herself. "If she believes he betrayed her, she'll believe anything of her Elio. But, how could her loving brother ever betray her? Hmmm..."

———

Captain's Ready Room
Tsunami's Bridge
Station-keeping Orbit over Caerus

"Welcome, Jadern," Commodore Vandu said as Brevet Captain Michael Jadern entered. "Glad to have you here." She motioned toward the empty seat on the left side of the table.

He sat. The two captains across the table glanced at him before returning to their wrist pads. He itched to be doing something useful. Hoping to look competent, he brought up the display on his own wrist pad and began reviewing quartermaster logs on his ship, the Torrent.

His ship. The words felt almost magical. He'd hoped for years to helm a ship. Then he'd ended up with Richard Morian, who pissed off the king and got shoved into the Orso Fleet's oldest rust-bucket—

Hey, stop that! came an errant, angry thought. The Avenger was never a rust-bucket. Richard saw to that.

He wasn't certain where the thought originated, but he would at least admit its truth. Avenger was the oldest cruiser in the fleet, but Richard's discipline refused to accept anything less than perfection. Jadern had seen newer ships with only half the attention to cleanliness. Richard was a stickler, but Jadern admitted that the cause had been just.

No just causes at the end, though, he thought darkly. *And now he's dead.*

"Gentlemen," Commodore Vandu began, "it's time to prepare for rotation." She called up a visual on the holo. "In two weeks, our task force is being sent out on patrols in the Eos, Suzia, Eleusis, and Cerian systems. We've had a pleasant time sitting here at home. Now it's someone else's turn."

"Commodore," Captain Seder said, "If I'm not mistaken, we've had a schedule change. Weren't we supposed to debark from Caerus in five weeks, not two? Why the change?"

"Recent attacks on various systems have left the royals in a fritz," Vandu explained. "We were supposed to patrol a different area, but they've increased the number of ships at every location. We will be traveling through the Tor system Slipgates to reach Eos, where we'll be relieving the Agitare task force, and sharing the system briefly with the Khaitan task force before they move on."

"What will this shuffling accomplish?" Captain Lavare asked. "It's like a carnival game, moving the bead between the shells."

"That is the sum of it," Vandu agreed. "The enemy showed us our weaknesses. Many of those systems only had a token force in play." She called up a holo of recently attacked systems, and the forces arrayed there. "Ships are to be deployed per emergency measures in the USF charter. The enemy hits somewhere, draws off vessels from larger forces, then attacks those depleted forces." The next holo, simplistic though informative, clearly showed the mining planet of Tyche. Several of their capital ships were shown leading commercial ventures. Nearby systems were attacked by small Swarm forces, and one by one the rest of the Tyche fleet was drawn away. Once the field was almost cleared, the Swarm attacked in force.

"The enemy is playing the shell game, Captain Lavare," Vandu said with a grim smile. "We are simply changing the rules."

She went to shut off the holo, but Jadern caught something else happening. "Wait, Commodore," he said, and her hand was stayed.

And they watched as a fleet of ships arrived in system and drove off the Swarm attack. "What are those ships?" Jadern asked.

Vandu frowned. "Apparently, a small fleet of Alastor vessels arrived to conduct business of their own. I'm not privy to the details. But I do know an ambassador is present. He's to negotiate something with their unions. Without his decommissioned destroyer, the planet would have taken a bigger hit."

"Ambassador?" Jadern asked.

"Elio Lorne," Vandu answered as she shut off the holo. "Though if we're arming the diplomatic vessels now—"

Jadern barely heard the rest of the briefing. The mere mention of the name Elio Lorne sent waves of... purpose through him. He knew that if he met Elio Lorne again, *he needed to... needed to...*

He didn't know exactly what. He just knew he needed to do it.

Strangely, the contradiction didn't even occur to him. He simply knew he needed to do something.

And he would, if he ever got the chance.

———

Tancovat Campus of Arts
   Monere District, Som Orsi

Duke Gyrich Rutta, head of the Gyrich dynasty, keeper of twelve generations of great fortune and responsibility, trembled at the thought of this one woman's displeasure.

It's not her I'm afraid of, he reminded himself. Helot represented someone much more powerful. The One King was brutal. He'd seen that. Helot had explained the One King's ambitions and sins, perhaps more than any other human knew. But he, Gyrich Rutta, was born to take the reins of power and whip the vehicle of state into place.

Which was why he'd called Genivei to his side this evening. She'd been his mistress for more than a year. Whatever passed for feelings in Rutta's ice-cold heart liked her very much. But he took his imminent rise to power very seriously. And if he was to kill someone for the One King, he assumed that a simple denizen of the streets wouldn't satisfy. He suspected the point was pain, and she was among those he cared for. Well, kind of.

They walked into the Tancovat Opera House, he in the same suit he always wore to such events, and her in a dazzling red dress that turned quite a few eyes in their direction. They made their way through the press of people, took the elevator to his private box, and there they settled into their seats.

"I've been wanting to see this for a while," she whispered excitedly. "The Emperor's Sandal has the best reviews of any such composition in years."

"I'm going to step out for a moment before it begins," he said, and rose to his feet and walked out. He waited until someone appeared in the hall, and called out, "Darling, could you come here a moment?"

"Of course, Gyr," she called back, and stood up.

Just as the man in the hallway drew close, Rutta used his TK to shove her over the railing.

Her scream rose above the murmurs of the crowd below and then was cut short.

He adopted an expression of terrible shock as the stranger rushed to the balcony, looking over at her death.

I had to pay for the tickets, he thought, and now I won't get to see it. Oh, well.

CHAPTER
THIRTEEN

PERPLEXITY
Unknown Location "Rat Cellar"
Som Orsi, Planet Caerus

FAXIL AWOKE and instantly knew what this day was. It was his birthday.

"Hey, Dad..." he began before trailing off. The container was empty.

Oh, he thought. Then he realized—*Oh! They must have let me sleep in so they could surprise me. With... something. Somehow.*

He pulled on his shorts and jogged out into the warehouse. No one was working on anything, but he smelled something. Was it... in the kitchen?

"Moment of truth," he heard Ms. Verso say. "Three blind redirects and a temporary university account. Once this goes out, I'll shred everything."

"Is it secure enough?" Mr. Rosst asked.

"How should I know anymore?" Ms. Verso said. "Oh, hi little scrub."

"Hi, Ms. Verso," he replied. She never used his name, but somehow that was... special?

"And... launch," Verso said, and tapped a key.

The screen fountained message icons. Faxil knew it was a silly thing, but it was thrilling.

"Auto-delete worked," Ms. Verso reported. "Deleting redirects..." Faxil barely understood any of that, but it didn't matter.

I'm Faxil Avestan. I'm twelve years old TODAY. And I helped create a game that will win a war. He blushed at the grandiose thought, but it was kinda true. That first meeting about the game—his idea—had created Perplexity.

It was a simple picture puzzle using actual locations in Som Orsi. Simplified into line drawings, the puzzle was slightly difficult. When you finished the picture, and stood where the picture was taken, it unlocked a short video. Eighteen of them were frivolous—

This was the hotel where they filmed the classic holovid, Will and Testament. It's said that the two principal actors, Zel Grase and Mallari Fenc, fell briefly in love during filming. Though they have always denied it, the crew claimed to have found the pair in compromising positions several times.

The Arazon halo manufactory once stood on this spot. They created thirty-five million Zone Halos in the factory, until their competitor Neva created the superior halo Nevashade. But without those first Zone Halos, we wouldn't have advanced communications at the level we currently have.

Then there were the two "rabid squirrels," as Verso insisted on calling them. Having never seen a squirrel, Faxil could only imagine that the beast looked as fearsome as Kuon—

I won't worry about Kuon today, he told himself. *Inoiae is fine, and Kuon is fine, and we're just waiting for them to come home.*

The two puzzle prizes weren't gossip or local history, but vids of the Som Orsi attacks. To avoid immediate scrutiny, Verso had chosen publicly available footage of heroic soldiers.

There were dozens of other vids, like random soldiers, casualties, Prince Elio and his team, fighting valiantly. Some denounced deals the Regency Council had brokered, public broadcasts, or private recordings. They would come later; now the point was to draw attention.

Someone punched Faxil's shoulder. Faxil expected Pinari, but it was Mr. Ferg.

"Well, kid, you lucked out," Mr. Ferg said, the smell of synth wafting around him.

"Wait," Faxil said. "What do you mean?"

"You spat out all that nonsense about a game," Mr. Ferg replied. "They chopped the idea up and made something stupid. A whole other level than my stupid."

"I don't understand," Faxil said.

"Of course you don't," Mr. Ferg said. "We keep sending out those games, and eventually someone will crack it open. Then they'll trace it here. The hacker lady said they found her personal system. They're better than her. She admitted it."

Faxil couldn't speak.

"Your stupid idea will get everyone killed," Mr. Ferg added.

The words sank into his mind. Faxil couldn't imagine it all, so he turned and walked away.

"Don't feel too bad, kid," Mr. Ferg said before Faxil turned the corner. "They would have picked some other idea. You were just unlucky this time."

Faxil turned the corner and ran. He needed somewhere to hide until he stopped crying.

———

Avrum Rosst walked back to his container. Grig had recently set up a layer of boxes around the door, saying, "If I'm retired, I'll sit on a porch to yell at brats." When Rosst asked how quickly the Avestan children would learn to avoid him, Grig only replied, "Oh, yeah, them too."

Grig had put out several cheap chairs, and Rosst had laughed, but quickly found the chairs a comfort. Something as normal as a "yard" almost immediately relieved some of the stress bunching his shoulder muscles. He found Grig already lounging in his seat, nursing a packet of citrus juice.

"Well, we just sent out the puzzles," Rosst said as he sat in his chair. "We're officially rebelling. What do you think the repercussions will be, Teyn?"

"Come on, Avrum," Grig replied. "You know as well as I do that no plan survives first contact. This was what? Twenty-seven thousand contacts?"

"It took weeks to compile the travel data for all those people. We needed to know who was likely to be in the right places to activate the first puzzles." Rosst sighed. "It feels like a terrible abuse, though. We're using citizens without their consent."

"Screw their consent," Teyn grumbled. "When you make decisions at my level, they stop being just people. Whatever might be good for one person may not be good for families or for communities or for cities."

"You can't generalize like that—" Rosst began.

"We have to!" Teyn insisted. "Twenty-two planets, Avrum. Tens of billions of people. What's best for each one?"

"Then why are we the ones doing the deciding?" Rosst countered.

"Someone has to," Grig replied. "The Regency Council

deposed the rightful ruler of fifteen systems. Was it greed? Ambition? What's their plan? What's their next step?"

"We lost those answers," Rosst said. "We can't trust anything we learned before."

"That's wrong." Grig pointed a finger at the wall. "They deposed Elio Lorne, which means they oppose his war hawk attitude. Otherwise, they'd profit off his policies while preaching against them. They're politicians."

"They've made governmental decisions for years, even decades," Rosst pointed out.

"They stood by while people died, and called it nonintervention," Grig snapped. "Are they going to protect Orso citizens? No, they will not. I know a prince who will, a prince who almost died heroically five times. You can't say that about any of those despots in the palace—"

"Excuse me?" a voice interrupted.

Deno Avestan was standing at the "fence".

"I'm looking for Faxil," Deno said. "It's... his birthday today. Has anyone had seen him?"

"He ran off toward the west corner," Grig said. "He didn't look happy."

"I hope he doesn't think we forgot," Deno replied. "I mean, maybe we did. But I thought we could do something... special?"

To Rosst's surprise, Grig said, "I understand. Let me drop some hints. We'll have something ready for him in twenty minutes."

As Deno walked away, Rosst said, "I honestly didn't expect you to—"

"Faxil didn't ask for this," Grig said. "At his age, every birthday is important. It's a marker of manhood. So we do something, and look happy about it, right?"

Rosst had nothing to add, other than, "Of course."

They sat in silence for a moment before Grig added, "I didn't forgive my brother for twenty years."

"What did he do?" Rosst asked.

"Stole my birthday," Grig replied. "He and his wife showed up and announced they were having a baby. Couldn't get any attention after that. Get after Lockwith. I'm not dealing with him if he's drunk. On second thought, lock him in his office."

"Yes, sir," Rosst said, and eased out of his chair.

————

Councilor's Quarters
Orso Royal Palace, City of Som Orsi

DUKE GYRICH RUTTA was sleeping when his comm tweedled loudly. He tried to silence it, but it rang until he activated it. "What is it?" he growled, but found a recording.

"King Targer Lorne summons Duke Gyrich Rutta to the central throne room for an emergency meeting. Time to arrive is 0100 hours." Then the message repeated.

"Insolent whelp!" Rutta muttered as he clambered out of bed.

He found his steward and dragged him to the dressing room. "I've been summoned to the king," Rutta said as he raised his arms to be clothed properly. "Why couldn't this happen after breakfast?" he complained as his steward carefully removed Rutta's bed wear.

"I don't know, sire," the steward replied out of turn as he pulled a dress blouse around his master.

Rutta glared at him until the clothes were presentable, then he marched out of his apartments and made for the elevators.

Ten minutes later, he walked into the throne room, his clothes slightly rumpled, and his attitude more so. All the other councilors were already there, sitting in near-darkness, the throne room lit only by accent lights.

"What's the urgency?" he demanded of his colleagues. "And where's his Highness? I thought he was behind—"

"Gyrich," Mezeke Bohne said. "Did you get dressed in the dark?"

Gyrich almost used his new TK powers to do something rash. Only inexperience held him back. He wanted nothing conspicuous.

"I called everyone here using the royal command codes," Pal Jiock said, "because we can't trust communications."

"Not even halos?" Hal Merca, Councilor of Trade asked.

"Certainly not halos," Jiock said. "Rogue programs are out in the world. They may have infected the halos. Halos could be listening devices now. The throne room has no recording devices. It is swept regularly for devices, and it wasn't being used, so..."

"So... paranoia. This sounds serious," Merca replied. "Please explain."

"We've just received word," Jiock said, "that this strange new program is some kind of game."

"Hah, Jiock," Rutta sneered, "you're really staying on top of things as councilor of technology."

"This isn't an idle summons, Gyrich!" Jiock snapped. "Over twenty thousand copies of this game suddenly appeared, distributed to wrist pads through a university mailing system. It slipped by all watchdogs. It invited users to assemble a puzzle. If you're in the right location, the puzzle matches some local landmark and gives you a vid. It seemed to be harmless, so no one reacted at first."

"Then why did they?" Comex finally asked.

"Our network security team received a call from the

university," Jiock explained. "They do not know where the messages came from. All relevant information immediately disappeared. Someone hacked them, someone as good as our specialists."

"You think it's whoever broke our prisoners out of Rising Tide?" Mezeke Bohne said. "We destroyed their computer mainframe. So they... what? Hacked the university for fun?"

"If I knew, I wouldn't have called an emergency meeting, would I?" Jiock replied. "I hoped someone might have an idea."

"Simple," Rutta asked. "Forcibly delete any copies from those devices, and then plant a virtual minefield in the university mainframe. The next time they surface, we'll find out, or their computers will be destroyed."

"What you don't know about technology is staggering," Jiock complained. "Number one, we can't just delete every copy of the game. We could release a self-evolving deletion virus into Caerus's comm network, but any programs with similar code would also be wiped leading to planet-wide chaos."

"Not the greatest option," Promeant agreed.

"Number two," Jiock continued. "Bohne, what happens when you tell everyone they can't have something?"

Everyone looked at Bohne, the Councilor of Social Analysis. Bohne clearly wasn't expecting that. "It's obvious," Bohne said. "Anything we tell them they can't have, they will want. The curious will seek out the information. If the culprit strikes again, more people will investigate."

"Thank you, Bohne," Jiock said. "The third problem. Is the game a goal, or a distraction? What was its purpose? We don't know. And the fourth problem is a simple one. They won't use the university again. Lying in wait only works on dumb animals. Wherever they strike next, we won't see it coming."

After an hour of that, Rutta finally made his excuses and left. His TK burned inside him. Helot had warned that the One King wasn't satisfied with his mistress's bloodless accident. Rutta needed to kill again, and soon.

It could be one of those idiots, he mused. But he couldn't do it yet. Once he was secure, he'd murder them all if it would please the One King.

He was prepared to do anything for power.

———

FAXIL CROUCHED behind a large metal pipe he'd found while playing hide and seek with Pinari. She hadn't found him yet. So his father's appearance was shocking.

"Heya, kid," Dad said. "What are you doing back here?"

"I don't wanna talk about it," Faxil mumbled.

"Are you sure?" Dad said. "Maybe things aren't as bad as you think."

Your stupid idea is going to get everyone here killed.

"We're stuck in a dirty old building, we live in a metal box, and we only eat canned food," Faxil said. "And we're gonna die."

"Who said we were going to die?" Dad asked. Faxil didn't answer. Maybe his dad didn't blame him for what was going to happen...

"Besides, what kind of dad would I be to let you die on your birthday?" he added.

Excitement raced through Faxil. "Wow! I mean, you remembered?"

"Of course I remembered," Dad laughed. "Come on, let's go have lunch. And then... dessert!"

Dessert was enough. Faxil crept from his hiding spot. "Don't let Pinari see my spot," he added. "She hasn't found me yet."

"I was pretty good at hide and seek myself," Dad bragged, but they went a twisty path that brought them out far away from the pipe.

When they reached the dining area, Faxil was shocked. There was a real cake, and it was covered with icing. It even had a few stubby candles perched on top. Everyone was waiting for him. Well, except Mr. Lockwith, but that was okay.

"We couldn't find twelve—" Dad began.

"It's perfect," Faxil whispered.

Dad lit the candles. "Make a wish, son," he said.

Faxil wondered for just a moment, then decided on his wish, and blew. Everyone clapped, and the ladies started dishing up the food. Faxil knew it had come from cans, but someone had tried extra hard to make it look... well, like real food.

Pinari came up beside him. "Hey, Fax," she said, clearly embarrassed. She not-so-casually threw an arm over his shoulders and squeezed him, like a sister's hug. "Um, sorry I hit you. I... freaked out. When you... yeah..." And she leaned over and kissed his cheek.

Then Pinari dropped her arm and shuffled away, her face red as the dill beets Mrs. Bree was spooning onto a plate.

My wish came half-true, he thought. That's good enough.

After the food came presents. Faxil was amazed that he'd gotten anything. Mrs. Presdon gave him a patchwork blanket she'd sewn together, and his dad gave him a folding knife—his first ever! "You've grown into a brave young man," he said. "I know I can trust you to use that responsibly. Though if you want whittling lessons, we'll have to get you a vid."

Mr. Arthon and Mrs. Bree gave him a reader with stories loaded, which was kind of neat. But the last package was just sitting on the table. "Dad, whose present is that?" he asked.

"I'm not sure—wait," he said. "No, I don't know."

Faxil untied the string, opened the box and looked inside. Inside was a battered sketchpad, and an almost full set of slightly used colored pencils. Inside the pad's cover, there was a note in Pinari's unmistakable hand. Don't lose this one. Draw me something pretty.

CHAPTER
FOURTEEN

HOLLOW
Esse, Monere District
Planet Caerus

Meera woke suddenly. She looked around. She was in her chair, not her bed; it had been smashed to bits.

"What was that?" she mumbled. "Did I hear something?" She'd been dreaming. She was in a battle against the Blues. But they'd had voices like bells, or—

Her wristpad vibrated on the table at her side. She picked it up. The display read Lifia Seleure.

"Lifia!" she said, and snatched the wristpad. "Hi honey," she said, before wishing she'd set it to voice-only.

"Sorry Mom. Did I wake you?" Lifia asked.

"No, of course not. I... needed to be up anyway," Meera said. She didn't want Lifia to know she'd hadn't slept well.

"Today was midterms," Lifia said, "and I just finished my last class for today. Mind if I pop over?"

"Of course you can. I'll be waiting," Meera said. "Do you need anything to eat, or—"

"Nope. I'm bringing a surprise." Lifia looked pleased. "I'll be there in an hour!"

"See you then—" Meera said, but Lifia had disconnected. Beset with purpose, Meera shoved her covers away.

It had been four days since visiting Dusti, and she hadn't left home since. She dragged herself into the hydro. At least Lifia had called, so Meera should clean herself. She dried herself off, dressed, brushed her hair, then almost ran to the kitchen and hid the dishes in the hydromatic. Then she set out clean plates, wondering what excitement Lifia was bringing. This tiny ray of sunshine was more than welcome. Looking around at the rest of her mess, Meera began shuffled around, collecting bits of paper and tidying up.

Lifia arrived minutes after Meera was at least halfway satisfied with her cleaning efforts.

"Hi, Mom," she called from the door. A wonderful aroma quickly wafted through the house. Crusted cichlid, from Meera's favorite fish house, Seascapade. She ordered it whenever she had the chance.

"Seascapade?" she asked Lifia. "Isn't that a little pricey for a student?"

"Wow, yeah, Mom, you're right," Lifia admitted, her expression downcast. "It really was. I guess..." her eyes brightened, and she smiled as she said, "so it's a good thing I put it on your account."

Meera laughed at that impish smile, and they sat down to eat. Meera kept the conversation on Lifia: life at university, her classes, even listening to social dramas Lifia endured for her friends' sakes. When Lifia tried to ask Meera something, she would deflect her. "I want to hear about you, sweetie," Meera said the third time. "I'm not doing anything important."

The visit was oh so welcome, but as soon as Lifia had gone, Meera looked at the unwashed dishes and realized that she was falling behind again. She forced herself to sort the dishes properly and turn the hydromatic on. She looked around the rooms she hadn't cleaned, and, in a moment of resolve, she decided she would do better! She would pick herself up by the bootstraps, and... and...

But then, resolve disappeared in a puff of reality.

"Oh, what does it matter?!" she yelled at nobody. "Why does any of this matter?" She collapsed into her chair, tears beginning to trail down her face. She recounted every moment of Lifia's visit and realized she'd lied to her daughter. Then, *I'm fine.* She thought. *Everything's okay. Nothing is wrong.*

"What is this all for?" she mumbled to herself. "Why am I even here?"

It wasn't so long ago that she'd felt purpose. She'd felt strong, and useful, if a little overwhelmed. But before that...

"Before that, I lost Sorge," she whispered. "And I was lost, even when Lifia was here. All that kept me moving were the Knights. But who am I, if I'm not a Knight, and not a mother?"

She got up before she could convince herself otherwise. She found the TraumAnon card again, looked at the schedules. The local meeting was in two days. She looked around the house at her mess and was filled with a new determination. Not an urge to run away from her problems, but a need to walk toward them one step at a time.

"In two days," she promised herself, "I'm going to be ready for that meeting." She scooped up a bag of groceries—mostly instant meals—and began putting them away.

———

GREASETOWN

. . .

Jude Cabeus crept toward the last building on his list. He'd planned infiltrations to twenty-three buildings. Each one was empty of humans, and most had been legitimate. A few had been full of stolen goods, but he made a note of them and moved on. He wasn't interested in police work; they could clean their own messes.

Nothing was certain; any building he missed could be filled with the fugitives. Potable water and access to food had been primary details, but there were alternatives to pipes and caches. No need to borrow trouble yet, he told himself. Just check this one off the list.

He found an ancient ID reader and held up his hacked passcard. The device whirred and whined. The ID reader flashed acceptance, and he eased the door open, stepped inside, and the door closed behind him.

He stood for a moment, listening. He could hear sounds, then voices, but couldn't make them out, so he moved slowly forward. The further he went, the more uneasy he became. The sounds were metallic, or mechanical. The voices were rough, angry. He heard foul language. *Certainly not with children around?* he thought, *Did my father ever hide his thoughts? Never!*

He found a section of wall that served as a makeshift window into the next area and carefully peered inside.

Grav cars lay on the ground, partly assembled. Some had mechanics working, though a few moments of observation proved they weren't putting parts in.

"What's going on here?" A massive hand clamped on Jude's left shoulder and hauled him away from the view. "I don't like strangers!" the large man snarled. He had to be a hundred and twenty kilos, and he swung a giant torque wrench at Jude's head.

Jude reacted without thinking, trying to use TK to shift the wrench and barely remembered to block instead. The wrench slammed into his metal arm with a reverberating clang! The large man swung again, and the head of the twenty-kilo-torque wrench missed him by only a centimeter.

"Please," Jude replied. "I mean no harm. "

"You shouldn't be here!" the man yelled.

The giant wrench began another swing. Jude simply side-stepped, letting the weapon pass harmlessly by. The man tried a backhand blow—

Jude punched his wrist with his mechanical hand. Bones shattered; the man bellowed in pain and the wrench skittered away into darkness. The man clutched his arm, screaming.

Jude tried to make for the entrance, but was blocked by two men and a woman. "What are you doing here?" the woman said.

"I...Um, I didn't mean to cause trouble," Jude replied, smiling at her.

The two men and the woman rushed at him, but Jude just continued to smile. *These two are only ninety kilos at best. Just like drills at assassin camp.*

The two men pulled knives, and he hastily reassessed the situation. They were proving to be more than he expected, and the woman seemed to have taken what he'd said person-ally, as an insult, spitting and snarling like an enraged khain, trying to claw his face off. It turned into mayhem and by the time he got out of there, all four of them needed immediate medical attention, and Jude had fared little better.

He limped back toward his hovel, pressing a wad of shirt against his side where he'd been stabbed. He thought about the criminal activities he'd witnessed. *Was that really so hard to find?* he wondered. *Shouldn't someone fix these problems?* He shrugged to himself. *The problem is endemic. Does one group control these and the others? Do they control local security, or maybe...*

He stopped. He'd learned that three companies controlled

most of the commerce in Greasetown, and that they, in turn, were controlled by a larger interest. But clearly the pyramid's top was larger and more inclusive. He needed to look at the bigger picture.

He shook his head, turned left, and headed toward the nearest Philanthropic Clinic. His ID would get him patched up there, regardless of the hour.

———

Philanthropic Clinic
Greasetown

Jude was awakened by a sudden bright light.

Where am I? He wondered, looking around at the bare white walls and the concrete floor, then he recognized the irregular sounds of blip, blip, blip in the background as an intravenous drip.

"Urgg," he muttered. "Not home." He checked his wounds. They were... competently bandaged, at least.

There weren't any large hospitals near the slums, but despite the severity of his injuries, he'd chosen the closest option, an emergency charitable clinic.

"Hello?" Jude called, but no one answered. Night shift, bad neighborhood, he thought as he carefully eased himself off the gurney, feeling it wobble as he did so. He stretched gently, but there were no unexpected pains. Can't blame any doctors or nurses for leaving the place at night.

Jude knew that the Wellbient Foundation had sponsored several health clinics in the area, though they were obviously a tax write-off, but the floors were clean, though the place looked like a detention facility rather than a medical facility. It stank of antiseptic and urine.

He heard a tired voice sigh behind him and say, "What are you doing out of bed?"

Jude whirled around, bringing his metal arm up to fire projectiles before remembering his good prosthetic arm was gone, replaced by a cheap copy. The nurse flinched back in fear.

"Sorry," Jude said as he lowered the arm. "You... startled me."

"I'm sorry, sir," she mumbled. "I didn't mean to disturb you."

"It's fine," he replied. "As you can see, I had a rough night. I'm just a little nervous."

"Yes, sir?" she replied, obviously choosing her words carefully. "If you say so, sir."

"Really," he tried to say, "you don't have to be afraid—"

"I saw what you looked like when you came in, sir," she said, fear replacing her polite demeanor. "When someone comes in like you did, it usually means someone else won't."

"It's not like that," Jude protested. "I didn't kill anyone. I just—"

"I saw your ID," she insisted, cutting him off. "It's none of my business. Please, if you want to go, we won't keep you."

"But I—" Jude began.

She flinched again. "I have a family!" she blurted out. "Please... I deleted your records. We have terrible security. Cameras are down. No video. So please..." Her voice trailed off, and he thought she was going to cry.

Jude gave up. He apologized, then nodded and turned away and left the clinic, and made his way back to his apartment. It was almost dawn, and Orso's light was creeping over the skyline. He supposed that residents of Greasetown were happy about that, but it only made him feel tired.

Once he closed his door and activated the security locks, he took out his ID. It looked like most military IDs. But this one had a security hash bordered in gold, and the edge had a dark blue stripe. When he held the ID up to the cheap light, he could see the holographic words SPECIAL ACCESS underneath.

"What does 'Special Access' mean?" he muttered. "What is my father doing?"

He remembered the nurse's fear. For a moment, he saw Maila's fear instead. Tag and Posie looked up at him as if he was a monster. Maila whimpered, *It's none of our business. If you want to go, you can.*

Jude closed his eyes, and tears trailed down his face. He'd been gone so long, and he didn't know anything about their situation. Now, strangers were reacting to him with... fear? No, terror.

What will I do to get back to my family? Jude thought. *Anything. I'll do anything.*

———

DOWNTOWN ESSE
Monere District, Som Orsi

MEERA MADE her way to Society Hall in Esse. She'd been there before. The local schools rented the space for events, and the indoor court was used by several sport teams. But today, she found the little room at the end of a darkened hallway. There were padded chairs arranged in a circle, some already occupied. Meera sat down, settled herself, and waited.

A few moments later, a tall, dark-haired woman in a business suit strode in, a briefcase and papers in hand. She sat down, and Meera wondered what problems she might have. But once Meera's wristpad chimed the hour, it was the woman who spoke.

"Welcome to TraumAnon," she said in a surprisingly melodious voice. "My name is Kirma."

"Good afternoon, Kirma," the rest of the crowd said.

"When I was twelve, my father died," Kirma explained without preamble. "My mother tried to raise me by herself, but she couldn't manage the stress, and I was blamed for her many problems. It took me six years to shed the guilt I felt because I assumed I was the problem. I wasn't. Today, I am more like the me I want to be, should be. Now I help others to let their pasts go, and deal with their hurts. Who would like to share first?"

A man stood up. "Hi, my name is Drey."

"Good afternoon, Drey," the crowd chorused.

"I was in a gravcar accident ten years ago," he began. "I was the only one who walked away. The rest, including a family of five, all died."

Drey talked about the family and about how he'd fallen into guilt and depression. Meera suspected there was a jail sentence in there, too, but if there was, he didn't mention it. When he'd finished, Kirma nodded, thanked him and moved on to the next person, and then the next. Each recounted a painful time and described the shambles their life had become.

Meera wanted to stand and talk, but something held her back. She listened to everyone, wondering why some fell apart so badly over much simpler problems than hers.

Then someone she thought looked vaguely familiar—a short tanned woman with springy hair and a pair of earrings the size of Meera's thumbs—stood up and said, "My name is Finia. I joined the Perceptual Expansion Unit to make a difference. I worked really hard, and I thought I could do something useful, but they told me I wasn't good enough, and they let me go. I... had to go back to my old life and problems and I..." she trailed off, tears rolling down her cheeks.

It was then that Meera remembered the almond-skinned

girl. Finia had worked hard. I thought she had gotten a post somewhere.

Kirma waited a few moments for Finia to compose herself and continue, but when she didn't, she cleared her throat and said, "Finia, we're grateful that you come to every meeting, and your desire to make a difference in other people's lives is commendable. But," she added, "you've mentioned only one time before about your problems and you've never told us about them. I think it might be good for you to discuss them, too. Don't you?"

"Look, it was hard for me, growing up, all right?" Finia grumbled. "I... don't want to talk to other people about that. They always get the wrong idea. Ask stalker-boy from the Cassa group."

"We at TraumAnon encourage our members to talk outside the meetings if they're comfortable," Kirma explained to the rest of the group, "but Finia had an incident, and we helped her handle it with the police. Please don't disturb others if they ask you not to." Meera expected Kirma to say something more, but she merely nodded to Finia, who sat down. "It's almost time to end the meeting," she said instead. "Does anyone else want to say something today?"

Meera wanted to talk, but she held back.

"Then I'd like to thank those of you who spoke today," Kirma said. "I hope you made some progress finding the 'you that you want to be.' For those who didn't speak, I want you to know that this is a safe place, and you can always share your innermost problems here. Let's be the 'me' that we want to be."

"I will be the 'me' that I want to be," the group recited, before the group began to leave. Some of them making arrangements to have lunch together; others simply shaking hands and saying goodby.

Meera was so lost in thought that she jumped when Finia appeared in front of her and said, "Meera?"

CHAPTER
FIFTEEN

CONFESSION
Royal Quarters
Royal Palace, Som Orsi

Eroa Lorne was queen, so it was quite natural for her to command those around her. At seventeen, she bore an authority that politicians thrice her age did not.

Why can't I get my mother-in-law to visit? she wanted to scream.

She'd tried the polite approach. She'd commed Kiaro Chiru, making small talk, dissembling her motive. But Kiaro had suddenly cut the call short.

Eroa had tried again, this time with a private meal together. Something light and crunchy that would give them plenty of time to talk. But Kiaro had postponed at the last moment.

Growing impatient, Eroa had sent her mother-in-law an official invitation to dine with the king. She would plead that the king had postponed his attendance. Kiaro said that if her son wanted to talk, he needed only to call her, which he did, twice a week in the evenings.

Finally, Eroa had had enough. She set a pair of operatives on the woman, watching her every movement. Kiaro Chiru didn't seem to notice, but her travels seemed to be quite random. The surveillance continued for two weeks before the pattern began to emerge, and a third before she was able to figure out what she was doing: Kiaro was meeting the women on the bastard list.

With great pleasure, Eroa arranged a small dinner party with caterers and a music troupe. The woman that Kiaro was supposed to see "won" a free spa day, all-expenses-paid courtesy of the royal account. And so the queen of seventeen planets awaited the arrival of a doctor in a small apartment. Eroa enjoyed the canapes and vegetable trays, and the music was lighthearted.

There was a knock on the door.

"One moment," Eroa called softly, and silenced the band. She swept toward the door, anticipating the doctor's reaction.

"Hello there!" she greeted. "Please, come in."

The pure terror on Kiaro's face was worth the effort.

Kiaro shut the door behind her quickly. "What in starblazes are you doing here?" she hissed.

"Careful, dear," Eroa cautioned her. "I am queen. I have indulged your fantasy of a life too busy to obey my summons, out of respect for my husband. Sit down, please."

Kiaro sat down in the chair opposite Eroa.

"Ladies and gentlemen," Eroa said to the caterers and band, "thank you for the lovely afternoon, but now to business. You may leave us. If you wait in the hall for a few moments, you will receive a bonus for your time."

"How is Targer doing?" Kiaro asked sweetly as everyone shuffled out.

"He's completely unaware that you're here," Eroa

answered. "If you'd like him to learn what you've been doing, you may merely walk out the door. Or you can stay and enjoy some of this wonderful food." Eroa picked up a crisp carrot and crunched it.

"Why shouldn't my son find out... whatever it is?" Kiaro asked. "Are you keeping secrets from him?"

Eroa smiled inside. Kiaro had already lost. "Why were you meeting with someone in a seamstress's home? Are you keeping secrets from him?"

"I was visiting a former patient," Kiaro said. "Professional courtesy."

"Oh, a former patient," Eroa repeated. "Nothing to do with the illegal breeding program you started while you were the royal physician?"

She was rewarded for her jab with a slight widening of Kiaro's eyes. "Illegal breeding program?" Kiaro asked smoothly. "I'm not sure what you mean."

Eroa had to give the woman credit for her poise. "You don't remember impregnating twelve women with Orson Lorne's genetic material? That, I would have thought, would have been difficult to forget, since I have your signatures all over these documents."

The physician glared at Eroa. "That's not how it happened," she hissed. "You didn't read everything."

"I read enough," Eroa stated. "You gave those women royal bastards to weaken the throne."

"The blazes I did!" Kiaro yelled. "Those are all my children!"

Eroa Lorne took a moment to recover. "What do you mean, they're your children?" she demanded.

"All twelve are children from my eggs!" Kiaro Chiru laughed. "After I got pregnant with Targer, I started bleeding. I knew the signs. I was a physician. I got treatments, and I took bed rest. The king was... disappointed. I was gone for months, and he lost interest. Then Targer came seven weeks premature. He was barely alive, but the king didn't care. I pried myself from my bed to monitor him, since he wasn't important enough to receive royal attention. And despite keeping me on, Orson never revived our relationship."

"Then why did you want more children?" Eroa asked calmly.

"I became a doctor to be more attractive to a noble family!" Kiaro was becoming increasingly more hostile. "My own family was almost destitute before they became the kingdom's source of cheap entertainment. That money was only enough to stave off creditors for a generation. I sought an education instead. I positioned myself where I could have leverage to restore my family's name. But no one took an interest... except for one man."

Now Kiaro's eyes gleamed in the light. A single tear trickled down her cheek. "Orson Lorne wanted more than a doctor. So I made a new plan. I'd have his child, stars, children! I'd birth an entire dynasty for him, if he would make them legitimate. Not heirs to the throne, but important enough to garner noble positions. And..." Kiaro's face twisted into a hateful grimace, "... I wasn't strong enough to do it more than once."

"But then... how..." Eroa's voice stumbled, but Kiaro filled in the gap.

"There was a physician who... looked fondly upon me," Kiaro continued. "My private life was gone. So, after several assignations and veiled promises, he examined me... intimately. My uterus was scarred. I would never have a natural birth again. So he harvested twelve eggs for me."

"What happened to this other doctor?" Eroa asked.

"I reassigned him." Kiaro shrugged. "He got a small promotion and got over it. One of his nurses resembled me. I hear they have three children."

"But that doesn't answer how these eggs became Lorne heirs," Eroa said.

Kiaro laughed. "Oh! It was simple to get Orson to give me a sample. I simply told him I needed one, and he gave me one. It was... nostalgic. Then I used my position to locate surrogates in need of money."

"So..." Eroa pieced it together. "You wanted a dynasty of royal bastards, so the king would acknowledge them, and your family could leverage new connections to the court?"

"All I needed was a few more years," Kiaro said wistfully. "Once they were old enough to be trusted with the news of their real parentage. The surrogates have been compensated, but everything changed after that attack on Orson. He grew weak, and he was always surrounded by security. I couldn't talk to him, and then his council approached me. They wanted to know about his love affairs. Who would know better than me?" She laughed a ragged laugh.

"So you told them you knew of a child," Eroa stated. "How convenient."

"Yes, I told them about Targer, and they said he would be king," Kiaro explained. "What could I lose? My bastard son would rule Orso. All his brothers and sisters would be sought after. My family could gain power and influence after all."

"You just had to betray the king," Eroa whispered. "Did you... kill him?"

"He would not have recovered!" Kiaro snapped. "And he betrayed me first, and his own wife I don't know how many times before she died. Because of him, Elio never took anything seriously. Removing him was a blessing for this kingdom!"

"Removing him was treason," Eroa said. "If this were ever to be spoken of you would be executed."

"And what about you, little queen?" Kiaro taunted. "Your

family started this. They promised us you could guide him how they wanted, but you've done precious little of that."

"Targer has a sense of honor that makes things difficult sometimes," Eroa said. "There's no telling where he might have picked that up."

"I know!" Kiaro replied. "It must be those vids he watched as a child. All about genuine heroes."

It says something of the nobility's mind, Eroa thought, *that my mother didn't realize I was insulting her*. But Eroa also realized how far she'd swung from her mother's goals. After only a few months married to a simpleton, she was finding hidden depths and emotions inside her convenient husband.

There was once a time when she would have dispatched him so she could rule as Regent... but those days were gone. Now she longed for his kind words, his simple praises, his affection; and he genuinely trusted her. And trust was addictive.

"So there's no intention of a coup attempt?" Eroa asked. "Because it's no longer necessary."

"Why would I want a coup?" Kiaro replied. "Targer can acknowledge them as kin, and they become exactly what I wanted. They'll be the most famous children of Som Orsi. House Chiru's stature will swell with influence. All my plans will come to fruition, and I—" She chuckled. "I will take a nice long vacation. Maybe somewhere in north Auspicia, where there are beaches and handsome lifeguards."

"Well then, may your retirement be long and restful," Eroa said. "You may leave."

Kiaro excused herself, and Eroa collected the hidden holo cams. Recorded confessions were, after all, too dangerous to leave lying around.

———

ROYAL QUARTERS
Royal Palace, Som Orsi

EROA'S meeting with Kiaro left her in a much-disturbed state, even a quandary, if you will. If she reported Kiaro Chiru, her own family would be implicated in the plot to steal the throne, and she feared for Targer should the confession become public.

It was supposed to protect him! she wanted to scream. Now there's a universe full of heirs with as much right as Targer to be king, and his mother created them.

Eroa had years of lessons in royal intrigue. She'd been forced to memorize lessons of logic and problem-solving, lessons on the tools of state and the history of political subterfuge. She'd spent her life learning why twelve heirs were the worst idea imaginable.

Perhaps Kiaro thought her medically conceived spawn, after she grew up in squalor with commoners, would be content with minor nobility. Perhaps half would be content. But the rest would hound Targer forever.

Her own family had kept their distance from each other, never growing close, never trusting. But for all that, they were family. Siblings with no connection, displaced from each other, having grown in the worst conditions, would have no problem murdering each other.

Or worse, Eroa realized. With no family bond, they might intermarry, cementing the bloodline. If all the law requires is Lorne blood, redoubling it would strengthen their claims. She knew the Regency couldn't dare trust the Chiru siblings. It would take only one public moment for Targer to denounce any councilor and strip them of their position and the people would believe he could do it.

She tried to get a grip of herself. *Wait a minute, am I*

being nonsensical? She wondered. *The councilors would never allow a simple blood claim...*

Except they already had. Targer had deliberately been conceived to take Elio's place. His own mother said so.

And they certainly wouldn't allow that kind of inbreeding, would they? She thought.

Except history had already proven that false hundreds of times.

Suddenly, she wanted to laugh.

This isn't complicated, she thought. *I have the children's names, and the names of their mothers. They'll all have accidents, one by one, until all the threats are gone. But...*

She tried to imagine herself trying to explain her actions to Targer. Don't you see? I did it to protect you! she would say. And he would look at her with a terrible sadness and say, But you killed innocent children. He would never believe that it was necessary.

No, she thought, *the safe option is to start by killing Kiaro herself. Eliminate the source of his problems. But he wouldn't approve of me killing his mother either!*

She didn't know whether to laugh or cry. Why am I more concerned with Targer's feelings than with keeping him safe?

———

EROA SPENT the rest of the day pondering her options on how to protect her husband and make him proud. The Regency Council was probably delighted by her absence, but Targer had spoken to her several times, and she was glad of his distractions.

Finally, the day was done, and the meetings had ended. The royal dressers had finished their duties and left for the night, leaving their king and queen clad in shameer bedclothes. Targer slipped under the covers without a word.

Eroa slipped in beside him. I just want a kind word, or a smile, she thought. And I already know all his favorites.

So she reached toward him under the covers, seeking him out. She would play until he responded, and she would set her troubling thoughts aside until morning.

But as soon as she touched him, he said, "What is it this time, Eroa?"

"Targer," she whispered. "I wanted to play a little. Don't you—"

"Eroa," he said patiently, as if explaining to a child. "Do you think I don't notice? Every time you 'play,' I'm badgered the next day. You should say, 'I'll do whatever you want if you promise to obey me.' At least that would be honest."

She wanted to protest, but her tongue wouldn't form the words. She had indeed started their marriage like that. She'd been proud of herself. But it wasn't his words that drove her away.

It was his eyes. They looked at her with what? Resignation? Pity?

It was his tiny frown. It was the same as those of her early teachers, disappointed that she hadn't applied herself to her lessons, and she'd become keen to please them.

Had he grown weary of her, even as she realized she loved him?

"Targer, I just..." She didn't know what to say. "I had a difficult decision to make today, and I've come to realize how much I appreciate you. I wanted to do something nice for you."

"You're a pretty present," he replied, "but it's very clear that you weren't shy or stumbling. You already knew everything there is to know. I don't know how many men came before me, but it—"

"There were no other men before you!" she snapped. It was true. Her mother had strict rules about that propriety being breached. But her daughter had learned all the lessons of seduction from her.

"Eroa," he said with the same resignation, "if you expect me to believe a lie, could you please make it a better lie?"

She wanted to protest that no man had ever been with her, and yet... she had touched men. Men had touched her. She'd felt pride in her abilities, but Targer was making her feel dirty. She lay there, silent and unmoving, for a long time.

"Targer, let's say that I want to give you a gift," she finally said. "I want it to make you the happiest you've ever been. What could I give you to make you that happy?"

"Oh, that's easy," he said with a sharp bark of laughter. "I don't want to be the king."

She was shocked, speechless.

"I was never this miserable before I got this stupid crown," he continued. "If I woke up tomorrow and someone else was on the throne, I would be ecstatic. And then you could stop pretending to care about me, and I could stop pretending I don't want to run to... Eos, and become a clothing model or something. Anywhere I don't have to talk to councilors ever again."

"Very well, my king," she whispered, but he didn't say anything.

She lay there until she was certain he'd fallen asleep. Then she crept to the Royal Archives. She quietly compiled everything about Kiaro Chiru's plot and attached the doctor's recorded confession. She packaged it into an encrypted file archive labeled for mid-level government officials. The military could crack the code, but dispatches between governors shouldn't attract attention.

She checked the proposed route for Ambassador Lorne. To her surprise, his flight plan had undergone changes. Appended to those route changes were reports of Swarm attacks.

I knew they were getting bad, she thought. *But why so many? And why are they attacking Elio?*

It didn't matter. Elio had left Tyche days earlier, and the next stop was Tor. She didn't know why anyone would let him get so close to an old ally, but surely he would be leaving Tor soon; she had to act quickly.

Hoping that her message wasn't too late, she sent the file archive to Governor Raymar Graynir on Tor.

CHAPTER
SIXTEEN

INTERLOPERS
Dregs Border Zone
Greasetown

Jude Cabeus was not a nice man, at least not today.

He shoved the grifter against the wall of the alley and snarled, "Listen, you cheap crook. I'm two days short of patience, so listen good. I'm looking for a doctor, someone who does nerve reconnection work."

"Stuff it up your... Urk!" the man grunted as Jude leaned on his chest with his prosthetic arm.

"You sent me on a crazy-ganse chase," Jude continued. "But I'm going to give you just one more chance. Where is this famous doctor?"

"He won't tell you anything," came a hard female voice from the alley mouth.

Jude had barely turned before he heard the grifter pull a knife. Without even looking, Jude clamped his metal fist around the wrist, gently. The man's whimpers were therapeutic.

"You see?" the woman said. "Charl only knows greedy and stupid. He took your money?"

"He did," Jude answered.

"Give him the money, Charl," the voice said.

Charl tried to reach into his right pocket with his left hand. "I... I can't get it," he mumbled.

Jude plucked the knife away with his natural hand and released his metal fist. Charl fumbled for the money and tried to dash away.

Jude grabbed for a sleeve, but a smoking hole appeared in Charl's back. He fell, Jude's credits fluttering to the grimy ground.

"He was going to get shot soon enough," she said as she waved her laser weapon, the ionized smoke trailing from the barrel. "It might as well have been me."

"That's cold-hearted, even for you people," Jude replied.

"You're a tourist here," she said. "Worse, you're a provincial. You've lasted this long, but you'll soon wear out your welcome."

"What do you know about me?" Jude said.

"Aside from that ID you flashed the nurse, not much," she admitted. "But you're looking for a doctor, one who specializes in mechanical replacements. Are you having a problem with that?" She motioned to his arm.

"Don't ask me questions," Jude snapped. "What can you—"

But now her weapon was trained on his chest.

"And you were being so polite," she chuckled. "Why are you seeking the White Room?"

He could almost swear she was... reverent? "Am I?" he said. "I'm looking for a man. He's looking for a doctor."

"Let me be clear," the woman said. "There's a rule here in Greasetown. The White Room is neutral territory. You aren't too subtle, so I'll make you a deal. You pay me five times what you paid Charl—and really, you expected information for that? And I will tell you when your person of interest enters or leaves."

"I need to speak to the doctor myself," Jude insisted, but she twitched the laser at him again.

"No," she replied. "The doctor has her own code of honor. She doesn't talk about other people's business, and everyone here respects that. The last person who didn't..." She shook her head. "Well, let's just say you'd pray for me to shoot you instead."

Jude was impatient now, ready to be done with the entire mission, collect his own arm, and go home. *If Maila will even recognize me*, he thought painfully. *If my children can stand to look at me.*

He picked the credits off the ground. They were filthy, but he pulled more out and held them politely to the woman. "Can I at least get your name?" he asked.

"No," she said. "But you can call me Veisti. What's your comm code?"

Jude was out of options. So he rattled off the string of numbers. She nodded, as though she didn't need to write it down. "I'll be in touch," she said. "But don't worry. I'm honest. It would be bad for business for me to be otherwise."

"What is your business?" he asked without thinking.

"I'm an information broker," she said. "Unlike the good doctor, I have no scruples about selling info. But it's always good and true info." She stepped back and sideways, and she was gone.

Jude hadn't even gotten a good look at her face.

That was pure idiocy! he berated himself. But staring at that smoking barrel, he couldn't call her bluff. Now he could only hope she hadn't robbed him.

———

REMAINER BLVD.
    Greasetown, Som Orsi

AVRUM ROSST HAD LIVED for two years with an eye patch but it hadn't affected his battle prowess one iota. He'd led a counterattack during the Battle of Som Orsi, but something was missing, just out of sight. Today he would remedy that.

Rosst checked his ocular implant case one last time. He confirmed the address on his wristpad, then walked through the heavily rusted door.

"Well," he muttered to himself, "you never know what to expect, now do you?" There were no guards or orderlies, just quiet inside the ancient and moldy factory. As instructed, he followed a trail of arrows marked on the walls. It was a maze of smells: rancid oils, fetid water puddles, heat-baked steel. But he quickly discovered the surgical room—a gleaming white bastion of cleanliness amid the decay.

In the operating theater was a striking blond woman wearing a traditional white coat. But when he met her eyes, he saw something; a woman who didn't view the world the way others did. He suspected her world was far more frightening.

"I'm impressed," he said, not wanting to insult his host. She did, after all, have a reputation for hasty action.

"Are you my 1300?" she asked. "Mr. Cyclops?"

He winced at the false name Verso had given him. "Yes, I am," he replied.

"Wonderful!" she said in a too-cheerful voice. "I'm Dr. Augon today. Did you have any trouble finding me?"

"Um, no," Rosst replied. "The décor, though... well, it was unexpected. Do you have trouble with criminals around here?"

"Oh, we're all criminals in Greasetown," she said dismissively. "Everyone knows my services and rates!" Her expression darkened. "Any scum that broke in here would be hunted down and shot by every lowlife for ten kilometers." She brightened suddenly. "So, I have good news and bad news. Which do you prefer?"

Her shifts were unsettling. "Bad," Rosst answered immediately. "Does it require shooting?"

"Oh, no!" she said with a smile. "The bad news is that my supply of exterocaine didn't arrive. That's the local anesthesia I was going to give you."

"Oh." The thought of not receiving the implant was depressing. "You could have contacted me to say—"

"Ah-ah, but you didn't hear the good news!" she cheerfully reminded him. "I have plenty of trizophine. You will be having your surgery today, but you'll be taking a nap as well."

Rosst felt relieved. "Well, let's do it, then," he said. He handed her the case with his new eye.

She told him to undress and put on a simple cloth garment. It wasn't regulation, but it served its purpose. He would be just fine.

It was only after he'd laid down on the operating table, and she'd fastened the safety straps across his body, that he thought to ask. "You said I would take a nap. How long before it wears off?"

She smiled at him, but her eyes didn't match her expression. She moved the anesthetic mask close to his face. "Oh, don't worry!" she said. "It wears off after forty hours. You'll be fine!"

She covered his face before he could object. And his objections faded quickly away as his first gasp of anesthetic pulled down the mist.

"You're lucky," he heard her say distantly. "I heard reports about a man needing an eye. Nice reward, too. But I'd already made your appointment. So that means you have patient confidentiality. I can't turn you in anymore. Make it up to me later, all right?"

Then he was asleep.

———

Spider clung to the high stonework like his namesake, spying across the street while hidden under a concrete ledge. He hated outside work, but Veisti had told him to do it, and Veisti always paid.

Usually, Veisti made him spy on stuff going on in the warehouses. Sometimes, he spied big bouncers yapping together. Spider was never spotted. He was the best hider spy in Gear or Grease.

But why am I watching the White Room? he wondered.

Everyone knew the White Room. No one dared to bring their fights there; the Lady never doctored any gang that broke that rule. But some old guy was supposed to show up, so Spider hid in the shadows until an old geezer came walking by. He didn't look scared, so Spider thought he might have been a bouncer boss, except he was wearing a black eye patch, just like Veisti said. He commed Veisti.

"What do you have, Spider?" she asked.

"Old guy, black eye patch," Spider whispered. "White Room."

"Thanks, Spider," Veisti said. "Come see me tomorrow, and I'll have your pay, plus a bonus." She clicked off.

"A bonus?" Spider whispered. Maybe he'd order two dinners tonight!

———

Resplendence Suites Room 813
City of Bariell

. . .

FOREIGN HAD FAILED ITS MISSION.

The mission was salvageable. But how could a non-biological construct trapped in a human body destroy the material universe when there were pastries?

Hacking human payment systems was effortless. Humans had "hotels" with rooms to sleep in and eat. With a stray thought, it paid for the room and the food.

It bought every food imaginable. Taste was addictive. The food from the forests and fields was unprocessed fibrous material, immature and bitter. In the hospital it had been fed through tubes, and jiggling protein cubes that tasted like insincerity.

Why it thought that it couldn't say.

Regardless, it had discovered food in infinite variety. If humans had created wonderful, glorious food, how could Foreign destroy them? And their servitude was extraordinary. Someone appeared with the food whenever it ordered from the computers. And someone else removed the garbage.

It had received icy stares from the servants, but humans weren't used to being ruled by an advanced non-biological construct. Foreign had also found information on "gratuities." Money seemed absurd, but it added gratuities to every order, and the glares disappeared.

Tonight it was trying pie. It picked up a piece and shoved it into its mouth, catching bits with its fingers before they fell.

Suddenly, there was a banging at the door

"Hey, you in there! Open up!" a voice demanded.

Foreign ignored the yelling. It was eating pie! They would receive a gratuity later—

The door beeped and opened. Foreign was outraged. No human had entered without permission before!

Then it took another look at these humans. They wore

uniforms and carried weapons, except for the fretful human in the back.

"Kasa Su Mei, you are under arrest!" a large, burly female announced. "You have the right to remain silent. You have the right—"

"By what authority do you barge into my dominion!" Foreign demanded.

The human female looked confused for a moment. "I'm a police officer. You're under arrest for monetary fraud, illegal tampering of credit systems, and... what is that smell?"

"My glorious human body!" Foreign declared. It had noticed a smell, but what came out of a human body was much worse. There were many vids teaching about body waste, with bright colors and catchy songs, and small humans. Foreign didn't know why small humans had such large heads—

The officers yanked Foreign off the bed. "Let me go!" it yelled. "I demand it!"

"If I could avoid that reek, I would!" the officer replied. "We're going to the elevator, and you'd better cooperate."

"No!" said the fretting human male. "Take her down the stairs, so our guests don't have to see or smell her."

The officers grunted, but they marched Foreign down the hall. "I will not comply," Foreign told the officers. "I won't walk downstairs." It picked its feet off the ground.

The officer—this one a burly male—said, "Listen. I was told to get you down the stairs. So you're going down the stairs. If we drop you, it will hurt."

"I doubt your conviction to harm me," Foreign said, and believed it. Until the officers dropped it.

Its knees hit the hard floor, and a terrible sensation lanced up Foreign's legs. It couldn't help crying out. Is this pain? It wondered as water leaked down its face.

"Now, will you cooperate?" the officer asked.

Foreign nodded. This time, when the officers walked, it obeyed.

But it could access all their comms. It infiltrated the systems and found commands to supplement arrest orders. With a few adjustments, everything was ready.

I can't sit quietly and eat food? It thought. *I will destroy your civilization!* Foreign wanted to laugh. *Deliver me to my goal and I will make your machines destroy you!*

Then Foreign would simply go to another planet and eat food there. Somewhere where they didn't question Foreign's authority.

When they reached the bottom of the stairs, fourteen hundred seventy-two steps later, Foreign's legs ached badly. But there was the officers' large black vehicle, and there were several humans waiting, wearing different uniforms and placards on their chests.

"Take her to Central and book her," the burly male officer said to the man with the largest, most ornate placard. He must be their leader. "And add resisting arrest, too. I want her to go down so hard."

"It isn't up to us," the leader said. "She's to be transported immediately."

"Who's claiming our collar?" the burly man said.

"Royal Task Force, Som Orsi," the leader said. "Seems she added 'records tampering' and 'identity theft' to her list, since Kasa Su Mei is a dead traitor. Gotta do your research, lady."

"Som Orsi?" Burly Man complained. "Who wants to ride with her for that long?"

Foreign smiled. *Such a simple task to go where I want to go.* It thought, but it said nothing to arouse more abuse.

Burly Man shoved it into a seat and attached its restraints to the wall. "Wherever you send her," Burly Man said, "hose her down first."

"Nope," the leader said. "Orders say all haste."

The doors closed.

Foreign's only regret was that it couldn't crush these humans in its moment of triumph.

————

GOVERNOR'S MANSION
Pricus City
Planet Tor, Pricus System

GOVERNOR RAYMAR GRAYNIR didn't dwell on things beyond his control. Such as being among the first Swarm targets. One had to accept that of the universe.

Six years of reconstruction had borne fruit. Yet every morning when he passed by his daughter's hologram he felt... alone.

How are you, Andra? he wondered, as he had every day since Avenger's rebellious departure. *Where have you gone? What adventures have you added to the Graynir name?*

He walked to her favorite window seat and wondered what she'd seen through the two-meter tall glass. Certainly not the gardens.

He was so proud of his daughter. She was bright, capable, and determined. There was that armed rebellion against his government, but she'd had good intentions, technically. After that, she'd dedicated her life to saving the Sovereign Stars.

Then Prince Elio disappeared. Some Regency upstarts had taken over and raised a puppet king. They could claim the man's royal blood, but Graynir saw the truth. His daughter was branded a criminal for associating with Prince Elio, along with everyone else who had.

"Sir?" one of his aides said.

Graynir turned to see him. "What is it, Benat?" he asked.

"You've received a governor's encrypted file archive from Som Orsi," Benat said.

"Som Orsi?" Graynor said. "The governor? Why would Swefen Draumer send me an encrypted archive?" At Benat's shrug, he sighed. "Get me my usual breakfast—moon biscuit and egg. Make my coffee a number three today." His coffee preferences were well known, and Benat had served a long time.

He went to his office and sat down. He pulled the file archive up on his holo projector and decrypted it. But it wasn't from Swefan Draumer. And it wasn't governor claptrap. It was a collection of genetic profiles.

Then he looked at the attached diplomatic schedule. Listed clear as day was the name Ambassador Elio Lorne. Official correspondence hadn't included that detail.

A slow smile spread across his face.

"We've got ourselves a game changer now," he whispered.

Graynir glanced up to find Benat carrying his breakfast.

"Benat, locate Dr. Volen," he ordered. "I have documents for him to examine."

"Volen? The geneticist?" Benat asked.

"Oh, yes," Graynir said.

CHAPTER
SEVENTEEN

SEARCHING
Afternoon Tease Cafe
Esse, Monere District

"So what is Prince Elio really like?" Finia asked.

Meera blushed. "Keep it down," she whispered. "I don't want everyone in the cafe looking at me!"

Finia had dragged Meera out for coffee after the first TraumAnon meeting together. Now, a week later, they were out again, this time having a delightful late lunch.

Finia shook her head and her large black earrings flashed in the afternoon sun. She took a long sip of her berry tea. "I don't know," Finia said. "If I'd worked with someone like him, I'd have made a pass at him, at least!"

"It wasn't like that, okay?" Meera insisted, trying not to blush. "We hardly ever saw him. He wasn't our leader or anything. He just started the Guardian project. Colonel Rosst was our leader."

"Well, what about you and that other Knight?" Finia said.

"The one standing next to you at the awards commendation on vid. What was his name?"

"You mean... Klaus?" Meera tried to concoct a perfectly normal reason. "Um, it was prearranged. Alphabetical order or whatever."

"You didn't stand together like two letters," Finia teased. "Maybe like a pair of I's, since everyone with eyes thought you were a pair, too. You can tell me. He looked young. Did you two have a fling? Was it a flash in the pan after the battle, or did you let it simmer a while first?"

"Really, we... didn't..." Meera gave up. "Fine. We dated for a little while. A few months. But he was being really immature, and I broke it off. In a way, he's lucky."

'The day you decide I fooled you, you can kill me.' Those had been his words, and Meera had clutched them to her heart for so long...

"He could have gotten worse than a break-up," Meera insisted to Finia and maybe herself as well.

"So, why did you break it off?" Finia asked as she sipped at her berry tea.

Meera could almost hear her own words from each pivotal moment.

'If I find out you've betrayed me, you'll wish you had died... If you had told me... You tainted every single memory I have of you... Never talk to me again! We're through!'

"It's complicated," Meera replied instead. "I didn't think I could trust him."

"Well, that's a problem." Finia finished her tea and stood up. "You want anything else? My treat."

Meera looked at the rest of her Vigorblend. "But I still have all this," she said.

"That?" Finia looked skeptical. "That's a responsible mommy drink. I'll get you something... fun." Her eyes lit up.

"I don't know..." Meera's refusal faltered.

"I'll get two. If you don't like it, it's mine!" Finia headed for the counter before Meera could object.

Meera couldn't decide who was taking advantage of who. *It's too sudden... unpredictable. Spontaneous. I should plan, not like when Klaus asked me out!*

But it hadn't been that way. Klaus had pursued her first. His feelings were never in question, she admitted to herself. *I only agreed after fencing him in place.*

She wanted him to talk about Sorge, but had she ever mentioned his name? *What about Lifia's achievements,* she thought, *or Gesc and baby Stevian? How could he approach me if I fenced him away?*

Finia returned with two drinks in clear containers, straws poking through the lids. Inside was a foaming mass of burnt orange shot through with snowy white swirls. "What are those?" Meera asked.

"A Laufmir Sunset!" Finia exclaimed. "Try it." She handed one to Meera.

Meera sipped the straw. There was the lauf, a bold, smoky citrus. Then sweetness, like tiny bubbles popping on her tongue.

"What's that other ingredient?" Meera gasped. "I've never had lauf like this!"

"Just keep going!" Finia urged her, and Meera wondered if this was a mistake.

Screw it! she told herself, and took a long drink. The citrus washed over her tongue, then exploded into sweet prickles. Then the citrus again, in a cycle of sensory pleasure. But she detected another hidden taste.

"Is there synth in this?" she asked, slightly embarrassed.

"Isn't it great?" Finia said. "I love these."

"But isn't it early for synth?" Meera protested.

"See, there's the good mommy again," Finia mock-scolded

her. "It's not that much. And sunset never comes soon enough. I need a head start."

Meera wanted to say something, but Finia looked so relaxed. Not the bitter Finia from TraumAnon. *Be the me that I want to be,* Meera thought.

She pushed the thoughts of Klaus away. Memories of him were painful.

Yet they persisted.

So, Meera took another long sip of Laufmir Sunset before asking, "What do you drink after sunset?"

"I'm partial to Sparkling Twilights," Finia replied. "You want to try one?"

"I think I do," Meera said.

Suddenly, Finia's wristpad deetled at her. She stabbed it with her finger. The screen changed, and her eyes lit with excitement.

"Oh, epic keen!" she blurted.

"Is it important?" Meera asked. "If you need to go, I can—"

Finia grabbed her wrist. "Come on!" she demanded. "I've got to show you this."

FINIA PULLED Meera out of the cafe with Meera carrying both drinks while Finia explained the fantastic new game everyone was discussing. "What are you talking about?" Meera asked. "I've heard nothing about it."

"You haven't heard of Perplexity?" Finia seemed astonished. "Oh... my gosh. Okay, watch."

There was a grid displayed on Finia's wristpad. Twenty-five spaces in a grid, but only twenty-four lines of pictures. Finia moved the pictures one space at a time. The pictures could only move to an adjacent empty space.

"If you get the squares right, it makes one big picture of a location," Finia explained. "If you go to that location, it unlocks a reward."

"What kind of reward?" Meera asked, trying not to drop Finia's drink. "You mean, like money?"

"Oh, stars, no." Finia kept trying the puzzle. "Whoever made this would be out a million a day, or worse. They tell you about something interesting in the city. In fact, the Afternoon Tease was a reward, the location, I mean. Did you know that the same family has owned and served there since... a hundred and fifty years ago? They came from Eos and set up a mokchon tea house and restaurant. Eos has a long tradition of tea houses. Most restaurants have moved about five blocks over since, so... wait! I think I've got it!"

The last puzzle piece slid into place, and...

It didn't seem like anything to Meera at first. It was just black lines on a white background, but it seemed familiar.

"I know this one," Finia said. "It's clear across Esse. You want to come?"

Meera frowned. It wasn't something she was really interested in doing, but it beat sitting at home. "Yeah, why not?" she said. "Let's go see what this thing is."

They hopped on a pub-trans, Finia sliding her chit through the reader twice. There weren't any empty seats, so they hung onto the upper railing.

"I didn't notice it before," Finia said, "but that's a really interesting necklace. Where did you get it?"

Meera started. "Um... I got it after I retired from the military."

"Retired?" Finia scoffed. "What are you, maybe sixty? Even the military doesn't retire before eighty."

"I mean—" Meera stammered. "I just, um, meant when I left."

"Oh." Finia's eyes lit up. "Oooooh-ho-ho. Was that a gift from Clause?"

"Klaus," Meera corrected without thinking. "No, it wasn't. It's just something I..."

Something I received for service to my kingdom, she thought. *What a joke. It's an insult, is what it is!*

Her vehemence surprised her. Where did this anger—

"Whoa, sorry," Finia said. "I didn't realize I touched a nerve there."

Meera blinked and realized she was scowling. "I'm sorry! I was... just thinking about, um—"

"No, it's okay," Finia said. "They made me leave, you know? They said I wasn't good enough. But they didn't help me get any better. The PEU closed down while that Odin thing was happening, and a lot of people got ditched. Not just me."

Meera wondered what might have happened if she'd stayed behind, been dismissed like that. She'd been so fragile already. Would she have—

"Oh! Hey driver! This is our stop!" Finia almost dragged Meera off the pub-trans.

Finia held up her wristpad, and Meera looked at the line picture again. She could see a part that was supposed to be a building... maybe. And that was a sign of some kind; kind of an oblong triangle... "Hey, is that the triangle thing?" she asked, pointing.

Finia looked. "Yeah, I think so! The part I recognized was this here:" she waggled her finger at several hooked lines like rotated check marks. "And it made me think of the old amphitheater, you know, before... the battle." She took a few steps left, right, forward, before saying, "I think we need to be closer."

Meera looked at the busy traffic. "Um, how much closer?"

"Finia shrugged. "Not sure, but I'd bet they didn't design

the game to get you run over by a grav truck. Let's cross to their outdoor festival area."

They crossed the busy elevated walk, where thousands of people were going about their business. From there, the damage to the amphitheater was much more noticeable. Meera spotted a cluster of onlookers a hundred meters from the north wall. "I think they found it too!" she shouted over the din. "Where do we need to be?"

"It uses geo-coordinates," Finia shouted. "Just stand near the original location. There are lists of them on the network. I've done twenty, but this is only my second on release day!"

"That's amazing," Meera said as they jogged toward the crowd. Once they drew close, Finia's wristpad beeped, and a holographic image appeared, showing the amphitheater as it once had been; tall, proud, and undeniably Orsan.

"This building is a triumph of neoclassical Caerus architecture," the recording said as the view zoomed into the air, then down into the fields. "It was erected for the New Orso-doxical Championship Games a hundred and seventy-four years ago. The games drew contestants from Orso's vassal worlds." Images faded between grueling feats of endurance and athletic prowess.

"In some cases," the recording continued, "the toughest competitors took home the prize before their world slipped away from Orso's control." A slender-looking man accepted the award. He stood well over two meters tall.

"What do they mean?" Finia asked.

"Saven Wister of Peros won a medal," Meera explained, "but Peros staged a coup for independence. My son studied that decade for history class. His teacher didn't like his report."

Then the scene switched to footage of the Battle for Som Orsi. "The south corner was destroyed by plasma fire," the voice continued, "and the east wall buckled under a crashed alien ship." The amphitheater disappeared to show a woman and a man. "The building hadn't been used in seventeen years, so the Councilors of Treasury and of Social Analysis, Thesa Monere and Mezeke Bohne, condemned this historical landmark to be demolished." Now seven councilors stood in a row. "Since Orson Lorne's death, the councilors have established a Regency Council—" they now stood behind the infamous "boy king," who had suddenly appeared, "—guiding King Targer Lorne in his duties."

The clip ended, the image frozen on councilors surrounding the uncertain boy. It seemed vaguely menacing. Then the image disappeared.

"Huh," Finia said. "I like that they're longer, because it feels like a reward if you play. But I think they're more political. Don't know if I like that."

"What do you mean?" Meera asked.

"Well, my first one was where the Slipdrive Strike happened," she explained. "The people got sick from the chemical tests they did, and they didn't get hazard pay. King Stolar stepped out to demand that 'his citizens' be protected. Real stand-up-for-people propaganda. Others are movie trivia or sports stuff, but they're getting anti-government."

"Well," Meera said cautiously, "if the people don't like those, the game makers will stop, right?"

"I hope so," Finia grumbled. "When everybody gets all political, it ruins everything, you know?"

But Meera had a hunch she wasn't going to share. These vids show the difference between old Orso and the Regency, she thought. Someone is stirring up trouble.

She forced herself to smile. And maybe I'll help them. Because I sure don't like how I feel anymore.

———

GREASETOWN

"I'VE HAD IT!" Jude Cabeus screamed at his father. "They've hidden themselves so they can't be found. I can't find them, nobody can find them! Just let me go home!"

Marshal Marrion stared with the implacable expression from Jude's childhood, from his brutal training, from Jude's first assassination order. He said only one word.

"No."

It was such a dead sound, so devoid of any thought or care.

Jude threw his chair at the marshal. The man didn't even flinch. Why should he? Jude's rational mind noted. It's a hologram. He isn't really here.

"Wayn, you have your assignment," his father said. And Jude hated him more than ever. "Carry it out, and you're on the first transport home. You can stay there, for all I care. But I have a tool, and I will use it."

"That's all I ever was," Jude snarled. "Just a useful tool."

"Yes," his father admitted candidly. "I used your mother to gain her father's support. I used her pregnancy to distract her from certain projects dear to me. I used you to prove my training method was valid, and I use every resource at my disposal to further my desires. Then I depended on you, Wayn, and you ran away. If I can't use you now, I don't need you or the hostages, do I?"

For a moment, Jude saw Maila, Tag, and Posie look up in fear as armed men kicked the cabin door in.

He knew exactly what it would look like. He'd been one of them.

Jude needed to do something, anything, to release the pressure in his chest. Instead, he said, "If you harm them, you'd better kill me first. Because if you don't, I will come after you and I will kill you, slowly, painfully."

"I'll take it under advisement," his father said, and disappeared.

After his confrontation with his father, Jude needed to get out, so he decided to take a walk.

The sun was just beginning to set. His shadow stretched out in front of him. It looked big, threatening. *I wish I was half this threatening,* he thought miserably. His metal arm did not intimidate people in Greasetown, and because he wouldn't kill indiscriminately, he was at a disadvantage.

His wristpad tootled. He checked it, afraid to find pictures of Maila or the children. It was only another puzzle. He'd solved a few perplexity puzzles, hoping to ease his stress. It was too simple. The video was footage of soldiers during the Som Orsi battle. He wondered if he could spot himself, but then he looked closer.

Avrum Rosst was directing soldiers after the orbital bombardment.

"Colonel Avrum Rosst," he remembered his father saying. 'He was slated to receive a replacement eye... He may have found a way to receive one...'

He needed to find a black-market expert in prosthetics.

Jude began mentally listing informants he'd met. There weren't many, but he'd manage.

CHAPTER
EIGHTEEN

HOSTILITIES
Central Dome, Business Offices
Planet Tyche

Drella Simond and D Squad were to the rear of Ambassador Elio's entourage to meet Commodore Lier. C Squad's trio was in the front, and A Squad's four surrounded Elio. It was such a perfect shape—two leading wedges, two trailing—that it looked intentional. But after losing four soldiers on Remanor and two here on Tyche, Blade Sergeant had decided all would be present for this "plenipotentiary meeting."

Drella's eyes were bloodshot behind her visor. Shifts were sixteen hours on duty, eight off. Everyone was ready to break. And they were all here, guarding against a phantom threat.

Why are we here? she wondered. *What could this meeting accomplish?* She didn't understand politics, except politicians argued about military funding, meaning her pay. And how in blazes did Alastor just claim authority over Tyche? The takeover made her shoulders itch.

Unable to keep quiet any longer, she thumbed a private

communication to Blade Sergeant. "Sir?" she whispered. "What should we expect? Is there anything... specific we need to be aware of?"

His response was something of a displeased grunt. "It's political buschwah," he murmured back. "If anything happens, it's Fish's fault, and I will be pissed. Off comms." Her link went dead.

When they arrived at the meeting room. C Squad opened the door despite the commotion up front. Ambassador Elio swept in dramatically, but he was flanked by ten royal guards.

"Excuse me, sir," some functionary complained. "You haven't announced yourselves properly. And there are too—"

"I am Elio Lorne," he interrupted, "Ambassador to all the systems in the Orso Kingdom. And... my retinue."

"You have too many in your retinue," the functionary continued. "And your retinue isn't under the proper classification—"

"Leave over, Indrew," called a familiar voice. "His retinue will firmly insist on being present. Besides, Tyche doesn't stand on such ceremony. Though it is irregular."

"I agree with you, Creg," Elio replied, smiling at Creg Granos of Extrock Corporation, from the meeting on Remanor. Elio walked over to the bureaucrat, and his "retinue" followed.

Drella immediately began to familiarize herself with the area. Despite the Tyche augmented-halo system, someone had dressed this room, though it was obvious to her that it hadn't been properly maintained in months. There was a marmorstone table, viridian laced with silver, four meters long and two wide, with chairs carved to match. *It must have been a tremendous expense*, she thought. *They mined the ore and carved it themselves, I suppose.*

The room was decorated to match, but the tapestries lining the glassy walls were faded and neglected. Her compatriots wearing aug-halos gazed at the virtual splendor. It's a distraction. She wanted to complain. *But Blade Sergeant doesn't like me right now. Best stay off his radar.* She thought.

There was another commotion at the door. An aide entered, followed by soldiers wearing Alastor's green and gold. At their heart stood two men—one military, the other in finer clothing than Elio. The aide announced, "Commodore Fermi Lier and honor guard accompanying Prince Padric Felder."

Drella's eyes locked on the soldiers, but the Prince detached himself from his retinue without a word and stalked across the room toward Elio, his face a complete blank.

"Prince Felder?" Elio asked with a smile. "What are you do—"

Prince Felder punched Elio in the jaw and Elio went down like he'd been sandbagged.

"Protect the Ambassador!" Drella shouted and raised her rifle—

Blade Sergeant slapped her rifle down. "Stand down!" he shouted. "That is a member of royalty! Anyone who lifts their rifle is court-martialed!"

Elio tried to stand up. "Pri-ince Felder?" he mumbled through bruised lips. "What's the meaning—?"

"You bastard!" Felder punched Elio again. The ambassador hit the floor a second time.

"Sir," Drella asked, "shouldn't we protect him?"

To her surprise, he smiled! "Nope," he said. "And for once I'm so happy to be wrong, Simond. The Fish is getting the stars knocked out of him, and legally I can't do a thing about it. This is the best day of the entire trip."

ELIO HIT THE FLOOR HARD.

He heard a guard shout a warning before Blade Sergeant clearly yelled, "Stand down!"

The guards aren't my protection, he reminded himself. Blade Sergeant is my jailer. He wouldn't risk harming Felder over me.

He tried to stand up.

"You bastard!" Prince Felder yelled and floored him again.

Elio could feel blood trickling down his face. His TK churned within. Even restrained, he could stop Felder.

No, he thought. *Don't show Blade Sergeant his mistake.* Instead, Elio rolled into a combat stance, feet planted, arms raised.

"My best friend's dead!" Felder shouted and swung again, but now Elio was ready. He stepped, blocked, and seized Felder's arm. He rolled backwards, taking the prince forward in a combat take-down Danis had practiced with him. Elio landed atop Felder before remembering how this usually ended. Struggling not to blush, he jumped to his feet and offered Felder a hand.

"Felder, if there's a disagree—" Elio cut off as four rifles snapped up. Without thinking, he seized the rifles with TK—

"Guards, stand down!" Felder barked. Elio released the weapons before the guards could move. "There is a disagreement, Lorne. Where's Tenilo's body?" Felder was trembling with rage, but he held back.

Elio took a deep breath. "Tenilo Barum was interred in the Caerus War Memorial. He was given the highest honors—"

"Not yours to give!" Felder yelled. "And you refused the Alastor rights of burial!"

"No, I didn't—!" Elio saw... felt?... a flash in his mind. "Wait... What did you say?"

Felder hesitated a moment. "After your great battle, we sent emissaries to claim his body. First, they were told his body wasn't recovered yet."

"Our shipyards were an unmitigated disaster," Elio confirmed. "Many fingers were pointing blame. We needed to—"

"Then, after all the bodies had been recovered, accounted for and processed," Felder pressed on, "we were not allowed to be involved."

Elio shrugged, but he was getting a bad feeling."I... understand why they didn't want—" Another flash of... something?

Felder scowled. "Then, they said they needed a prompt military funeral so they could have their Odin war. We dedicated three ships to that war and lost seventy Alastorians."

Elio winced. Odin had been militarily necessary, and a diplomatic nightmare. And then his father had died—

"We approached your government afterward," Felder spat, "but your diplomatic councilor—"

Duke Gyrich Rutta, Elio thought. *Why did my father even keep him around?*

"—explained that he couldn't be bothered to release the body. The Barum family visits an empty patch on Alastor, and our soldiers at Odin were left to burn!"

This flash was brighter than the others. Elio's head was starting to hurt. "I didn't have any say in—" Elio tried to say.

"You, of all people, had a say!" Felder exploded. "You've never taken anything seriously. Everyone in Orso knows that, and most people in other kingdoms know it too!"

Tenilo! Elio heard so clearly, yet so briefly. *Why? Why!*

Elio realized—Felder's emotions were so strong, his Psy could sense it!

That's what I felt on Remanor! he thought. *Fears were so strong in the shelter, they leaked past my inhibitors.*

For the first time in a month, Elio attempted to use his Psy. He reached out to Felder, and dredged every paralyzing worry that Elio had kept tamped down, and pushed those emotions toward the prince.

My father is dead—!

How could they remove me from the succession like that—!

How dare they call themselves a Regency Council—!

Is Danis dead—?

Was Danis captured—?

Is Danis being tortured—?

How far will Blade Sergeant's abuse go—?

Am I in danger here—?

I need to know more, but they've maneuvered me out—

They could kill me at any time—

We barely survived the attack on Tyche—

The people on Remanor were so afraid—

We need to protect the other systems—

—and for a brief moment, he felt the prince's mind. Then he lost the connection and crashed back like a fallen stone.

Prince Felder wore a shocked expression, which he quickly removed. "I see," he murmured. "So those rumors are true?"

"Yes," Elio murmured back.

Elio waited several seconds.

"Ambassador Lorne," Felder spoke normally. "I regret my actions and would like to have a conference with you after this small ceremony. May I call on you?"

"Of course," Elio said, a sudden thought taking him.

Careful not to let the sergeant notice, Elio palmed one of a pair of information chips he carried on his person at all times. He'd only managed to make the one copy in secret, and that had been a chancy affair. But as he reached out to shake Felder's hand, he managed to slip the black chip into his hand.

"I look forward to a longer discussion," Elio said. "But in the meantime, please continue your 'temporary authority' with Tyche's government. I'll send a glowing report." He turned and walked back to his guards.

Blade Sergeant was there, next to a guard he thought was

Drella. The sergeant smirked. "A pity," he said. "You'll barely notice it tomorrow."

Elio continued walking. From the corner of his eye, he saw Drella. Her bandage peeked out from under her greave as she and her squad followed him.

When Elio turned, Blade Sergeant's visor hid his eyes, but not his scowl. Elio suspected D Squad had just made a point: they were choosing Elio over his authority.

If he didn't like me before, Elio thought, *he really hates me now.*

———

DRELLA FELT GIDDY. D Squad had walked away from Blade Sergeant? Then she caught his glare. His menace radiated across the room. She and the others stood near Elio, watching the room carefully for any threats, which included her superior.

The crack of stone on stone reverberated through the room. Creg Granos now stood at the head of the table. "I call this ceremony to order," he announced. And everyone found seats at the table. Except Elio, who stayed where he was.

"On behalf of Extrock and the workers of Tyche," Granos began, "We thank Commodore Lier and the Prince of Alastor for their intervention. Without their assistance we would have been annihilated. After three days of rescue efforts, we've managed to recover one hundred-twenty-seven trapped miners. Our list of missing is still unacceptable, but we thank you."

That wasn't bad, Drella thought, before Prince Felder spoke up.

"You speak for Extrock and the workers," Felder snapped. "Where are Metaglione and Zeetsteel?"

Drella was shocked. First by the imperious tone, then by

the truth. Three corporations were involved in mining the planet. Where were the executives of the other two companies?

"Several of Zeetsteel's executives are among our dead," Granos said.

"Then their plenipotent powers devolve to the successor," Felder argued. "Where are they?"

"Their executives make such arrangements, not I," Granos replied. "And I am not privy to the details—"

I bet he knows, Drella thought. *He doesn't know legally. Spies, however...*

"—and it's not my position to air their internal issues," Granos finished diplomatically, "but I know that Metaglione announced an internal audit before the Swarm—"

"We can't establish martial law without the consent of the protected!" Felder slammed his hand down on the table. "Our emergency aid ends in five hours, by the Sovereign Stars compact. If they don't agree to this, we are obliged to pull out, including all medical and rescue personnel."

Drella heard Elio sigh dramatically. "I suppose that a member of the Orso government could, in theory, ask for your continued presence?" he called.

Prince Felder looked over at him. "You... could invite us to participate in a joint Orso/Alastor operation, per the Charter," Felder admitted. "But that would only last for... one standard week? And requires authorization from your government."

"I do hereby request a joint operation," Elio said lazily. "I'm sure you and I can work out the details."

The ceremony wasn't complicated, but it entailed a lot of formal language that essentially boiled down to "We're legally obligated to establish martial law until your people get their act together." Documents were signed, witnessed, and officially stamped. Hands were shaken and promises made, again in unnecessarily political language.

Governments are good at generating paperwork, Drella

thought sourly. When she joined the Redemption unit, she'd seen her service record. One hundred sixteen documents including reprimands, warnings, negative appraisals, along with her vocal—and usually private—complaints about the Crown's incompetence.

The meeting concluded, and D Squad followed the ambassador until Blade Sergeant intercepted them.

"C Squad, see the ambassador to his next appointment," he growled. "I'll want a full report." As the three-soldier squad covered Elio's exit, Blade Sergeant rounded on Drella's team. "What in the purple voidfire are you pulling, you gutless ingrates?"

"Sir, we just—"

He cut Drella's partner off. "We are on station here for two days now. There are a hundred and seventy thousand pox-poor civilians working in a rock hole. I've secured permission to replace our lost squads. I could strip your commissions and give them to any of these idiots. Any of them are preferable to you. The only reason I don't—!" He shook his fist for emphasis. "—is that you already know which end of the rifle to hold! So consider yourselves trainer candidates tomorrow. You're on backup detail while A Squad gets rack time. You'll get six hours of sleep, starting in eleven hours. Dismissed." He turned and marched away.

"Eleven hours?" Drella's partner grumbled. "What happened to the eighteen-hour shift thing? Twelve hours on, six off, right? We've already been on for thirteen hours, and C Squad got up seven hours ago. We're due!"

"Remember that A Squad is overdue," Drella replied. "But you're right. We showed some spine, so he'll break it. We're here for doing the wrong thing. We're written off."

"What if he adds five or six new grateful trainees to the roster?" her partner asked.

"No," Drella corrected him. "He's tired, and he's made a

mistake. Why would he share that, unless he was going to anyway?"

"But what happens to us?" her partner asked.

Drella waved at their surroundings. Her meaning was clear.

If he stripped their commissions, why return them to Caerus?

CHAPTER
NINETEEN

GENTILITIES
Central Dome, Business Offices
Planet Tyche

Elio sat in a small conference room waiting for Prince Felder. It was time to settle Elio's questions.

He knew he couldn't ask directly, because he had a pair of guards nearby, and another outside each of the two doors. Blade Sergeant hadn't liked that distribution, and Elio knew they were stretched thin. But the four here weren't the ones he recognized, except for the complaining corporal from before. Clearly, Blade Sergeant suspected something, so he removed any of the guards he thought Elio might be able to sway.

I'll soon find out how much sway I really have, he thought as the door opened and Prince Padric Felder entered the room.

Felder was dressed in modern noble fashion, with a glittering ensemble of medallions like Elio once wore, and a princely circlet. Neither of them wore a reality-enhancing halo, so the room was gray stone.

"Ambassador Lorne," Prince Felder began. "It's been... awhile."

Elio was taken aback for a moment, before realizing that the last time they'd met, they were equals, with all that implied. "Ambassador Elio" didn't rank near as high as a prince.

"It has indeed, sire," Elio said carefully. "The years have suited you well."

Now Felder looked surprised. "I'll offer an apology for, er, punching you," he continued.

"That's appreciated, sire," Elio replied, "but not necessary."

Prince Felder looked nervous. "May I offer compensation for—"

"That is also not necessary, my prince," Elio said with a smile. "I'll apologize for getting in the way of your fists. if you so desire."

Felder returned the smile. "That won't be necessary. Thank you for your intervention at the ceremony. We were justified in taking action, but the courts would be a nightmare. I wouldn't want to leave before things were settled."

"Your appreciation is noted, sire," Elio said. He was getting a little tired of layering honorifics, but he needed to maintain form for the guards. This conversation would get back to Blade Sergeant. "I wondered why an Alastor flotilla was passing through here, though."

"Come now, Ambassador," Felder said. "USF treaties allow unrestricted Slipgate travel."

"I've seen the battle holos, my prince," Elio corrected. "You didn't arrive by Slipgate. You used ungated travel, a method that's new and untested. It's dangerous to travelers and bystanders."

"As it happens," Felder said with a grin, "we've applied an easy fix to that. Additional shield generators at the fore and aft synchronized to activate when using gateless travel. Those shields disperse hyper-speed particles perpendicular to the flight path instead of as a focused beam forward or back."

"Interesting," Elio said. "You've solved a problem only discussed in a closed meeting a few months ago. Almost as interesting as Alastor sending a flotilla into Orso space. My ship's captain received no warnings of this."

"As I recall, Orso just sent a flotilla into Dianesis space," Felder countered.

"Irrelevant, Prince," Elio said, feeling more perturbed by the moment. "Are you involved with the corporate malfeasance that I was supposed to adjudicate?"

"Malfeasance?" Prince Felder repeated. "That's a strong word."

"An Orso-aligned company operating under royal charter is selling their stockpiles during an extermination war," Elio stated. "If that's true, they could be charged with war profiteering. Sire."

"And my flotilla flies right into your investigation," Felder concluded.

"And your flotilla flew right into my investigation," Elio agreed. "And Metaglione didn't come to the safety compact."

"Zeetsteel didn't come, either," Felder pointed out.

"Zeetsteel's building was targeted by Swarm fighters," Elio countered. "They lost seventy-five percent of their administration on-planet. Survivors are traumatized. And their executive warned me about Metaglione's dealings."

"Did you ever think," Prince Felder asked, "that Metaglione is 'committing malfeasance' because Orso almost bankrupted them? Obviously, your government doesn't care about anyone else."

Elio was speechless. That was quite an accusation.

He pointed a finger. "Felder, how in the blazing stars do you—"

"Tut, tut, Ambassador," he said. "That isn't very diplomatic."

Elio tried to regain composure. "My apologies, Prince," he managed to grate out. "Now, are you conducting unauthorized business with Metaglione?"

Felder frowned. "Metaglione needs my business—"

"Are you admitting culpability, Prince," Elio interrupted, "or your government as a whole?"

"Your officials blackened Metaglione publicly," Felder retorted. "Metaglione had fifteen military contracts, and one person vindictively canceled them, Marshal Secerna Hyde. The corporation went into free-fall."

"Secerna Hyde was charged with treasonous incompetence and the deaths of over a hundred military personnel," Elio stated. "She was stripped of all rank and jailed. If Metaglione wants that order negated, I'll send a message and—"

"In your circumstances, Ambassador," Felder said with a hint of scorn, "do you have that authority? Can you really do that?"

Felder was right about that. Elio wasn't certain anyone read his reports.

"So, then," Elio replied instead. "What can you tell me about this business?"

"Alastor has been building ships for nine months," Felder explained. "Our mining concerns are strained. But a top-tier metals company was abandoned during mobilization. They had five years of stockpiles waiting to ship. If Orso wouldn't accept them, why can't Metaglione sell elsewhere? We certainly needed them."

Elio recalled the charter they granted to companies like Metaglione. 'If in the course of fiscal quarter production, that the product is not purchased for the agreed-upon price by the Orso government or its authorized agents, thus will the company be allowed to seek a buyer for that fiscal quarter's production—' Elio hated the stilted language, but it was clear; Orso had abandoned those contracts, so it was legal for them to sell wherever they could and at whatever the prices.

"Speaking of advancements," Elio redirected, "what about those new missiles? We haven't seen anything like them; they're effective."

"Typical Orso thinking." Felder's humor seemed different now. "With your vast mining resources—so vast that you didn't notice the loss of one of your largest company's resources—you've mustered ten new prototypes that feature dutrinium bearings! Very expensive. Not all kingdoms are so lucky."

Elio ignored the jibe. "How do they work?" he asked.

"It's simple," Felder replied. "Their ships operate like Slip-drive shields, by accelerating particles across their hulls. They veer by changing the particle's direction across their hulls. This creates hard radiation. So our missiles close the distance by tracking that radiation. No radar pulse needed."

Elio's mind spun. "That's incredible. Missiles jink to change direction. Your missile just follows a trail."

Felder grinned. "We called them Switchblades. The tip is a knife that drives into the hull, then they explode. Very effective in the heavy transport vehicles they use."

"The spearheads?" Elio asked. At Felder's nod, he added, "Our pilots call them ballistas."

"Appropriate," Felder replied. "We have similar vehicles now, with heavy armor that can withstand abuse. We named them Javelins."

Quite a development, Elio realized. Alastor was driving where Elio wanted to go. Clearly, they should ally themselves closely, but he needed to gain Felder's trust without alerting his guards.

"So," Elio ventured, "can we examine these Switchblade missiles?"

"Will your government apologize for Tenilo Barum?" Felder said.

"I can't promise anything of the current administration," Elio hedged. "But I will do anything I can."

"My government doesn't trust Orso, you understand? Not even this much." He raised his hand to gesture just how much.

Elio glimpsed it. The info chip disappeared from view again. Only Elio could have seen it. Felder's meaning was clear. If Elio was willing to share information without an agreement, it might help relations between the kingdoms.

"Shall we discuss how to bridge that gap?" Elio replied.

"Of course," Felder said. "That's what ambassadors do, is it not?"

Felder clearly wanted to collaborate, now that his frustrations had been aired and allayed constructively. Elio simply had to work around his own government.

"How might we cooperate?" Elio said. It would be a busy discussion, but terribly boring to his guards.

So sad.

Elio was pleased. This was a real meeting of the minds, though the use of honorifics had slipped a few times, but Felder hadn't minded.

But now Felder seemed uneasy. Elio assumed it was time to end the meeting.

"Well, prince, this has been delightful—" Elio began, but Felder held up a hand.

"Elio," he said in a low voice. "I need to ask you something."

Elio was concerned. The prince hadn't used his name for most of the meeting. "What is it, sire?"

But Felder's words were completely unexpected. "What happened to Richard Morian?"

Elio's emotions crashed down. He'd enjoyed sparring with

the prince and forgotten most worries. One name brought it all back.

"The Avenger disappeared," Elio replied finally. "The whole crew is missing, save for refugees on Thorn."

"Refugees? Thorn?" Felder repeated. "What do you mean?"

Elio hesitated, then plunged forward. "Before my father died, Prince Tarak Tudor and I spearheaded a mission to retrieve or kill escaped criminals with Psy and TK. They'd fled to the Dianesis system. Richard Morian led four capital ships, and I... stayed behind when my father died. And then someone scrapped the mission."

Felder gave the slightest nod. He knew how Orso's leadership had changed.

"Every captain in the flotilla chose to follow the mission, against orders," Elio continued. "After that mission, they followed another... objective. They entered an unaligned star system and found a Swarm incursion. Three ships Slipped without gates. The Avenger never reappeared."

Elio paused, took a deep breath.

"Because of that battle, fighter pilots or shuttle crew took whatever refuge they could to escape. But Orso had a fleet waiting at the rendezvous point. Prince Tarak and Sasha Crowe weren't from Orso, so they couldn't be detained. That left the Thorn. If Richard had joined them, he'd have been arrested and tried for treason. They waited for a week, then declared him dead and returned to Orso."

Prince Felder began whispering. Elio caught just a snatch of it... the Igar Catechism for the Dead. Many Alastorians remembered the common prayers of Igaris, even if Alastor had shed state religion three hundred years ago. Elio's mother had practiced it and prayed often.

Elio had whispered this catechism at her funeral. His father hadn't noticed.

Prince Felder finally raised his head. "Richard Morian was an honorable man. Affairs of state kept me from reacquainting myself with him before his death. I... am sorry."

Elio couldn't help himself. Thoughts of Richard led to Danis. He tried to keep his emotions leashed. At least he didn't cry in front of his guards.

"It's been a trying day, hasn't it?" Felder asked gently.

Elio composed himself. "You did start it by punching me," he replied with a smile.

"You accepted it graciously," Felder replied. "I'll make it up to you."

"Thank you," Elio said. "If I think of anything, I'll call you."

Felder reached to shake hands, and Elio felt fingers brush inside his sleeve. Wait a minute—!

But the prince turned and left the room. Elio cupped his hand to catch whatever Felder had slipped him. He knew it well.

It was another info chip.

———

WHEN ELIO EMERGED from the conference room, Blade Sergeant was there, his chin more imposing than usual.

"Get your things," he growled at Elio. "Just because you get attacked by aliens is no reason to piss on my schedule."

Elio bit back several responses before saying, "If you insist, Blade Sergeant. Let's head out. Perhaps we'll avoid the next Swarm attack."

Blade Sergeant turned to a platoon's worth of ragged former miners. "Recruits, a-ten-hut! You will march in formation like actual soldiers! When your feet hit the deck, it should sound like a single step! Ready, march!"

Their feet, Elio noted, did not sound like a single step. It sounded like a box of shoes falling down the stairs. With Blade Sergeant berating them every eighth step, they sounded better before they reached the shuttle. Takeoff was quick, and they reached the Ataraxis in under an hour.

Elio was immediately taken to his quarters, allowing the Blade Sergeant to break in his new troops. *If he doesn't just break them first*, Elio thought with a grin, but it quickly faded.

He was once again confined to his quarters with guards. This was Squad D; he recognized the woman who had her legs injured before. *What was her name... Stella? Adella?*

They looked tired, so it was no surprise they had trouble concentrating on him. After making sure they were focused elsewhere, he slipped Felder's chip into the port on his halo. He watched carefully, but no one reacted to his sleight of hand.

"I'm going to review some information about our next stop," Elio said. "Tap my shoulder if you need anything."

The guards didn't say anything, but the one with the bandaged leg gave him a nod.

He activated the halo, and was surrounded by his virtual office space. He accessed the info chip and found only one file, a slideshow. He tapped it and found a news article dated a few months ago. Thorn Crew Return To Caerus Amid Serious Allegations.

He skimmed it a moment, then flipped to the next slide. It was another article in a similar vein. Returned Bridge Crew Held For Possible Mutiny. The next was different. Former Avenger Commander To Receive New Posting. The attached pictures were of... Michael Jadern? He scanned the article and found some disturbing commentary. *How could Michael Jadern turn against Richard like that?* he wondered as he read the man's vitriolic comments. *It's like he's become a different person. The Michael Jadern that I knew...*

His thoughts froze. *The Michael that I know is as loyal as* the sun is bright, but that isn't him, is it? There must be a Psy working for the Regency, tampering with people's minds. It would explain some things.

Disturbed by those implications, he flipped to the next slide. But this wasn't an article, it was a vid, taken from a distance. Prisoners were taken off a shuttle by armed guards. Elio highlighted the center of the image and it zoomed closer. He highlighted the same area, and it got even closer—

Was that Jadern? Elio thought as the face disappeared behind... It was just a glimpse but... He ran the vid back a few moments.

There he was! Michael Jadern, looking haggard. And walking just in front of him was... Was Danis Morian. Thrashing and kicking a guard, but most definitely Danis. He had only one thought left.

She's alive... She's ALIVE!

CHAPTER
TWENTY

PERCEPTIONS
Remainer Blvd.
Greasetown, Som Orsi

Jude Cabeus sat atop the same building that Spider had so recently used. Whatever relationship Veisti had with her comrades, she'd delivered.

The first thing he'd done was splice a signal repeater into the comm receiver nearby. If anyone nearby used a comm, he would know. Signal repeaters couldn't decrypt the data, but they could read senders and destinations. Police and investigators built up profiles of comm traffic this way.

Now he waited. The hum of the building's heat exchanger provided a steady backdrop to the city buzz. He pulled a Vitax from his pack and dry-swallowed it. The stimulants would keep him awake.

I just hope that Rosst hasn't already left, Jude thought as the sun sank. He needed this information to be accurate. His father would run out of patience soon.

———

The White Room

AVRUM ROSST WAS FLOATING in a milky haze. It was a happy haze.

"Oh, you look so handsome when you smile," said a friendly voice.

He realized his eyes were closed, and he carefully opened them. It was bright, but he soon realized the room was barely lit and that he was on a hospital bed.

I must have had my surgery... he thought, blinking his eyes.

Eyes. He had two eyes.

He blinked both eyes again and stared at the grimy ceiling. One eye was unfocused.

Did I hear a voice? he thought. He tilted his head backward, and his good eye saw Dr. Augon smiling down at him, her blond hair like a halo around her face.

"You looked so peaceful," she said. "I didn't want to wake you, but your friends contacted me. That's a breach of agreement, I'll have you know. The only communication is supposed to be the arranging of the appointment. But I'll give them a little slack because of your unusual situation."

The barrage of words was annoying at first, but then he realized she was lonely; living by herself, doctoring criminals all day. And with the rumors about her husband's death, few would want to get close to her.

Now I'm babbling to myself, he thought. But then she said, "Not babbling. You understand me pretty well, Avrum Rosst."

"How did you—?" he tried to ask, but his voice cracked with every word.

232

"Have some water, Colonel," Dr. Augon said, and handed him a plastic cup. He looked at it with suspicion, but she snapped, "I didn't have to wake you up, genius! Show a little faith."

He took a sip, then a swallow. His throat protested even as it absorbed the life-giving moisture.

"I'm sorry. Maybe you don't remember," the doctor said, her expression calmer. "I told you there were reports about someone of your description. The missing eye and the patch weren't your friends. You weren't able to hide very well."

"I'm not used to hiding," Rosst replied.

"I know. I never could manage it either." Dr. Augon sighed. "But why should I hide? I was betrayed; but you see, I have marketable skills and a large pool of potential clients. Those Wellbient clinics can barely handle the smallest, most common injuries."

Rosst wasn't sure what to say. "I really need to be going soon," he said gently.

"Oh, you shouldn't leave yet," she said. "You haven't even tried to walk, let alone test that new implant."

Rosst tried to squint. His unfocused eye could "see" fuzzy lines superimposed on his vision. With an attempt at focus... they were still fuzzy.

"You can't see because we haven't yet calibrated your new eye," Dr. Augon said. When he frowned, she added, "Do you think I can't figure out what squinting means?" She shook her head. "Here, put the calibrator glove on."

She held up a strange little thing of wires and rubber caps, with a tiny button box on the end. He held up his hand. She expertly slipped the caps over two fingers and a thumb, strapped the box to his wrist, and pressed the button. Instantly, his left eye showed words.

TAP HERE, it read. He raised the glove, reached forward, and tapped the words. They transformed into little bulls-eyes.

"Now for a series of depth exercises," Dr. Augon explained. "The glove will measure the programmed distance from your eye."

Some targets looked closer than others. A few seemed just out of reach. After he'd touched all of them he could, the targets changed, and he repeated the test.

"Good," she said. "Now for focusing. Watch the moving ball. When you see the pattern clearly, tap your fingers together."

A virtual ball bounced around the room. Up close, he could see the checkered pattern and tapped his fingers. The ball disintegrated, and a different one appeared.

"You know exactly what to do, don't you?" he commented.

"You're not my first eye implant," she said, but something distracted Rosst. He left the ball bouncing and turned to look at her eyes more closely.

Her eyes weren't real.

———

"Surprise," the doctor said. "Your surgeon also has ocular implants. Mine have better resolution than yours, but you chose well!" She looked proud. "I know everything there is to know about ocular implants. Now, finish your exercises."

Rosst sensed something deeper. "Why did you have to get implants?" he asked.

She sighed, and her bravado faded. "It was a stupid grav car accident! One minute I'm a surgeon, the next I'm blind. I told my husband to pay whatever it cost to fix me. Six months later, I saw him leave me."

"Did he ever explain?" Rosst asked, before remembering that she was wanted for murder.

"Oh, yep," she snapped. "I lost some muscular control around my eyes. I have a wall-eyed stare now. It's creepy."

Rosst said nothing.

"Oh, I know what everyone thinks; what you're thinking," Dr. Augon said, "but I didn't do it."

"So, why did you go into hiding?" Rosst asked, confused.

"It's really quite strange," she replied. "I had to replace my old eyes with new ones to see what a mess my life was. At least here, the people like me for what I do, and they're honest compared to our society snobs."

"So how did he die?" Rosst asked, glad for the explanation.

"His onboard brake controls failed." Dr. Augon turned her head shyly, but not before Rosst saw a smirk. "It was another stupid grav car accident. Finish your exercises; doctor's orders."

Rosst focused on following the ball and tapping it. Once complete, a congratulatory message appeared, and his left eye snapped into focus. The entire room was right there, just like it had been before... And he felt... whole, in a way he couldn't describe.

"Thank you, Doctor," he said. "It's good to feel like... me, again."

"I'd like more than that," she replied. "When can I see you again?"

"See me..." Rosst was confused. "You mean a follow up appointment?"

"No, silly!" she said, facing him once more. Her bout of melancholy had disappeared. "I turned down a huge payday by not collecting your bounty. So I thought we might have dinner together."

Rosst tried not to gape. "Like a date?"

"Well, if you're asking me out, sure!" the doctor agreed.

"But I don't even know your name," Rosst said, stunned.

"That's easy," she whispered. "It's Jan Loko. It's my maiden name. So, would you like to go out this afternoon?"

Rosst's mind spun with the sudden change. *Should I put her off? Should I give in? She's insinuated she'd turn me in. A meal with her would be the least of my concerns.*

"How about lunch?" he said, hoping he didn't sound too suspicious. "I'll let my friends know I'm awake, and we'll go."

"Call them," she said with a smile.

But she watched him intently. *Who do I call?* he thought. *Bree and Emila Preston are the only innocents I know. But if I call a woman, she might get jealous. And if she's seen my dossier, she might know the others. She has to be well-informed working here.* He made his choice and tapped the command on his wristpad.

What shall I say? He wondered as he waited. *Hi, I'm fine. I'm taking the doctor on a date?* He tried to believe she wasn't staring, that it was just the wall-eyed expression.

"What is it?" Lockwith's slurred voice blared from the tiny speaker.

"I'm awake and fine," Rosst said. "Tell everyone I'll be back around..." he checked the time, "...1800, in time for dinner." He suddenly noticed a warning message blinking on his wristpad.

"Signal echo detected," he snapped, then, alarmed, he blurted, "I think someone's—"

"Got it!" Lockwith snapped and cut the connection.

"Who was that?" Dr. Augon—Jan Loko asked.

"An unfortunate acquaintance," Rosst said. "But he'll get the information to my friends."

"If you say so." Dr. Loko didn't seem sure, but then she smiled. "What are you in the mood for? I know a great place for Suzien noodles near here."

———

Remainer Boulevard

Jude wanted to scream.

The temperature exchanger was a clattering buzz that drowned out half the city sounds. Every few minutes, someone nearby sent a message. He was almost at the point of stopping checking the data.

Jude was almost manic from the constant noise and Vitax. He was about to get up and start pacing when the signal repeater tootled an incoming comm message.

Jude pulled up the data without thinking and lost the call almost immediately. But his wristpad proudly displayed the captured information. The sender was masked, listed as Ann Onymouse, but the destination was a warehouse several kilometers away. And the origin—he triangulated—was right across the street.

That is the White Room, he thought. *It has to be.* The frustrating days, the lack of sleep, and the stimulants had taken their toll, but now this was the time.

So he waited.

And waited.

He glanced around so quickly that he saw the door open three times before he noticed. Two figures stepped outside. One was an attractive woman with blond hair. The other was Avrum Rosst.

It was Avrum Rosst, but he no longer wore his eye patch.

Jude ducked down in a panic, though he knew if Rosst was looking for trouble, it might already be too late.

What kind of sensors could he have? Jude wondered. He doesn't know anyone is here... unless Veisti sold me out.

He realized that the heat exchanger might be masking his presence. *It's warm enough to cloud body heat.* He thought. *The noise would mask my movements. The metal might even block back-scatter X-ray.* He doubted Veisti had considered any of that. He risked peering over the edge.

Rosst and the doctor were walking away.

The White Room is neutral, Veisti had warned him. If something happened to the doctor, Veisti would sell him out in an instant, and Jude didn't trust the idea that she had nothing on him. Gutter-level info gatherers lied as easily as they breathed.

He followed Rosst discreetly. He couldn't know what Rosst's prosthesis could do, so he kept two hundred meters away. Jumping alleys and maintaining visuals was difficult, but it was what he was trained to do. And he couldn't dwell on whose lives hung on his next decision.

———

JUDE FOLLOWED THE PAIR TO... a restaurant?

What does the colonel think he's doing? Jude wanted to shake that answer out of Rosst, but from what he could see, Rosst was simply conversing with the doctor. He'd expected to accomplish his hit after they parted, but they'd foiled that plan.

My family is at stake here! he reminded himself. He looked at the short rifle he'd appropriated. *I can't be sure of a decent shot with this. I might hit an innocent by mistake.* His father wouldn't care about casualties, but Jude couldn't allow it. *If I had TK,* he mused, this would already be over.

Finally, he decided to accomplish something instead of sitting on a rooftop, waiting for them to choose dessert.

It took forty-five minutes to trek across the district. He didn't follow avenues with obvious security. He took side streets, watching for cameras—they could be hacked—until, finally, he reached a ramshackle warehouse. He reconnoitered the building from every angle. It looked decrepit.

But it was intentionally decrepit. The windows were uniformly filthy. Despite the old doors, the locks gave it away. No fake corrosion could hide their age from him. The "rusted" locks were just more window dressing.

He found an entry point, used a metal fingertip to crack a windowpane and, with a large enough hole, he reached through to deactivate the security sensor. Once that was accomplished, he broke the pane open, crushed the lock and the window opened freely, and he slipped inside.

This was his element. He avoided the security cameras, noting the tracks in the dust. They were recent. Someone had been here several times, and not too long ago.

He followed the trail to a cargo elevator. He almost pressed the controls, then swore softly. The elevator was an obvious place to put a camera; they could trap him between floors. He took the nearby stairs.

On the next level, he found piles of metal crates. Most were fastened shut, some open, empty. *But what's in the others?* he wondered. *Weapons? Explosives? What kind of rebellion are they plotting?*

He found a ramp down to the subbasement. Fresh black marks from industrial lifters marked the top and bottom of the ramp. He reached the doors at the bottom—one for cargo, one for humans. He looked around. There were no cameras nearby. He grinned. *This won't be too difficult,* he thought as he eased the door open and stepped inside to be confronted by several men with weapons trained on him. One of them was retired Air Marshal Teyn Grig.

The marshal glared at him, then said, "They say curiosity killed the cat. That arm suggests curiosity gave you a warning shot," Grig said. "Now come in nice and slow."

———

Baroque Street Cafe
Geartown

Avrum Rosst's wristpad trilled an incoming message. He answered it immediately, not caring if Dr. Loko watched now.

"Thanks for the two-minute warning," Grig said. "He says he knows you."

Rosst sighed in relief. They were safe. "Anything interesting?" he asked.

"He's got a mechanical arm," Grig said.

Rosst was dumbfounded. *Could it be Jude Cabeus?* he wondered. Aloud, he said, "He might have Psy, or TK."

"We have him secured," Grig replied. "See you shortly." And his image winked out.

"Oooh, this sounds interesting," Dr. Loko said. "Take me with you."

"Our location is a secret—" Rosst began.

"I can keep secrets," she said, interrupting him. "Besides, you need someone to examine the prosthetic arm. You never know what tricks it has. Not taking no for an answer."

Rosst suddenly remembered, if the man was Jude Cabeus, he had ammunition in that arm and everyone might still be in danger.

And this woman wants to walk into that? Best keep her happy, Rosst thought. The situation was getting worse, and he had another worry in the doctor's trustworthiness. Take her with him or risk her anger?

"Let's hurry," he said. He left the table and the restaurant. The doctor kept pace with him all the way back.

CHAPTER
TWENTY-ONE

PRETENSION
Ataraxis's Guest Quarters

Elio fought to keep his emotions from spilling out.

The Regency kept Danis from me!

Rationally, Elio knew why, to keep him under control, but that didn't alter the bone-chilling rage he felt inside.

He carefully tapped search terms into his wristpad. The vid was time-stamped five days after the Ataraxis left its berth. With a few rough guesses, the Thorn might have arrived at Caerus within hours of his departure. But with Blade Sergeant and a punishing schedule, he'd been distracted and exhausted for days.

They needed to keep me in the dark, Elio fumed. *Without Prince Felder, I wouldn't know any of it. Would he have told if he hadn't punched me?*

Getting home was his highest priority now, but how could he manage it without committing murder?

Captain Carrica wouldn't respond to his pleas. If he tried,

Blade Sergeant would immediately arrest him. What he needed... was to be summoned.

Except they don't want me there, he mused. *I duped Targer into making me ambassador so I could escape. What would entice them to bring me back?*

He would have to consider his next moves carefully.

———

Ataraxis's Troop Deck
En route to Planet Tor, Pricus System

"Fall in!" Blade Sergeant's voice cracked. Drella Simond and the rest of the guards formed up.

Assembly Room A was the largest room on the troop deck. Destroyers normally carried a single complement of marines. Four squads had been a tight fit.

"We're changing things up," Blade Sergeant announced. "We've lost five marines. Another is recuperating in the med-bay, watching Thunderball replays. Is that what you want?"

"No, sir!" Drella was drowned out by the new recruits.

Rooms for four squads of four now housed four squads of six. Blade Sergeant and his second had their own quarters. Everyone else was hot-bunking. Uniforms were at a premium. Everyone had two, but visors were scarce. Only veterans had them, creating a stark difference between them and the recruits.

"Everyone on board at Caerus, step forward," Strike Sergeant continued. Drella and the others came forward. "You just got a field promotion. Second Corporals are now First Corporals. First Corporals are now Provisional Sergeants with a Lance Sergeant test on our return."

Drella couldn't believe it. *Lance Sergeant! I mean, it's my second time. But if I focus, I can keep it!*

"You will lead off your new units," he continued. "Sergeant Hanson, you will lead E Squad, along with—"

He rattled off names and roles. Drella felt giddy at her new role as head of F Squad—Blade Sergeant's hateful look on Tyche flashed through her mind.

He needs me now, she thought as he gave her what she'd wanted back, command of her squad. Without D Squad as leaders, he would head two squads himself. *But D Squad is split up, and his new recruits will report anything I do for Ambassador Elio. He's neutered any disobedience.*

"I'll take questions," Blade Sergeant said, with an air of fond concern.

He's never talked like that before! Drella thought. *Somethings not right!*

"Why do we need so many people to guard the ambassador?" one of the recruits asked.

"Well," Blade Sergeant shrugged, "the ambassador has a history of dodging responsibilities and slipping away from punishment. I was provided fifteen soldiers to watch over him."

"What happened to the other soldiers?" someone said.

"We've had unexpected losses," Blade Sergeant explained. "The Swarm attack on Tyche, and we lost B Squad to a collapsed tower. I've expanded our operations."

"Why is the Swarm attacking like this?" another called.

"We don't know, but we adapt," Blade Sergeant replied. "That's what's expected. So we're altering our schedule, in case our ship was the target."

"Why would the ship be a target?" came the next question.

"Elio Lorne made the first contact with Blue soldiers," the strike sergeant answered. "Then he stumbled into early Swarm attacks. Afterwards, they targeted Orso Kingdom with increasing force. It's possible the enemy is focused on him... personally."

Drella couldn't breathe. *Did he just say the war is Elio's fault? And did he just hint that if Elio dies, the Swarm will leave?*

None of that made sense if you knew the events of the war, the scouring of worlds that had never seen Elio Lorne. But Drella had been a soldier for a decade, had seen the murdering aliens, and the awards bestowed upon those who died fighting.

Blade Sergeant had served continuously too. But she couldn't say anything. She had glimpsed the most important information she could have.

During every attack, Blade Sergeant was off-duty, away from Elio. During any Swarm attack, Elio could suffer an "unfortunate accident." Drella knew the blade sergeant was a TK. He could hurt Elio without touching him. Thousands had died during this tour, but that wasn't enough.

Blade Sergeant doesn't just dislike Elio Lorne, she thought. *He's his sworn enemy. And if Blade Sergeant ever has his moment alone with him, he might even kill Elio.*

———

Shuttle Goodwill
    Approaching Tor Planetary Orbit
    Pricus Planetary System

ELIO LORNE WATCHED the clouds of planet Tor grow closer. So much of his life had changed here. The war began for him here. Fighting for his kingdom began here. His relationship with Danis—

I can't dwell on history, he thought. *I need to focus.*

Governor Graynir is a trusted ally. Blade Sergeant can't keep us apart without raising suspicions. If I slip him the second information chip, he will find someone to use it.

It took time to build a fleet, but it might be enough to put the information out there.

"Enjoying the view, Ambassador?" Blade Sergeant appeared beside him. Elio couldn't miss the mocking tone.

"It is a lovely planet," Elio offered diplomatically.

"Too bad we won't see it," Blade Sergeant replied. "Meetings, meetings, and then off to another port. Like a traveling salesperson."

"Salesperson?" Elio said cautiously. "I'm certain that isn't my title."

"But it is your job, isn't it?" Blade Sergeant taunted him. "You knock on their door, extol the virtues of Orso, and the benefits, with no power to produce either. Then they accept that they shouldn't rebel against your authority... I mean, the king's authority."

Elio couldn't help himself. "I'm not selling them anything."

"You're right," Blade Sergeant agreed. "You're keeping the serfs in line, explaining the freedoms they'll lose if they rebel against authority."

"You have layers I've never seen," Elio commented. "And a better grasp of history than I would expect. Your education does you proud."

"I'm a complex man," Blade Sergeant said. "Not just a pretty face."

"I couldn't say," Elio replied, dryly.

"Hmm." The man's cheek quirked. "Maybe sometime when I'm off duty. Enjoy the view, Ambassador." Then he turned and strode away.

"Maybe if you ever consider yourself off-duty," Elio

muttered. Whatever Blade Sergeant had against him, it was complicated.

It didn't matter. Elio would get free, and he would find Danis. It was only a matter of time.

———

DIPLOMATIC LANDING ZONE
New Memorial Airfield
Pricus City
Planet Tor

ELIO STEPPED down the landing ramp to find a suitable delegation: a military honor guard, a bevy of dignitaries, even a crowd of onlookers. The crowd began to cheer and wave pennants with the Orso seal. This is much better than Tyche, he thought. And twice the size of Remanor's.

"Greetings and welcome back, Elio Lorne!" Governor Graynir announced. The man had aged well. A few more wrinkles and lighter hair, but he looked a hundred and ten. "It's been six years since we've seen our hero," the governor continued, then stooped to bow.

"Please, Governor," Elio quickly interjected. "I'm not here as... I'm an ambassador."

But as Graynir bowed, so did the dignitaries. The soldiers gave a raised-rifle salute.

"You don't need to do this," Elio insisted. He glanced at Blade Sergeant. If he decided that Elio wasn't sincere enough...

But no. He was enjoying Elio's discomfort. I wish I could see past that visor, Elio thought. I always feel like he's hiding something.

Finally, the governor stood and reached for Elio's hand. He feared Graynir might kiss it, but it was only a handshake.

"Welcome back, Prince Elio," he whispered. "We remember the man who ran across the enemy's killing field for us."

"It wasn't my last, either," Elio admitted. "Can... we meet privately later?"

"If you ask me to fetch your robe in the mornings," Graynir replied, "I will clear my schedule and attend you myself."

"Why are you... behaving like this?" Elio whispered.

"Because others do not," Graynir replied just as quietly. "But we remember."

"My guards will take exception to it," Elio pointed out.

Graynir smiled. "None of your soldiers outrank me."

"Guards, not soldiers," Elio said. "They watch me closely."

"We'll see about that," Graynir said. Before Elio could reply, Graynir turned to the crowd. "We're going to break for refreshments, and then there will be a press conference with the man who saved Tor from the Swarm!"

The crowd cheered again, and wouldn't disperse until Elio and his entourage reached the hangar. It wasn't long before Blade Sergeant caught up with him.

"That wasn't your itinerary," he growled.

"I didn't want this," Elio said, and he meant it. "I came here to do my job, not attend a party."

"Even if I believed that," Blade Sergeant replied, "do you really think I'll let you parade around—"

"Blade Sergeant," Elio said, regretting he couldn't properly excoriate him. "I never liked this fuss when I was the crown prince, and I don't have time for it now. But I serve my people. You can't stop them, despite your orders. And I suspect this government will have words for a sergeant who embarrasses the ambassador."

"My orders are from—" Blade Sergeant cut himself off and smiled. "Play your cards well, Elio Lorne. When you realize exactly what game this is, I will be more than amused."

Well, I didn't win a friend, Elio thought. *But that wasn't likely to happen, anyway.* He watched as Blade Sergeant walked away to rejoin his troops. *But maybe he slipped there. Maybe I now know more than I did.*

Someone obviously had an agenda, but Elio suspected how high the Blade Sergeant's orders went, and what the final play would be.

And Elio didn't like this game.

———

OBSIDIA GOVERNMENT HOSTELRY
Pricus City

DRELLA SIGHED in relief as F Squad entered their barracks.

This time, they'd were in a decent hostel. It wasn't much, but everyone got three days of hydros and a warm bed.

"Everyone, break down and clean up!" she ordered. "I want everyone washed and bunked in an hour. Whatever sleep we get needs to—"

"F Squad!" Blade Sergeant's voice snapped from the hallway. "Fall in!"

"Now what?" Drella said to herself, wondering what abuse Blade Sergeant planned.

"Simond," he said when they were at attention, "I'm shuffling assets. I need the conference room inspected for a meeting in two hours. Check for recording devices, concealed weapons. Use scan depth three."

"Two hou— I mean, question, sir," Drella recovered herself. "We just ended our shift. Shouldn't we bunk down?"

"Simond," he repeated, "I'm shuffling assets. I need the conference room inspected. Use the scanner."

"Understood, sir," she replied stiffly.

"Dismissed," he said, and waited until they broke ranks before turning to leave.

"What's up, Sergeant?" one of her recruits said. "Did you piss in his porridge or what?"

"First off," she replied firmly, "insubordination will land you on latrine duty. Second, keep piss jokes to yourself or I'll put you in the latrine myself."

She must have been convincing, because the grunt paled. "Yes, sir!"

"Collect scanners and mount up," she ordered, fighting weariness. *It's only two hours*, she told herself, but nothing was certain.

CONFERENCE ROOM 1A
    Prica City Government Offices

TWO AND A HALF HOURS LATER, F Squad had almost finished the conference room when her comm pinged. "Sergeant Simond," she answered.

"Simond," Blade Sergeant snapped, "I need F Squad on The Fish for an hour. G Squad will reconnoiter."

"Where will he be?" Drella asked.

"In his room," Blade Sergeant answered. "He isn't to leave or contact anyone."

"What if the governor stops by?" Drella asked. "He seemed really into the ambassador."

"Then he is asleep!" Blade Sergeant snapped. Landing to

find the Elio Appreciation Society had apparently scorched his calm.

"Understood, sir," Drella said, and the comm winked off without another sound.

"What did we ever do to him?" one of the grunts asked. Drella hadn't marked him as cunning, but two others eyed her with distrust. They'd figured out that she was the reason for the punishment.

"Well, you heard him," she said to her squad. "Be positive. G Squad can do a simple reconnoiter. Sergeant Hanson isn't incompetent." Unlike, say, Corporal Complainer from Tyche, who had been promoted to Sergeant Complainer. He led H Squad now.

It took ten minutes to get across the city to Elio's room in the Balkanfisher Suites. It was two blocks from the governor's mansion and the parliamentary building.

They rode the elevator to the fifteenth floor and disembarked into a long hallway. It took but a moment to find the correct room—The ambassador didn't rate the penthouse?— and entered to find G Squad... and Blade Sergeant.

"You're late," he accused without preamble. Sergeant Hanson said nothing. "I want six rotations every hour. Nobody is to spend more than ten minutes in any location, or with any partner. The three positions are at the front door, patrolling the hallway, and wherever the ambassador is standing. Am I understood?"

"Yes, sir," they answered.

"You will receive positions every ten minutes, starting... now." Blade Sergeant pressed a button on his wristpad, and everyone's wristpad lit up. Drella looked at hers. It read Ambassador.

A recruit also had the Ambassador. When he turned toward her, she recognized him as the suspicious one.

Great, she thought as Blade Sergeant and G Squad filed out of the room. *I wonder if he'll betray me?*

CHAPTER
TWENTY-TWO

DEVISING
    Balkanfisher Suites, Room 727
    Prica City, Planet Tor

Elio sat at the desk in his suite. It wasn't large enough for the holo screen and the few papers he didn't need, but he wanted to look busy, because he needed a distraction.

He'd pass the info chip to a guard. They would deliver it to Governor Graynir, who wouldn't betray him. But who could utilize it? No Orso planet had a suitable shipyard.

Prince Tarak does, he thought. *And the Odin kingdom is ideally suited. These plans could begin a new fleet of anti-Swarm vessels. But who to trust with the chip?*

He'd marked out a few guards he might trust. The medic Hanson, the female guard who pushed him to safety, and perhaps two others. But Blade Sergeant's reorganization had split them all, and the recruits weren't trustworthy.

Why did he rotate the guards? he wondered. *Did I let something slip? Or is Blade Sergeant paranoid? With enough emotion, I can pierce the Psy inhibitor,* he reminded himself again. *If one of them comes close, I can project my feelings...*

But could he really? His experience was limited. He'd managed to send Prince Felder a few flashes, but only when the man himself hit an emotional peak.

If I don't try, he told himself, *that's worse than failure.*

But how could he pass the chip? With the rotation, he'd have minutes to make an emotional contact. And any guard he trusted had a partner he couldn't.

Returning to Caerus was another problem. Could he forge something rescinding his ambassadorship? That would make Blade Sergeant happy, and "punishment" might distract him from his involvement.

How would Blade Sergeant or Captain Carrica respond? he wondered. They... would ask the Palace for confirmation, the Palace would deny it, the result would be Elio's imprisonment. So, he would need to forge confirmation. With an official-looking contact, and spoofed codes...

This required thought.

The guards changed. He faked disinterest, but glanced casually to see if it was their sergeant... *What was her name...?* he wondered. He still couldn't remember. *Stella, Adella, Delphia... I'm close, but it's not right.*

He came to a reluctant conclusion. Any documents to move him would look too suspicious. But, if the orders weren't about him...

Governor Graynir would be an ideal distraction, he decided, just as the guard's comms trilled. The guard shifted again. Two new recruits, with their sergeant by the door. He couldn't move the chip without them noticing. But he had about two hours before his next meeting. Could he forge the documents without being spotted?

If I learned one thing with Danis, he thought with a smile, *it's run to the one you want.* He picked up a datapad and began drafting an official document to call Governor Graynir to Caerus.

The wording was going to be a pain. It had been a while since he's done anything like it. After a few moments of thought, he concocted what he thought was a plausible reason for Graynir to travel across the galaxy and started to write the letter. After a few minutes, the comms trilled, and the guards switched again. This time their sergeant was nearby, along with a recruit.

Delphia, Darellia—Drella! He finally remembered her name. Drella Simond. And he owed her dinner.

If she pulls this off, I'll buy her a restaurant! he thought. *Now, to make certain his misdirection works. The closer it happens to me, the more suspicious.*

Without being able to see the hallway guards, he was limited to his room. That meant a door guard.

But first, make contact with Drella.

He fought the urge to close his eyes. Instead, he concentrated on need, hope, trust. Desires like Free Danis! and Defeat the Swarm! Sorrows like Richard are dead and family is gone! He pushed those as high as he could, then reached out to Drella.

Help me, he thought.

She started slightly. "You okay, Sarge?" the recruit asked.

"Just tired," she replied, and the recruit turned away.

I need to get information to the governor.

He hoped his thoughts were showing through. *It will help win the war. It needs to be sent to Prince Tarak Tudor of Odin.* The thought of winning this war created such hope in him, he worried it would weaken the message. But she nodded.

He reached out with the thinnest thread of TK. He touched one of the door guards, careful not to be noticed. He wouldn't injure him, just jostle his intestines. They filled most of the abdomen. Just a simple nudge to—

The comms trilled, and Elio jerked, his concentration broken.

"Ugh!" came a yell from the door.

Oh, stars! Elio almost gasped out loud. *I didn't hurt him, did I?*

"Um, Sarge!" the door guard exclaimed. "I need to use the refresher!"

"What?" Sergeant Drella snapped.

"Sorry, Sergeant. But I need to use the head? Right now!" He waited only a moment longer before rushing toward the room's private refresher.

Elio slipped the info chip onto the corner of the desk and Drella slid it away and it disappeared.

"Lowens," she barked. "Stay here. I'll take his place."

"But Sarge," Lowens said, "aren't we supposed to—"

"Are you the sergeant, Corporal?" she barked, and Lowens backed down. She joined the other door guard.

Elio appreciated the maneuver. Him being alone with a recruit deflected any suspicion of collusion. Blade Sergeant might see through the trick, but it might not be reported.

He blew out a breath in relief. Using TK had been a gamble. He hadn't considered the consequences before committing. It had been foolish, and reckless, but... necessary. And Danis always made him feel reckless, and he wanted that back in his life.

He noticed Lowens trying to peer at his datapad.

"Sir?" Elio asked politely. "Are you reading my classified documents?"

"What classified documents?" Lowens asked. "Blade Sergeant said you didn't do anything important."

His opinion spreads quickly, Elio chuckled to himself.

"I'm not doing anything critical," Elio cautioned, "but details of state aren't available to the public. Viewing these documents without clearance is punishable with prison time."

"How did you get that clearance, if Blade Sergeant thinks you're useless?" Lowens demanded.

"Did he tell you my name?" Elio asked.

"No," Lowens replied. "He just calls you 'ambassador.' Or, you know, other things."

"My name is Elio Lorne," Elio said. When that didn't merit a response, he added, "My full titles were Elio Lorne, Royal Family of Lorne, regalis pluris centum, Prince of Caerus, hereditary Seat of Orso System and applicable territories. Surely you've heard of 'Prince Elio'?"

Lowen's eyes grew wide. But when Elio finished, he said, "But now you aren't, right?"

"They said I'm not a prince anymore," Elio admitted. "What do you think a prince is?"

Lowens smirked and turned away. The comms trilled again before the other guard returned.

"Stick to your partner and move out," Drella ordered. "I'll report this when we're relieved. Trig, you're on the door with me."

Lowens was in the hall and Elio was left with another pair of recruits, but he didn't mind. While they made certain nobody contacted him, he edited his false documents, with separate versions for Graynir and Captain Carrica. He carefully embedded contextual metadata "from" Caerus. and an official-looking halo contact for Captain Carrica to confirm the orders.

They were as believable as Elio could make them. Now he needed the halo contact—

There was a knock at the door.

"Who is it?" his door guard demanded.

"I'm to escort the ambassador?" the voice on the other side said.

Elio noticed Drella's expression. She was exhausted, and their relief hadn't yet arrived.

"I'm running behind," Elio stated. "I need a few more minutes to get ready."

The guard opened his mouth, but Drella glared at him before replying, "The ambassador will be ready shortly."

Elio closed his files, his letters unsent. He went into the bedroom and sorted through his clothes, stalling for time, hoping Blade Sergeant would let them rest. But he couldn't stay forever, so he chose a dark-blue suit with military styling, black shoulder panels, crimson trim, and gold buttons: the image of Orso.

He checked his appearance, adjusted his hair, patted the sweat from his forehead, then emerged to find F Squad still there. His heart sank.

"I'm ready to go," he announced with little fervor.

"F Squad, form up!" Drella snapped. The recruits made a passable Square Guard formation. She opened the door and found H Squad outside, led by Sergeant Complainer. F Squad's hallway guards were there, and the aide waiting for Elio was wringing his hands.

"Our relief is here," Lowens announced.

F Squad slumped in relief. Elio couldn't blame them. They'd been on duty for more than twelve hours. They had to be drained.

"Lance Sergeant... Clament," Sergeant Drella said with only the slightest hesitation, "I deliver the ambassador's safety into your hands." It was a ritual Elio had heard a thousand times in years past.

"I accept the obligation of the ambassador's safety," Clament replied, then added, "You deserve this rest, Sergeant. Make the most of it." H Squad formed up around Elio, and they marched him away to his conference. The aide tried to engage Elio in discussion, but he paid little mind. This was just one more public appearance..

Instead, his thoughts were of reaching Caerus and Danis.

―――

Obsidia Government Hostelry
Pricus City

Drella awoke.

Nothing was familiar. The walls were yellowed beige, with geometric vines painted along the ceiling. She needed the refresher. Then memory came crashing back.

She was in F Squad's temporary barracks. Around her were five sleeping soldiers.

Twelve-hour shift! She checked her wristpad, which she hadn't removed before crashing to the mattress. She had only slept for six hours.

But there was something else—

The info chip! She panicked. She stumbled off the stiff mattress and grabbed her uniform. She felt in her pockets, then started turning them out. She almost missed the click on the tile floor. She bent over to retrieve it and heard a groan.

Drella whirled to see who it was, but Lowens rolled in his sleep.

Help, the ambassador had said to her. Get to the governor... will help. Prince Odin... win the war with received information.

Garbled, but direct. The governor will help me. The prince of Odin can win the war with this information.

How could the ambassador contact her with his restraints? He was remarkable. She respected Elio for fighting alongside his soldiers. He thought of those he commanded, and risked himself to help.

The war was everything now. Elio wanted to end the war. And by disobeying orders and handing this info chip to the Tor government, Elio could become king.

If she could manage it.

She looked at her rumpled, sweaty uniform and debated the risk of waking someone over clean clothes.

"Why didn't I pack civvies?' she muttered as she pulled the sweaty uniform on. Clean wasn't worth the risk. She ditched her wristpad, knowing it might be tracked. Then she grabbed her coat and headed out the door.

It took Drella a half hour to retrace the route to the government district.

She regretted her clothing choice; it made her memorable and it was smelly. She discreetly followed some journalists and found Elio heading into another conference with H Squad. She ducked out of sight, and spotted the governor off chatting with his aides, all dressed in similar uniforms. Two aides followed the governor, and three broke away on various tasks.

When one of them left the immediate area, Drella followed him for several blocks. As he passed between two buildings, she dashed forward, grabbed his arm and pulled him into the alley. She glanced out, hoping no one had noticed.

"What's the meaning of this?" he demanded, and tried to pull away. But Drella had surprise and leverage and pushed him to the wall.

"You're one of the governor's aides," she said. "What's your job right now?"

"Unhand me, you... you..." His nose wrinkled in distaste. "Ugh. You stink. I thought it was the garbage."

"Shut up!" Drella ordered. She didn't have time! "What's your job?"

"I'm a governmental aide!" he gasped. Drella stopped pushing him so hard. "I do whatever Graynir tells me. Right now I'm getting him and the prin— ambassador drinks from a cafe."

"Does he trust you?" she asked.

"Of course he... I mean, I guess he does?" The aide suddenly looked uncertain. "I've worked for him for five years. I hardly ever screw up. And—"

"Fine!" Drella snapped. "Look, I have something for the governor. It's vitally important, and it's from the ambassador."

The aide looked confused. "But he's with the governor! Why can't he—"

"Elio is a prisoner," she whispered. "I'm one of his guards. My superior would be really pissed off if he knew what I'm doing. This chip needs to go to the governor. The Prince of Odin needs information, immediately. Elio says it will win the war."

The man looked at her strangely. "You're crazy, right? You're a loony in stinky clothes."

Drella frowned. "The clothing is a Caerus' honor guard uniform. Just like the ones escorting him to that conference. Except mine are twelve hours used."

The aide still looked uncertain.

"Look," she snapped, "just deliver the chip, right? Tell the governor to take every precaution. This chip is worth blowing my career for."

He stared into her eyes. "You're really serious, aren't you?" he asked.

"Absolutely," she replied.

"Fine," he said. She placed the chip in his palm. "It will be my career that goes up in smoke if you're wrong, but, hey. A chance to end the war? I'll take the gamble."

Drella sighed in relief. "Thank you," she whispered. Finally, she'd done something right. "I need to go, now."

She left the alley and jogged back toward the hostel. She hoped no one had noticed she was missing.

Drella returned to the hostelry and crept along the hallway. Everything was silent as she made it back to her room, carded the door lock, and pushed it open, to find Blade Sergeant on the other side.

Drella blinked in confusion.

She hit a wall with bone crushing force; the impact knocking pictures and furniture down. Blade Sergeant hadn't moved. And she was pinned above the floor.

He's using TK! she thought savagely. *The rat bastard attacked me!*

She struggled against the invisible grip, but Blade Sergeant only smiled.

Then she was crushed through the wall, wood and plaster raining down. When she opened her eyes, Blade Sergeant was standing over her.

"Sergeant Simond," he said softly. "It seems you are disloyal, which is not surprising." His words dripped condescension. He turned to her squad, standing behind him. "Sergeant Lowens, arrest her."

CHAPTER
TWENTY-THREE

Bautan Beta-Max Penitentiary
[CLASSIFIED]
Solitary Block, Cell A

"Dear Elio."

Danis Morian sat on a white bed, in a featureless room, and wished to die.

"I've been worried sick ever since we left Caerus."

She could feel claws digging inside her, dragging away feeble excuses, flimsy denials.

"I've been desperate to talk—"

Richard had betrayed Orso.

"I know you worry about me—"

Elio had toyed with her.

"Sometimes I get scared, and you're not here—"

Elio had disposed of her.

She had failed. Utterly.

Her message to Elio had been playing continuously for...

what? Days? Weeks? There was no time in a cell that didn't exist.

There was no way out. So she did the only thing she could.

"Please!" she called over the incessant repeats. "Please, I want to change! I promise I won't betray Orso ever again! Please, I'll do anything!"

When begging failed, she implored her unseen listeners.

"I'll do anything you ask!" she called. "I'll make myself into whatever you want. Just please—!"

And then her world crashed.

Danis struggled in the sudden blackness, after what seemed like months in the gleaming white room. Her limbs were weak and refused to move. She finally realized she was strapped down.

A voice nearby said, "You've rejoined us in the land of the living."

Danis felt herself lifted into a seated position.

When the mask was lifted off, she saw the dingy walls and realized she was strapped to a motorized gurney. There were two men present: one appeared to be a doctor. The other was...

"D-d-duke Rutta?" Danis croaked.

"Yes, it's me," he said with a gracious smile. "And you're alive and kicking. But you haven't been very reasonable, have you?"

Danis wanted to throttle him for the weeks of torture. But fear of the cell stayed her tongue.

"See? Finally reasonable," Rutta continued. "You want to serve again, don't you?"

I'll do anything to stay out of that cell! she thought, unable to forget the endless noise, the abyss of guilt. "I want to serve again," she mimicked him.

"Perhaps on my... personal staff?" His words were innocuous, but his eyes... said so much more.

And she would do whatever he asked. Anything to stay out of the cell.

She was disgusted with herself, working up the courage to accept.

"No, I think not," he said after a few moments. Danis hid a sigh of relief, then panic swept over her. *What is he going to suggest? Is it my cell—!*

"Pilot duties!" Rutta said. "Of course. We'll plan a recovery schedule, put you in sims, get your mojo back, or whatever pilots call it. Courtesy of... me."

Your courtesy put me in that cell! She thought, but then the thought of being confined again silenced her.

"I'll write out a release for you," Duke Rutta said. "You're in prison, don't you know? It's a good thing I took an interest in you." He bent over a small table, scribbled a few lines on a piece of paper, and affixed a seal to it.

"Thank you, sire," Danis said, every word bitter. But if she was away from here... well, she'd already considered worse sins than to escape.

"Sign here, please," Rutta said to the doctor. "You're the official witness. Show this to the warden. Have her things released from impound, or whatever it is you call it."

The doctor signed and left the room, leaving them... alone.

"So we're clear," Rutta murmured, "no matter who you report to, you belong to me. Understand?"

Danis tried to swallow her rising bile. "I understa-and," she stuttered as the duke's hand rested on her leg.

"Good." With that word, the duke lost his friendly smile. Without another word, he swept out of the room.

Danis was left in a drab room, on a gurney.

"It's better than the cell," she told herself.

"I still want to be a pilot," the message echoed.

It's better than the cell.

"We're all born to be something," the message echoed.

It's better than the cell.

"Do we really have to choose?" the message echoed.

"I choose not to be in the cell!" Danis screamed. But there was no one to hear her.

Police Transport
En route to Som Orsi

Foreign rode toward its destiny in a transport with no windows, but that didn't matter, since Foreign was also hooded.

Foreign's human eyes saw nothing, but that didn't matter either. The vehicle was linked to dozens of outside systems, including maps, both representative and topographic. Foreign was on the most direct route to Som Orsi.

Finally, Foreign sighed to itself. *The long journey is nearly over. Once I reach my army, I will destroy the city that has impeded the Will.*

Foreign decided to make a special effort. *I will find the Will's enemy, the one called Elio. He is a powerful threat. He led the attack that captured me. The Will's stratagem to place me here was successful, but Elio represents risk. I will find him, and the Will shall see his death.*

Foreign reached through computer networks, searching for Elio, and found surprise instead.

How could humans remove their leader? it wondered. It pondered removing the Will and replacing it with lesser creations. *This human society destroys itself!* Foreign crowed to itself. *If humans throw him aside, then Elio is weak.*

That reasoning was flawed. If Elio is weak, how does he prevail against the Will?

It pondered this. *Humans are corrupt, just as the Will has said*, it thought. *Anyone powerful enough might lead them.* Someone like Foreign. A human, but one who controlled all computers.

I am not human! it insisted, as it also reasoned, *This body has advantages, so I will use them. I can conquer this world and expand the Will's base in this universe. I can spread, take over the human's lives with their computers. I can destroy them with their weapons, just like the Heretic attempted to do.*

Foreign noticed that Som Orsi was growing nearer. City networks were coming into range, and Foreign digested the information at speeds humans thought only theoretical. It quickly found its army in a human building called the Rising Tide Group Psychiatric Facility at the Resdon Military Facilities Annex. So it touched the police vehicle's computer and changed its destination.

"Hey, Kein?" the driver announced. "Our orders just changed. We're not going to Special Crimes anymore. Now we're supposed to go to the Resdon Annex?"

"Maybe they changed their minds?" Kein replied. "Or maybe they're busy, and they're shoving the fraudster on a back burner. It means no downtown traffic. Count your blessings."

"Guess you're right," the driver said. Foreign felt the vehicle shift direction as they headed toward Resdon and its army.

If the police removed the mask, they would be frightened of its smile.

———

DANIS STOOD in a grimy prison hydro, letting the water flow over her body. After the unending, unchanging sim, the sensation was sharp and unpleasant, but she bore it stoically.

When she got out, her skin prickled in the chill air. Whoever had monitored her had also cleaned her; not knowing who, or how, kept threatening her calm. She pulled a towel to her dripping body and scrubbed away the water, focusing on her freedom now instead of the past. The towel was heavy and plush, far nicer than she'd expected.

I'm getting a second chance, she thought as the steam slowly dissipated from the mirror. *It's like a dream. I mean, my life before feels like a dream, and my time in the cell feels like one, too. But now I'm clean and free...*

She looked at herself in the mirror and recoiled.

"What the stars?" she gasped and reached a hand up to her face.

Her face was too thin. Her hand and arm were thin and bony, not her corded muscles. She wondered how many calories they'd allotted her; clearly not enough. *If I'd accepted their offer sooner...* But she let that thought die. She understood better now. That was all that mattered.

She found a full set of pilot uniforms as well as feminine undergarments on the bench when she emerged from the prison hydro. Glad to receive a familiar uniform, she slipped the undergarments on only to find they didn't fit.

I've lost weight, she thought as she pulled the uniform on over them. If she was underweight, then she would build it back with diet and exercise. Jogging to the mess and lifting heavy forks sounded heavenly.

She emerged to find Duke Rutta waiting. "You look splendid!" he said, though politicians lied all the time. "I have wonderful news. You have a posting. Are you ready to fly?"

Danis was shaken. So soon? Back in command, just like that?

"Sire," she began, "I don't think I'm ready to lead—"

"Temporary reduction to Lieutenant Commander, retroactive Commander's pay when you assume full duties,"

Duke Rutta explained. "I have a ship leaving on standard patrol, with lots of sim time and an excellent rehab specialist."

Danis couldn't believe it. "You'll just... let me go back to being a pilot?" she asked.

"You're one of our best," the duke assured her. "It's foolish not to use every asset. Incidentally, I'll be on board to watch some of your training."

"Sir?" Danis asked, dumbfounded. "You're going with me?"

"As a passenger," Rutta said. "I'll take a shuttle to Tor when we pass through."

We're going near Tor? Danis almost blurted. Her life had changed on Tor. Shot out of her fighter, she barely survived the chute deployment. The Swarm devastated the system. It was where they'd learned how to kill their enemy.

It's where I met Elio Lorne.

She pushed all that aside. It didn't matter; they were just dropping off the duke. No big deal. None at all.

Rutta paced back and forth after Danis left the room.

"Do I need to go to Tor?" Rutta asked Helot impatiently. "And why are you going?"

"I will work with Danis Morian," Helot said. "She must not resist me."

"I still think she needs an inhibitor," Rutta argued.

"No," Helot ordered. "That will blunt my touch. Besides, she needs Psy to find Elio Lorne, or she is useless to me."

Morian shouldn't need to find Elio, Rutta mused. His blood belongs to me.

Rutta paced some more before asking again, "Why do I need to visit Tor?" A thought occurred to him. "Is it... because Elio is there?"

His vision flashed before his eyes once more. He and Elio battling like gladiators of old in the streets—

Wait, that isn't right, Rutta remembered. *Our fight is on a starship. I saw that.*

Rutta's new TK powers would overwhelm the former prince. And then... Elio would collapse at his feet, begging.

"Yes, Duke Rutta." Helot's voice slithered like a snake over sand. "All you desire and more awaits you there."

Good, Duke Rutta thought. *Because I desire it all.*

————

RISING TIDES GROUP Psychiatric Facility
  Resdon Military Facilities Annex
  Som Orsi, Planet Caerus

LANCE-SERGEANT DASCHER BIKK sat in the observation chair, keeping one eye on the patients, and the other on his squad.

Bikk shook his head. He could have had one of his squad sit in the chair, but if they were to doze off... Surprise inspections were rare, but squads were reprimanded for negligence. Much better to do the work while the others played games.

Besides, his squad was eclectic. Today they played a dice game of Corporal Linny's devising called 101 where they used the six numbers they rolled to make math problems, getting as close to one hundred and one as possible. It was too intellectual for Bikk's taste, but two of his squad had been demoted for back talking their superiors. *They spend too much time thinking,* he thought. *That's what gets them in trouble. I'm just a simple man, here to do a simple job.*

Do the job and get paid. The other three bet actual money on their game. The last time he'd tried the dice, he'd managed a 54, and lost six hours' pay.

And then, all the patients stepped out of their enclosures

and onto the catwalks. They often did this. Maybe they'd do the thing of quietly pointing instead of that weird warbling song they'd started recently.

They all raised their arms, and Bikk sighed contentedly. Finally, he mused, they're back to normal—

"EeEeEeEe-EeEeEeEe!" the guard room speakers shrieked, and he clapped his hands over his ears.

"What the stars was that?" Linny said as he dashed in, followed by the rest of the squad.

A distraction from your stupid game, Bikk thought, then said, "Our patients are singing again, idiot!"

"But where are they pointing?" one of the others asked over the warbling din.

Bikk looked at the overview screen. They were all pointing to the west... No, wait, they're turning, he realized. Their arms were moving to point closer to the south... And then they were pointing to the north?

Suddenly, the noise stopped and all the patients stood, arms extended in the same direction

"Hey, Bikk," Linny whispered, "what are they pointing at now?"

"I don't know," he whispered.

They waited in silence to see what would happen next.

"Monitor station!" the comm erupted.

Everyone jolted in surprise. Bikk reached out and tapped the comm. "Um, yes, sir? What can—"

"Be advised that we are accepting a new patient!" the comm shouted. "We will be entering the first-floor patient area!"

That must be Dillos on the other end, Bikk thought. The man has no idea of volume control. "Understood," he replied. "Be advised that the patients are out of their rooms at this time."

"Who cares?" Dillos yelled back. "They never do anything except point! Be prepared to cycle all appropriate gates!"

Don't you read the reports? Bikk wanted to ask.

He frowned. The patients weren't holding still. They were all moving their arms. Some to the left, some to the right, all of them downward until they pointed toward Patient Processing.

When the light blinked, Bikk punched the door control. The doors opened to reveal four guards, leading one small adult female. He closed and locked the door as soon as they passed.

All the patients continued to point. Their fingers followed the young woman as she was led to an empty cell room on the ground floor, a double unit with its own bathroom. Bikk touched the lock control and the door swung open. The woman stepped behind the clear plastic and the door closed. One of her guards locked it with a swipe of his badge. And the woman sat down on her bed.

And so did all the patients. They returned to their rooms and sat on the bed.

"Now that's just downright creepy," Linny said.

The comm chirped. "Monitor station, this is Higgs," one of the guards said. "I am to inform you that Unknown-Prisoner-8K21 has been added to the patient population. She is under no circumstance to leave that room. Food will be delivered under armed guard and eaten under direct observation by Medical."

"Understood," Bikk replied. "UP-8K21's delivery is acknowledged. Exit will open momentarily."

The guards walked to the door, and Bikk pressed the button to let them out. Once they'd passed, he closed and locked the door again.

"That was... really creepy," Linny said.

Linny was usually verbose. Hearing him repeat words was... a little odd.

"What does it matter?" Bikk said. "We keep them inside. If they do something weird, it takes ten minutes to do the report, which I will do now, so you guys can go back to playing dice."

But he kept one eye on the monitor screen as he wrote the report. If there was something wrong, he wanted to be the first one out of the way.

CHAPTER
TWENTY-FOUR

Danis Morian felt the shuttle touch down on the deck. "I have business to attend to," Duke Rutta explained, "so you wait here while I meet with the captain. Someone else can greet you and give you a tour."

Nobody dared say anything, not even Danis. She felt a retort bubble inside her, but she was too afraid to speak. She wanted, needed, to return to duty.

The ramp descended.

"Entourage!" Rutta barked. "Time to make the scene."

He swept down the docking ramp, followed by his courtiers and assistants. Only after the group had moved away did anyone else make their way off the shuttle.

Danis stepped off the shuttle and looked around. Maintenance techs were servicing fighters, F-31s. Fast but less armored than her F-32; more ammo, but fewer missiles. She'd flown every fighter in sims, and most in combat. It was an easy adjustment.

The hanger was clean, but not polished. She'd known a few ship captains. Either the ship sparkled or maintenance checks abounded while morale suffered. She never appreciated either approach. Discipline wasn't found in overbearing attention. Discipline was found in readiness and competence. Whoever ran this ship understood. It made her feel almost at home.

A stray thought caught her attention: Richard had believed this and passed it to her. But she ignored that. Richard was no longer her concern. Her new role was.

What is my role? she wondered. She was to train in sims, exercise vigorously, consume twice her usual calories.. And then she would take the fight to... *Who will I fight?* It was strange, this feeling that she almost understood...

"Hello, there," a dry, husky voice said. Danis turned to find a much older woman, rail-thin, wearing a black skin-thin under an abbreviated shipboard tunic. Danis wasn't familiar with the uniform.

"Hello," Danis replied, unsure of what to say. "I haven't had the pleasure..." She offered her hand in greeting.

The thin woman touched Danis's hand with a little laugh. "I'm sure you will. My name is Heloise," she said without shaking the offered hand. "I'm your therapist for the journey."

"I don't need therapy," Danis said immediately. "I can deal with my issues."

"I meant your physical therapist," Heloise said, still smiling. "You have many things to accomplish in a short time. And I expect you to reach your goals."

There it is! Danis thought. *It made little sense until she explained it. I need to have goals. A set of goals to achieve to put myself back on top. I need to fight complacency. And then I'll be ready for anything.*

Heloise was smiling at her fondly, like a pet. Danis would

have been insulted, but she realized Heloise wasn't like that. *She just wants to see me improve,* Danis thought.

She could hear Rutta talking loudly to the officers, including someone dressed in a captain's uniform, but they were too far away to identify.

"The duke enjoys being the center of attention," Danis observed dryly.

"It is his most useful fault," Heloise replied, a little cryptically. Danis might have pressed for more, but Duke Rutta quickly left the hangar, and the other passengers gathered their things. Danis followed suit. "So," Danis asked, "when do we start training?"

Heloise smiled. "As soon as you've had a meal. You look starved."

As they walked to the mess hall, Danis couldn't help but think, *If there was ever a pot calling a kettle black... she is it.*

———

TORRENT'S BRIDGE

"SIR?"

Michael Jadern looked to his comm officer. "Yes, Lieutenant Desquar?"

"Incoming call from Commodore Vandu," she reported, her voice quivering.

Jadern sighed. "Broadcast or private, lieutenant?" he asked.

"Um, oh... private," Desquar replied.

"I'll take it in my ready room. Jasson, you have the conn," he said to his first officer.

He still felt that thrill as he said it. My ready room. He walked out as Desquar rerouted the message.

Lieutenant Desquar wasn't the ideal choice for comm training. Her previous superior had placed her, but the Torrent would be patrolling contested areas and he needed efficient officers on the bridge.

He activated his holo projector. "Good morning, Commodore Vandu," he greeted. "How may I serve today?"

"I'm just checking on your readiness, Captain," she said. "We reach the Slipgate in six hours."

"I have a few assets I'd like to shuffle," he said. "I've tested them, and I'm convinced they aren't in their best positions."

"I'll overlook this the once," Vandu said. "But I can't have captains who are afraid of disappointing their subordinates."

"Not fear, Commodore," Jadern insisted. "I avoided capriciously moving members of the crew into new positions before knowing their strengths."

"You're being softhearted, Jadern. The eve of battle isn't the time to make these decisions," Vandu snapped. "Get your house in order, Captain." Her image disappeared.

Jadern sighed. Being a superior meant that you placed people where they would do the best job and keep morale high. He'd even needed that gentle push once upon a time, back when... back when Richard...

Best not to think about that. He had plenty more problems to deal with.

He returned to the bridge. "Lieutenant Desquar, a word, please," he said quietly, but the way the bridge silenced, he knew everyone was listening. "Meet me in my ready room," he said.

When the young woman joined him, he didn't offer her a seat. This needed to be quick. "I've watched you for two weeks," he said gently. "I don't think you're ready for comm officer."

Desquar stood rigidly at attention, "But sir, my redemption was..." A tear worked its way down her cheek. "I mean, I understand. Yes, sir."

"I'm not overlooking your hard work," Jadern said quickly. "But I'd like to transfer you back to comm maintenance, and give you another opportunity when we return to Caerus. We're leaving on patrol, and I can't give points for trying if we're attacked. You're a good officer, Desquar. I just think you need a few more months' experience."

She didn't move, even as another tear leaked out. "Your concern is appreciated, sir," she said. "Permission to withdraw, sir?"

"Permission granted, Lieutenant." Her expression broke his heart, but it was the right decision.

She turned, and the door opened for her. He watched her stride off the bridge as he walked through the door and felt the eyes of the entire bridge crew upon him, but when he looked, they were all busy at their tasks.

Six hours passed seemingly in a blink. He was still going over readiness reports when Commodore Vandu's voice came over the comms. "The time for the Tsunami task force to Slip has arrived," she announced. "Navigators, set your course for the Tor system. From there, we'll slip to Eos. We have no changes to our schedules at this time. Tsunami's Slip to begin in four minutes... mark. I want a ship through the Gate every three minutes, and I want an arrival every three minutes. You will be timed. That is all. Vandu out!"

Jadern couldn't help feeling a little chagrined. Such unnecessary attention to minor details went against his beliefs about command. Richard had never—

He stopped. *Richard was never in good graces,* he thought. *Maybe he shouldn't be my role model.*

"Nav officers," he ordered. "The commodore has given her order. I want to see a clean entry and a timely exit."

Their entry into the Slipgate thirteen minutes later was

almost textbook. But a last-moment acceleration to compensate for a tiny delay caused them to revert in Tor space nineteen seconds earlier than ordered.

Commodore Vandu wasted no time in comming the Torrent and letting them know they had failed.

———

DANIS THREADED her F-31G through a hundred Blue ships. Her rail-guns stuttered kinetic trails of destruction as one Swarm fighter after another spewed energy before they exploded. She killed them one after another, counting on luck and enemy stupidity to allow her to live another few seconds—

The canopy glowed brilliantly white, then went dark. She sat in that darkness until her KILLED announcement appeared, along with her kill totals and resource expenditures. Fuel was high, I think, she mused. I'll check that against the spec sheet. Ammo is expected, kills...

Twenty-seven.

Seven minutes and three seconds into the simulation, she'd only downed twenty-seven in a target-saturated environment.

Her canopy lifted to show Heloise outside. "I know it was bad," Danis said, avoiding criticism from the fashion antique. "This wasn't my best run. Let me try again."

"You did well," Heloise said. "I altered the difficulty rating to fifteen. Your heart rate stayed steady, your reactions were natural, no overcompensation. Many people lose their fine control when surprised. You've made a good start. I expect you will do better tomorrow, after a good rest."

Danis hadn't heard so many words from her yet. But something was amiss. "How do you know all that?"

Heloise pointed to the side of the simulator. "All simulators have a bio status screen." Danis looked, and there was indeed a display on the simulator she hadn't noticed.

Heloise cocked her head, considering something. "You must be hungry. Go have dinner and wash up. We'll have an evening stretch to relax you for bed."

Danis's desire for a hot meal and a long hydro were immediately apparent. "Great idea," Danis said. "I think I'll grab dinner to go, and head back for a soak."

"Just the thing," Heloise said. "1900 hours, then."

Danis walked to the officer's mess. She ordered her meal: grilled guinea carbonado, and a side of butter-lentil soup. All high in protein and fat, just the thing for muscle mass and energy. She swiped her wristpad across the pay scanner and made her way to the door.

It opened, and Michael Jadern walked in.

Danis stopped. What's he doing here?

TORRENT'S BRIDGE

HALFWAY THROUGH THE SLIP, Jadern's shift ended. "Commander Ames, you have the conn," he ordered his helm officer, and excused himself. He felt oddly drained, as though this day had been more exhausting than any other. *I wasn't the captain then,* he thought. *Perhaps it's different when everything stops with you. I could always pass things to Richard if—*

He cut that thought off. There was no need to bring up Morian again.

He passed the captain's stateroom. He hadn't taken it as his own, and possibly never would. He wasn't a real captain yet. Besides, Richard had preferred to leave the room open for dignitaries—

Will I not be rid of that man's voice in my mind? Jadern thought as he swiped his wristpad across the door lock to his current quarters. It was a standard officer's berth, and he hoped that others noticed that he didn't feel himself above them. If this post was permanent, he needed the crew behind him.

Desquar's quivering lip came to mind. *There's one who won't vote for me,* he thought as he changed out of his uniform. He put on standard shipboards. They bore rank insignia, but they were more comfortable for dining. Attired, he headed to the officer's mess. He walked in to find a face too familiar by half. She jerked away as he recognized her.

"Danis? Danis Morian?" he asked incredulously.

"Michael," she said flatly, her voice betraying no emotion.

Wait, he thought. *Was that... fear in her eyes? Hope? Or something else?*

Her eyes traveled to his shoulder. "You're the captain of the ship?" she asked.

"Brevet Captain," he corrected her. "But... you didn't know this was my ship?" *And why didn't I know she was aboard?* he wondered.

"I was brought on board yesterday," she said. "I'm working with a trainer. She had me on the simulators all afternoon."

Her shipboards were baggy, sweat-stained. They looked like a flight suit at first. Now he noticed the hollow cheeks, shadows under her eyes. "Are you all right?" he said. "Do you need anything?"

"I'm recovering," she offered, nothing more.

As captain, he could order her... but this was Danis Morian. Conflicting loyalty and betrayal warred in his mind, but he composed himself.

"Well, good luck," he said. "I hope your recovery goes well."

"Thank you, Captain," she said, with a hint of irreverence, and pushed past him.

Heading to her bunk, he supposed. *She looks tired.*

His concern warred with the anger. She isn't her brother, he thought. She was used, like I was. He felt a kinship now. They had both been abandoned.

And he'd never distrusted Elio before. Maybe I'm finally shedding my naivete, he thought. But what better way to reconcile our feelings against them than by cementing a new relationship?

Something surged through him. It was perfect for the two of them to join: the ship's captain, the flight commander.

If everyone else was throwing rules to the void, why wouldn't he?

———

Torrent's Officer's Mess

Helot smiled.

She'd noticed Jadern's admiration for the Morian girl. It was no effort to pierce his mind and nudge that from attraction to lust. She almost laughed. Such a stalwart man, loyal and reliable, turned to his own base desires. A touch of betrayal, a hint of revenge, and Michael Jadern followed her song.

She left the mess. She had done enough today, between Danis's training and Jadern's new hunger, she deserved to open the '82 Aufeltz she had in her quarters.

Helot felt the One King's thought brush her mind. She tensed before she realized his approval. That feeling suffused her the entire evening.

———

CONFERENCE ROOM 1A
  Prica City Government Offices

ENOUGH OF THESE MISERABLE MEETINGS! Elio Lorne thought as he entered the fourth one of the day. He'd spoken to every semi-important functionary on Tor, each expressing remarkable gratitude. This was the price he paid for pushing himself onto the front lines.

He'd arrived on Tor. He'd had latent TK. He was also a PsyOp who had connected with a beautiful, dangerous, and utterly distracting pilot named Danis Morian. Then Richard had used that link to pinpoint the enemy Swarm and snatch the first victory.

Now Elio wanted to leave.

I will escape, he thought. *I will find Danis!*

Governor Graynir ambled over, shaking Elio's hand. "It's a pleasure seeing you again, my prince," he said quietly. "I have something to share, something urgent. But your shuttle has already requested departure. Are you leaving so soon?"

"It seems so," Elio murmured. He wanted to be away, and time was too short. "I wanted to finish my work here first. Don't be surprised if you receive an invitation shortly."

"I look forward to it," Graynir said. "Where am I going?"

"Ambassador?" a guard interrupted. "We are to report to the shuttle launch with all haste."

"Shouldn't I wait until the party dies down first?" Elio said, waving a hand across the room.

The guard glanced over a room full of murmuring bureaucrats. Some were sipping synth, and a few were arguing about some legal point.

"Blade Sergeant says not to wait," the guard ordered. "And I don't think they'll miss you. Sir."

"Then he won't mind if I finish this conversation later," Elio said. "Governor, you have my comm code? Contact me before we leave the system."

"We need to go now, sir." The guard touched Elio's arm, a not-subtle reminder of who ordered whom.

Elio shared a meaningful glance with the governor. "Then lead on," Elio said. "We won't keep the boss waiting." The guards escorted him to the shuttle, but his mind worked furiously.

I'm out of time, he thought. This has to be fast and perfect. Step one, finish the false halo contact. Step two, send the letters. Step three...

CHAPTER
TWENTY-FIVE

APPREHENSION
　"Rat Cellar"

Faxil was sitting with his sketchpad, trying to decide what to draw. But somebody had tried to get inside their hideout, and the grownups had captured him right away. All the commotion meant Faxil couldn't concentrate.

They'd tied the prisoner up in Ms. Verso's container. It had been the easiest to clean out. Just the bed, and a big rack of clothes. Ms. Verso had huffed a bunch and then stomped away in her sparkly red dress.

Maybe I could draw Ms. Verso... he thought. But the idea of drawing Ms. Verso, especially in her pretty dress, made Faxil feel weird inside again.

"Hi, Fax," Pinari said as she flounced into view.

"What was that walk?" Faxil asked. "And what are you wearing?"

Pinari was wearing a long shimmery green dress, down to her knees. Underneath, she was wearing her usual pants and sneakers. There were ruffles hanging down her arms and around her knees at the bottom. Every time she moved, the shimmery ruffles swung. Faxil had trouble not staring.

"Ms. Verso gave me this," Pinari said. "I mean, she gave her shirt to Mrs. Presdon two days ago, and she sewed it up like this."

"It's really pretty," Faxil said. A thought struck. "Could I... draw you?"

"Draw me?" Pinari looked nervous? Shy? "Um... how long?"

Faxil wasn't used to shy Pinari. "I don't know," he said. "Just sit down over there and I'll get started. Maybe I could finish it later, if you get tired."

"Yeah, sure," Pinari said, and sat down on a box. Faxil started to draw, but every time he glanced back up, Pinari was looking toward the prisoner's container.

She's just nervous about him, Faxil thought as he tried to get her shoulders right. She had very strong shoulders.

———

Outside Rat Cellar

Avrum Rosst approached Rat Cellar's decrepit warehouse. "I make no promises that you'll leave right away," he said once again.

Dr. Loko's wall-eyed glare was unnerving. "Let me explain myself," she said. "For four days, the people I've helped claimed a man with a metal arm was looking for one of my patients. I don't take threats like that lightly."

"Well," Rosst admitted, "this man was specifically looking for me."

"Is he a friend?" Dr. Loko asked.

"I assumed he was," Rosst said. "But if not, he's dangerous."

"Take me to your friends," she insisted. "I'm sure we'll get along fine."

She strode north, as Rosst instructed.

He shook his head. "Doctor?" he called after her. "You've gone too far."

She turned and found him motioning toward the warehouse. "You almost left me, didn't you?" she asked with a smile.

"Not almost," he defended himself. "I was merely considering your safety."

"Oh well," she said, "then no harm done. But next time you want to be inconspicuous, look at the building a few times. Facing the wrong direction is a dead giveaway."

He smiled and followed her into the warehouse.

FAXIL AND PINARI crouched behind some boxes near the prison container.

"When can we go back to drawing?" Faxil asked. "You said you just wanted a quick break."

Pinari sighed.

"Why do you keep doing that?" he finally whispered.

"Doing what?" she asked.

"That 'huh' noise," Faxil imitated. "You keep doing it."

"No, I don't," she said.

Faxil decided to approach this the smart way. "What do you think of the prisoner?" he asked.

"What?" she said. "I don't... I mean... hey, don't call him that."

"What should I call him?" Faxil countered. "He's a prisoner."

"Maybe he isn't bad," Pinari said.

"He broke into our secret hideout?" Faxil reminded her.

"Maybe he didn't know," she said. "It could be an accident."

"Kids?" Dad said from behind them, and they both jumped.

"Oh, Dad," Faxil said. "Um, we..."

"The difference between 'he didn't know' and 'he knew where to look' is that he still broke in," Dad said. "Security was breached after Rosst reported he was being tracked. We can't take that lightly. Either way, he knows where some of the fugitives are. If he goes free, we're in danger."

"But what if he's innocent?" Pinari demanded.

"At best, he's a thief," Dad said. "Lock and Verso haven't heard of him. His manners aren't from Geartown or Greasetown. Mr. Rosst is due back soon. Hopefully, he'll have answers. So... keep away from here, all right?"

"All right, Dad," Faxil said. Pinari murmured something that sounded agreeable.

As Dad walked away, Faxil said, "Well, I want to go get something to eat. You wanna come with me?"

"No," Pinari said. "I'll just... make sure he doesn't do anything."

"Suit yourself," Faxil replied, disappointed. He didn't know what her kiss meant, but he'd watched enough of her shows to know what sighing meant.

He glanced at the chrono. Passion's Flame was on. Pinari was missing it?

He heard her sigh again.

Fine, he thought. *If some stranger's more interesting than Equard's love for Merelda's sister, then she can have him.*

He stomped off toward the kitchen, only for the adults to rush past and open the door once again. Mr. Rosst walked in... with a woman?

Wait. Mr. Rosst has brought another intruder. He thought. "Where are we gonna tie her up?" he muttered. "It's getting crowded in here."

———

"...AND she insisted on coming with me," Rosst finished. "But I think she'll be useful."

"You think?" Dr. Loko said. "I think I'm gonna boot you out of your bed and make you sleep on the floor. Where do you sleep, anyway?"

"Across from him," Rosst laughed, pointing to Grig.

"Oh wow," she said, looking closer at Grig. "I thought you must have got up on the wrong side of the bed, but if you have to wake up looking at Avrum, it's no wonder."

"Ha!" Grig laughed. "Nice try, girlie. But you can't handle me."

"And Avrum can?" she replied.

"More than you'll ever know," Grig said, and walked away.

"Don't worry about Teyn," Verso said. "He's a bit stiff, but that was almost a compliment."

"Oh, really?" the woman asked. "What do the insults sound like?"

"Silence," Rosst said. "He uses silence and silent glares very well. And then there are the threats."

"I can't wait," she said. "Well, let's go see the patient."

"I'm afraid not, Dr. Loko," Deno said. "First, we need a discussion about why a highly paid surgeon works in a slum and follows fugitives home."

"If it makes you feel better, I supported the monarchy," Dr. Loko said. "At least until I became a black-market surgeon. Law Enforcement didn't make good friends."

"So you befriended fugitives?" Arthon Daire asked.

"I've never met a nicer bunch of Most Wanted," she

reported. "Unlike your prisoner, who has government IDs and beats people. People gossip."

"And you decided to check him out. Why?" Deno asked.

"I want to know why he was looking for me," she replied.

Rosst looked at Deno Avestan, who looked at Arthon Daire, who looked at Verso. They each gave a shrug of consent.

"All right," Rosst said. "I want him unconscious, I want his arm detached. He's exceedingly dangerous. Best to remove the obvious weapons."

———

JUDE STOOD IN A SHIPPING CONTAINER, his arms chained.

His mechanical arm could break the links. But his arms were bound to a single chain, looped through cargo rings on the ceiling. Any attempt to escape would pull his real arm out of socket.

Someone warned them. Veisti sprang to mind immediately. *Or her accomplices*, he thought. *Or someone I bribed. Charl wasn't the only cheat.*

A head poked around the door. "Hey, mister," a high-pitched voice said.

"Hello," he replied. "Who are you?"

The figure came further in. The bright light outside made details difficult. "I... wanted a closer look," the young girl said.

"I'm sorry," Jude said. "This is a misunderstanding." He felt bad lying to a child, but he needed to finish his mission.

"I knew it!" the girl said, her voice growing excited. "You wouldn't hurt us. But you can't leave yet. It's a secret. Okay?"

"I understand," Jude agreed. "I just need to see my friend."

"I heard Mr. Grig tell New Dad that you knew... I mean

Dad!" she corrected. "Don't tell him I said that. He's a nice dad."

Jude thought of Posie, trailing after her mother, and Tag running through the woods. He missed his son. "Are you adopted?"

"Yep," the girl said proudly. "My parents died two years ago. But my new mom, Inoiae, is a soldier, and she's off fighting the Blues, so we have to hide. And Ms. Verso says I need to be a proper girl, but she acts like the ladies on my shows, so I don't know what she wants to teach..."

Jude barely heard anything after that.

She's Inoiae's daughter, he thought. *Inoiae's family is in hiding. I'm here to kill the colonel in front of her children.*

But he felt the same drive to finish the mission. He should, but didn't, care about traumatizing children.

"What's wrong with me?" he whispered.

"Pinari!" a voice snapped. "Get away from him!"

The girl fled, and several adults blocked the light. It looked like Jude's soul, darkened by shadows he couldn't identify. One of them came closer.

"Hello there, sir," a chirpy voice greeted him. "I'm a doctor, and I'll give you a look over before we talk. The kind of look where—" Her hand shot forward, stabbing him in the neck with a needle. "—I administered some helpful chemicals! This is going to be fun, but not for you. Why were you hunting me?"

Jude parsed her words together. "Hunt... you? You... docker... white..."

"Doctor White? Hmm," she said. "That alias sounds really cool!"

Jude's mind slipped into the shadows.

———

"WHY'D YOU DO THAT?" Rosst demanded. "I didn't get a chance to talk to him."

"I told you," Dr. Loko said as she shone a light in the dim container. "He's been very aggressive. I'm not taking any chances."

Rosst peered closer at the captive. "This is Jude Cabeus," he said. "He's a soldier, and a TK. Did he say why he was hunting me?"

Dr. Loko inspected the mechanical arm as Deno replied, "We didn't give him time. We hustled him into the container and chained him. Then all he talked about was you."

"He wants to be here," Rosst said. "Or he wouldn't have let you do anything."

"You were lucky," Dr. Loko called. "This prosthesis is internally coupled to the socket. If it wasn't, he could have detached it and killed you all." The entire group turned toward her and stared. She stared right back. "What? I don't soften the blow. I say it like it is."

"I wonder what your patients think of your bedside manner," Rosst said.

"You mean, 'Be sure not to get to shot' kind of talk?" she cooed. Then her voice hardened. "You lose patience with your patients. Now, I need some tools." She rattled off a list of precision hand tools. "And hurry. The Solumnix I gave him is only good for an hour."

As Rosst left the container to look for tools, he glanced back. She stood there, imperious, controlled, examining a dangerous soldier with about the same concern he would give a field-stripped weapon.

He was seeing the real her for the first time, and she was impressive.

———

Office of Military Affairs
    Private Wing

"Sir?" Nila Dyens said. "We just lost signal to Operative Fist. Awaiting orders."

Marshal Marrion stroked his chin, pursed his lips. Nila was very familiar with his mannerisms. His son Wayn—now Operative Fist—had abruptly left their previous assignment together, and she had been reassigned to his scanner division for the last six years. Sometimes, his manner and charisma distracted her, though she'd managed to hide it. He was an impressive man.

"Why did we lose signal?" he asked.

"Vitals show an abrupt increase one hour ago, then returned to baseline," she reported. "They just dropped, indicating... sleep? Then we lost signal—" She hesitated. "Is he dead, sir?"

"Not sleep," the Marshal said after a moment's consideration. "Captured. Vitals spike. Restrained. Vitals stabilize. Then unconsciousness. Look:" He pointed to the moment before the vitals dropped. "A flutter upwards, then slowed. Probably drugged. And then either killed, or his arm removed."

"So what should we do, sir?" she asked again.

"He's a liability," Marshal Marrion said. "Whether or not he succeeded, someone dies."

He turned to Technician Bobel. "Initiate Closed Hand. Send the signal and whoever has him will reap the consequences."

Nila turned away. The Marshal was a hard man, and his decisiveness was part of the attraction. But she hadn't expected him to order Wayn's death so easily.

—

RAT CELLAR

"WELL, THAT WASN'T TOO COMPLICATED." Dr. Loko hefted the metal arm like a trophy. "That wasn't an internal lock, just someone who didn't want it to come off."

"Cabeus couldn't have removed it?" Rosst asked.

"Unlikely," Dr. Loko confirmed. "And I have other questions. Have you linked up your sensor packages yet, Avrum?"

"I've only started the base level," he admitted.

"I want spectral scans," she said. "My eyes are top-resolution civilian models, but they don't have sensors. This arm is confusing me, and I hate that." She started disconnecting the outer plates. "And what's this thing?" she added, pointing.

Rosst recognized it from his briefings on TK-criminal restraints. "That's an inhibitor. Someone didn't want him using TK? How very odd."

Dr. Loko started removing the inhibitor. "Sounds like a handy thing. Let's weld it to a nice collar for him."

"We can't weld that," Rosst said.

"Whatever," Dr. Loko dismissed with a wave of her hand. "When will you scan this?"

Rosst brought up his menu and found vision enhancements. "Where should I look?" he asked.

"Why does it have two power supplies?" she asked, pointing to the square black box hidden beneath the upper pistons and armatures. "See? Identical," she added, pointing to a second box in the forearm.

Rosst blinked through different modes of vision. "Infrared shows the forearm isn't warm," he said. "Magnetic induction doesn't show power. Back-scatter X-ray..." he frowned. "The upper arm power pack has... parts inside, metals, wires. The forearm is... a block. I get no reading."

"Shielded by metal?" she asked.

"No, it's like..." he tried to find a description. "A sponge, or cake, or whipped paste. There's texture, but no parts." His brain tried to pull an answer from that description from...

Something lit up his enhanced vision. Then it beeped. A very familiar beep.

"It's a bomb!" he yelled.

CHAPTER
TWENTY-SIX

ARROGATE
Monere District, Som Orsi

Meera sat at her dining table, reviewing the vids she'd received.

She'd spent the last week hunting down the Perplexity Puzzles. Grainy capture vids weren't enough. She wanted to see the real ones. She curated from lists on the network only the ones of the Battle of Som Orsi. If she studied those, she was certain to understand the people making them.

Meera couldn't describe why. And it had nothing to do with Klaus. There were several, even though she and Klaus hadn't been with the main group.

We were killing some sort of Imperator knockoff instead, she thought.

Thinking about Klaus was getting dangerous, and she was realizing her reactions weren't appropriate, and she was perilously close to forgiving him.

She'd shoved him on the Avenger shuttle. And the Avenger never came back.

"It wasn't my fault," she whispered. "I didn't know. I just wanted to get... It wasn't my fault."

But what if it was?

"It doesn't matter," she mumbled. "If I'd been on the Avenger, then we'd both be gone. I'm here, with my family, and that's all that matters."

But what about Klaus's family? she wondered. All they have left is the traitor's mark on his record.

She reached for her wristpad, but then she stopped. She'd been warned not to contact former teammates. While the prissy-faced commander probably hadn't expected her to visit anybody's family, he might wreak havoc on her family. And baby Stevian flashed before her eyes again.

After Sorge's death, she'd stopped using her wristpad. She couldn't bear the temptation to watch the vids of him. When she finally reclaimed that wristpad, she'd given the new one to Lifia, who hadn't used it since.

She removed her wristpad and retrieved the blank one from the drawer of forgotten things. It connected to the nerve couplings on her arm and lit up, displaying first-time data. It still had basic search functionality, but if she used it here the search would be traced to her address.

I think I know someone who might be willing to help. She tapped a comm code.

"Hey," she said when Finia answered, "wanna meet at the Afternoon Tease?"

———

AFTERNOON TEASE
   Esse, Som Orsi

. . .

"I CAN'T BELIEVE THIS." Finia took a long drink of her Laufi Sunset. "I came out here for juicy gossip, and you want me to help you find your ex-boyfriend's mom's comm code? You, my friend, are so very gimp."

"Look, I have my reasons," Meera said. "I'm not... gimp." What does that word mean, anyway? "But if I go looking for it myself, it might attract attention," Meera finished.

Finia gave her a look. "Okay, fine, I believe you. What am I searching for?"

"His name was, is, Klaus Brekan," Meera said. "He was stationed aboard the Peacemaker during the Battle for the Slipgates."

Finia searched for those details. "It says he's dead." She showed Meera the death notice.

"His ship went rogue and disappeared," Meera said, defensively. "Is there anything else?"

"I'm not getting much," she said. "Just a few official announcements. 'Paucus Par celebrates Klaus Brekan... determination... joining the TK Guardians.' After medical discharge—"

"Does it say anything about his medical discharge?" Meera asked.

"Not this one," Finia muttered. "Um, 'Paucans welcome hero home... fought against the alien menace... mother Enith Brekan asks that well-wishers let him adjust...'"

"What else about his mother?" Meera interrupted.

"Will you stop that?" Finia's large earrings flashed darkly as she shook her head. "I hate it when people do that! It's so annoying."

"I'm sorry!" Meera said. "I just can't do it myself, and everything makes me want to look up something else." She saw Finia adding Enith Brekan to the list.

The first result was a death notice, dated just after Avenger left the system.

"Um, other family?" Meera asked quietly as several people came in the cafe doors.

Instead of complaining, Finia simply shrugged. "There's a couple of Brekans listed, no direct relation. No announcements related to Klaus or Enith except a state funeral service. His medical discharge gets no mention why, except that he spent three months at Seabreeze Medical for observation..." Finia tapped that into her search. "Oh. Seabreeze isn't a hospital. It's psychological rehab."

Meera tried to wrap her head around everything she'd learned. Klaus had no living family. Klaus had been mentally traumatized and put through psych evaluation before returning to civilian life, then reenlisting a few months later.

"He never seemed traumatized," Meera said. "He was just... goofy and pushy sometimes. He wouldn't take no for an answer. I gave him every chance, but... he never seemed to take it seriously. He never wanted to talk about his service time. I thought it was because of Sorge..."

"Meera, sweet darling," Finia said, "everything you just said sounds like 'traumatized.' Maybe he really liked you, but ignoring recent events, insisting on his way, joking at bad times. I think he must have been hurting pretty bad."

Meera couldn't find words. Conveniently, someone walked up to their table holding what looked like a... warrant?

"Good afternoon Meera Seleure, Finia Mell," the man said in a strangely nasal voice.

"Who are you?" Finia demanded. "And how did you know our names?"

"My name is Adiro Estar, and I needed your names to file this arrest warrant," the man said, flourishing a paper to the table. At the top it claimed "Warrant of Arrest," with "Meera Pelic Seleure" highlighted further down in the text. And then a second one bearing the same title as "Finia Hurn Mell" below that.

"What is this about, sir?" Meera asked politely.

"Meera Seleure," he announced, "you are charged with collusion with member or members of former units, in violation of the plea agreement you signed."

"I am not!" Meera exclaimed. "I never served with Finia. I don't even know what her job was. We met at—"

"While Ms. Mell's involvement is troubling," he replied, "you are also attempting to contact Klaus Brekan, whom you did serve with."

"How is looking up his mother the same thing?" Finia argued.

"Not my problem," the man said. "Either come quietly, or you will be restrained."

Meera looked at Finia, who looked at Meera.

"If we don't make a scene," Meera said, "it should be easier to get you free."

"Me?" Finia said. "What about you?"

Meera carefully glanced around the restaurant. The people she had noticed coming in were soldiers in civilian clothes, stationed around the room. The cafe was a box trap.

"I'm going to cooperate fully," she said. "Because I want to see my kids again."

———

RISING TIDES GROUP Psychiatric Facility

LANCE-SERGEANT DASCHER BIKK looked at the chrono. Five minutes until guard change. "Finally," he grumbled. "Except for that weird prisoner coming in, today was as dull as... an old knife."

"That phrase was underwhelming, sir," Linny remarked.

"Whatever! Metaphors aren't my strong suit," Bikk replied.

"Apparently not, since that was a simile," Linny said.

"Shut it," Bikk ordered. "Shift change in four minutes. Clean up and sparkle, so we can go home."

"Sparkle, sir?" Nejaz said.

"Someone's showing up this afternoon," Bikk said.

"Says who?" Nejaz asked.

"Says Nunya Bizness," he replied. He saw no need to reveal his source. They had a date tomorrow night. "We want to look like we paid attention all day, instead of shooting math dice."

"Seems pretty unlikely they'll show during the guard change," Linny said.

"Now I can really expect something to go horribly wrong," Bikk retorted.

Two minutes later, Bikk was proven right. The shift change came in, accompanied by two officers and three science types. They were dressed like civilians, but Bikk knew they were here for the prisoner.

"Before you go home," one of the officers said, "These gentlemen want to ask your squad members a few questions."

Bikk managed not to sigh. *I should kick Linny. He jinxed us.* "I'll answer your questions," he said carefully. "As their superior, it's my responsibility."

"They might add valuable insights," one scientist said. "Who knows what details are pertinent?"

Bikk wanted to curse. *They can't add anything, they spent the whole day gambling!* But he couldn't say that.

"Can you tell us anything the new patient said or did today?" the scientist asked, already tapping at his wristpad.

"The prisoner remained calm and silent," Bikk said truthfully. "She never spoke to anyone, not even the guard."

"Well, she wasn't shy to the police!" another scientist joked. "She swore punishments on them. It's in his report."

"Shut up, Jurgins!" the other scientist complained. "You'll taint their testimonies!"

"Ahem!" the first scientist said. "Second, did anyone notice... unusual behavior from the pris— I mean, patient?"

"I already said she was calm—" Bikk began.

"I meant eating habits or ablutions," the scientist said curtly. "Strange movements or exercises?"

"Nothing," Bikk said.

The scientist looked at the guards behind him. "What about any of you? Did anyone else watch the patient today?"

He heard a general muttering of "Well, yeah," and "Of course, and nothing happened." He stifled a groan.

"This is premature," Jurgins said. "We'll review the footage tonight, and—"

"I'm not watching security footage all night!" the third scientist complained. "I have a reservation at Nescire Dijen—"

"Um," Bikk heard Linny say. "Is that the kind of weird thing you want to look at?"

———

FOREIGN SAT IN ITS PRISON, overjoyed at being in the presence of its minions.

It could feel each one, just like on Odin. The human vessel diminished its senses, but they were so close now. Foreign had discovered the sensation of wrapping itself in a soft blanket. It felt comfort again and armed with the means to finish its mission.

I am too human, Foreign thought. It enjoyed food. It drew comfort from objects and minions. It would conquer the world to eat pastries. *These are all human desires. If I desire human things, what am I?*

But they weren't just human desires it felt. It was a deep appreciation for human accomplishments. The Will could conjure anything it desired. Foreign had experienced wilderness, had proved how hard humans worked to accomplish... almost anything. And human food showed their ingenuity in common tasks.

But I must complete my mission, Foreign thought. *I cannot be swayed by these distractions.*

It must destroy this planet's ability to wage war. Once that was accomplished, Foreign would control the computer networks, and reign here until the Will burned it. This wasn't Foreign's purpose, but the Will would triumph.

And Foreign would, too.

It reached into the facility's computers connected to the military base, and Foreign easily reached inside the military network, disabling anything that could hinder its progress. From there it spread to every military computer on the planet.

The process had taken seconds. Foreign was now the most powerful entity on Caerus. It merely thought the command, the cell door opened, and it stepped into the light.

———

BIKK, Nejaz, and everyone else turned to the monitors. The new patient's cell stood wide open. The patient walked out, and suddenly other patients appeared next to her.

"Interesting!" Jurgins said. "How does this compare to the usual behavior?"

"Sound the alert!" Bikk ordered. "Linny! Contact Lieutenant Pasdar. Tell him we have a Code One-Zero-Five!" He pushed past the scientists and started tapping out commands on his console.

The controls were unresponsive.

"I don't understand," Linny was saying behind him. "All base communications are cut off."

"This isn't necessary—" one of the scientists was saying.

"The blazes it isn't!" Bikk snapped at him. "This is a break-out!" He grabbed the intercom mic. "Attention all Rising Tide Personnel! We have a Code One-Zero-Five! I need all on-duty guards to arm themselves and report to the common areas now!"

———

FOREIGN'S MINIONS were on the catwalk, singing its praises. It took a long time to teach humans to sing in a proper language. Binary wasn't as elegant as the Will's trinary, but it was a start.

And this was the end.

"Come!" it announced, for the humans' sake. "We go to fulfill our purpose!"

Minions scrambled from every level, joining Foreign in a massive throng. Guards appeared, brandishing weapons. But they had been complacent for too long and there were too many minions. Foreign smiled as minions seized the guards, stealing their weapons and beating the guards helpless.

Go into every corner, Foreign commanded. Find every weapon. Subdue every human. Let none escape!

CHAPTER
TWENTY-SEVEN

DESPERATION
Ataraxis's Guest Quarters

The guards marched Elio to his quarters as soon as he walked down the shuttle ramp. Now he was flanked only by a pair of guards, both recruits. Per Blade Sergeant's rotation schedule, their sergeant was patrolling the hall. With little else to do, Elio picked up his datapad and set to work.

His first task was to finish the false letters to Graynir and Carrica. Once they were complete, Elio placed his halo on his head.

Elio was constructing a new halo identity: his antithesis. He'd used publicly available holo images to render a virtual construct. He didn't neglect the surroundings. He knew the necessary decorations after perusing the ship's archives. The background only needed to pass muster for a few minutes. He used a waveform analyzer to copy the voice he needed; it should be enough to fool one man for five minutes.

There was a tap on his shoulder. Startled, he resisted the

urge to clear his interface; no one else could see it. He lifted the halo just enough to break the nerve connection.

"Yes?" Elio asked the guard.

"You've been on there for a while," the guard informed him.

"I'm researching Sterium," Elio replied. "We're heading there next."

The guard looked skeptical. "We're supposed to restrict your communications."

"I'm not communicating. See?" Elio pulled up connection information on his wristpad. "Everything is local interface, or from ship archives." He made a note to alter the history. Blade Sergeant might be able to guess something from the data. The guard stepped away and let Elio continue working.

It took twenty minutes, but Elio cobbled the avatar and background together. Then, hoping it would hold together long enough, he sent the messages to Graynir and Carrica. Then he spent five minutes removing his searches and replaced them with Sterium and their foibles.

He had to hope that Carrica or Graynir didn't question the messages. With any luck, they should pass any filters and send him back to Caerus.

They held Rosst and Grig as hostages to my good behavior, Elio remembered darkly. *But their vids quickly repeated themselves. Either they're safe, or they're dead. But if the Regency isn't flaunting Danis in front of me, she's in danger. I won't let them stop me!*

"Sir, are you listening to me?" the guard demanded. "Or are you deaf, too?"

Elio removed his halo and stood to face the guard. The guard had changed. This one was perhaps twenty-five, uniformed as Blade Sergeant would expect; a real soldier, not a recruit. But Elio gave him the most withering look of condemnation he'd ever learned from his father.

"When I was your age," Elio snapped, "men and women in that uniform protected me from assassination. Four lost their lives doing so. When you are ready to die honorably as they did, you will have earned the right to speak to me like that." The guard opened his mouth, but Elio glared until the man backed down.

But Elio knew that when the time came for him to escape, these guards would not be slow on the trigger so he would need another plan.

One step at a time, he thought. *Som Orsi wasn't built in a day.*

―――――

Ataraxis's Bridge

CAPTAIN BHOR CARRICA watched the star-field shift as Ataraxis lifted out of planetary orbit and Tor quickly become a colorful disc among the stars instead of the dominating feature.

At least our time here was short, Carrica mused. I didn't need any more reminders of the old days.

He'd met Pieda here. She was a refugee on Tor after the Swarm attacked. He'd served aboard the Stalwart, ferrying relief supplies. She'd stolen his heart, and he'd swept her away to Caerus. Six months later, he was First Officer aboard the Ataraxis. A nice, peaceful post while he started his family.

The fighting came to Caerus four years later. Now, his family was still buried in the rubble.

Carrica had sudden episodes of "incompetence," and had been on a short list for discharge. But then he'd met a lieutenant commander, working for a marshal he'd never heard of, who asked him to join the Redemption Unit. His record would be fixed in exchange for fulfilling a few extra "special duties." In a moment of uncertainty, he'd accepted.

"Sir, you have a communique," the comms officer announced.

He snapped to attention. "A communique? From Tor?"

"No, sir," she replied. "It's from Caerus."

"Send it here," he ordered, and his readyboard lit up. He expected something from Marshal Morrison, but instead of the Office of Military Affairs, it was the Regency Council's new sigil.

"What is this?" he murmured as the elaborately graphed data scrolled out before him.

> *Whereupon it behooves our noble personages to meet with members of the governments we do support, thus we hereby request a meeting with GOVERNOR RAYMAR GRAYNIR in a closed session to discuss matters of state.*
> *CAPTAIN BHOR CARRICA is thus ordered to provide transportation for GOV. GRAYNIR at the earliest convenience and will offer all the amenities of his diplomatic ship, The ATARAXIS, and deliver GOV. GRAYNIR to our noble person forthwith, and exercise the utmost discretion in this endeavor concerning any concurrent military duties and orders from this council. Signed and sealed on this day..."*

There was a comm code at the bottom, with scrawled signatures and pages of official justifications for their decision, but Carrica had only one question.

Why?

His orders had been very specific: keep Elio Lorne away from Caerus. What had changed?

. . .

"Sir, vessel approaching," the Sensors officer called. "A shuttle-class, seven to twelve passengers only. The Forthright, registry number 0901-5B. It's broadcasting official government codes."

"We have a hailing call," Comms announced. "Shall I put it on speaker?"

"No," Carrica replied. "To my station."

The call appeared immediately, and Carrica held the earpiece to his head.

"—is Governor Graynir's shuttle Forthright, requesting docking clearance. We have received official documentation requesting the governor's presence—"

"How did they get off the elevator so quickly?" he murmured. Cursing the sudden change, he tapped the transmission control. "Shuttle Forthright, you are cleared to land in Hangar Bay Two. Please wait until a delegation comes to greet you."

He waited through their official acknowledgments, cut the signal and trembled. What would this do to his orders? Or his promised redemption? What would the blade sergeant say?

He imagined the man's temper was dangerous. The meek didn't rise to that rank. And he was certainly prejudiced against the ambassador.

But this looks so official! he thought.

So he did the only thing he could. He tapped the comm code at the end of his new orders. Hopefully, someone on the other end could straighten this out. He'd like to keep his career and his immediate health.

———

ATARAXIS'S GUEST Quarters

• • •

Elio pretended to continue working, but he couldn't concentrate. His messages were out, and he could only wait for his plan to bear fruit or be plucked and crushed underfoot.

There was a knock on his stateroom door. The guard glanced at the annunciator, then Blade Sergeant walked into the room.

Is this my arrest? Elio wondered. Instead, he said, "I didn't expect you this afternoon. You normally accompany Squad E."

"I despise predictability," Strike Sergeant said. "If you'd paid closer attention, I've watched you three times today."

Three times? Elio repeated to himself. *But no accusations yet.* Blade Sergeant seemed unaware of Elio's plan. But when would he receive his comm contact? And when would Blade Sergeant suspect something?

Elio's wristpad vibrated silently. He'd set it so the guards wouldn't immediately be alerted.

I guess this is the moment, Elio thought as he reached for his halo.

"What are you doing, 'Ambassador?'" Blade Sergeant asked as Elio picked it up.

"Just taking a call," Elio replied.

"From who?" the sergeant demanded.

"It must be Governor Graynir," Elio said easily. "He wanted to continue our conversation."

Blade Sergeant looked at the guards. One of them nodded.

"You have fifteen minutes," Blade Sergeant growled. "Be done by then."

Elio bit back a response. He slid the halo on and found himself facing Captain Carrica.

But Captain Carrica was not facing Elio. "Duke Rutta! What a surprise," Carrica blurted to Elio's avatar. "Of all the people I thought... I mean, I had no idea it—"

"I have no time for babbling," Elio replied in his best Rutta voice. "Why have you contacted me?"

"Sire, I have done as you requested, carrying... the Ambassador on his missions," Carrica replied carefully. "But I've just received your message, and the governor's shuttle has already docked. I'm to return to Caerus?"

Elio wondered about that pause, but he couldn't ask. "Returning briefly," Elio-as-Rutta scoffed. "Though I'd like that royal pipsqueak off planet, I need you to deliver the governor—"

"My lord?" Carrica interrupted. "Didn't you say... um..."

"Spit it out, man!" Elio ordered.

"Elio Lorne isn't a royal, sire," Carrica finished.

Elio kept from cursing. "Thirty years I've called him that!" he pretended rage instead. "Who are you to correct me?"

Carrica's eyes glinted, even in the sim, and Elio wondered if he'd pushed the charade too far. But the captain only said, "I will deliver the governor in all haste. Did you have any instructions about the Ambassador?"

"No, leave him be. In fact," Elio added, "if Graynir wishes to visit, let him. He trusts the brat. Pricus has been slacking on taxes anyway. Either it will improve matters, or Graynir will prove himself a traitor. A win either way."

Carrica stood silently, as if waiting for some sign of dismissal.

"Well, go on!" Elio ordered. "Get the governor out of the system before 1700."

"Aye, milord," Carrica said with a salute, and vanished.

Elio's eyes shifted from the sim to the light of his rooms. His halo was gone—

Blade Sergeant stood over him, Elio's halo dangling from his finger.

"I warned you to be quick," Blade Sergeant rumbled. "Did you finish your call with the governor?"

"No, I didn't," Elio replied truthfully. He reached for the halo.

"Good," Blade Sergeant said. He stepped back before Elio's hand could reach. "I don't think you need this for a while."

Blade Sergeant's wristpad bleeped, and he glanced at it, then glared. Elio's Psy caught a flash of rage. Carrica and some old crone Elio didn't recognize...

And... Drella?

He grabbed that image, but it faded as the blade sergeant stormed out. Drella was next door, bound and gagged.

And it was his fault.

Elio's TK flexed against his limiters. He could push hard enough to rescue Drella, but then what? Guards knocked unconscious, the ship on alert, Blade Sergeant hunting him down with uninhibited TK.

He just needed to wait. He needed to—

His door opened.

Elio blinked. None of the guards had—

Stun blasts rained in, striking the guards along the walls. The other two immediately drew close to Elio, though he noticed their weapons were not pointed at the door, but at him. A dozen armed men—in Pricus City colors!—stormed inside, weapons raised. And behind them was Governor Graynir.

"By the authority vested in me by the government of the Orso Kingdom, I demand you release Ambassador Lorne from custody," Graynir demanded.

"Elio Lorne stays right here," the guard insisted. "And our orders come from higher than yours. If Lorne tries to escape, we're to—"

Elio's TK push knocked them into opposite walls, where the Pricans stunned them.

"How did you get here so fast?" Elio asked Graynir as he got up from his desk.

"You said to be ready," Graynir replied. "My shuttle was orbiting at three hundred klicks. And then I received a message from Caerus. I assume that was yours?"

"A bit of trickery on my part," Elio admitted.

"Humility serves you well, my prince," Graynir said. "Now, why in the blazing stars didn't you just escape before?"

"Short version? I didn't have a good plan then," Elio said as he stood. "Longer one? It started with hostages and got worse. I refuse to climb stairs of blood to claim my throne."

"It's still your throne," Graynir said. "And I have the evidence."

"I'm happy to look at it," Elio said. "But you're going to rescue Drella next door. I'm going to take over the ship."

"But how can you take over the entire ship by yourself?" Graynir asked.

"There's only one person in my way," Elio replied. "I'll just ask him nicely."

———

DRELLA DIDN'T KNOW how long it had been since her last blackout. She'd been beaten with TK and rifle stocks and then drugged. After that, she became very disoriented.

Now, her head was pounding and her eyes felt puffy. She was hungry and thirsty, and the silence stirred new fears in the recesses of her mind.

That silence was broken by a resounding thump that rattled the wall.

She jerked upright as she heard the whine of stun blasts. After another minute or so, a fuzzy light appeared. She tried turning her head to see, before realizing that her eyes were swollen shut.

"Look at her," an unfamiliar voice said. "That's what they do to people who help him?"

"None of that!" snapped a voice laden with authority. Not like Blade Sergeant's, but power and compassion. "Anyone who beats their own like this should be court-martialed. I'll see to that. Jenes, break out the med-kit and stop that swelling. I want her walking in five minutes."

"Who... who are you?" she rasped, her throat parched.

He must have understood, because he replied. "I'm Elio's friend, and I'm here to get you to safety."

"No," she blurted out, still dry and hoarse. "I need to help him. I'm... his—"

"He'll be fine," Elio's friend said. "Have a drink."

Drella felt a water bulb touch her lips, and she drank greedily.

CHAPTER
TWENTY-EIGHT

SHOWDOWN
Ataraxis's Enlisted Level

Elio ran.

He'd studied the destroyer's layout in-depth and he knew which elevators to take and he knew which ones would be watched. So he took the less direct route through the enlisted barracks.

He halted and pushed himself behind cover. There was a full squad of his guards in uniform heading for the elevator he'd just vacated.

I didn't know they bunked here! Elio thought as he glanced around. He yanked open the first unsecured door, the emergency pressure-suit storage. Shoving past the hanging suits, he closed the door just before his guards appeared.

"—you hear some—"

"—probably just—"

The voices were faint and passed quickly. Elio waited until they'd turned the corner. Then he pushed the door open and made for the bridge.

"That was too close," he muttered to himself. It was obvious the Ataraxis couldn't bunk twenty-five marines on one small troop deck. He should also have kept track of the guard changes. They would reach his room and the alarm would sound.

Elio summoned the elevator to the bridge and stepped inside. Every moment he rode in the elevator felt like an hour. The weeks of playing ambassador hadn't helped his physique.

When the doors opened, he found the blade sergeant on the bridge, arguing with Captain Carrica.

"I spoke with him!" Captain Carrica said. "I'm telling you, it was Duke Rutta, and he ordered—"

"I don't care what he said!" Strike Sergeant bellowed. "You don't take orders from him; you take orders from me!"

"Forgive me," Elio called out. "Since when does a captain take orders from an enlisted sergeant?"

All heads swiveled toward him. Elio caught his breath as the blade sergeant glared at him.

"For that matter, are you even enlisted?" Elio asked, as pieces fell into place. "You wear no name tag. You don't introduce yourself. Yet everyone knows who you are, and everyone believes you because you're a Psy."

For the first time, the blade sergeant's face broke out into a genuine smile. "Finally. Someone with brains in this entire kingdom. Having TK blinds everyone to the obvious, because no one has two powers, do they, Elio?"

Blade Sergeant pushed everyone away, leaving a clear path between him and Elio. "Nobody will remember this except me. My superior will wipe everything away."

After weeks of abuse from this man, Elio could finally ask him the question. "If you hate me so much," Elio said, "why not just kill me?"

"You see, kid, I've got orders," he said, his voice changing to something... almost casual. "You were a tool to take over your government. We have forces removing every person who can't be controlled. We failed at Regis Magnum, but everything's in place now."

"You're with the Dawn Fan?" Elio asked, confused.

"I'm so much higher than the Dawn Fan!" he laughed. "I'm the One King's Red Knight, and he will rule."

A TK blow sent Elio flying. Elio's own TK cushioned his landing. He fell into a combat stance.

"Enough talk," the Red Knight laughed. "Let's fight."

———

Ataraxis's Guest Quarters

Drella was holding a cold compress over her eye when the drugs hit. She went from tired to alert in thirty seconds. Her aches and pains began to fade. She stood, her legs still shaky.

"Now, how many crew are loyal to Elio?" the friendly man asked, "and how many are against him?"

"The captain follows orders," Drella said, dabbing her other eye. "I don't know about the bridge crew. The original guards are from Caerus, like me. Three or four of us are on his side, but all the new recruits are the blade sergeants. They don't have armor; just uniforms."

"Good information," the friendly man said. "We need to remove them from the field immediately."

"Sure," she said. She reached for the door. "Wait," she realized. "Who are you all?"

"I'm Raymar Graynir, governor of the planet Tor," he said. "Prince Elio saved my world. I'm returning the favor."

They stepped out of the room and found six guards waiting at Elio's door.

"Simond is escaping!" one of the recruits shouted and reached for his wristpad. A stun blast took him down.

"Listen!" Drella said. "The blade sergeant is not who we think he is. We have to stop him! Some of these men are loyal to Elio." She turned to them and said, "Who will join us?"

"I will," said the visored sergeant. She wasn't certain who it was—

"Fire!" the governor shouted. A flurry of stun blasts took down the others before she could ask the guard his name.

"Why did—" she began.

"They didn't join," Graynir replied. "You!" he ordered the visored guard. "Open the door and shove them inside and lock it down. Drella, take us to the barracks."

"Wait, we need him," Drella said as she helped shove the stunned recruits in Elio's room. Only then did the soldier take off his visor.

It was Hanson.

"I was worried about you," he whispered. "I'm really glad you're safe."

Drella tried not to blush. "We need you to open the other barracks," she said. "Follow us!"

———

ATARAXIS'S BRIDGE

THE RED KNIGHT GESTURED, and dozens of small objects hurtled at Elio. With his limited power, Elio was able to deflect most of them. But then the objects came faster and faster; some he was able to deflect, some he missed until finally, in a burst of rage, Elio mentally struck at the light panel above the Red Knight's head. The Red Knight changed focus to deflect the debris, and Elio used the distraction to smash every piece of the Red Knight's ammunition into a tiny ball.

"Impressive," the Red Knight mocked as he began firing TK shots at Elio. The invisible blows felt like rocks striking his body. He tried to create a TK shield, but it was too weak, and he was pelted on all sides.

"You don't know how to fight, do you?" the Red Knight laughed. "Didn't you run a school for the TK Knights? What weaklings they must have been!"

"Why call yourself a Knight?" Elio asked as he tried to guess his opponent's attacks. "Are you mocking the Knights I created?"

"Mocking?" the Red Knight laughed as another dozen shots struck Elio's body. "The One King created his knights more than a decade ago when the first Swarm ship came out of the Inherence and he took them all down! Then he began to—"

"The first Swarm attack was six years ago!" Elio countered, throwing a surprise attack that the Red Knight easily blocked.

"You fool! The Swarm destroyed an entire planet!" The Red Knight crushed Elio's shield, and the blows pelted him. "The One King defeated them! And the One King will stop them now, since you nobles won't deprive yourselves to aid the masses!"

Suddenly, the blows ended and before Elio could capitalize, an invisible hand grabbed him and hauled him across the room to a spot just in front of the red.

And the Red Knight grinned at him in triumph.

———

ATARAXIS'S ENLISTED Level

. . .

DRELLA LED the governor's troops to the enlisted barracks. She pointed out the doors where her comrades slept. It only took a wave of her wristpad to open the doors. The recruits were stunned in their beds, and the few Caerus guards that were left happily joined the Pricans.

But when she got to Lowen's room, he was nowhere to be found. Neither was Sergeant Complainer, nor Sergeant Sidray, who was still supposed to be convalescing in his room.

"We're missing the three I'm most worried about," she told Graynir.

"You four, check the communal hydro down the hall," Graynir ordered his men. "You four, check the mess hall. Take Hanson with you to identify the recruits." Nine people sped off to do the governor's bidding, leaving just two to protect Graynir and Drella.

"What about us?" she asked.

"We're going to the bridge," Graynir said. "If the prince needs backup, we're it."

"Wait a second," she said, and ducked into her own bunk. She unlocked her trunk and took out her sidearm, a DEW pistol. She checked the charge—almost 75%. "I'm ready," she said.

"Can you see well enough to shoot?" Graynir asked.

"Mostly," she replied.

Graynir gave her a slight nod, and they took off for the bridge.

Drella emerged from the elevator just in time to see Lowens and Sidray dash past. She took off behind them, Graynir's guards a full second behind her. She found the pair crouched by the bridge doors, aiming slug rifles. She burned two warning shots just above their heads.

"Drop your weapons!" she shouted. The men turned their heads. "Both of you, get down—!"

Someone attacked her from the side—Sergeant

Complainer! He'd hidden in the doorway just behind her. He wrenched the DEW away and pinned her arms from behind. "Let me go!" Drella shouted.

"You're taking shots at your own team, Simond!" he laughed. "Blade was right, you really are nuts!"

She glimpsed Graynir's guards arriving, but Complainer had too. He moved himself—and her—into their path. "Nope, you stop there," Complainer warned. "We'll deal with intruders as soon as we finish this internal matter. Put your weapons down or I hurt the girl."

"Girl!" Drella snapped. She stomped her boot down on his laces. "That's Sergeant to you, you pus-sucking traitor!" His grip relax slightly, and she jabbed an elbow into his solar plexus before smashing his nose with the back of her head. As she turned, she saw twin stun bolts take down Sidray and Lowens.

Complainer staggered back, and Drella swept her leg up in a powerful kick that caught him on the temple. Complainer's head bounced off the bulkhead before he sank to the floor.

Graynir finally caught up to them. The fight had taken only seconds.

"Good job," he told her, as he retrieved her pistol. "If you decide to leave your current job..."

Drella took her pistol and peered through the door onto the bridge. Elio was floating in front of the blade sergeant. She raised her pistol and aimed at his head.

For a brief moment the blade sergeant saw her, and she saw fear in his eyes.

———

"YOU REALLY ARE AN IDIOT," the Red Knight taunted Elio. "You could have left any time you wanted. Just kill a few guards and remove your restraints. You could have done anything you wanted."

"I did do what I wanted," Elio replied. "I saw what the Regency Council had wrought across my kingdom. If they'd done everything right, I'd have let them win the war. I never wanted to be king."

The Red Knight's focus shifted and his triumphant expression became one of fear as he saw Drella, and Elio struck. His TK blow slammed into the knight's face, and the invisible fist dropped Elio to his feet and his fist again slammed into the Red Knight in a bone-shattering uppercut.

The Red Knight was lifted off the ground from the force of the blow and crumpled to the floor unconscious.

"I've been trained to fight since I was seven," Elio said as he leaned down to rifle through the man's pockets. "But killing Blues is easier than killing humans.

He found the hash-encrypted security key that held his restraints. He pressed the key to his wrist restraints. They clicked open and fell to the floor. Next was his neck restraint, and finally the neural mesh circlet that inhibited his Psy.

For the first time in months, he could feel people around him, could understand the buzz of thoughts nearby. It was overwhelming, and he almost—almost—placed the circlet back on his head.

No, he thought. *This is part of me. This is what the people need right now. Not just purpose and strength but understanding as well.*

His Psy was immensely stronger than he remembered. He thought of all the days he'd strained against the circlet, trying to speak to others mind-to-mind. *I don't know how this is possible. Is it like exercising a muscle? I feel like I could control the entire ship if I wanted.*

And that was the danger. He'd thought he understood

such temptation before, but with his powers, he could command an army to do anything.

"Captain Carrica," he said. "Do you understand what this man admitted to? He isn't an Orso soldier. He used his powers to confuse people's minds. He works for an organization that wants to destroy us. If I ask you to serve Prince Elio Lorne, what will you say?"

The captain hesitated. "Ambassador—"

Elio didn't take that as a good sign.

"—I don't think you understand the situation, sir. I was... coerced into this... the Redemption Unit. I have orders, and if I don't follow them, they'll destroy what career I have left. I should have just resigned when I had the chance."

"When I take my rightful place—" Elio began.

"But you aren't there yet, sir. Respectfully," the captain added. "The Regency Council—"

"—will be lucky to keep their lives until next week," Governor Graynir's voice boomed across the bridge. He held up an information chip. "I have the proof right here. The entire Regency Council plotted to murder the king, depose the rightful prince, and put up a puppet. The boy's mother confessed to it all. I have the recordings, and I have the genetics files that show Targer Lorne was part of a second plot to flood the aristocracy with marriageable but illegitimate Lorne heirs."

"When I arrive on Caerus," Elio declared, "this information will be broadcast across the kingdom, on every receiver. And then I will take my throne by force of law and punish everyone involved in the plot."

"Will that be enough?" one of the officers called out. "What about the Redemption Unit?"

"Coercion isn't involvement," Elio clarified. "But those who created it and forced citizens to betray their own consciences will be brought to justice. And I see a place for this ship under my rule. You will all have a place here on Ataraxis. What say you all?"

From the series of smiles that broke out, Elio thought he had them convinced.

And now, he thought, *I just need to make all that happen.*

"Sir!" someone called out. "We have ships appearing in system from the Slipgate! Four capital ships led by the Tsunami."

CHAPTER
TWENTY-NINE

DAMAGES

JUDE FELT HIS THOUGHTS FOCUSING. He could hear people talking.

"—why does it have two power supplies?" he heard a woman say. He opened his eyes and saw the woman who'd stabbed a tranq in his neck.

"Infrared shows the forearm isn't warm," a man said, and Jude focused on him. Colonel Rosst! He was right outside, holding Jude's mechanical arm.

The arm that prevented his TK. He could feel all the tiny particles nearby that he could use as weapons. He wrenched the retaining pins from his shackle, and the cuff began to separate.

"Like sponge, or cake, or whipped paste..." Rosst was saying. Jude understood instantly. Spongy paste perfectly described pyrominxe, a chemical explosive commonly called shatterstone.

There was a block of shatterstone, and Jude heard the activator beep.

"It's a bomb!" Rosst yelled.

Jude had only one thought: Kill the targets!

The bomb could take out Rosst in a blink. Whoever the bomb didn't kill would be distracted, allowing him to kill Grig. It was a perfect plan.

A plan that would kill children. Inoiae's children.

Jude panicked. He used TK to fling the arm as far from his prison as possible. It needed to clear their little community—

The bomb exploded, and the force of the blast slammed the container doors shut.

He was trapped in darkness.

———

SOMEONE YELLED, "BOMB!" and Faxil turned to look. He couldn't help himself.

The explosion was brighter and louder than anything ever. Something struck his chest, and he was thrown backwards, and landed hard on the concrete floor.

Then the fire rushed past, but he could barely see it, because his view was blocked by Pinari on top of him.

"Hey, Fax," she grunted, and rolled off. "Ouch!"

"You okay?" Faxil asked, scrambling to his knees.

Pinari rolled onto her stomach, revealing her blackened, smoldering dress. Faxil tried to pull it away.

"What are you doing... ow!" Pinari screamed.

"Your dress is on fire!" Faxil said.

"Get off!" she snapped, but then she sat up and yanked it off. "What about my back?" she asked.

Faxil looked. Her undershirt was crinkly and brown in a few spots. "Um, it's not on fire," he said.

Pinari looked at the ruined dress. "Sorry, Ms. Verso," she said. "Your shirt was nice."

Faxil glanced around. Things were on fire, and the air was getting smoky. But then he heard a screechy metal noise from Mr. Grig's house. It was turned over!

Faxil ran over and found Dad and Mr. Rosst trying to open the container door. Mr. Rosst screamed and let go, but Dad didn't.

"Dad!" he yelled and ran to help.

"Stay away, Faxil!" he shouted back. "It's too hot! You'll get burned!"

Faxil stayed, watching Mr. Rosst go inside the container. He dragged Mr. Grig out.

"Faxil," Dad yelled, "go get the doctor, now!"

Faxil spotted her and ran to Mr. Ferg's container. Mr. Ferg was crying and holding his mom.

She was burned, and not moving.

"I'll take care of her," the doctor said, just before she poked Mr. Ferg with something.

"What the... blazing... stars..." Mr. Ferg said. He sounded sleepy.

The doctor saw Faxil. "Get over here and help me."

Faxil helped Mr. Ferg inside his container. The doctor dropped him on his bed. "Best I can do. Now what do you want, kid?"

"It's Mr. Grig! He's hurt bad," Faxil said.

The doctor ran so fast, Faxil couldn't catch up. But when she got there she told Mr. Rosst to, "Get to the cell. I want that bastard watched; you hear me?"

"What about—" Mr. Rosst started to say, then he turned and left.

"This is the best I got," she told Mr. Grig, and poked him like she had Mr. Ferg.

"Now, what about you, Papa Bear?" she said to Faxil's dad,

and he couldn't help but laugh a little. She started spraying his hands with something, then poked him in the arm. "I need a few minutes before I can properly work on that. You kids get your dad to his bed. He's going to be really sleepy really soon."

Faxil and Pinari walked Dad to their little home. It suddenly looked sad and fake, with things knocked over by the explosion. Dad slumped on the bed and mumbled something before he started snoring.

"Is he going to be okay, you think?" Faxil asked Pinari.

"Yeah, he's plenty tough," Pinari said. "But I don't know about some other people."

———

ROSST ENTERED THE PRISON CONTAINER, laser rifle in hand. He couldn't risk bullets. Cabeus might deflect them.

"Well, son, you did something here," he said. "Why?"

Jude just hung there, saying nothing.

"Answer me, Cabeus!" Rosst demanded. "What was your purpose?"

When Cabeus finally looked up, his face was twisted in confusion.

"To kill you, and Grig," he whispered. "I did it because they threatened my children. But there's something else... wrong with me."

Rosst scoffed. "Burning right there's something—"

"No, sir!" Cabeus said. "Someone did something to me. I stopped caring about things. I made mistakes, a lot of mistakes searching for you. Things I should know better."

Rosst thought back to the way he'd behaved when he first joined Prince Elio's Guardians project. "You think you were being controlled by a Psy," he stated.

"I don't know how to prove myself," Cabeus pleaded, "but I'll do anything to make this right."

"But you can't do anything to fix this!" Dr. Loko said as she marched in. "It's beyond even my ability. Great job with the murdering."

Cabeus hung his head in shame.

"Avrum, did you know your first aid kits have these wonderful muscle relaxants?" Dr. Loko said, and stabbed Cabeus with another syringe, this time in the arm. "I should have looked for it earlier! I also dosed some guy crying about his dead mom, and the one with the burned hands. I have to help him soon, so he has hands later. But I absolutely wanted to visit my very special patient, Mr. Murderpants!"

She gave Ferg and Deno drugs already, Rosst thought. "What about... Grig?"

Her glare softened a little into something like pity. "He... doesn't need relaxants. I gave him some lutanyua, but I don't have enough. Not for... that."

Rosst felt something stir inside him. Something more than his anger at Cabeus. "I'll... go see him," he said. "Keep Jude sedated."

"If you insist," she said, and Rosst left.

———

TEYN GRIG LAY on his cot in a dark room.

He could feel pain. That was all. They'd given him lutanyua, but it wasn't enough. There was nothing they could do.

"Grig?" he heard Rosst say.

"Good man," Grig croaked. It hurt to talk. "Come to give me... a send-off?"

"There's still time—" Rosst started to say.

"Shut it, colonel," Grig tried to bark. It came out as a wheeze, but he pressed on. "I had two... attacks. One in that van... the other after we arrived. My heart seized up... thought I was gonna die. No time... left."

"But... Dr. Loko—" Rosst tried to argue.

"I want to live... as much as... the next bastard," Grig mumbled, then coughed. It felt like something ripping his throat. "Lasted this... long. Just... tell my son... not..."

"Grig..." he heard Rosst say, but it seemed like he was already outside. He tried to raise his voice.

"Tell... Huis not to... do... anything... stupid..."

It hurt too much to say any more. And Grig was so tired. He let himself slip into sleep, wondering how many more times he would wake.

———

FAXIL HELPED Pinari bandage his dad's hands. Now he stood in the middle of what had been his third home in a year. He didn't know how to help anyone else. He wished someone would tell him what to do.

This is as bad as anything that had ever happened to me before. Well, maybe except for being shot at by aliens. But every time, someone was there to help.

Kuon helped fight the aliens so I could run away, he recalled. The medics helped get Pinari to the hospital. Dad and Inoiae helped fight the scary men, and those TK Knights helped get us out of the rubble.

But nobody knew what to do now. A bomb had exploded! Mrs. Presdon was hurt bad, and Mr. Grig. He didn't know where Mr. Lockwith was.

Faxil couldn't describe his feelings. It was like everything he wanted to be the same kept changing and getting worse. He just wanted all the bad things to stop happening!

Suddenly, he heard all the speakers in the room come to life. "Emergency broadcast!" he heard Ms. Verso yell.

"In what appears to be the largest prison break in history," the announcer was saying, "thousands of prisoners have broken out of a penitentiary—"

Now Faxil was confused. Did this new problem have anything to do with them? Did they do something wrong?

"Your stupid idea is going to get everyone here killed," Mr. Ferg had told him before.

The thought chilled him. Did this happen because of my game idea?

He ran over to Ms. Verso. "What's happening?" he begged as she frantically tapped at the keys.

"There's a major communications failure throughout Som Orsi," Ms. Verso said. And now there's some kind of mental-health crisis writ large in Som Orsi."

"Is it... our fault?" Faxil asked, instead of what he really wanted to ask. Is it my fault?

"Someone tracked Rosst here," she replied, still concentrating and tapping. "Bounty hunter or something. This other stuff has nothing to do with us."

"Um, okay." Faxil felt a little better, at least. "What's wrong with the communications?"

"I can't figure it out," Ms. Verso said. "The outage isn't complete, and there's no pattern. Sections of the network drop. Some come back on, then disappear again. Maybe it's a self-evolving virus in the system, and someone manages to scrub it long enough to bring their network up?"

"But why would someone do that?" Ms. Bree asked.

Faxil turned and found that everyone who wasn't injured was there. Except for Mr. Rosst.

Ms. Verso tapped some keys and hummed. "It targets communications between military units by taking out whatever grid the signal passes through," she said.

"So... it reads all the messages first?" Mr. Arthon said. "Then it stops the ones that it doesn't like?"

"That's the only thing that makes sense," Ms. Verso said.

Faxil churned his brain, trying to come up with something, anything, that would save everyone. Ms. Verso managed to get the news back twice, and he had to turn his head away to concentrate. He felt like there was something, an idea just out of reach...

And it hit.

"What if it couldn't read everything they say?" he asked. "What if it had to solve a puzzle first?"

He turned to find everyone staring at him. "Every message could start with a puzzle," he continued. "It would take people a second to solve it, but the virus couldn't solve puzzles, could it? So if we send out a copy of the puzzle maker, someone in the military could use it to communicate!"

"You're right, scrub," Ms. Verso said, her fingers dancing across the keyboard again. "I'm packaging it now. Sent. And now a message to everyone. If you are near Royal Boulevard and the King's Highway, the military needs reinforcements. Package with an image and... sent." She looked at Faxil. "If this works, kid, your game idea just saved a lot of people."

"Thanks, ma'am," Faxil said. "I'm... gonna check on my dad now." He turned and ran away before they could see the tears run down his face.

Maybe I didn't mess everything up, he thought.

———

JUDE SAT IN THE DARKNESS.

I'm not a killer. I'm not a killer. I'm not a killer.

It was a lie. He'd killed for his father before, so many times. He'd balked at killing Elio Lorne, because it sickened him to lure the child with electronic trinkets. The young man's trust in his father felt dirty.

His father blamed his mother. But Jude had realized his

father treated him the same way Jude treated Elio, with just enough praise and attention to manipulate.

The doors suddenly yanked open. Rosst appeared in the doorway, holding the laser rifle again.

"I'd kill you in a second except that I might believe you," Rosst said. "Whose idea was it?"

"My name isn't Jude Cabeus," he finally admitted to someone. "It's Wayn Marrion."

That made Rosst's rifle twitch. "Marrion? Jonn Marrion sent you to kill us?"

"You and Marshal Grig," Jude said. "He'd claim it was a Regency hit, and Huis Grig would retaliate, possibly from orbit."

"He might, either way," Rosst agreed, but dropped the rifle. "There's a major riot going on right now and people will have a lot of questions for this government. The traitors in the Council will receive justice, and we'll deal with the false king. But what do we do with you?"

Jude thought about going home to Maila, to Posey and Tag, but a surge of anger obliterated his feelings. "I want... I need to kill you, sir," Jude said. "It burns inside me. You should kill me now."

Rosst didn't respond to that. Instead, he said, "Son, do you consider me a man of honor?"

"Of course," Jude replied.

"I mean real honor," Rosst said. "I have one piece of business left. If you'll help me finish it, I'll let you kill me. You can pull the trigger. Will that satisfy whatever urges they planted in you?"

Jude imagined going with Rosst on whatever errand he needed, and that was fine. Accompanying Rosst to certain death left his anger at a slow simmer.

"I can do that," Jude said.

"It will be good to have you along, son," Rosst said as he carefully entered.

Jude thought he was trusting to walk past the debris by the door. Jude could have flensed him at any time.

Rosst walked up to him, behind him, and suddenly wrapped a cord around Jude's neck. Jude tensed for strangulation, but instead Rosst tied a knot of some kind.

"Sorry if I'm not entirely trusting," Rosst said as he unlocked the wrist manacle. It clicked open and fell. Then he knelt and unlocked the ankle shackles. "Which is why you'll wear that inhibitor from your fake arm until I say so. Understand?"

Jude stood unburdened, a freer man than he'd been in weeks. He came to attention and saluted. "Yes, sir," he replied.

"Quit that, you idiot," Rosst barked. "We'll start by asking you what reactions we should expect from your father about this riot."

CHAPTER
THIRTY

King's Highway and Royal Boulevard
Som Orsi

Foreign controlled the news.

Foreign controlled the traffic.

Foreign controlled eight thousand completely loyal, instantly obedient shock troops.

Viewing every camera, Foreign saw where the police gathered, where the military ambushes were, where citizens huddled in fear. Its minions overwhelmed the feeble resistance and appropriated their weapons. Weapons would cow the populace.

Power coursed through Foreign. Its body reveled in power, chemicals flooding Foreign with vigor and purpose. "Yes!" it cried out over the pandemonium. "This is what I was meant for! I will conquer this place and make it my own, and then—" The possibilities seemed endless. "What other worlds can I conquer?" it wondered aloud. "How many millions of humans can I control?"

It reached out to the city's broadcasting stations. The citizens would all be watching right now.

Foreign manipulated the signals. Every receiver emitted the frequencies Foreign used to turn the citizens of Odin into minions. It would take more time without a direct connection, so best to start now. Soon, eight thousand minions of Odin would swell to millions with Som Orsi, then other cities, then other planets.

Would it give all these worlds to the Will?

When the Will came for them, the Will could claim them. Until then, Foreign would take all that it wanted.

It would be glorious!

ROYAL QUARTERS
Royal Palace, Som Orsi

EROA LORNE SAT on the royal bed, watching the news reports with growing concern. When she couldn't stand anymore, she called in her night dresser.

"Fetch me a gown," she demanded. She shed her evening clothes even before the woman returned and then hastened to dress. She marched out of the room without even brushing her hair. She needed to find Targer.

She found him with his Council and military advisors, though Duke Rutta wasn't there. She hadn't seen him for... two days? Three?

"What is being done to quell this riot?" Targer demanded.

"We are trying to coordinate our forces," one of the Marshals' aides was reporting, "but they always attack our planned ambushes!"

"How do they know where they are?" Targer asked, but no one answered.

"Sires!" one of the technicians called. "We have a message from the hackers behind Perplexity?"

"Those bastards!" Pal Jiock exclaimed. "Are they taking credit for this fiasco?"

"No!" the tech said. "They offered us the program they use. They said that whatever is hacking communications would have to solve every puzzle to read our orders."

"That's absurd!" Jiock snapped. "As Technology Councilor, I refuse to—"

"You'll refuse nothing!" Eroa couldn't believe it. "This is an invasion! You'd refuse to hamper the enemy because of pride?" When Jiock didn't answer, she declared, "All communications centers will commence using this program. No complicated pictures. Just use snapshots of each other. We will use whatever we can to slow the destruction."

"We'd be handing everything over to those rebels!" Jiock retorted.

"If thousands of rioters attack the palace," Eroa said, "they'll kill us all. But at least the rebels won't win."

Jiock stormed out. Eroa saw the technicians already following her orders.

———

Balteus Higher Freeway

Meera sat in a police transport, ankles and wrists chained to a bar. Finia had attempted to punch Adiro Estar in the face. As a result, Finia was also chained.

"This is an abuse of power!" Finia complained for the

third time. "You can't arrest people for talking to each other? This is a kingdom of laws, you tight-pantsed bastard!"

Officer Estar sighed. "Meera Seleure was in violation of her plea agreement and her military parole—"

"What military parole?" Finia challenged him. "Why don't you explain that? Why is the military discarding its assets during a war?"

"Finia, please calm down?" Meera pleaded.

"I'm not at liberty to discuss—" Estar began.

"You didn't mind yakking before!" Finia said.

"Look," Meera finally said, "under Military Police Provision Article, um… seven, I think, I'm entitled to know the crimes I have been arrested for. Since I'll have a lawyer, you might as well tell me now."

"I'm not at liberty to share this information—"

"Then let me read the warrant," Meera suggested. "It might calm her down?" She shot Finia a pointed look.

Officer Estar looked pained, but he held it up. Meera looked it over.

"Every one of those is false," she said.

"Not according to our records," Estar replied.

"Klaus Brekan is missing in action. I couldn't talk to him," Meera said. "He's got an arrest order in place if he sets foot on this planet. Talking to his mother isn't even close."

"Enith Brekan died seven months ago," Estar pointed out.

"So I couldn't contact her, could I?" Meera said. "This list is useless in court. And I have witnesses to testify against you."

"Any witnesses you claim are criminal accomplices, subject to additional charges of perjury," Estar remarked. "You'd best leave them out of this."

Meera felt a blind rage. "Did you just threaten my family?" she said. Her TK surged, and it took no effort to find weak points in her chains. Her TK freed both Finia and herself.

Estar grabbed for his sidearm, but he'd barely pulled out the grip when—

Meera smiled. "You can't have my family."

She pushed with TK. The entire panel behind Estar simply fell away, seat and all. She heard him scream as he was quickly left behind.

"Brace yourself," Meera warned as the driver slammed on the brakes. The transport came to a stop, but Meera and Finia were already out of the vehicle.

They stood on one of the busiest freeways in Som Orsi. Traffic whizzed by them every moment, but Meera read their vibrations and simply avoided any hazards. Finia followed closely until they reached the edge of the freeway.

Even Meera, who had seen the spectacular natural beauty of stars and alien worlds, had to admit that the sunset behind Som Orsi was breathtaking.

"So," Finia said, her face a mask of awe, "are you gonna fly us out of here or something?"

Meera shrugged. "My TK doesn't work like that. I can manipulate things that I'm touching, kinda."

"But you destroyed those weapons, and part of the van," Finia argued.

"I was touching the van," she corrected. "The van touched him, and he touched the gun. Direct line of connection, or something like that. I could never explain it. It makes no sense."

Meera's wristpad beeped, and so did Finia's. Meera opened an unexpected message. It was a Perplexity puzzle. But it said, Important Information. Solve Immediately! at the top.

"What could this be...?" Meera said, but the puzzle was too simple. It only took seconds, and she found a message.

If you are near Royal Boulevard and the King's Highway, the military needs reinforcements!

"Well, Finia," Meera said. "Apparently, there's an invasion of some kind. Let's go."

"Are you trying to get pardoned or something?" Finia asked.

"That would be nice," she answered. "But I won't let these bastards touch my kids."

"How are we supposed to get out of here?" Finia asked.

Meera pointed ahead to where there was a parked grav truck idling a kilometer up the highway, and two men running back to them.

"What's going on here?" the tall one asked.

"What happened to those police?" the pudgy one said. "Are you criminals?"

"We were illegally detained for pissing off the Regency," Meera said. "We need to get to Royal and King's right now."

"We?" Finia sputtered. "You're insane!"

"Lady, don't you know there's all sorts of crazy going on near the palace right now?" the first driver asked.

"Yes! It's another alien invasion," Meera snapped. "Someone has to stop the madness."

"I don't!" Finia argued.

Meera took her by the shoulders. "You've been a big help to me, and you're my friend. They can take you wherever you need, but I'm going to fight, if I can."

Finia sighed. "Fine," she muttered. "I'll come with you."

"Then let's go!" Meera said, and they ran for the truck, the two bewildered truckers following behind.

DOWNTOWN MONERE DISTRICT
Som Orsi

. . .

Rab Grein walked toward the gravrail station. His life hadn't changed much lately. He was still a lowly assistant in a medium-level programming company who's techs were panicking at the recent network troubles.

Even after the government changed hands, things mostly continued on. But they hadn't been great for a while, and after the King's death, it just seemed to Rab like more of the same. Once, he'd hoped that Prince Elio would fix things, but then Elio disappeared, and the new King Targer showed up.

His wristpad beeped. He checked and found a new puzzle. This one differed from the others. It read Important Information: Solve Immediately! in the header.

"Hey, if there was ever a time for distraction, this is it," he muttered, and opened the puzzle.

Fortunately, it wasn't difficult. It was full color and a regular building. He solved it in moments. It was the old amphitheater.

There was no image, only a gender-less reading program. As he listened, his heart raced.

"To all Perplexity players," it said. "There is a crisis near the palace. Thousands of people have been brainwashed into attacking the populace. We have to stop them. If you're near the King's Highway and Royal Boulevard, they need help. We wanted to change things for the better and we began by disseminating information. But if you want your kingdom to change, it starts with you, right now!"

The message ended.

Rab found himself standing still, staring at where the picture had been. But if you want your kingdom to change… it starts with you. Right now.

There were people in danger. He didn't know what that actually meant, but he was tired of feeling helpless. He was tired of feeling worthless.

He ran to the gravrail station. If he could get to Royal Boulevard, maybe he could help. Somehow.

————

POVRE District
    Som Orsi

"BUT IF YOU want your kingdom to change, it starts with you, right now!"

The message ended.

Damir Piel rolled out of bed. He'd retired from the Orso Royal Order of Police twelve years ago after he lost his left leg in the line of duty. He couldn't afford a proper mechanical replacement, just a spindle leg attached to his knee stump.

He crammed his stump into the socket and tightened down the locks. It was going to be a busy afternoon.

————

MESOT DISTRICT
    Som Orsi

"BUT IF YOU want your kingdom to change, it starts with you, right now!"

The message ended.

Wynda Grommon pushed away from her table at the Tea Nook, thinking how her son had only that month taken a position with the Royal Guard and that he'd probably already been dispatched to the scene.

She'd served ten years as an Orso marine. She'd taught him

everything she knew about hand-to-hand fighting. Now she was going to show some upstart terrorist what she knew, too.

———

Upper Geartown
Som Orsi

"BUT IF YOU want your kingdom to change, it starts with you, right now!"

The message ended.

"I knew it!" Baine Fendol cackled. He looked around the diner, but no one seemed to notice him.

"Of course not," he muttered to himself. "The Blind Watch isn't going to let on that they've noticed me. That would tip their hand!"

It was all connected. Prince Elio hadn't really disappeared. Knowing the Darkens' assassins were waiting for him, he'd gone into hiding. Elio had left a loyal puppet to take the throne while he worked as head of a shadow government, orchestrating the Eclipseon Order's downfall.

Baine had posted all about this on the network and he had dozens of loyal truth-followers now.

And now, they were retaliating with this revolt that masked their true intentions.

He had to get to the scene. He ran from the diner in the hopes that the Blind Watch wouldn't follow him. He found his gravcar in the parking tower and zipped out into traffic. If he could help stop the revolt, that would end the news coverage and allow the real crime to be revealed.

He smiled as he remembered the bag of quickloop restraints in his trunk. At least two thousand pairs. He always carried a few with him, just in case, and now there was a revolution at hand, and he was prepared for it.

His therapist had always told him he took things too seriously and now he couldn't wait to mention this at his next session. Vindicated yet again!

CHAPTER
THIRTY-ONE

Severed
   Outside Tor Planetary Orbit
   Prica System

As the Tsunami entered planetary space, Elio felt a shiver of dread. *Why are they here? Are they a threat to us here?*

"Captain, we have a hail," the comms officer reported. "It's... oh. It's for Ground Control."

The speakers hissed on. "—en route to secondary Slipgate. We'll be in-system for sixty hours. Over."

"Copy that, Tsunami," Ground Control replied. "Be advised, we are coming up on our annual Aerian meteor shower. Your course may experience debris inbound, so please be aware. Over."

"We are advised, Ground, and thanks for the tip. Out." The speakers went silent.

"Sorry I didn't mention before," Governor Graynir said. "It's a patrol group, heading to Eos. They altered the schedule a week ago."

But Elio couldn't put his finger on it. Something seemed off about their arrival.

I've been wearing that Psy dampener for too long, Elio thought. *There's no reason to suspect—*

And then Danis's mind brushed against his.

He couldn't even be certain she'd felt his mind, but it was all the evidence he needed. She was there on one of the ships. Was she a prisoner?

He needed to find out.

"Captain Carrica," Elio said, "I need to take a shuttle. Can you spare one?"

"The Goodwill is at your disposal, Ambassador," Carrica replied. "I'll have a pilot and honor guard waiting."

Elio felt no duplicity. Carrica was an honorable man.

"Thank you, Captain," Elio said, "but the governor's men will escort me. And I will fly the shuttle myself." He heard the crew's whispers and ignored them.

Now is not the time for mistakes, he thought as he made for the shuttle hangar. *I will only take people I can trust to find Danis.*

Torrent's Pilot Country

Danis felt a familiar, repulsive touch on her emotions. She'd longed for it all these months. It had never appeared, had left her to rot.

It was Elio Lorne.

Emotions whirled as she ran for the fighter bay. She skipped the lift, taking the maintenance ladder down two levels. She'd be filthy, but that didn't matter.

When she reached Fighter Bay Two, she saw an F-31,

already checked out and awaiting a test flight. She shoved a mechanic out of her way and climbed the ladder as quickly as she could manage.

"Hey, get down from there!" someone shouted. Danis ignored him. She didn't do preflights. She simply flipped the engines from a cold start to full burn. That played havoc on maintenance, but she only needed this fighter for a few minutes.

"Unidentified pilot, you have not requested clearance," Flight Control blared in her ears. "Shut down your engines and—"

She slapped the comm control off and nudged the yoke forward. The fighter slipped into the vacuum. She oriented toward planet Tor and goosed the throttle. In two minutes, she'd be hitting twenty kilometers a second.

Thirty thousand kilometers ahead was some shiny, fancy little destroyer. Her board listed it as the Ataraxis. And heading straight toward her was a shuttle called the Goodwill.

But Elio was on it. She was certain. And she had no goodwill.

She called up her weapons panel.

———

Oh, it's no problem. I'll just fly the shuttle myself, Elio thought as he stared at the rows of unfamiliar switches and knobs. *And I'm pretty sure my pilot rating is expired by now.*

He had to remember all the preflight lists he'd watched Danis do a hundred times. But he had watched, and he remembered most of it. Once he finished, he keyed the comm to Flight Control.

"Ataraxis, this is shuttle Goodwill," Elio announced. "We're ready to depart."

"Confirmed, Goodwill," Control replied. "Safe flight."

Elio eased the Goodwill out of the hangar. Once he was in space, he set course for the incoming patrol cruisers.

"Unknown pilot, you have launched without flight plan or clearance," Elio heard on an open comm channel. "Identify yourself immediately."

But there was no answer.

Suddenly, he heard an alarm sound. It took only a moment to recognize it—

A missile!

He checked the scanner board. An Orso fighter was coming in hot. But the missile was faster still. It would arrive in... fifteen seconds.

Everyone's life would be forfeited unless he did something. He stretched out with his TK and seized the missile.

He tried to hold it, but his control was shaky. He barely kept his hold on the missile. Is it set for a proximity fuse or timer? he wondered. He was flying toward the missile, and the fighter had accelerated—it was quickly approaching the missile, unaware that Elio had caught it.

I can't hold it much longer! he thought, and he put mental dexterity aside for brute force. He crumpled the missile with his mind, detonating the warhead, creating a brilliant flash as the pilot flew past the explosion.

Elio thumbed the intercom on. "This is your ambassador speaking," he announced to his guards. "Prepare for acceleration and possible turbulence."

He felt the engines leap under full acceleration. In moments he'd avoided the fighter and sped toward Tsunami—

He felt a surge of Psy power coming from one of the other vessels. Could that be... Danis? he wondered. If so, she was far more powerful. He adjusted course and made for the Torrent instead.

TORRENT'S BRIDGE

MICHAEL JADERN WATCHED the drama unfold. An unscheduled flight was heading towards the embassy ship? He was stunned.

"Flight control!" he finally barked. "Get me a pilot ID. Comms, contact that fighter. This action is unauthorized and the pilot will be disciplined."

"Sir! Fighter has a confirmed missile launch!" Sensors announced.

"Artillery, detonate that missile remotely!" Jadern yelled. "I won't be responsible for this embarrassment!"

"We can't detonate!" came the reply. "Codes are locked and scrambled."

"Who has that authority on my ship?" Jadern demanded, but no one answered.

A burst of light flared in the distance. "Casualty report!" he ordered.

"We have two signatures, sir," Sensors replied. "The shuttle has passed the fighter. They're en route."

"I want weapons trained on that fighter," Jadern said. "If that pilot tries again, blow it to pieces."

"Sir, we have an incoming communication," Comms announced. Before he could say anything, the bridge speakers hissed to life.

"Attention Torrent, this is shuttle Goodwill," a familiar voice said. "Prepare to be boarded by the Orso ambassador and his honor guard. If there's another attack, my men will defend with extreme prejudice."

"To whom am I speaking?" Jadern asked.

"This is Elio Lorne... wait, Michael Jadern? Is that you?"

An unthinking rage overtook Jadern. He redirected

weapons control to his station. He shifted aim from the fighter to the shuttle.

He activated the ship's railguns and five streams of high-velocity rounds lit up the space between the Torrent and the shuttle.

———

200 Kilometers off Torrent's Bow

Danis looped her fighter to bear on the retreating shuttle. Her unthinking rage drove her to watch him die.

She locked on and launched another missile. She watched with satisfaction as it closed the distance.

Up ahead, the Torrent unleashed the rail-guns' kinetic fury. A storm of death flew toward the shuttle, and her missile boxed it from behind. There was no way it could escape! Sensors showed the shuttle fly straight to its doom.

The shuttle jinked in a maneuver that Danis had done a dozen times. The rail-gun barrage breached the missile warhead. There isn't another pilot who could reverse exhaust flow like that, she thought before she realized Elio was flying the shuttle himself.

Thus distracted, she flew right into the second wave. Her hull shredded, her emergency life-support tried to seal the breaches, but it was pointless.

Something inside her screamed for help. Only one person could help.

ELIO!

———

ELIO!

"She's in the fighter!" Elio muttered as the third barrage of railgun fire hammered his shields. He wanted to jink, but the fighter was directly behind him. Sensors said her hull was leaking air fast.

I have to save Danis!

Elio reversed course and adjusted his shields. Putting all power to the rear deflectors for more than a few minutes wasn't advisable, but Danis had less time than the shields did. He toggled the intercom.

"All hands! We have a derelict ship off the starboard stern and it's under fire," he announced, only bending the truth a little. "I'll tractor the fighter close enough to rescue the pilot. Everyone get into in pressure suits, now!"

He could hear his guards busying themselves. Two of them entered the cabin. "Help the pilot," Elio ordered as bullets crashed into the shields. Several pierced the shield, and he adjusted the deflection again.

"Your Highness, that pilot fired on us," one of them said. "You may be merciful, but we are responsible for you."

Elio tractored the fighter, pulled it close enough to make the rescue. When he had a lock, he opened the docking hatch. Another pattering of bullets rang out on the rear hull. The excess power was burning out the shield coils; every moment weakened the shields further. Shutting them down was suicide.

The soldiers pulled Danis aboard and activated the pumps to restore the shuttle's atmosphere. He immediately aimed the nose and the shields back at the Torrent. His hand hovered over the shield controls, but no more shots came.

"Torrent, you had a forty-second weapons malfunction," he called over the comm. "Care to elaborate?"

"We are happy to explain once you've arrived, sir," the comms officer replied. Before Elio could question the logic of approaching a ship that had fired on him, he heard a too-familiar voice.

"Hello, Elio. Are you having a bad day?"

It was Duke Gyrich Rutta.

———

TORRENT'S BRIDGE

"DUKE RUTTA," Elio said. "To what do I owe this displeasure?"

Rutta almost cackled as his armed security escorted Michael Jadern from the bridge. "Today has been unfortunate," Rutta said. "If you come aboard, I can explain everything satisfactorily."

Rutta could only imagine the thoughts in Elio's mind. He couldn't understand everything Rutta had done to create this moment. His vision reappeared Rutta striking Elio with tools and discarded ship parts until the boy knelt on the greasy floor in defeat. Rutta had loomed over that defeat so many times, and the ship was the perfect place.

He would kick Elio's lifeless body into the void.

"Fine," Elio replied. "I'll come aboard. And I won't leave until I'm satisfied." The comm cut off.

"Well," Rutta murmured gleefully, "at least one of us will be."

———

TORRENT'S HANGAR Bay One

. . .

Elio landed the shuttle, jarring the occupants. As soon as engines were down, he unbuckled his harness and stumbled into the passenger area, where Danis lay in a reclined seat. Her skin shone with vacuum-exposure gel, and a mask wafted fresh oxygen and medicines through her lungs.

Her appearance frightened him. Sunken eyes, hollow cheeks, gaunt frame—she appeared half-dead already. *How was she able to be on active duty without a proper fitness review?* His anger burned into rage, but he cut those feelings off. He needed to keep his emotions in check.

"Danis?" he said. She said nothing, just breathed gently.

He reached out with Psy. He found a snarled mess of contradicting thoughts and emotions, barely repressed urges, helplessness, anger, fear, and rage. Her mental state was close to psychotic. He could only feel whispers of her mind as it had once been.

He whispered into her subconscious, "I love you with all my heart. When we are free, I will help you find your way out of this mess."

He felt something change, but the hull rang with dozens of impacts. Small arms fire. Someone wanted to get his attention.

"Lower the ramp," he instructed. When the guards hesitated, he snapped, "Do it! You can't guard against that many soldiers. But I can, I have TK. You'll have clear shots."

His guards lowered the ramp and surrounded him on every side, following him down the ramp. Elio immediately raised a TK shield to block the bullets.

There stood Duke Rutta, with twenty guards holding smoking rifles.

"Welcome, princeling," Rutta said. "I've been waiting for you."

CHAPTER
THIRTY-TWO

REUNIFICATION
Torrent's Detention Bay
Officer's Ward, Cell II-38

Security threw Michael Jadern into the cell. His head bounced off the wall. Before he could turn, the door had already slammed shut. "Sorry about this, Commander," one of the guards said.

"You will be sorry!" Jadern snarled as he launched himself at the bars, trying to grab them, to yank them into the bars. But he couldn't reach, and then the guard touched the bar with a tase-baton.

The shock burned him, and he fell backwards, cursing them, their mothers, anything he could think of even after they'd left. With no outlet, he seized the cheap mattress from his bunk and hit the walls, the floors. He clawed and kicked the mattress, then gnawed it like an animal. His rage seemed infinite, and he wouldn't rest until he had killed something to appease the unspent wrath against Elio Lorne!

———

Torrent's Hangar Bay One

Duke Rutta watched Elio walk down the ramp. The whelp looked worse than Rutta ever remembered: no confidence, no attitude. Elio had aged fifteen years in a month.

He let his trollop die out there! Rutta realized. Glorious and perfect.

"This is over, Gyrich," Elio called across the hangar. "We know everything. Targer's mother, her genetics experiments. Once the people hear that you've overthrown—"

"Nobody cares that you're gone!" Rutta laughed. "They respect whoever holds power. And now that's me."

"Your Council is under arrest the moment I set foot on Caerus," the brat countered.

"You'll never make it back, you little prick," Rutta said. "And soon it will be King Gyrich the First and Forever, if I have my way."

Elio looked past Rutta. "Who is that woman?" he demanded.

Rutta glanced aside. "That's my... compatriot," he said when he saw Helot. "She helps divert your Psy talent while I do this."

He used TK. My own TK, how delicious! He thought, as a crate of tools rocketed toward Elio. The metal tools battered his guards as Elio tried to defend them.

"Put those toy soldiers away," Rutta chuckled. "Let's have this just between us. Noblesse oblige, and all that."

Elio motioned the guards away. Rutta could sense Elio's shield grow stronger to protect them.

That's fine with me, Rutta thought. It's just power he can't use against me.

He seized a metal pole with TK and hurled it like a spear. Elio shifted his shield to block, and Rutta kicked up a rain of steel from every workbench in the hangar, pelting Elio and everyone behind him.

"You don't fight fair, Gyrich!" Elio said without emotion.

"I fight to win!" Rutta laughed, and pressed his attack.

———

Aboard Shuttle Goodwill

DANIS DREAMED of a fierce battle in space, fighting her betrayer. Elio was no match for her. She bracketed him with gunfire and rammed a missile into his exhaust port. He exploded like skyrotechnics every Freedom Day.

She'd killed Elio! She cheered until she was hoarse. He'd abandoned her to die, and she gotten revenge!

But... that wasn't right at all.

Suddenly, she found herself in a completely white room. The air was dead, stale. In a room so large she couldn't find the walls, Elio lay in a bed of sveta lilies, though he couldn't smell them. His body was whole despite his fiery death, but she couldn't think of that.

She tried to touch him, and a single tear rolled down her cheek.

"I just wanted to be with you! Why can't I be with you now?" she screamed, begged, sobbed. But she knew the truth.

She'd killed him. "I didn't mean to!" she tried to say, but she knew the truth. It had taken only a little push to make her kill her love. Only a little loneliness.

She stared at her hands, watching Elio's blood flow from her sleeves, dripping down her fingers. "No," she murmured as the blood gushed. "I didn't want to! I didn't mean to! Please! Please give me another chance! I want Elio! ELIO!"

———

Hangar Bay

ELIO WAS BATTLING Rutta with everything he had, but his shield was weak. He couldn't make it any larger and still deflect Rutta's savage blows.

Suddenly, a shriek of Psy shattered his concentration.

ELIO!

Duke Rutta stumbled, and his assistant staggered from that single word. Even Rutta's soldiers broke formation, looking for its source.

He felt his core strength return to him.

Danis, he thought. Everything's going to be all right—

Elio ducked as Rutta sent a chunk of fuselage zipping past his head.

———

Aboard Shuttle Goodwill

DANIS SURGED out of her seat, staring in panic at her hands. They were clean. No blood.

Danis, she heard, and a thousand emotions flooded her with that single word. She'd connected with Elio before, but this was entirely new. Whether it was her or him, she didn't know or care.

I need a weapon, Danis thought. She glanced around the passenger cabin, but it was empty. So she staggered to the shuttle cockpit. Next to every pilot's seat was a small knife to be used in an emergency to cut them loose. It only took a push of the thumb and a flick of her wrist to pull the ten-centimeter blade free.

She stepped out of the shuttle into the hangar and... chaos. Elio was waging a battle with... was that the idiot politician Rutta? And then she saw her "therapist" Heloise standing a few meters behind Rutta. She could sense the aura of wrongness around the woman. Heloise was even more skeletal and emaciated than she remembered, and her antique funeral dress reminded Danis of her dream.

Foolish child! Heloise said as she stabbed at Danis's mind with a Psy attack.

Danis felt Elio easily guide her around the attack. Heloise tried two, three more times, but Danis battered them away.

How did you hide this from me? Heloise's voice demanded in her mind. You cannot be this powerful!

She ignored the crone and focused on the duke.

Hey, she said to Elio. Want to trade?

Elio nodded and sprayed a cloud of shrapnel toward Heloise. It wasn't enough to kill her, but the old woman screamed as Danis readied a spear of thought and stabbed into Rutta's mind.

Pain lanced through Rutta's temple.

In a rage, he pushed everything near him toward Elio like a gale of steel. Elio parried, staggered and fell to his knees.

Yes! This is it! Rutta crowed to himself. He'd finally reached the moment of his vision. The point from which all his glorious futures would flow! He felt Elio's TK shift—

Elio's shields collapsed.

"Everything I have done, Elio, was to reach this moment," Rutta said as he loomed closer, wanting to savor this final moment. "I would kill thousands more for the privilege of killing you."

Then something grabbed what hair he had and yanked him backwards. He caught a glimpse of olive skin, dark hair, and a fiery gaze.

Danis Morian? But she was dead! How did she get here?

"Killing Elio isn't quite that easy," she spat, before dragging the knife across his throat.

Rutta gasped, clutching at his throat, trying to halt the flow of life from his body. But all the TK in the universe couldn't heal him. He sank to his knees, eye to eye with Elio.

Elio glared imperiously at him.

My last vision in life... is to be brought... down to... his level? Rutta wanted to curse. It... isn't... fair...

He slumped to the ground, grateful to avoid Elio's self-righteous stare. It was over.

———

HELOT STAGGERED from Morian's mental blows. It was absurd! How had she not detected her power?

She looked up. Morian had sliced Rutta's throat open. Helot shrugged as the duke bled out. I would have killed him myself, anyway, she thought. His ambition was a threat to the One King.

But now she would crush these two herself. She aimed to disable their minds with a single blow. She launched twin attacks—

And slammed into a block she couldn't penetrate.

What are they doing—? She wondered, helplessly. But then Helot saw what they'd done. There was a link between them of pure Psy power like a steel beam.

She stabbed at their minds over and over, and each time her efforts were simply... blocked.

"How are you doing this?" she screamed. "I am the Red Rook! I have served for decades! None can resist me!"

She snaked a tendril of thought into Danis's broken mind and found Elio's plan to use something against her. He was trying to hide his intention, but from her, not Morian. Helot forced Danis to shut Elio's TK down. She snapped his will, and there was a clank of chains above her.

That was her only warning. She looked up to find an F-32 fighter hovering above her.

She screamed. It fell, And her decades of service were over.

———

ELIO SLUMPED to the hangar floor. His head ached, his body was sore, and he had a thousand questions. Unfortunately, the answers lay beneath the F-32.

He turned his head just as Danis collapsed. Her thoughts disappeared from his mind.

"Medic!" he called. "Someone call the ship's medic!" He realized he could do it better—he lifted her with TK and ran past the other crew gathered in the hallway.

He burst into the med-bay. The tech took one look at Elio and then busied herself with the obvious problems. It was over, but, as Elio sank into a nearby seat, his wristpad chirped. "Sire," the Torrent's comms officer said, "Commander Jasson requests your presence."

"I'm busy," Elio said.

"The commander says," the officer continued, "there's a message from Caerus."

Elio had no desire for any more betrayals from his father's councilors—!

But he sighed. "Inform the commander that I will be there as soon as I can."

It was ten minutes later when Elio walked painfully onto Torrent's bridge to find everyone staring at the giant holo of the chaos in Som Orsi.

It's happening again. Elio couldn't believe it. They had attacked his home again—

No. They're humans! He watched as people in tattered white rampaged through his city. From above, it seemed like they moved like flocks of birds. One moved, dozens followed. It was coordination the likes of which he'd never seen—

Humans can't do this, but I've seen the Swarm do it hundreds of times.

Something was terribly wrong.

"Commander?" Elio said. "The Torrent will set course for Som Orsi."

"But Ambassador, we... it'll take hours," Commander Jasson tried to explain. "And Commodore Vandu—"

"I am Elio Lorne, Prince of the House of Lorne," he said firmly, his eyes never leaving the holo. "The commodore can follow if she wishes. Take me home."

Then he turned and walked swiftly off Torrent's bridge, pausing only long enough to hear the commander relay his order.

———

Torrent's Detention Bay
Officer's Ward, Cell II-38

MICHAEL JADERN SAT on the metal plate that served as a bed. The remains of his mattress lay on the floor, the cloth ripped, the stuffing shredded.

In his rage, he'd sworn a blood oath to kill Elio Lorne. Now the source of his rage was gone, and he had a long list of shameful things to consider.

He'd betrayed Richard's memory. Somehow, he'd believed the worst possible things about his good friend.

He'd tried to kill Elio Lorne, a good man and the king he should have sworn allegiance to. Jadern didn't know how it had happened.

And, perhaps worst of all, he'd disgraced his friendship with Richard and his honor to his king by lusting after Danis Morian in the most despicable ways. He still had feelings for her, even after his rage had disappeared, and he didn't know what to make of it. He'd known Danis for years. Had he harbored some secret longing for her all that time? He didn't know.

But the things he'd imagined were... not befitting an honorable soldier. His shame burned deep within him, and he didn't know how to extinguish it.

Jadern didn't know whether he would be court-martialed, or imprisoned for life, or executed.

At that point, he would have welcomed execution.

CHAPTER
THIRTY-THREE

CONDESCENSION

THE GRAV TRUCK had to force its way through the traffic and Meera wondered if she should just use her power.

I could just take the limiters off. It would be easy, but—
She discarded the thought. Her power was devastating. She'd wreaked mass destruction in Som Orsi fighting the Swarm, and she also had the deaths of dozens of humans on the Ikalvan mining asteroid.

No, she thought. I don't want that power. I won't kill humans. I will find another way, so I don't need to kill them.

Did this make her brave or foolish? Righteous or selfish?

Finally, the driver pulled over. "I can't get any closer," he said. "Traffic is whacked, and we need to make our delivery."

"I'll go," Meera said, and opened the door.

A hand grabbed her arm.

"I'm going too," Finia mumbled.

"You don't have to—" Meera began.

"And what if you die?" Finia interrupted. "What happens if I bail and you die?"

Meera sighed in relief. "I'm glad I have a friend like you," she whispered.

"You like dumb and gullible, huh?" Finia said as she got out and slammed the door. "Can't say I blame you, though. Where are we going?"

Meera consulted the map on her wristpad. One of the news stations is showing a map of hazardous locations. "Up ahead, two blocks, then north about half a kilometer," Meera said as she started to run with Finia following. It took almost ten minutes to find the source of the chaos.

Thousands of rioters were surging around everywhere, seemingly in abandon. Some wore regular clothes, others wore filthy, ragged prison jumpsuits. They all carried weapons—firearms, metal poles, sticks and rocks. They beat anyone who stood in their way and when they saw Meera and Finia, they charged forward.

Meera used her TK to lock the rioters' feet to the ground. The front wave stood fast, unable to move their feet. Those behind quickly found themselves unable to run, too.

"How can you have that kind of power?" Finia asked in awe. Meera ignored the question. They walked forward, Meera carefully sweeping the patients aside until she reached the center of chaos where she was confronted by a young woman in a pristine white jumpsuit.

"Who are you?" Meera called.

"I am called Foreign," the young woman said. "Why are you here?"

"You are an alien, an invader," Meera declared. "You've infected all these people, but you'll not infect anyone else."

"These humans," Foreign waved its hand across her crowd, "don't feel your pains. You don't need to feel them, either."

Meera hesitated...

"I can give you peace and eternity," Foreign continued. "I think you will join me."

"I would never... join..." Meera trailed off. She'd joined the TK Knights to be something more, but they had failed her. These people understood something bigger. It would be so easy to give in... never to feel pain...

Oh, blazing stars! Really?

She heard the words distinctly before something clamped down on her ear. The sharp pain shocked her out of her trance.

"What the—?" she said as she grabbed her ear. She turned to see what had happened. It was Finia, and she was only wearing one earring. The other...

Meera felt her ear again. The large heavy stone was now locked onto her ear—no, not stone; it was metal, and it was humming.

"Wow," Finia said. "That creepy girl is doing some major mind-churning. I could feel it even through my limiters."

"Limiters?" Meera suddenly remembered their conversation that day. It seemed so long ago, and yet it was just the other day.

They made me leave, you know? They said I wasn't good enough. They didn't help me get better. The PEU closed me down...

"You were in the PEU... you're a Psy?" Meera exclaimed. "Can't you do something, like... a Psy blast?"

"I'm not very strong," Finia said. "And my control is terrible. Everything I feel leaks out to other people."

Meera looked at Finia, then at the immobilized rioters, then at Foreign. "Wait... I think we can do something here," she said. "Take off the other one, then read my mind."

"Why would I—" Finia said.

"I want Little Miss Invader to know what I feel," Meera

said. "Let's see how much human misery she can really handle."

Finia took off the earring, and Meera felt a strange wash of emotion surge through her mind. The flow increased. It took a moment, but Meera quickly realized what she was feeling were the emotions of people around her. Some of them were Foreign's troops; most were innocent civilians. So much for that promise, Meera thought just before she felt something distinctly not-herself wade into the pool of her mind. It was Finia's over-hyped, exuberant voice. Then she connected with Miss Invader.

So Meera thought about Sorge.

Sorge's life flashed over and over. His death. The despair, pain, loss. Crying, sobbing, weeping.

Finia moaned in Meera's mind. *It's too much... I can't take this...*

In that moment, Meera could feel Finia's crippling anxieties as well.

Yes, you can! Meera thought as the compounded emotions washed through her, and into the minds of the thousands of rioters. They were all humans with wants, needs, fears, and their emotions churned together in a vast wave of human misery. Meera, her eyes closed, rode the wave for what seemed like forever before she opened her eyes again.

Hundreds of Foreign's rioters had collapsed, moaning in agony from the emotional bombardment. And yet, others were moving; police, moving quickly with determination, binding wrists and ankles with quickloops. Some of them were civilians, hundreds of them, helping the police while Meera had to keep the patients locked down and disordered.

She thought of Klaus. He'd tried to persuade her to try again. He'd always made her laugh. Maybe if he was older, more mature... He'd loved her in her own way; she knew that.

But she'd rejected him, pushed him away. Now he was gone, and it was her fault.

If only I'd let him speak.

That guilt had been eating at her for months, but she'd pushed it away.

Meera half-watched the military bully their way through. They put Foreign in full locking restraints, then strapped a giant, ugly helmet over the woman's head. It was only then that the strange music in Meera's head ceased. And she watched as they carted Foreign away, leaving thousands of victims lying on the ground, squirming in agony.

Finally, Finia's touch receded, and Meera tried to halt the painful memories. But she couldn't. She'd opened a floodgate and she couldn't close it.

"You... have some real... issues, don't you?" Finia panted as she clipped her limiter earrings back in place. "But I'd love to talk to you about that later, yes?" She held out a hand.

Meera took her hand and squeezed it gently. "Yes," she replied. "We'll talk about your problems, too. Right now... I need a drink."

"Oh, yes," Finia said. "You think the Twilights are good? Wait until I get you a Sparkling Midnight. You've never had anything like it..."

———

Ataraxis's Guest Quarters

DANIS DREAMED OF HER CELL, her message to Elio droning on, and on, and on... driving her mad. *Please make it stop!* she repeated over and over.

And then she heard voices, talking, and explosions...

An attack? She panicked and forced herself awake. She sat

upright. She was in a strange bed, in a strange room, to find Elio sitting beside her in the dark, staring at his wristpad.

He covered the image. "Hey. How are you feeling?" he asked. "You're safe now."

"I was startled," she snapped. "What are you doing here?"

When he hesitated, she quested for his mind. To her surprise, he let her in easily, and she saw everything he'd seen and what he planned to do, swirling through the mists of his mind.

"See?" Elio said. "The worst is already over."

Danis felt the tremor of a completed Slip run through. And she knew they were home, and together, finally, after all this time. But that couldn't distract her.

"Som Orsi is a wreck," she said.

"Yes, and something needs to be done," Elio said as he grabbed his clothes from before. "I have to convince them that things will be better."

"You... shouldn't go alone!" Danis whispered as he oh-so-calmly stood and adjusted his shipboards. "The Council will have locked everything down. It's too dangerous."

"I won't be alone," he said. "I'll have Prican guards, and I know my way around." His love brushed her mind, and she shivered. "There won't be any trouble," he said. "The emergency communication systems are broadcasting the doctor's confession. Most of the population will storm the palace to help me."

"You don't know that!" Danis said as she stumbled off the bed. "They could revolt against you! You have no idea—!"

Elio silenced her with a kiss. "I know these councilors," he whispered. "The mob may have already deposed them."

Danis stamped her foot. "How can you always be so... infuriating?"

"Well, I'm glad neither of us has changed," Elio teased as

he looked in the mirror and straightened his collar. "These clothes... aren't fresh. I should switch to something cleaner."

Danis caught a glimpse of her reflection. She forced herself to look away. "Keep them," she said, despite the smell of sweat. "You said we shouldn't change."

"That's not what—" he said, then he laughed. "Oh, I love that twinkle in your eye. I've missed you, Danis."

"And I've missed you, too," she said. A flash of betrayal stabbed her heart. She pushed the feeling away. "So I want to be there with you."

He opened his mouth, but then the comm system tweeted. "Ambassador," the commander said. "We are thirty minutes out from Caerus. Your shuttle is prepared and leaves in five minutes."

Danis grabbed her pilot's uniform as Elio dashed out of the room.

"Jerk," she muttered. "He's not leaving me behind!"

She stumbled, trying to dress, still a little off balance. Then, dressed, she jogged down the hallway toward the hangar.

But when she arrived, the shuttle was already through the atmo shield.

"Hey!" she yelled at the nearest mechanic. "Get me an F-32."

"What? Who are you?" the mechanic said.

Danis pointed to her lieutenant commander insignia. "This is who I am. Now get me a fighter!"

"I can't. They're all in maintenance!" he blurted.

She looked around, saw a nearby shuttle. "Is that shuttle under maintenance?" she demanded.

"Err... No?"

She dashed up the loading ramp, into the cockpit and began the preflight sequence, flipping the comm on. "Flight control, this is shuttle, um, this is shuttle Concord, requesting accelerated liftoff procedure."

"Who is this?" Flight control responded.

"This is Lieutenant Commander Danis Morian, Three-Alpha-Three," she replied. "And... I'm leaving with or without clearance."

There was a moment of silence. Then another. Danis finally punched the engine controls—

"Concord, you have been cleared for liftoff," the Flight Control replied, sounding more than a little upset. But she didn't care. She wasn't letting Elio out of sight for one second longer.

CHAPTER
THIRTY-FOUR

JUDGMENT
On Approach to Royal Palace
Som Orsi

Elio watched the clouds part as the shuttle broke through and saw the majesty of Som Orsi laid out like a glittering jewel in the dawn light. He also saw the Smoke rising from the center of this jewel where thousands of rioters had caused millions—if not billions—in damages. He shook his head. *I never should have let it get to this.* But he'd taken the high road, not wanting to bully his way into power, but at what cost?

He wanted to believe that the Council deserved all the blame for the mess and destruction, but he knew that, had he taken power early, this destruction would never have happened.

The Goodwill landed on the Palace rooftop pad. It was the first time he'd used the pad since... returning from the Battle of Som Orsi, he thought. It was after that he'd been stripped of his titles, imprisoned, and then sent on a fool's errand across the Sovereign Stars. But the doctor's confession of regicide was even now playing on every viewscreen and holo. The revelation of the false king had destroyed the Regency's claims.

He exited the shuttle and walked quickly through the screen just inside the roof entrance, followed by his retinue of Pricus Guards.

"You're not sure you remember impregnating twelve women with Orson Lorne's genetic material?" he could hear Queen Eroa saying. "That seems quite a thing to forget, since I have the documentation with your signatures all over them."

"That's not how it happened. You didn't read everything." Kiaro Chiru replied, her credibility in shreds.

"You gave those women their own royal bastards to weaken the throne."

Eroa had confronted the woman, then released the damning information to the public, knowing she would be punished.

Something had to be done, Elio knew, but he didn't know what. I have to punish them, he mused. But fairly, considering that she revealed this.

But first, there was business that needed to be done. He arrived in the hallway outside the throne room, where a crowd awaited him. He passed through the news crews he'd alerted.

"—and then the council approached me," Kiaro's recording was saying. "They wanted to know specifics about his love affairs. After all, who would know—"

He would interrupt the broadcast—its eighth repetition—to announce his return. He would claim his birthright and be king.

"—my own royal bastard child would rule all Orso. And all his brothers and sisters—"

But what next? He needed to make changes. But the war was paramount.

"All you had to do was betray the king," Eroa replied once more. "But instead, you... killed him?"

"He was never going to recover!" she snapped. "And he betrayed me first."

He entered the throne room and the news crews spread out behind him.

This is it, Elio thought. The moment when everything changes. Again.

———

ON APPROACH to Royal Palace
  Som Orsi

"THIS IS SHUTTLE CONCORD, approaching Som Orsi Palace," Danis informed Ground Control. "I'm looking for a place to park."

"Shuttle Concord, you are on screen," Ground Control replied. "Be advised the palace is not accepting landings."

"I'm with Elio Lorne," she only half-lied. "He just landed the first shuttle."

"We were not provided with your flight plan," Ground Control said. "Palace security has been informed of your approach. Anti-aircraft batteries are being readied."

"I'm Danis Morian!" she snapped. "Three Alpha Three, Twenty-Nine Eighteen Avenger!"

"Listen, whether you're lying or not," the controller yelled, "It doesn't matter if you're the mayor of Auspicia or Old Laude Sancire with his bag of gifts, the palace is closed today! Land on the nearest non-government pad or they'll spread pieces of you across the metro area." The comm cut off.

Danis brought the shuttle down atop a gravcar parking

tower. She lowered the ramp and found a pair of bewildered parking attendants.

"Hey, um, you can't park that thing here?" one of them said.

Danis looked back. She'd taken up eight spaces. "I thought I did a good job," she said, and walked away. "Gimme a citation if you have to," she yelled over her shoulder as she headed for the elevator and rode it down to ground level where she found... chaos.

Hundreds of prisoners were being herded by a combination of police, military, and civilians.

Carefully, she opened her Psy.

She couldn't distinguish one person from another. Emotions were running wild: anger, indignation, fury, but none of it for Elio. He'd been right.

But I was right to worry, she told herself. He couldn't have known all that before... could he?

Suddenly, she felt a burst of Psy on the far side of the street. Fearful of an attack, Danis readied herself to fight, but then she saw a familiar face.

"Hey! Hey you!" she called, and ran across the street to the woman who'd been with her in the hangar on the Thorn.

"Danis!" the woman called. She dragged her friend over and embraced Danis. "It's so good to see you. How are you? Did you ever..." she trailed off.

Did you ever find out about your brother? Danis heard the question clearly. She tried to remember the woman's name, but... She cheated and peeked into her mind. "It's been really... terrible, Meera," she answered, and then she had an idea. "But none of that now. We need to get a crowd of people to the palace right now."

"What for?" the other woman asked.

"Prince Elio is back," Danis said. "He's overthrowing the

Council and establishing himself as king. But a coronation needs to be public, right?"

Meera and the other woman looked around at the crowd. "I'm sure these people would want to," Meera's friend said, "but they're kind of busy right now."

Danis opened her mind again, feeling the emotions of the crowd. "They're... confused," she replied. "Nobody knows where to go. How can we direct them?"

Meera's friend sighed. "I can do it... I think. But we need someone who knows what to do."

Danis spotted a military man among the nearby police. Surely he would have a comm. She walked over and yanked her ID out. "I'm Commander Danis Morian," she announced. "I'd like to offer assistance."

"Yeah, you and half the— a commander?" The man shot to attention. "Lance Sergeant Bikk. Sorry, ma'am. It's been... quite a day."

"Where do these prisoners need to go, Bikk?" she asked.

"We have, um, nothing," he said. "Eight thousand patients escaped. They just ran out. We don't have that many buses."

"Then let's walk them back," Danis said.

"But... that's klicks from here!" Bikk protested.

"Then they're getting some exercise today," Danis said. "Come on, Bikk, it's got to be better than chasing them, right? Just tell us what direction we should go."

Bikk nodded, but when he saw Meera and her friend, he paused. "Wait. You're the one!" He pointed at Meera. "I saw you in my mind! You're the crying lady!"

Danis looked at Meera.

"It was a thing," Meera said. "You missed it by five minutes?"

"We need your help," Danis explained. "This woman here —" Danis realized she didn't know her name, "—will help guide everyone back to your jail."

"Psychiatric facility," Bikk snapped.

"Whatever," Danis said and looked at Meera's friend. "What can you do?"

"All right," she told Bikk. "Think of the place where we need to go. We need to go there. We need everyone to go home."

Then she took off one earring, and Danis felt a sudden urge to visit the Rising Tide Psychiatric Facility in the Military Annex of Resdon Military Base. She turned before she even thought about it, and she saw ten thousand people doing the same. They walked in unison, picking their way over debris and around vehicles. It was the strangest thing she'd ever seen, and her feet simply went to the same steps as everyone else.

"You are very powerful," Danis said to her.

"I'm not that powerful," the woman replied. "His emotions are driving this. He really wants to go back to work right now."

"I want to keep my job," Bikk was muttering. "I need my rank. Everyone go back to your wards. Everyone go back. I need to keep my job..."

———

PUBLIC VIEWING THRONE ROOM
Royal Palace, Som Orsi

ELIO GAZED around the throne room his father had once dominated.

His half brother stood there next to his queen. They'd held the throne for just one year, a year during which Elio had been lost and confused, but not anymore.

Kiaro Chiru and Eroa's parents were sequestered to one side and guarded by a pair of officers. The Regency Council stood to the other side of the room, also under close guard. Some of them were dressed, some were still in their night-clothes. None of them wanted to hear Elio speak. Instead, they were all shouting at once.

"The recordings are faked!"

"This is a sick fantasy—!"

"You know the treason laws—"

"—a twisted mind to accuse—"

"—rake you over hot coals for—"

This is just posturing. Elio thought, something he'd predicted. They want to be heard before I accuse them.

"Enough!" Eroa called over their commotion. They turned to her in surprise. "I made those recordings. You killed King Orson Lorne, and you tried to execute Prince Elio Lorne. And you would have had my husband had I not stopped you. I won't be a party to this plot any longer."

Elio brushed her mind with his, but he felt no dishonesty. She wasn't repentant, but he felt her disgust. He wondered what made her betray them.

"We now have a verbal confession from two of your party," Elio said. "Everyone on Caerus has heard it. The rest of Orso Kingdom will know tomorrow."

"What about Gyrich?" one of them demanded. "Duke Rutta was the key player in all of this!"

"No! He wasn't," Elio countered. "He was a puppet who, in turn, dragged all of you into his treason. Gyrich Rutta is dead. "

"How did he die?" Exical Promeant asked. "As your father's legal advisor—"

"He attacked me using TK in front of dozens of people," Elio interrupted him, "and was executed by a member of the ship's crew." He hoped Danis's involvement would not be revealed.

"Gyrich didn't have TK!"

"This is an absurd fabrication—"

"Dozens of the ship's crew witnessed it," Elio snapped. "All of whom were chosen and manipulated by this... tyrannical government. I've had enough of it and—."

"It doesn't matter," Promeant argued. "The Lorne family was removed from power. Whatever you attempt is irrelevant."

Elio shook his head. "You were my father's legal advisor? Conspiracy to murder the king is treason. Traitors don't get to make laws." Elio motioned with his hand, and the guards along the walls came forward. "There will be a full investigation, though I don't expect the courts will depose me. Guards, take them away."

The guards immediately secured, then shuffled the former council members out of the throne room. The sentries guarding the parents of the former king and queen were more, slightly more spurious, but they were soon gone as well.

And then there were two, Elio thought as he looked at the false king and queen.

"The courts will deal with them in due course," he said. "But only the king can decide what happens to you two."

———

ONE KILOMETER FROM
Rising Tide Psychiatric Facility

DANIS COULD HARDLY BELIEVE IT. She was jogging a garbage-strewn highway, even though her body was ready to give out. Behind her jogged some ten thousand people, most of them wearing filthy white clothing with their arms in restraints. Danis wondered how they could keep their balance.

"Hey, how much farther do we need to go?" she asked the sergeant.

"It's just up ahead. See?" Bikk said.

And there they were, the Resdon Military Base gates. The last time she'd gone through those gates...

I was kicked off the base, she remembered with a grin. I'll have to find that Air Marshal and apologize. Maybe he'll let me come back.

As they approached the gates, she could see the armed guards there were panicking, reaching for their weapons.

"NO! she shouted as she put on a burst of speed and went to the front of the crowd, her hands in the air. "I am Commander Danis Morian!" she shouted. "We are returning these people to confinement! Do not engage!"

"They already engaged us today!" a guard shouted as she approached the gate. "They kicked the living crap out of me and my men!"

"I said don't engage!" Danis snapped as the crowd approached the gate. "They were under Swarm control, but no more, We're returning them to their cells."

Danis stood by as the crowd filtered through the gates until only the civilian stragglers were left, most of them exhausted.

"Hey, are you all right?" one of the guards asked.

Danis tried to say she was fine but, as she collapsed, she felt someone grab her and lower her gently to the grass verge.

"Take it easy there, commander," Bikk said. "Hey, someone get her some water!"

Danis heard unfamiliar voices and opened her eyes. She was seated in a hard plastic chair, in a room full of... She was confused. Everywhere she looked there were officers, guards, civilians.

"Hey! Meera, she's awake," someone said. Danis squinted in the harsh light. It was Meera's friend.

"What's your name, soldier?" Danis asked weakly.

"Me? Oh, I'm not a soldier," she said. "My name's Finia. I, um. I flunked out of Psy School."

"Your power is incredible," Danis murmured. "Why would they turn you away?"

"I can't stop my power once I start. It takes hours to shut it down." Finia touched her earring self-consciously.

"You're not broadcasting now," Danis observed.

"Well, no," Finia said with a shrug. "I'm wearing my limiters."

"Those earrings?" Danis said, and Finia nodded. "They're strong enough to stop you." Ideas began swirling around in Danis' mind. Finia used her power over a square kilometer almost without trying. Could she cover a field of engagement? Danis wondered. Could Finia help direct pilots from outside a battle?

"Finia, if you could help the war effort, would you?" Danis asked.

"I really wanted to," Finia replied. "But they said I wasn't good enough."

"That's what some stylus-twiddler with no imagination would say." Danis couldn't believe the incompetence of the government. Then again, *I'm surprised they didn't have her in prison. The Regency Council should have feared her.* "Luckily, I think differently. How would you like to be reactivated?"

Finia's eyes grew wide. "I... What? Really? You mean I could help?"

Danis nodded. "I have no doubt, and know someone who will agree with me." Danis eased herself out of the chair. She was sore. She spotted an officer, a lieutenant. She limped over to him.

"Lieutenant... Treben?" she read from the tag. "I am Lieutenant Commander Danis Morian." He looked at her, came to attention, and saluted.

"I want you to get every available transport at this door in fifteen minutes. I want to go to the Palace with five hundred new friends. Understood?"

"I can't request clearance for five hundred people to enter the Palace!" he said.

"I didn't ask for clearance, I asked for transport. Now go!" she snapped, and he turned and marched stiffly away.

She turned to face the room. "Everyone, listen up!" she called. "I'm going to a coronation today. Anyone who wants to meet the new king, stand up now and start forming lines!"

Half the room immediately stood and cheered. Finia stood at the front, her eyes gleaming with tears. As the word spread, there were more cheers and more people stood up.

Oops, she thought. I think I may have miscounted.

CHAPTER
THIRTY-FIVE

PROMOTION
Public Viewing Throne Room
Royal Palace, Som Orsi

Even as Elio... Prince Elio, the former queen Eroa reminded herself—banished his usurpers, he displayed no self-righteous attitude. He seems... melancholy.

He just condemned men and women he'd known his whole life, Eroa thought. And I played a part in that.

She and Targer would be imprisoned as well, but they were left on the precipice as Elio asked the holo-news people to stop recording.

This is where we see the real man, she thought. Secret orders, media blackouts, death squads behind a veil of smiles...

"Thank you," Elio began. "I've never seen a coronation?"

Eroa's jaw dropped.

Several snickers arose in the crowd of reporters, but Elio simply smiled. "I know," he said. "But when in my lifetime did we need one?" He looked at each reporter in turn. "I would imagine there are recordings of Targer's coronation, but I... Well. I missed that one."

More snickers.

Did he... just mock his imprisonment? Eroa wondered. She couldn't begin to Imagine what his plan might be.

"There are traditions, I know," Elio continued. "But I need something more. I don't want recordings of a dozen people declaring me king. And if the people don't want me, I'll step aside for someone who will do the job the way it should be done. That means protecting the people, defeating the Swarm, and saving our way of life."

Eroa, unbelieving, shook her head. He's offering to relinquish the crown? Why not leave us in place if he doesn't want it?

"Do you think you can do that again and let us record it?" one of the reporters called from the back of the room.

"Of course, but first I need to freshen up and change my clothes."

Murmured agreements arose, and Eroa just stood there, stunned. Who are we, she thought, that they accept a fop like him? Will he return in a belled cap and dance for their amusement?

"I'll be back shortly!" he said, and then turned and left the chamber.

Eminent Residences, First Floor
Royal Palace, Som Orsi

Elio stood before the door to his room, the one he hadn't seen since he left for the airfield and boarded Sasha Crowe's shuttle.

"It's just a door," he told himself as it slid open silently.

And he entered the room for the first time in more than a year. He breathed in the familiar scents of his childhood, fine wood and clean clothes and just a hint of himself.

"I'm home," he whispered. After so much fighting and uncertainty, this was where he belonged.

He stripped off his clothes and went to the hydro. The hot water was a relief, but he couldn't linger, and it was over too soon, far too soon.

He toweled himself off, then went to his closet and dressed in a simple dark blue uniform trimmed with gold, then he went to the velvet box, delivered more than a year ago. And slipped it in his pocket, almost giddy to be carrying a keepsake from treasures of Orso. It will mean everything to Danis, he thought, then frowned. It should mean everything, he hoped. If I have a chance to give it to her, I will, he thought. I don't care who sees me. If I can't marry who I desire, then...

He would propose today and that would be the end of it.

He rehearsed all the way back to the throne room. He was so distracted that at first he didn't notice the crowd gathering in the hallway. "Pardon me,—" he mumbled before noticing the woman's rumpled clothes and sweaty sheen.

"Hey, everyone! He's here!" the woman shouted, and everyone turned to look at him. "Our king is here!"

A cheer broke out, laughter and catcalls mingling with hails for the new king. Where did they all come from? he wondered. He reached the front of the crowd, where he found Danis. And he saw her eyes light up.

She stepped forward, hugged him and whispered, "I didn't want you to be lonely."

Before, he'd have felt awkward hugging her. Now, he was thrilled and said, "I couldn't ask for a better gift today. Thank you." She beamed at him as he walked to the throne. He reached out with Psy, touching the memories of each citizen. He relived the rioters' attack, felt their worry and pride.

I need to show my people I can be there for them, he thought. And Danis, bless her, had brought the solution right to him. He motioned for the holo-news crews to begin broadcasting.

"Citizens of Som Orsi, I am Price Elio Lorne," he announced. "I should have inherited the throne from my father. It would have been delivered to me without question, but the people I trusted murdered my father and in so doing they weakened us. Their lust for power destroyed our city and forced thousands of our people into poverty and destitution."

That's one point down, he thought.

"As you know," he continued, "I supported and fought in the war against the Swarm." He took a deep breath. "And, as king, I will continue to do so. I will reorganize the Orso military and give the commanders the autonomy to do what they think is right without the restraints of bureaucratic rules and I will encourage the other kingdoms in the United Sovereign Fleet to do the same."

The crowd cheered at his words.

He paused, fearing he was being overly dramatic, but then he pressed on. "But I will accept the crown only if the citizens of Orso accept me. These ordinary people gathered here," he waved his hand, and the cameras followed his direction, "fought to protect their city from the Regency's mistakes and they represent you, our people. I will rule only by public acclamation."

He stepped forward. He took a woman's hand, knelt before her, bowed his head, and said, "Please allow me to serve as your king."

She looked shaken, but she placed her other hand on Elio's head and said, "I... accept you as my king? Yes, I do."

She stepped away. An older man with one artificial leg stepped forward.

"Please allow me to serve as your king," Elio repeated.

The man touched Elio's head. "You have my support, sire."

He stepped away, and another man stepped up. "Please allow me to serve as your king," Elio said again.

"Will you stamp out the Blind Watch and their stranglehold on the lower government offices?" the man blurted.

Elio, taken aback, looked up at him and "Um, yes, I will end government corruption, but my concern are the aliens that want to destroy us."

"That's important, too," the man said, and ruffled Elio's hair. "Yeah, I'll take ya as king."

Elio didn't know how long he knelt there, but, as he was about halfway through, Danis stood before him, placed her hand on his head, and said, "I already accepted you as my king." And then stepped away, smiling at him.

And then he received another surprise. A TK Knight stepped forward. He couldn't remember her name, but she placed her hand on his head and said, "You'll do a great job, my king," she said with a smile. "I know it." And she, too, stepped away.

Then another person came forward, and another, and another.

Meera Seleure, the name finally came to him. Hero of Som Orsi.

When they had finished, he stood and looked at the cameras, hiding a grimace from the cramp in his knees.

"These people can't speak for everyone on seventeen worlds," Elio said, "but it is enough, and I vow to serve you my people to my last breath. Our people are strong, and when we work together we can overcome all obstacles. And we will work together."

He turned to the two prisoners behind him. Targer paled and Eroa shook with fright.

Elio pointed at them. "And that is why I've already decided—"

Eroa trembled. This was when he would show that he was fair to his friends and harsh to his enemies. She couldn't let him.

"As my first act as king—" Elio began.

"Please, King Elio," Eroa gasped, "kill me, but spare Targer. He was a pawn. I... I was key to many of the council's plans. I deserve whatever fate you decide."

"Interesting," the new king replied. "Targer, do you have anything to say?"

"I, um." Targer hesitated. "I never wanted to be king. And I knew what Eroa was, but she was nice to me when she didn't have to be. So, please, my King. I'd rather she didn't die."

Wait—he really thinks that? Eroa thought. About me?

"What about you?" Elio asked.

"I don't want to die, sire," Targer said.

"So both of you plead for the life of the other. Interesting." Elio stared thoughtfully at them.

Eroa grew desperate. She wasn't nice, whatever Targer believed. But Targer? If not for his kindness, Elio wouldn't be alive. She would have lived in luxury, ordering legions of servants while deciding how to rule seventeen planets in Targer's name.

She felt a whisper of breath on her mind. It withdrew as soon as she noticed. Was that Psy? Eroa began to panic. He read my mind. He heard all those things!

"This is my verdict," Elio stated, and Targer drew up stiffly beside her. "All lands and titles of the Disiac family whom you represent shall be taken and held by the crown in respite per Article One-hundred Twenty-three. And I shall appoint you, Eroa, to a new position."

"What?" Eroa blurted out. "You're giving me a job?" She was stunned.

"You will be my new ambassador," Elio replied. "I have a diplomatic ship waiting for you and a captain I trust. Your first port of call will be Alastor, because I need you to open new diplomatic channels with prince Padric Felder. After that... well, I have plans. Are you ready and willing to serve?"

"I... I mean—" she babbled.

"Ambassadors don't stutter," Elio said, smiling.

"Yes! Yes, I will be your ambassador," Eroa replied. "But... what about my family's estate?"

"I will keep it safe from any other claimants until you return," Elio said. "Much like you did for me," Elio said, still smiling.

She looked into his calculating gaze. They both knew he could have chosen death. And they both knew the irony of the punishment.

Then Elio looked at Targer and said, "I have a job for you, too. I want you to act as Eroa's advisor."

"But how could I do that?" Targer looked confused. "I wasn't a good king. She's been trained to do this. I haven't"

"Exactly," Elio replied. "You must be the person who helps her see through the twists and barbs of court. She needs someone like you to balance what her mother taught her."

Targer turned to Eroa. His expression, a thread of hope waiting to snap under the strain of disbelief, almost undid her. "So do you... really want someone like me following you around?"

"No," Eroa snapped, without meaning to. But then, before Targer could react, she added, "I mean, I don't want someone like you, I want you! I would refuse to do this without my... my husband. I overthrew the monarchy for you. I threw it all away, so that you wouldn't hate me." Her face reddened, and she turned away.

"Very good, then. So it shall be," Elio declared, and then continued, "My first official act is to pardon you both of any and all crimes you may have committed prior to this declaration. I'll have my secretary draw up the papers and you will be assigned to the Ataraxis under Captain Carrica."

Eroa lowered her head, then said, "Thank you, my king." Then she looked at Targer. The expression on his face stole her breath.

"Await your orders in the Palace guest quarters. I'll send someone to get your things," Elio was saying seemingly somewhere far away. "And now... for the final act of my first hour as king."

But Eroa was past caring what Elio said. She was looking into Targer's eyes, and what she saw was love, pride, and acceptance.

He leaned forward and kissed her lightly on the lips.

———

DANIS COULDN'T HELP but smile.

He's finally done it, she thought. He takes the throne and pardons them. Now they serve happily. A master stroke, turning an enemy into an ally.

She tried to keep her thoughts private, because he was busy, but she couldn't help but notice his glances. Why do I feel such a silly thrill every time he looks at me?

But she knew. This was what it felt like to need someone. She longed for him, just like she hoped he longed for her.

"This one is personal," he said, and suddenly she felt his attention on her. His Psy reverberated with feelings, though he kept his thoughts hidden. What are you planning, Elio? she wanted to ask. But all too quickly, he descended from his throne and knelt before her.

"Danis Elanaetos Morian," he began, gently pulling a velvety box from his uniform pocket.

She was simultaneously impressed and embarrassed. *How did he find out my middle name? Was it Richard?* She shoved Richard aside, and Elio continued what might be the worst thing ever.

"When I met you, I couldn't believe our connection," he continued. "We have always fit perfectly together. But you were a pilot, and I was a prince. I couldn't maintain responsibilities while flying around the galaxy with you. That time is past now. But I look to my future, and I see no other woman there except you. So I ask you to accept... this."

Danis couldn't believe it. *He is asking me this in front of twenty news holos? Everyone in the Orso kingdom will see this by tomorrow, and the other kingdoms by next week!*

Then he opened the box, but instead of a ring, or brooch, or necklace, it was a service medal. It wasn't like any she'd ever seen: a gold bar with an arc of five diamonds underneath, and a crown of chased platinum atop.

"This is the only one there is," Elio said. "Three hundred years ago, Colonel Willan Sathaz inherited the throne after his older brothers died. He made this medal to show his allegiance as he took the throne. But I want you to wear it, his original medal, on the deck of your ship. I want you to command our troops and bring peace and security to our kingdom. Danis, will you marry me and be my warrior queen?"

Everything he said sounded wonderful, fantastic, even. Except he'd said it in front of several trillion people! *Did he just ask me to marry him?* He had, but what could she do here, now, except...

"I will," she said, and smiled at him.

Elio jumped up and kissed her, her mind whirling with emotions: love, joy, sadness, fear. And now this huge expectation.

"Danis, what's wrong?" he whispered.

In response, she hugged him fiercely. She trusted Elio. He wouldn't manipulate her.

"Nothing. I love you," she whispered back.

Whether it was right or wrong, she'd deal with this. Somehow.

CHAPTER
THIRTY-SIX

Satisfaction
Office of Military Affairs
Orso Royal Palace

Marshal Jonn Marrion stabbed his comm board again. "Are you in position yet, Operative Eye? Report!"

There was no answer.

He switched comm channels. "Operative Ear, status report of the medal ceremony, over." No answer. He swore and pulled up monitor windows on all his operatives. All had active vital signs. All were awake and on duty.

But none of his palace operatives had reported in for two hours.

He checked their bio-signs again—

They all had exactly the same vital signs! Heartbeat, oxygen intake, lividity, all perfectly aligned.

"We've been hacked," he said, and checked the office security. Every post was unmanned, though all vitals displayed as perfect. He brought up the restricted security system. From these angles, he could see dead guards, sprawled under desks or shoved in corners.

His office door creaked open. He shot to his feet as an old man entered carrying a laser rifle.

Not an old man, he realized. Colonel Avrum Rosst.

Rosst's rifle whined, crimson fire flickering to either side of Marrion. He ducked uselessly as the shots continued, the acrid smoke of burned stone filling the air.

When the laser fire stopped, Marrion looked up to find Rosst admiring his handiwork. "Nice office you had here," Rosst said. "A shame something happened to it."

"You've a lot of nerve," Marrion said, reaching for his office security panel. But when he pressed the activator, nothing happened.

"No need to bother with that," Rosst said. "I destroyed your defenses. My new eye has auto-tracking linked to the rifle sights. Perfect shot every time."

"And I suppose you're going to burn a hole in me?" Marrion snarled. "End years of work with a single pull of the trigger? But no, you won't. There are more of us, all dedicated to the—"

"Two hundred and thirteen, to be precise," Rosst said, smiling. "We've obliterated your command. False reports, hacked bio-signs. You won't get the opportunity to kill King Elio."

Marrion had to keep from gaping. "How could you—"

"Once I set this off," Rosst said as he pulled a metal cylinder from his pocket. "a chain reaction will detonate the dozens of explosive devices we've laid here. The Office of Military Affairs will need to be completely rebuilt. We have less than twenty seconds."

Marrion turned. He had an escape tube behind a false panel. If he could just reach it, he might have a chance—

The cylinder landed in front of the panel.

"Ten seconds!" Rosst called.

Heedless of Rosst's rifle, Marrion ran for the office door. If he could escape the first explosive, he could hunker down in the shelter as the rest of the bombs exploded—

But his son Wayn was waiting in the hall, knife in hand.

"Hello, Father," he whispered.

"But... you're dead!" Marrion said.

"No! But if it makes you feel better, the bomb you planted in my arm killed Grig," Wayn said. "And then Rosst made me an offer I couldn't refuse. It was a lot of work, killing more than two hundred of your soldiers with just one hand—"

Marrion charged forward, decades of combat training overriding instinct. He struck at Wayn's carpal bones, to force the knife hand open. Then a swift kick to Wayn's stomach, a knuckle punch to the trachea—

But Wayn bent the wrist, twisted away from the kick and nudged the punch. Then the knife slashed across his father's throat. Blood gushed out before Marrion's hands could reach the cut.

"But..." Marrion's voice bubbled, "I'm your... father..."

"That means nothing. It never really has, has it?" Jude said. "It was time for you to die, father."

Marrion collapsed in a puddle of his own gore.

Jude Cabeus stood over his father's corpse then looked up as Rosst strode from the office.

"You owe me a can of synth," Rosst said. "It leaked all over his carpet."

Jude ignored that. "Bombs all over?" he said. "That was a little over-dramatic, don't you think?"

"You wanted to do it yourself," Rosst said. "So I chased him out for you. I could have just shot him."

Jude thought back over the years of abuse and brutal training. "I owe a lot of people a debt because of him," he said. "Maybe I can set some of it right."

"And what about me?" Rosst asked. "Do I need to watch my back?"

Jude searched for any lingering rage. "No," he said. "Whatever it was, was gone before Prince Elio returned. The Psy must be far away by now."

"Maybe they're dead," Rosst offered.

"Maybe they're waiting," Jude replied.

"Go home," Rosst said. "Be with your family."

"No," Jude snapped. "We need to leave. I'll go somewhere no Psy can find us."

Rosst pulled something from his pocket and handed it to him.

Jude looked at the knife in his hand; the knife his father had given him so many years ago, and he dropped it onto the corpse. He wiped his hand clean on his pants and took the small document file. He opened it. Inside were identity cards and a stack of credit chits.

"I took the liberty," Rosst said. "Verso was happy to oblige. Very official, and it all passed the strictest backgrounders."

The pictures were right, but the names were nonsense. "These might work for a time," Jude said, "but they'll leave a trail."

"Then cross a stream and hide your scent," Rosst said, and handed him a second file.

He tucked the first file under his stump and looked inside the second. This time, the top card read "Ajuud Gabios," showing a happier Jude than he'd seen in twenty years.

"The name is close enough," Rosst said. "One for you and one for your wife Omaala. Juvenile IDs for your children. Dump the first set and use the second."

Jude Cabeus held freedom from his past for the first time in twenty years.

"You'll never find me," he told Rosst. "I'll disappear."

"I expect you to," Rosst said. "We have enough soldiers to win this war without you. You've done your part. Go in peace."

Rosst lifted his arm and tapped his wristpad. "The target has been neutralized, sire," he said, but Jude was already walking away from the carnage. It was over. He didn't want to be Wayn ever again. He didn't even really have to be Jude, the royal traitor. He could just be... himself. Whoever that was.

I am a father, and a husband, he told himself. Everything else means nothing.

———

Outside the Throne Room

DRELLA SIMOND STOOD PROUDLY in her Royal Guard uniform. She was still a Lance Sergeant, but she and C Squad stood ready for the hand-off. The King was due in five minutes.

She resisted the urge to check her wristpad. Strike Sergeant Mattis was probably watching remotely. B Squad arrived right on time, six soldiers surrounding King Elio.

Lance Sergeant Hanson called "Halt," and about-faced toward Drella, as did the rest of C Squad.

"Hold," the king said, and lifted his wristpad. "Yes, Colonel?" Drella could hear the other person murmuring. "Neutralized, good. He didn't stay? I understand. Let him be at peace with my blessings." The king turned back to his guards. "Now, you may begin."

Lance Sergeant Hanson began the ritual hand-off.

"I release the safety of the king into your hands," Hanson snapped, and his soldiers stepped back.

"Thank you, Lance Sergeant Hanson," Elio said. "Thank

you for your service. And welcome, Lance Sergeant Simond. I appreciate your honesty and integrity, and I wish I could find more like you."

Drella blushed. "I will look after you, my king," she replied.

"And I you, Sergeant," King Elio said. "It's my duty to keep my people happy."

Drella took her position, and they marched to the ceremony. It was then that her wristpad tweedled.

"Ooh, you might want to check that," King Elio said.

"It's not urgent, sire," she replied. "It isn't tagged for emergency viewing."

"Still, you might want to check it," he said. "You never know when an opportunity might be missed."

"Sire?" she asked, but he said nothing. He was doing a perfectly terrible job of looking innocent. Intrigued by his Majesty's behavior, she peeked at the message.

LSgt. Simond - I would like to discuss troop training and deployment possibilities with you. Are you available to meet at the Fox Hole at 1800 tonight? LSgt. Hanson.

"I'm sure it's important," Elio said. "Just make sure you kit yourself out properly. You wouldn't want to show up unprepared."

She resisted the urge to stare at the king. How much does he know? she wondered. He'd survived the blade sergeant's abuse for months because he wouldn't kill his own citizens. *How can I resent him after that?* she thought

So she marched alongside the king she could respect, someone who looked out for his people, even though it might occasionally be embarrassing. *Well, he'll probably grow out of that.*

But privately, she hoped he wouldn't.

———

Lorne Presentation Pavilion
  Royal City Gardens
  Som Orsi

"—and to the citizens who came forward, I say once again that you are heroes!" King Elio intoned.

Meera sat with Lifia, Gesc and Dusti on outdoor bleachers, all bearing the Orso Crest. She bounced baby Stev on her knee.

Elio is still handsome, she couldn't help noticing. *But he's... different. He really is a king now. And Orso will be the better for it.*

"To all who are gathered here!" King Elio continued. "I have five hundred awards to give, the Orso Crest of Gallantry, our highest recognition to civilians. This award has never been presented to so many!"

The crowd of thousands cheered behind her.

"But first," King Elio said, "I found seventeen valiant defenders who were listed as civilians. The Perceptual Expansion Unit was founded as an extension of our military. The Regency Council disbanded it, and many PEU soldiers risked prison sentences to help our cause. So I present these forgotten warriors with the Honorable Star!"

The crowd cheered again, heartier than before. An aide brought a cobalt-blue tray chased in silver. King Elio picked up the first red-ribboned medal.

"Meera Seleure, step forward!"

What? Meera couldn't move.

"Go on, Mom!" Lifia shouted. Gesc cheered madly as Meera walked to the stage.

As Meera reached the stage, King Elio called "Finia Mell, step forward!" And then King Elio leaned forward.

"Thank you for my kingdom," he whispered as he draped

the ribbon around her neck. The medal was platinum, with a sapphire the size of her thumb set in the center of a golden starburst.

"It wasn't me," she said. "Lots of other people—"

"Meera," he said, "you've lost so much to this war, and still you fought on. I will grant you any reward within reason."

"I want to make a difference," she answered. "But I want to stay here. Let me be a... reservist. I can help train others in the PEU."

"I couldn't have chosen better," he said. "Granted."

She walked back, wondering what he whispered to Finia. Danis Morian had already rewarded Finia with officer training.

As she sat with her family, she wanted Klaus to be there. He'd made mistakes, but so had she. She'd been broken, and so had he. When he came home, she'd give him a chance to explain.

Another aide brought a crimson box covered in gold filigree. King Elio pulled out the first blue-ribboned medal. "May I present this medal to Dyron Abren," he paused for the family to hoot in appreciation, "who selflessly defended this city!" He continued quickly, "May I present this medal to Deno Avestan—" Abren arrived on stage, breathless, and Elio placed the ribbon around his neck. "May I present this medal to Faxil Avestan—"

———

NEUJAZ APARTMENTS
Feducere, Som Orsi

DAD OPENED the door and Faxil stepped into his own home for the first time in months. Everything looked the same, but the air was stale.

"Finally!" Pinari gasped, and flung herself into the room and onto the sofa. Her medal flashed in the waning sunlight. "I thought that weird party would go on forever."

Faxil felt the same way standing among so many grownups who'd fought against the rioters, and he'd felt so very small. But King Elio had shaken his hand and told him he'd done a good job.

I didn't really do anything, Faxil kept telling himself, even as he fingered his medal. *I just said people liked games.*

He looked behind him. "Hey, where's Dad?" he asked.

Pinari sat up. "Ooh, I wonder what they're talking about," she whispered. And then she jumped off the couch and pulled Faxil toward the door. She peered around the edge. "There they are."

Faxil could barely see around Pinari's head, but Dad and Ms. Verso were still down the hall.

"I don't think that's a good idea, Werta," Dad said.

"Young girls need a role model," Ms. Verso replied.

"You didn't even attend the award ceremony—" Dad began.

"It's obvious why I didn't," she interrupted.

"Why not? I think you're a wonderful role model," Dad said.

"What are they talking about?" Faxil whispered, but Pinari shushed him.

"You weren't a good role model," Ms. Verso said, "but Faxil turned out fine. Why can't I have that chance?"

"Because I don't want them thinking that we... are anything," Dad said. "Their mother is so far away. I don't want Inoiae coming home and—"

"You're afraid for the children," she snapped, "or yourself?"

Dad didn't answer.

"I don't understand," Faxil said.

"You goof," Pinari hissed. "It's like on All My Broken Hearts when Abya and—"

She jerked back, and yanked Faxil with her.

"It's just the children," he heard Dad say, but Ms. Verso got quiet.

"You know me," Ms. Verso finally said. "I'm very practical. My only weakness was you, though I suspect it wasn't shared."

Dad didn't answer that, either. Pinari peeked around the corner again, and so did Faxil.

"I feel something for the girl," she admitted. "You'll have a difficult time with her soon, trust me. My mother threatened to abandon me when I was fourteen. She, and you, you need a woman in your lives."

"What is she talking about?" Faxil asked. "What are they going to do?"

"I dunno," Pinari said.

"You can't stay here," Dad insisted. "Your crimes are pardoned, and you have a contractor's license with the new regime, so you can live anywhere. But not here. Understand?"

"So serious now," Ms. Verso said. "I'm not sure I'd want someone so tense. But I'll follow the rules. Think of me like your wife's sister—"

"That'll be difficult. You're nothing alike," Dad said.

Ms. Verso laughed. "Many sisters aren't. I promise I'll hand you back to her as inflexible and as honorable as you are now. Do we have a deal?"

Dad sighed. "Fine. I guess that's what I get for ditching my mom before my sister turned thirteen."

"You saved yourself a lot of fighting," Ms. Verso said.

"And I lost a lot more," Dad replied. "They haven't spoken to me in years."

"Family trait."

"What?"

"Nothing."

Pinari yanked Faxil back into the room again. "What did you do that for?" he asked, but Pinari had already thrown herself on the sofa again.

"They're com—" she started to say, but then Dad was in the doorway, and Ms. Verso was right behind.

"Give it up, scrubs," Ms. Verso snapped. "We know you were listening."

"No you don't. I mean, weren't. I mean, we weren't," Pinari lied.

"Kid, I gotta teach you how to—" Ms. Verso stopped and glanced at Dad. "Be more honest. I'm gonna be around sometimes, okay? Auntie Werta. What do you say to that?"

"Um," Faxil said. "I, um, don't like it when you call me funny names."

"What funny names?" she asked.

"Like scrub, or urchin," he said.

"Those aren't names, they're..." Dad cleared his throat, and Ms. Verso, Auntie Werta... He sighed. "All right, Fax-man, I'll go easy on the insults."

"Well, I want you to call me names twice as much!" Pinari said as she bounced off the sofa.

"Deal, scrubmuffin!" Verso replied. "I'm glad your dad and I could agree on this, because I already took out a lease on the fifty-third floor."

"What?" Dad said and pulled her into the kitchen. "That was... I mean, you can't just..."

Pinari laughed and hugged Faxil from behind. "Thanks for saving me," she whispered.

"That was a long time ago, wasn't it?" Faxil asked.

"Nope," she said. "I kinda feel like you save me a little more every day."

And while Dad and Auntie Werta argued in the kitchen, Pinari kissed his cheek again.

EPILOGUE

TORRENT'S DETENTION Bay
Officer's Ward, Cell II-38

Michael Jadern had given up hope.

He'd been in this brig for a week. He'd been allowed two supervised hydros and two square meals a day. Nobody had seen him except the guards. They'd just delivered another meal and wouldn't be back for hours. It was time.

Jadern removed his uniform shirt. There was a section of bars above the cell door, protecting the air vent. But with a little agility, Jadern thought he could thread his sleeve through the bars. A pair of slipknots would make an improvised noose. He would tie one end to his neck, yank the other end, and the slipknots would both pull tight, leaving him suspended enough to suffocate. There was no need to wait—

The door at the end of the detention bay clanged open again, and Jadern pulled the shirt back on.

"Hello, Michael," a familiar voice said. Jadern looked up to see, "Prince Elio?"

"I'm afraid you must call me 'King' now," Elio said. "At

least around other people. And I won't tell them your plans if you don't." Elio tugged at his own shirt to let Jadern know he knew what he'd been thinking.

He's a Psy! Jadern wanted to curse. Of course he knows! And then he realized that Elio could see everything else, too! He tried not to think about Danis—

And failed.

"I can't punish a man for his thoughts, Michael," Elio said. "But you need to know something. You and Danis were both warped by a powerful Psy. The thoughts you had weren't real. And two different people have assured me that when the Psy died, her control ended."

"I... I don't want to kill you anymore," Jadern said. "But... I swear I never thought of her that way before, but now it's all I can think about! I'm unfit to command even the lowest soldier."

"What would you do if I removed that feeling?" Elio asked.

"I would be loyal until death," Jadern said.

"I know you would," Elio replied. "Let me try to help you. Just relax and open your mind. Don't worry about what I might see. I know this isn't your doing."

Jadern relaxed as much as he could. He thought about the endless void of space, of planets and moons of spectacular beauty. As beautiful as Danis stretched out on—

He jerked away from that thought.

"Relax," Elio said, and Jadern tried a different memory. Sailing with his father on the Arboran Sea. The salt spray, the setting sun on the waves, the birds winging like star-fighters in formations—

"Calm," Elio whispered.

Jadern felt something touch his mind, and the unwanted images faded. He sighed in relief.

"The Psy used two different memories to create a bridge,"

Elio said. "I've blocked it, but my technique isn't perfect. My advice is to find someone to create new memories with. Go make new friends, maybe date someone. You've dedicated years to the Fleet. Michael It's time you spend a little time on yourself, Captain."

"Captain?" Jadern was stunned. "You mean I'll still have a ship?"

"No one deserves to command a ship more than you, Michael," King Elio said. "Though I'll take you off the Torrent. Commander Jasson is due for a promotion, and placing you in command there would be awkward, given... everything that happened."

"Thank you, sire," Jadern said. "For your grace and your tact. Do you have a ship in mind?"

Elio smiled at him. "The Precarious."

Jadern frowned. "But sire, that's an Angel-class destroyer. Their frames can't mount enough armor to protect them against Swarm weapons."

Elio smiled. "We've adapted some of the Angel-class ships and with the recent advances, like ablative armor and new rail-guns, well, it's a rather messy conversion, but after the Regis Magnum debacle, my father shifted his thinking. We have a full flotilla, and a desperate need to formulate new tactics. Are you the man I need?"

Jadern couldn't believe the opportunity before him. Elio was placing him in the same position Richard had found himself in when the Swarm first attacked.

He recoiled at the thought, but anger at Richard didn't materialize. He was... at peace.

"Yes, sire," Jadern said. "I'll take the Precarious. Where will you send me first?"

———

Chapel-Hall of Vega
Signa, Monere District
Som Orsi

"You really said that? 'I hear you need a new Palace Physician?' And the king just gave it to you?" Rosst said as they entered the chapel doors.

"Who else would he trust now?" Doctor Jan Loko said. "Though I think you convinced him most. He likes you. I like you too, by the way," she said, shyly.

Rosst looked around at the chapel walls. "How did I let you talk me into this?" he demanded as Jan dragged him into the hall in his dress greens.

Jan laughed. "My parents were strict Vegalyrs," she said, "so I have to get married in a chapel."

"But why am I here?" he demanded.

"Because I promised you," Jan said, unhelpfully.

They reached the front of the hall, where the Deudocent waited in a cinnamon-colored bloused shirt. His hair was combed to stand tall, and his glasses had a strong green sheen to them.

"What's up, lovebirds?" he said. "You ready to yoke up the marriage wagon?"

"Informal," Rosst observed.

"Vegalyrs don't pontificate much," Jan replied. "Now, take me and all that."

She stood there, with her long satin dress, black with silver thread sparkling throughout, her hair up in some kind of twist, and her impossible stare. And he found himself, once again, gripped by apparent insanity.

"Yes, let's do this," he said. "What do I say?"

"You want to marry her, and keep her forever, and all that?" the Deudocent asked.

"Yes," Rosst said, and he really meant it.

"How about you, missy?" the Deudocent asked.

"Why not?" she said. "Third time's a charm."

"Then you're now one!" the Deudocent declared. "Gotta grav. I'm doing a thing across town. Juvenescence party." And he turned and left them standing there.

"Wait, what did you mean 'third time's a charm?' I thought you were only married once," Rosst said.

"I meant your third time, darling," Jan said. But he knew she was fibbing, and she knew he knew, so there was no telling if she really meant it. Women are confusing.

He sighed. "So what do we do now?" he asked.

"If you don't know what happens now, it's no wonder they both left you," she pouted. "I suppose it's a good thing I'm a doctor. I can explain the basics to you."

Blonde and sweet with a little spice, Rosst thought. *Never thought I'd switch from black coffee to cappuccinos. Guess I'd better give it a try.*

———

ONE MONTH LATER
Alastor Royal Palace
Chalcedone, Planet Gern
Alastor System

Eroa and Targer Disiac strode into Prince Felder's diplomatic chamber, attended by their honor guard. While not as resplendent as his father's suite, the prince had decorated it with taste and restraint. His only concession to luxury was a filigreed white marble table, with a silver holo projector at its center.

"Welcome again, Lady Eroa," the prince said, gently

shaking her hand, then Targer's. "It's been three days, but I have something exciting to present. My shipwrights have finished the preliminary blueprints."

It had been two weeks since Eroa and Targer had arrived on Gern, the capital of the Alastor Kingdom. She might think the Alastor Royal Palace was more opulent than Orso's. Alabaster and ivory tones gleamed with every ray of light in contrast to Orso's darker marble.

"That's good news," she replied. "I hope I can inform King Elio shortly? He's eager to receive news."

In response, Felder activated the holo in the center of the table. A warship appeared before them, but it was like nothing Eroa had ever seen.

"This is the first of a new breed," Felder explained. "The armor is radically different. It imitates some of the Swarm vessels' properties. The beginnings of that research came out of Regis Magnum. Before the... trouble."

Eroa remembered that catastrophe too well. Her family had financially backed the Vindication Fleet, and its loss had prompted replacing King Orson and Prince Elio.

"Energy blasts striking that crystal armor will be redirected to the ship's capacitors," Felder continued, "and can be used to power weapons or shields. Studies of Swarm energy prompted new shields, weapons and reactors. These reactors generate the same power at sixty percent of the mass. With the same ship engines, we can redistribute thrust for more speed or agility. This vessel is smaller than a cruiser, with ground-breaking science and engineering. It is a falcon among pigeons, which is why they've named it the Peregrine."

"The Peregrine..." Eroa murmured as she gazed at the design. "A bird of prey, ranging far and wide. King Elio will be pleased." She thought of Danis Morian, the warrior-queen-to-be. "And I think someone else will be, too."

AUTHOR'S NOTE:

In previous novels, each of the characters played an important role in the story. But now our characters have been flung to the far reaches of the galaxy. In these next several novels, all subtitled Isolation, our characters will be forced to face and solve their problems without the help of those they most relied on.

This book, Sword of Diplomacy, focuses on Elio and his struggle to find his place in a world turned upside down. As the series develops, there will be many more challenges for Elio to overcome, and for others - Danis, Tarak, Richard, Jadern, Manda, Sasha, Tiger Wok, some familiar, some not.

In the coming Isolation stories, the familiar characters will take center stage in their own stories and we'll learn a great deal more about the universe of the Sovereign Stars.

Thank you for reading *Sword of Diplomacy,* the seventh book in the Sovereign Stars Series. I hope you enjoyed it, if you did please help others find Blair Howards Books by leaving a few words about it in the form of a review.

Follow Blair C. Howard on Amazon!

Get Exclusive Deals (As Part Of "The Family")
SIGN UP FOR ANNOUNCEMENTS & GREAT DEALS!
PLUS you'll Unlock 20% Off
Visit www.BlairHowardBooks.com
If you don't see the pop up to join, just click the blue unlock 20% off icon and enter your details.
Don't forget to confirm your email and whitelist (save as contact)Blair@blairhowardbooks.com to your email system.

FROM BLAIR HOWARD

The Harry Starke Genesis Series

8 Books in Series as of 2024

The Harry Starke Series

24 Books in Series as of 2024

The Lt. Kate Gazzara Murder Files

20 Books in Series as of 2024

Randall And Carver Mysteries

2 Books in Series as of 2024

The Peacemaker Series

3 Books in Series as of 2024

The O'Sullivan Chronicles: Civil War Series

5 Books in Series as of 2024

FROM BLAIR C. HOWARD

The Sovereign Star Series

7 Books in Series as of 2024

ABOUT THE AUTHOR

BLAIR C. HOWARD

Blair C. Howard is a Royal Air Force veteran, a retired journalist, and the best-selling author of more than 50 novels and 23 travel books. Fascinated by the heavens almost from childhood, and a sci SciFi fan for almost as long, he decided to try his hand at writing a military space opera. His first journey into this genre resulted in the Sovereign Stars series. Book 1 in the series, Avenger is followed by Gods of War and Armored Fleet.

Blair lives in East Tennessee with his wife Jo, and Jack Russell Terrier, Sally.

Visit www.blairhowardbooks.com

Find and follow the author: